Legends say a syphon can drain a mage dry. He'll brave the danger. Will she?

Someone's playing pranks. The body of the late Casteel patriarch has been stolen and gifted to the family's enemy, the powerful Rallises. As far as Bronte Casteel is concerned, they can keep it. She hasn't spoken to her family in thirteen years, not since they exiled her from society for her lack of mage power. But she's a syphon mage, able to drain another mage's power. Syphons' destinies are always the same: death by fiery stake. She hides her secret by living among the Nons--powerless humans and the lowest class in the Republic. When her family orders her to go plead for the body's return, she comes face to face with the one man who knows her secret.

Colonel Vincent Rallis isn't letting his syphon get away this time. Not when she's under suspicion of body-napping and aiding anti-mage terrorists. He'll prove her innocence whether she wants him to or not, and then convince her they belong together…forever.

Vincent's help comes with a steep price: Bronte must reveal her power. The inevitable ensuing witch-hunt and trial would be bad enough, but even a tough girl might buckle if her prosecutors are her own parents.

Books by Anise Rae

Syphon's Song

Published by Kensington Publishing Corporation

Syphon's Song

Mayflower Mages, #1

Anise Rae

LYRICAL PRESS
Kensington Publishing Corp.
www.kensingtonbooks.com

Lyrical Press books are published by
Kensington Publishing Corp. 119 West 40th Street New York, NY 10018

All Kensington titles, imprints, and distributed lines are available at special quantity discounts for bulk purchases for sales promotion, premiums, fund-raising, and educational or institutional use.

Special book excerpts or customized printings can also be created to fit specific needs. For details, write or phone the office of the Kensington Special Sales Manager:
Kensington Publishing Corp.
119 West 40th Street
New York, NY 10018
Attn. Special Sales Department. Phone: 1-800-221-2647.

First Electronic Edition: March 2014
eISBN-13: 978-1-61650-211-9
eISBN-10: 1-61650-211-8

First Print Edition: March 2014
ISBN-13: 978-1-61650-763-3
ISBN-10: 1-61650-763-2

Printed in the United States of America

For Katie, for L and C, and as always, for my mom.

Chapter 1

Bronte Casteel had eleven hours, ten minutes and five seconds before her Non-mage pass expired. Her nerves crackled like the groomed pea gravel crunching beneath her old Volvo's tires. The car limped down the grand estate's long driveway. She looked up at her cracked rearview mirror to see the gates closing behind her, locking her inside the den of the most potent mages in the country. Ahead, the gray stone mansion sat tall and proud. Its symmetrical wings sprawled to either side. Rallis Hall was as imposing and majestic as she remembered it.

She passed beneath the arch of the gatehouse, circled the driveway, and parked the car. Its dimpled nose pointed toward the gates for a quick escape. She glanced at the plastic clock stuck to the dashboard. Her neck muscles tightened with every *tick-tock* of the second hand. Eleven hours, eight minutes. Her mother—a mage powerful enough to intimidate most of the Republic—had allotted just enough time for her powerless daughter to make the trip north, deliver the Casteels' morbid message to Senator Rallis and scamper back to her assigned city.

The ticking clock wasn't her only problem. After all, the Rallises would likely kick out any member of the Casteel family in a flash of mage vibes anyway. And that was the best-case scenario. For Bronte, the worst case was much…well, worse. Burning to a crisp was as bad as she could imagine. She took a deep breath to loosen fear's tight grip. Senator Rallis had no reason to suspect her of anything. To his eyes, she was nothing but a struggling Non-mage musician. All she needed was a little luck, the goddess's grace, and a lot of poise, to pull this off.

It wasn't as if she had a choice. She either obeyed her mage sponsors or she'd be exiled from the Republic of Mage Territories forever. A chord of sadness rippled through her at the thought. Her soul would wither if severed from the enchanted music that existed only here. She craved the sound of the mages' songs as much as she yearned to play them, though no mage would ever let her on stage. Mage citizens would never see past her true self, no matter how magical she could make her violin sound.

Forging ahead her only option, she leaned forward to get the car keys. Her fingers brushed against them as a gentle whisper of mage energy spiraled into her. She recognized it immediately. Vincent. He wasn't supposed to be here. She froze as her forbidden power reawakened and soaked up his blissful vibes, but terror overpowered the bliss.

"No. No. No." The denial puffed from her lips. Her pounding heart competed with the sound of her words. If she were the powerless non-mage she pretended to be, she'd never sense him.

She dropped her head to the steering wheel, tense muscles creaking in protest, as the warmth of his vibes fed into her. His energy felt so familiar even after all those years. It touched her lightly, faint from the distance between them, but the bottomless pool inside her drew his vibes with a constant, steady strength.

Syphon mages were long forbidden, now relegated to mere legends.

But the death sentence still applied.

She sucked in a hard breath of the car's rapidly warming air, held it, willed his energy away. Her head drummed with the fruitless effort. She wished she could stifle her energy signature, something an average mage could easily do.

Maybe Vincent wouldn't sense her presence. After all, she had spent her entire life without anyone else noticing her unique vibes. Her energy signature registered as faint as a black hole, a fact she knew thanks to a lifetime of insults from her family. Today her faint vibes were her only hope at getting out of here unscathed. He couldn't reveal her secret if he didn't know she was here. Her meeting was with the senator, not with the famous Colonel Vincent Rallis.

She squinted through dark bangs for another glance at the clock. Eleven hours and five minutes. Her fingers itched to shred that darn pass into a thousand pieces. Her frustrated sigh seemed to blow against the second hand of the clock, speeding it along its circular path.

She peeked at the rearview mirror, half-expecting to see Vincent dashing down the stone stairs, an army of mages behind him with a big stake. The only person around was a gardener mage, spying from behind one of the fat trees lining the drive. Bronte craned around to look at him. Even from this distance, the tuning spirals tattooed on his temple appeared dark and thick. The permanent circles channeled the universe's energy into his sixth sense, providing more mage power than he naturally possessed.

For his sake, she should get out of the car. It couldn't be easy to keep the red and gold leaves of autumn neatly on their trees when they only wanted to tumble to the ground willy-nilly. The gardener wouldn't dare let that happen in front of a guest. Autumn was too messy to tolerate for a powerful founding family. The unnatural trees gnawed at Bronte, their strangeness reminding her of the odd, new tune her songwriting partner had composed for her. Even now it grated against her ears. She'd changed Claude's song onstage last night, improvised new notes in a disobedient but beautiful melody that sang from the strings of her violin. She'd get an angry earful the next time they spoke.

As she watched, the leaves began to shake on their branches like Claude's angry fist. The gardener mage smiled at her beneath the fiery canopy's shimmy. He was putting on a show. Though it was a distraction from Vincent's invisible presence, she couldn't afford to encourage any mage's attention. She didn't smile back. Instead she looked away, curled her fingers around the car key, and slipped it out of the Volvo's ignition.

She reached for the straw cloche hat resting on the passenger seat and placed it just so for its short ride to the entrance of the house. Her thin cardigan was next. Her brooch acted as a pretty version of the required letter *N* for *Non*. A constant reminder of her status, it pulled heavily on the knitted fabric. She buttoned the pink sweater to support it. Respectably attired, she stepped out of the car.

The unusual September heat tried to force her back in. She would have preferred to comply, but her orders were not optional. She reached under her hat to check that her low chignon was still neat and then dropped her keys into her secondhand leather purse.

Coiffed and composed. That was her life's formula, her self-defense.

She pulled the black violin case from the backseat. Subjecting it to the scorching temperature of a closed-up car was unthinkable. She never traveled without it. The instrument was an extension of herself. It would brave the Rallises with her.

The car door gave an impolite groan as she pushed it closed. With the violin in one hand and her purse tucked under her arm, she set a fast pace to the grand entrance, making up for lost time in the car. Her low heels scuffed against the pebbles of the drive.

She didn't get far, halting as movement to her left drew her gaze. She looked up from under the brim of her hat. A solitary red leaf danced on invisible currents of heat. Bronte followed its pattern as it glided up and down, first by its tail end and then its tip. It drifted toward her. She couldn't resist. Setting the violin case down on the stone, she held out her empty hand. The perfect red leaf landed there with a whispered grace.

She glanced back at the mage. He stood beside his fat tree trunk and stared, daring her to do something. She opened the discreet latch on her purse and tucked the rebel leaf carefully inside. It was as daring as she could get. The leaf was now a companion to the cursed note she was to give to the senator, her identification papers, and her car keys, which she moved into the zippered interior pocket to better protect her delicate refugee. Picking up her violin case, she marched toward her task in the stone house.

Had there been a moat, the steps could have been replaced with a drawbridge that angled up to the gray structure. The tall rectangular windows, over a dozen of them on the front, saved Rallis Hall from looking like a medieval fortress. The glass left a wavy impression, warped by generations of mage energy. There was a stark beauty to the manor's straight lines. Rallis Hall hadn't changed since she'd been here thirteen years ago for the Gathering ceremony.

The two dark wooden doors, a story and a half tall, were punctuated by knobs in their middles like matching belly buttons—unusual since mages didn't need door knobs to open a door. In a mage home, energy was the universal key.

The twin doors opened before she'd climbed to the top of the stone steps. Bronte stumbled, expecting Vincent's face. Instead, a gray-haired man in a dark suit and a gray silk cravat stood in the doorway. His hand fell to his side. He'd used the knobs instead of his mage power.

"Miss Casteel." He nodded once, a formal gesture accompanied by a smile. "I wish you a warm welcome to Rallis Hall."

She nodded back, though she wished to be most anywhere but here.

"Thank you." The automatic words were part of the coiffed and composed façade. She couldn't remember his name but did recall his face. He'd been the one to open the door then, too, as her parents rushed her out for daring to socialize with a mage. They'd been blind to what had just happened to the girl they'd all thought powerless. Their ignorance was a blessing from the goddess. From the moment Vincent brought her power to life, Bronte knew she had to hide it forever if she wanted to survive.

After that Gathering, her parents had banished her to the South. Another blessing. Though the Republic's small population of Nons was scattered throughout the country, most lived in the three territories of the Southern Alliance. It was simple to hide her power among the Nons in her adopted city of Chattanooga in Locke Territory. From what she could tell,

Vincent's energy frequency was the only one she could influence. No one noticed she wasn't really a Non.

The grand front doors clicked shut behind her. She jumped. Vincent's vibes flowed into her, stronger now as if the doors held his power inside the manor, that much closer to her syphon.

The butler politely ignored her nervousness. "May I take your hat and your violin? I'll see that it rests safely in our coat closet."

She lifted the case, handing over her livelihood as if she weren't really trapped with a dark fate lurking somewhere in the shadows of this house. She repeated her thanks, her voice thin from too little air. Another of the Rallis staff hustled over, his footsteps silenced by his mage power. The servant took her things from the butler.

"This way, please." The butler held out his arm toward the double doors on the other side of the grand foyer and left her to follow him. She didn't. Instead she kept her eyes on her violin until it was tucked in the massive closet. She needed to know its hiding spot in case she had to see herself out.

"The senator is waiting, miss." The mild reprimand was nothing compared to her need to keep her violin safe.

Certain she knew its location, she paced to the butler, her heels clacking and echoing in the vast entryway. Her mother would be mortified. Manners dictated mages always silence their steps.

A Rallis sentry stood in front of the closed doors, his dark gray uniform embellished with a scarlet sash and the family's crest. Like the butler, the stern sentry opened the office doors with his hands, a courtesy to her. Mage vibes bothered Nons and made them anxious and jittery.

The butler stepped into the senator's sanctum. "Miss Bronte Casteel." He announced her name slowly, a pause between each word, drawing out the final syllable, and then stood aside.

She passed him with three shaky steps into the dark entrance of the office. The doors latched shut. She clutched her purse to her chest. Its leaf, the only one to escape the doomed fate of the others, was a talisman of hope and freedom. Every nerve was alert to any sign of Vincent's presence and his unstoppable vibes. She crept forward one foot at a time as if the floor might rot from beneath her, and ventured into the light shining through the tall windows at the end of the huge room. Two masculine silhouettes, black shadows against the bright light, waited motionless.

She couldn't sense any vibes from those two. Relief flooded through her. Vincent was not among them. With the exception of Vincent's frequency, Bronte was blind to all mage energy, more so than a Non. She set her shoulders and headed toward them.

Senator Rallis, Vincent's grandfather, stood behind the desk and wore the Rallis medallion. The medallion linked the land, its energy and people to the goddess's blessing. Whoever wore it controlled the territory and its mages and had a vote in the Senate. The medallion hung heavily against the senator's barrel-sized chest and gleamed with a polished bronze stone in the center.

Vincent's brother, the other person her mother had told her to expect, stood to the side of the desk. Bronte's mother had reviewed all the names and standings of the entire Rallis family, but she hadn't needed it. Bronte remembered everything about these people. Anything connected to Vincent was too indelible to forget.

"Miss Casteel." Vincent's brother, Lord Edmund Rallis, greeted her first. He reached out a hand for hers. She shook it quickly. She didn't want to linger if he didn't like touching Nons. Most mages didn't.

"Lord Rallis, it's an honor to meet you." She repeated the gesture with the senator. His right pinkie finger was missing, a casualty from a famous battle at the Rushes where the Senate met. It was a dangerous place even for the most powerful mages. "Thank you for seeing me on such short notice, Senator Rallis."

The senator inclined his gray head. "We are always pleased to meet with a fair-minded ambassador from the Casteel family."

Those were in short supply. In fact, she didn't know one since she didn't count herself a part of the family. She gave the senator a small smile, but couldn't resist a glance behind her. Vincent lurked somewhere nearby. His energy was strong.

She turned back, determined to focus on the senator. "How do you know I'm fair-minded?" She regretted the lighthearted words the moment they reached her lips.

"I'll tell you." The older man leaned forward. "I can read your energy."

She froze. If he could read the energy around her, it might very well be Vincent's. She hardly registered to any mage's sense.

"You're the only Casteel who doesn't have the energy of a donkey's behind." Senator Rallis's voice took on a wry edge.

Her laugh escaped from shock. She hoped no one heard the desperation behind it.

"Please have a seat." The senator gestured to a chair in front of his desk.

She moved on shaky legs to the plush wingback and darted another glance to the back of the room. Those perfect vibes originated from that direction. Nothing there but shadows, though she didn't trust her eyes. The Rallis men took their respective seats as she smoothed her skirt over her lap with a silent lecture to stop looking.

"Just last week we had a visit from your brother," Edmund said. "Fair-minded is not how I would describe him. Claimed he needed access to our land for some sort of research. He was lying."

Bronte blinked. Her options clarified with his warning. Some mages could sense lies. Apparently, he was one of them. Lying wouldn't help her get out of this.

"A visit from two Casteels in one week is extraordinary." The senator's voice carried through the entire room. Probably from practice at the Rushes, named for the various herbs scattered on the floor of the Senate to dampen the dangerous energy levels from so many powerful mages in such close proximity. "She won't lie to us, Edmund. I can feel it."

"There are whispers of riots and growing discontent within the Casteel boundaries. Are the rumors true?" Edmund asked, his handsome face intent on hers.

"I have heard no rumors." She tried to keep her expression free from her shock. "I'm rather uninformed about the happenings within Casteel." An honest answer.

Senator Rallis's fingers came together in a thoughtful pyramid. "That's a shame, Miss Casteel. Family is meant to stay close together and provide support for one another. That's a lesson the Nons exemplify."

Bronte cocked her head. "The Nons have to be diligent in sticking together, senator. There is safety in numbers. A large mass of living energy is harder for mages to manipulate than one single source. Or so I'm told." She could have rolled her eyes at herself. What was she doing? Poking at the senator was not the way to ensure a safe escape. She bit her tongue to prevent anymore verbal prodding.

The senator's half-smile was accompanied by a raised brow. "An enlightening point, Miss Casteel. Like the Nons, the Rallis family sticks together too."

Bronte knew the Rallis senator usually voted for Nons' rights, unlike the Casteels, who were famous for their anti-Non stance. The Casteels would prefer to round up all the Nons in the Republic and stick them in the South, much like they'd done to their daughter. Bronte's family believed all Nons should be forced to work in the South's numerous manufacturing plants. Their smokestacks towered over the region like industrial forests.

She swallowed against the knot of bitterness stuck in her throat. "Support of my family is what brings me here, sir. As you know, my grandfather recently passed on."

The senator bowed his head briefly. "Yes, our condolences on your loss. Senator Casteel will be missed by a great many."

But not the many Rallises. "Thank you. My father is, of course, stepping up to take his place at the Rushes."

"When does he plan to do that, Miss Casteel? It's been three weeks." Edmund's voice was perfect for taking over the family's Senate seat someday. Clear, enunciated, and with just the right pitch. He looked enough like Vincent for one to recognize they were brothers, but not to guess they were twins. Edmund's features blended into a handsome sophistication. His dark hair waved across his forehead over blue eyes. A perfect nose complimented his concerned, friendly smile, and his shoulders were broad enough to carry the weight and responsibilities of the medallion. She'd heard he was a mage of considerable power, like the rest of his family. She couldn't sense it for herself, but it was common knowledge that Nons avoided the entire area surrounding the estate, unable to tolerate the Rallis clan's collective vibes. The Nons' ancient instincts recognized a greater power and, therefore, a danger to their lives. It was hard for Nons to resist the need to flee, or worse, to fight.

"Lord Casteel plans to take the Senate seat soon, but there is a problem." Bronte faced the senator. "I'm here to ask for your help."

"Help with what, Bronte?" His gruff, hoarse words came from behind her, accompanied by a flood of vibes.

She wouldn't have recognized his voice except for that energy pouring into her. She wrenched around in her seat to see the lion prowl out of the shadows.

His gaze targeted her like she was prey that might escape. "Tell us how we can help you. And then you can explain why you ran away from me."

Her mind recorded him like a pencil scratching away at paper to save his image—his dark hair clipped short, eyebrows that formed stark lines with a skeptical bent near their ends. A crease pulled between his brows that hadn't been there before. His rugged face had weathered storms his brother had avoided. Those storms had chiseled away any softness.

She closed her eyes, stopping the mental sketching—a necessity to save her sanity. She turned her whole body back toward the senator and only opened her eyes when she knew Vincent wasn't in her line of sight.

"Vin!" Happy surprise colored every note of the senator's voice. "How long have you been standing back there? Your energy is so subdued I didn't even sense you until now."

"I didn't either." Edmund's voice was equally surprised. "Miss Casteel, your beauty has distracted us."

Bronte fought to keep her calm mask intact. Her heart boomed like the senator's voice and threatened to shake that mask right off her face. She couldn't let that happen. Diplomatic words and composure were her only weapons in this battle, a quick escape her only viable strategy. She stood, one move closer to getting to the door. At her cue, all the men stood as well.

The closer Vincent came, the more his energy reached out to her. It touched her, filled her in places she'd forgotten were empty. Dangerous memories spilled back. If she knew how, she'd dump his vibrations out of her hidden vessel, turn it over, and sit on it like a metal bucket until it sank into the dirt with the force of her weight. She'd seal her hollow spaces shut and keep him out forever. To do otherwise would only invite death to creep close.

Vincent strode toward her.

She held her ground and looked him in the eye. "I do not need your help. I am simply the messenger. Here on behalf of the Casteels." She cleared her throat to try again and turned to the senator. "Senator Rallis, my family requests your assistance."

The senator's wise gaze locked on Vincent, his expression thoughtful and full of silent words Bronte lacked the power to hear. Curiosity lit the dark depths of his gaze as they landed back on her.

Vincent leaned toward her. "And they sent you as their messenger?" His voice was soft, a caress against her skin. "The most vulnerable and weakest of them all, to fight their battles."

"I am not weak." She risked a quick glance at him. "I have plenty of strength to fight whatever battles I need to." She bit her tongue to stop her aggressive tone. Arguing would not help her cause.

"Vincent, you are making our guest uncomfortable." The senator's tone went quiet. Deadly. The boom was much safer, she realized.

"No, I'm not. At least not with my vibes, Granddad." Vincent's reply was matter-of-fact. He held all the power between them, and he was going to use it. Running for the door would not help her now.

"My mage vibes do not make her uncomfortable."

Her hold on her tongue wasn't tight enough to stop her gasp. She'd messed up. Goddess, but she'd messed up. She closed her eyes for a moment at the realization. Instead of drinking Vincent in, she should have faked a reaction to his power, imitated the jittery anxiousness Nons felt around a mage who wasn't suppressing his energy. Maybe that would have saved her.

"Vincent. She's a Non. Of course you're making her uncomfortable." The senator's reprimand was deceptively soft.

Bronte stared at Vincent as desperation swirled inside her. "Please. Don't."

"She's not a Non." Vincent's words shattered her hope of escape.

Chapter 2

"Of course I'm a Non!" Her denial was automatic. "My parents wouldn't have banished me to the South if I was a mage." Betrayal ripped through her, but Vincent had done nothing more than what she'd expected from a mage. A sense of doom sat heavily on her shoulders. If she weren't careful, it would sink her. She needed to shrug it off and fight back.

"Look at her, Granddad." Vincent's voice sounded rough. He, too, was preparing for a fight. "Is her aura grated? Does her energy seem agitated by mine?"

Bronte squirmed under their scrutiny.

"I can't sense any energy from her," the senator said. "But her aura doesn't seem unpleasantly affected by your vibes. Why is that, Miss Casteel? I would expect a Non's aura to be twitching from all the energy Vincent puts out." His voice was quiet, but the force behind the words was clear.

She had no hope of fooling them with lies. She'd have to make the truth work for her.

"Mage vibrations don't bother me." She kept her admission soft and humble. "I grew up among one of the most powerful families in the Republic, after all."

Truth.

Senator Rallis stared back, testing her. She knew what he was doing. Like opening a river's dam, he released his mage energy. Though she couldn't feel it, it was written in the quirk of his eyebrow. The urge to run flooded through her, but some fleck of age-old instinct warned her if she ran, they would hunt her down.

"Can you feel my grandfather's energy? Or Edmund's?" A hard curiosity lurked beneath Vincent's words.

She swallowed against her fear. "No."

Vincent nodded as if she'd given him the answer he'd expected.

She closed her eyes for a moment. There was no truth that would save her from these questions. Nor was there any point in railing at fate and demanding to know why she'd been put on the path here. *Why?* was not a question the goddess answered.

"But you can feel Vincent?" Senator Rallis asked.

"She can," Vincent spoke for her. "But I'm not hurting her." A silent tension coiled around the room.

"Interesting. I'd like to hear how a woman who claims to be a Non can tolerate mage energy, yet she can only sense one of us. Should be an entertaining story. Let me get you a chair, Vin, and you can explain." Edmund strode to the back of the room, grabbed a chair from a shadowed corner, and carried it over. Vincent scooted it next to her. The men waited; politeness demanded they stand until she took her seat.

Her knees simply gave way. Her chair met her body.

The Rallises took their seats once again.

Vincent looked at her, waiting for her to speak, but this story would never form on her lips. He broke the silence. "Bronte is a syphon mage."

The senator and Bronte protested at the same time.

"Vincent! Syphons do not exist. Not in today's world."

"I am not a…" She couldn't even say the word.

"Let's hope not," Edmund chimed in. "We can't let such a lovely face burn at the stake."

A horrified gasp flew out of her mouth.

Edmund flinched back in his seat as if an invisible hand shoved him. "Vin! Chill!" Exasperation drenched the words. "Sorry. My apologies, Miss Casteel, for my thoughtless words. I certainly don't feel you syphoning anything from me." His voice trailed off as if he had second thoughts about that. From his expression, the senator reconsidered as well.

Bronte's stomach roiled. Every school history book told the story of syphon mages. Long ago in the Old World, most of the witches burned at the stake were syphons, women who could supposedly steal the power of other mages. Magekind had been happy to turn syphons over to the inquisitions. It kept the focus off the rest of them and got rid of a feared problem. Nowadays, most mages believed syphons were mere myths, untruths that mages had invented to justify handing over their own people to a horrible death in order to save themselves.

"Bronte, no one is going to hurt you," Vincent said. The pressure of his words pounded against her ears despite his low volume. There was power in his words. The senator and Edmund must have felt it in their sixth senses. They all shifted in their seats. "I would never let that happen."

She lifted her chin and glared. "I do not need, nor do I want, your protection. I can take care of myself. Thank you very much, though." Manners took over out of habit.

"Vincent, are you sure about this?" The senator studied him. "Is it possible you're not quite as recovered as you thought? Your sense was fried less than twelve hours ago."

Vincent's arm brushed against her. His heat seared right through her sweater. His sky blue gaze cut to her soul. "What do you think, Bronte? Am I making this up? Am I crazy?"

Yes, you're crazy.

Lie.

I don't know you well enough to say.

Lie.

Her syphon knew him. The sharp bite of truth gnawed against her with inescapable teeth. She took a breath, her own shoulders doing the rubbing this time with her inhale. "I'm sure you're not crazy." She sounded like a peasant appeasing an all-powerful lord.

Vincent narrowed his eyes. She could feel him changing tactics as if he were shifting gears in a car. "Granddad, how do you feel? Edmund? What's your power sensing?"

Bronte tried to swallow under their silence, but her dry, dusty mouth wouldn't cooperate.

"Comfortable," Senator Rallis finally answered. "Dare I say…almost peaceful."

"When was the last time that happened? I'm not the only one whose sixth sense aches from the power." Vincent's words were directed at his family, but his gaze was on her.

This had to stop before it was too late. If it wasn't already. But she still had to deliver the cursed message.

Bronte cleared her throat. "If we could get back to the reason for my visit, senator…" She opened her purse and extracted the letter a Casteel servant had hand-delivered to Bronte's trailer home. She set the envelope on the gleaming desk with a glance at the senator.

He didn't reach for the letter but gave her a small smile, indulging her. His pleasant humor wouldn't last long.

Edmund spoke before she could begin her spiel. "After last night's bomb, Mother was ready to call General Wilen to tender your resignation on your behalf, Vin. Despite the promotion you have coming. And that's saying something." He rubbed his hands over his face. "I've never seen you so sense-sick. Quite a recovery." He glanced toward Bronte.

"I'm not resigning. Lifetime commitment," Vincent said, his gaze still on her.

She'd had enough. "It's not polite to stare."

"If I look away, you might disappear again. Now what's in your letter?" He surprised her, handing her control of the conversation.

She took a fortifying breath and dove into her message while she had the chance. "A servant found this letter in the laying-out room where the late Senator Casteel's body had been. The body was missing."

"So you're missing the medallion," Vincent stated. He went straight to the heart of the problem.

"The medallion was still around his neck." She recited the message as instructed. "Lord and Lady Casteel ask for your assistance in retrieving the medallion. Lady Casteel awaits your communiqué." Done. She could say her goodbyes and leave. Before she was an inch out of her chair, the senator held up his hand. She sat back down. He ruled here. She could not disobey.

The elder Rallis pulled out the letter.

Edmund gave a disbelieving chuckle. "So that's why your father has yet to take the Casteel Senate seat." He looked at his grandfather, who was still focused on the letter. "This is our chance to get that school bill passed. No Casteel to stop it."

The letter suddenly hit the desk with a *crack*, flattened by an angry current of wind that glued it to the shiny surface. Senator Rallis shot up from the desk. His chair rolled away behind him. He leaned forward on arms as thick as a young man's. "The body is on Rallis property? In our gyre?" His voice boomed around the room. "How long ago did you receive this?"

Bronte's heart pounded like a runner racing for the finish line. "The letter was found two weeks ago."

"Where were you?" Vincent's voice snapped like a whip.

An outraged gasp exploded from her throat. "Me? You think I did this? I'll tell you where I was! I was in Chattanooga. Where I have been for the past thirteen years! Except for once. A year ago." She only added that part because she didn't want them to think she was lying.

"I'm not accusing you of stealing a body. I know you didn't do this. Just tell me you have witnesses to back up your alibi." His blue eyes morphed to steel even as his tone softened.

"We'll find some if she doesn't, Vin," Edmund said.

She looked away, ignoring them both. Her mind was too clouded to think back two weeks. She faced the angry patriarch seething behind his desk. "The Casteels did not feel there was a threat to you, sir, so they chose to keep the information to themselves."

"No threat?" His roar echoed.

His angry words pierced right through her skin. Her ears popped with the pressure of his energy cast. Power arced sharply into her chest. His finger jabbed in the air as if he would strike at her stuttering heart. "How long have *you* known about this?"

She struggled for breath. The force of his angry spell hovered, suffocating her. Bronte put a hand over her heart to shield it. Unlike other mages, she had no way to defend herself against a mage spell. Her power didn't work like that. She was going to die. Right here. Fretting about burning at the stake had been misplaced worry.

Vincent laid his hand on her shoulder. The pain from the senator's vibes eased in an instant, but her head still spun with nauseating speed from the aftereffects.

"Breathe," Vincent ordered, his face intent on hers. He stood, breaking the contact between them. He turned to his grandfather, his fingers pressing like claws into the desk. "Back down, senator." His whispered voice ruffled the hair on the back of her neck. "Syphons cannot shield themselves from spells. She is helpless against a mage. You don't want to hurt her."

Air pressure built until she thought her ears would implode. And just like that, it was gone. Silence rained down around them. It took a while before she had the courage to break it, but she spoke up, claiming the innocence that was hers.

"My mother informed me about the missing body late last night. She sent the thief's letter by messenger. It arrived at the same time as her landline call. She instructed me not to read it. I don't know anymore than I've told you." The words rushed out.

The senator's red face glowed as he read the letter aloud. "*The body of Walter Casteel lies in the Rallis gyre, along with the Casteel Medallion. We will no longer tolerate being ignored. Use the power to better our land for all mages and Normals.* It's unsigned." Senator Rallis looked up from the letter, anger shining from his eyes. "Only one group refers to Nons as Normals. Double-Wide."

Double-Wide…terrorists…it resonated through her mind. Bronte swallowed hard and clutched at her purse. The leaf was a lousy talisman. Her mother had neglected to mention anything about the horrific anti-mage group. How was it possible that Double-Wide, named after the trailers so many poor Nons lived in, including Bronte, had targeted a founding family?

"Put the letter down, Granddad." Vincent gave the order softly. "Goddess knows it's been handled so much the vibes are all blurry, but maybe there's something left for the energy readers."

"I doubt that." But the senator dropped the letter.

"They've managed to pick up vibes from the bomb's residue. There's a chance. We're getting closer. Just not close enough."

Bronte had read the newspaper accounts of each bombing over the last several months. The latest attack was early this morning in a minor city of Rallis Territory. She'd heard about it on the radio station during the drive here. According to the reporter, the explosion demolished a new apartment building that was only partially full. A young family of Nons had perished. The bombing obviously hadn't gone as intended. Nons wouldn't have been the target. Plus the device had been capable of a much bigger explosion. Thankfully it malfunctioned.

"Double-Wide has invaded our home and yours, Miss Casteel," the senator said.

It's not my home.

She bit back the words along with the urge to offer an apology. This was not her fault. She was just the messenger.

"The enforcers don't know?" Vincent glanced over his shoulder at her. His mage power drifted into her and heated her soul, the total opposite of the cold chill of his grandfather's anger. A strange combination.

"Of course the enforcers don't know," Edmund scoffed. "If word got out that the Casteels lost their medallion, they'd never get their Senate seat back."

Vincent leaned over the desk and read aloud. "*Use the power to better our land for all mages and Normals.* That's nothing Casteel would ever do. Double-Wide has to know that. Considering they hid the body on our land, I'd bet Double-Wide anticipated the Casteels handing the letter over to us." Vincent shrugged, his face intense and thoughtful.

"We're the intended recipients of a letter from those damn terrorists?" The senator's voice filled the room.

"A political strategy. That's a new approach for them." From Vincent's frown, she wasn't convinced he believed it, but it wasn't her business. Her sole focus was on a safe, speedy exit.

"The medallion is a gift and a threat all rolled into one package. Maybe they're smarter than you think." Considering Edmund's relaxed posture and tone, he might have been chatting about the weather.

"No." Vincent was quick to dismiss the suggestion.

The senator gave a furious growl. "A gift from Double-Wide." He narrowed his eyes at Bronte. "We do not tolerate terrorists. You'll get your body back. And the medallion." The older man's words rang with the weight of the promise.

"Thank you," she replied, though she had no claim to either the body or the medallion. Her shoulders knotted tighter than ever as the meeting came to a close. Her escape inched closer. She swallowed down the regret at leaving Vincent's energy. It flowed through her, a delicious warmth that would haunt her for the rest of her life.

Vincent crossed his arms over his broad chest. "Getting him out of the gyre isn't going to be easy."

As Vincent thought aloud, images of tiptoeing out of the meeting undetected flitted through her mind. He raised an eyebrow at her as if he read her thoughts. He stepped closer to her. "The energy's too high right now. We'll have to wait for the moon to wane. Three days at least." He nodded to his grandfather. "I'll call General Wilen and have him send an analyst to come pick up this letter. Since there's a body, they're going to send a bone witch and that means the Council. Edmund, make sure we have all our loose ends tied up before they get here. We don't want anything they might find to slip through our fingers and into theirs."

"Already planning on it."

Vincent glared down at her. "You wait here. No disappearing this time."

Edmund cleared his throat, loud and deliberate. The two brothers faced off. Edmund's mouth moved with silent words.

Bronte had never witnessed a mage throwing his voice. Whatever Edmund was saying, the sound waves jumped straight to Vincent's ears. No one else could hear them. Directing sound waves was a talent that ran in families, one the Casteels didn't have.

Vincent frowned at her. "My brother tells me I'm being rude."

"Not my exact words." Edmund gave her a wink.

"If you would, Bronte, please wait here. I might really go crazy if you run away again. But I'd find you this time. I'll be right back. My call will only take a few minutes."

A wisp of energy stroked along her cheek, as real as a physical caress. She'd never felt anything like it. She lifted her hand to her face and traced the vibes' path.

Vincent pulled a handkerchief from his pocket, turned to his grandfather's desk and gently picked up a corner of the Casteel letter. He strode through the office and walked out a side door that blended into the wall. His vibes faded to a trickle, steady but soft.

The remaining Rallis men stared at her. She felt like a deer in a meadow full of wolves. Bronte cleared her throat. "On behalf of the Casteels, thank you for your help." She stood up, leaving despite Vincent's order. She took a deep breath. "Unfortunately I'm not able to stay. If you'd convey my goodbye to Mr. Rallis." Her heart drummed against her ribs, fear and regret pounding in rhythm.

Edmund stepped toward her. "Colonel Rallis." His masculine smile, warm and friendly, softened his correction.

"My apologies."

"I know my mother would love to meet you. Vincent's her current favorite, but I think you might sway her to my side if I were to introduce you to her."

She couldn't find a smile in herself to respond to his teasing. "I can't. My pass is only for twenty-four hours. I have to get back to Chattanooga before eleven tonight. Locke Territory is a long drive away." Her cheeks burned with the admission. The two men were silent at her statement, too polite to question the Casteels' close control of her. Her mother had made sure she couldn't linger.

"Good day." She turned away, not offering to shake hands with them. The thick carpet muffled the sound of her escape. She stopped short as she crossed into the shadows, out of reach of the windows. There were no knobs on the door.

She was trapped.

* * * *

Vincent listened with half an ear as General Wilen spouted questions and orders from the other end of the landline connection. Two trains of thought tunneled through his mind. First and foremost was Bronte. She'd returned. For so long he'd only had her in his dreams. She was scared, but he'd fix that…show her she was safe here. Though how was he going to do that when Double-Wide had dumped a body in the gyre without tripping over any of their security wards or personnel? That was the other thought barreling through him.

Bronte's tug on his energy softened.

Edmund strode into their father's office, ignoring the fact that he was on the landline. "She's leaving, Vin." His brother was right. Bronte was moving away from him.

Edmund nudged him hard in the shoulder. Vincent stiffened. No one touched him.

His brother's whisper hissed into his ear. "Hurry up. We can't force her to stay. Unless you want me to tie her up. There's probably some rope in Jasper's closet."

Vincent interrupted General Wilen's stream of orders, a necessary breach of protocol. "Our lead is leaving, sir."

"Don't let her out of your sight," Wilen said.

"Yes, sir." He had no intention of letting her get away. "Rallis out." He dropped the receiver into its cradle. Using Nons' technology was easier on his mage sense than using vibes to communicate with Wilen.

"Your lead? She's a suspect?" Edmund wrinkled his brow.

Vincent moved to the far end of the office. It was an ingrained habit to keep his powerful sixth sense from overloading. He was the most powerful deflector mage in the country. The more powerful a deflector, the more sensitive he was to energy. It was an unfortunate paradox. Edmund's energy brushed against him, but for once, Vincent's mage sense remained relaxed. Bronte's syphon power worked even from a distance.

"Look at it from Wilen's point of view," Vincent said. "She's a Non, or so everyone believes. Maybe she's angry. Resentful of her controlling sponsors. As a Casteel, she has access to their house, or would if they treated her like family. Then she shows up here, finagles her way into our household. If she's a DW agent, now they've snuck someone into both Casteel and Rallis."

"She's hardly terrorist material. She's terrified. Did you tell Wilen she's a syphon?"

Vincent looked at him without an iota of guilt. "No."

Edmund leaned against their father's empty desk. "You don't trust what he'll do with her."

His brother's guess was right on target. Wilen would sacrifice anything and anyone for the good of the Republic.

But Bronte was off-limits.

"We need to keep her safe," Edmund said.

Vincent braced himself for one of his twin's plans. Edmund was smart, devious when needed, and a crack at winning against the system. But Vincent didn't need his brother's interference to win over Bronte. He cut him off at the pass. "Here's the plan. You get her sponsorship with the Casteels voided. Today. Transfer it over to us. I'll handle the rest."

Edmund slipped on a smile. "Come on, Vin. You need me for more than that. When it comes to women, you're out of practice. Hell, you've never had practice. Women just hop out of their clothes and into your bed at the crook of your finger. They all know not to waste time before your sense can't tolerate them. But this pretty little Casteel is going to be a challenge." He held out his hand like a knife, slicing it back and forth through the air. Their grandfather used the same gesture when he formulated plans for a Senate bill. "You're gonna have to woo her. I've got some ideas on that." Edmund paced toward him.

Vincent stepped out the door and slammed it behind him. He sent a stream of energy into the lock. It clicked into place.

"I only want to help." The laugh in Edmund's voice came through the door. His brother could unlock it in seconds, but Vincent had made his point. He didn't need Edmund's schemes to catch his girl.

"Let me know if you need some rope." Edmund threw the words to Vincent's ear, making it sound like he stood at his side. Vincent swatted at the air as if he could shove him away. He picked up his pace and strode down the marble hallway toward the main entrance. He was confident Jasper had delayed her from leaving—without involving rope.

Two groups waited for meetings outside the senator's office. One was the chief of the territory's enforcers and his lieutenant. The other two made for an odd pair: a fluffy woman in pink and a man with a sour face. Vincent dismissed them all with a glance.

Bronte stood by the front door, her back to him. The sun shone through the glass of the windows, highlighting her slender silhouette. She wasn't tall, but her composure and the quiet way she carried herself lent her the illusion of height. He'd never seen anyone with such pale skin and dark hair. Those red lips had tempted Vincent at nineteen. They still did.

"Bronte." His voice sounded louder and harder than he'd intended, echoing in the marble entryway.

She turned. Her lips parted. Her dark blue eyes went wide. Edmund was right. She was terrified. He wanted to see her lit up with joy and happiness. Someday soon, he promised himself.

Jasper exited the coat room with her hat and violin case. "My sincere apologies for your wait, Miss Casteel." The butler spared an exasperated look at Vincent. It vanished as he turned back to Bronte. "There was some confusion as to which violin was yours."

"Thank you." Her tone made it clear she didn't buy Jasper's story about multiple instruments. She donned her hat. Its low brim concealed most of her face. With long, graceful fingers, she tamed any errant strands of hair, tucking them in place. He couldn't remember ever noticing a woman's hands. Hers were delicate and slender.

Vincent reached for her violin, but she beat him to it.

Jasper left them to battle it out while he attended to the other visitors.

"Stay." An order. "Please." A small improvement, but it made no difference.

"No."

"Thirteen years ago—"

She cut him off. "We were kids. Ignorant kids."

"No. We weren't." He'd already spent a year under Wilen's command. He hadn't been a kid. Considering the family she'd been born into, her childhood hadn't lasted long either. "We deserve a chance—"

"I deserve a chance to keep my head on my shoulders." Her whisper crackled with fury. "Hanging around you isn't going to help me achieve that goal."

"You'd be safe here."

She lifted her chin. Blue eyes peeked out from beneath the hat. "Goodbye, Colonel."

He took a quick, short breath. "Hand me your purse, please." Somewhere in his mind, a red flag waved a vicious warning. He ignored it and held out his hand.

"What?"

"Your purse." He crooked his fingers.

"There is nothing in my purse except my keys and my identification papers." Her voice retained its cultured, proper timbre.

What would it take to make her lose that composed shield? What had it taken for her to build it? He would regret this, but it would keep her by his side for a little longer. He needed that time.

For a moment, she stood her ground. Her gaze drilled into him. He admired her determination, but it worried him as well. Defiance was dangerous for a Non-mage, even if she only pretended to be a Non.

Finally she held out the small bag. Her chin dropped. That hat once again hid her expression, but he'd bet anger lurked beneath.

He flicked the purse open and pulled out the red leaf. He'd watched from the window. He'd sensed her presence the instant she'd pulled through the gates. "What's this?"

"That is a leaf." She didn't look up, but he could see her lips tighten.

"Is there a problem, Colonel Rallis?" The territory's chief enforcer approached with pounding feet, a rhythmic warning that reverberated through the quiet foyer.

"Chief Masset." Vincent nodded at the older man. Masset knew him well enough not offer his hand. They'd worked together after the first Double-Wide bombing. The chief's son had died in the explosion.

Bronte lifted her chin, revealing her stubborn expression to the enforcer.

That red flag inside him waved another warning.

She stared right into the chief's eyes. "I stole a leaf, Chief Masset." She was calling Vincent's bluff.

"Colonel." Masset's voice boomed through the house. "Would you like me to arrest the Non? She has confessed to stealing from a mage." He thrust out a hand. "Papers, Non."

Vincent ground his teeth at the question, but Bronte stood perfectly composed under the threat to her freedom. Her courage ran deep. Her life hadn't been like the rest of the Mayflower heiresses'. No pampering or coddling. She been ordered around, forced to live at the whim of someone else and eek out a living in the South. Did she work in the sweltering factories among their dangerous machines? With hands like hers, he knew the answer was likely no, but it didn't erase his horror at how she must live.

"Papers!"

"Certainly, Officer." Bronte lifted her small purse out of Vincent's grasp, the closest she'd come to touching him. Her hand stayed as steady as her voice. How many times had she faced men like Masset? Vincent wanted to step in front of her and order the chief to stand down.

Bronte tugged a folded white paper from her purse. A short, gruff growl escaped his throat. The white paper indicated her sponsorship was valid for one year. The darker the paper, the longer the sponsorship. Black indicated a sponsorship for a lifetime.

He'd expected black.

Instead, the Casteel family required their own daughter to reapply for sponsorship every twelve months. If they denied her request, she had fourteen days to find a new sponsor, or she'd be deported. Though a few Mayflower families had changed their sponsorship policies because of the outcry over the Double-Wide attacks, a Mayflower daughter ought to have a permanent sponsor.

Vincent slipped the paper from her fingers and stepped in front of Masset, cutting off the chief's access to Bronte. He'd meant to use her theft to cajole her to linger, giving Edmund time to transfer her sponsorship.

Gentle blackmail. Not jail. His plan threatened to spiral out of control thanks to the man's overly zealous attitude.

He looked down at the top of her hat. "Have lunch with me." He winced at his order. Thank the goddess Edmund couldn't hear him bumbling this yet again.

"Ooooo!" The squeal came from behind them. The woman in pink hopped up from her bench and skipped over.

"A lunch date! Yes! A date would be perfect." The pink lady stopped beside them. "You two are an exemplary energy match! I've never seen anything like it. And I get around!" The woman's round face beamed with pure joy. "I'm so excited to get to meet the match already! You found each other all by yourselves!" Her smile grew so large it caused her eyes to squint. She turned the squint on Vincent. "It's usually our job to find the woman. That's how it works, you know." She nodded, her head bouncing on her neck.

Her stern companion paced over and whispered in her ear. The woman's face fell flat but perked right back up. "Oh trust me, Frederick." She shook her finger in the air like a schoolteacher reprimanding a naughty boy. "He's the right man! And she's the right woman! Their vibes match perfectly." She clapped her hands and tucked them under her chin. If her smile grew any larger it would hang off the edges of her face.

Frederick's pointy nose flared. He gripped the woman's elbow and dragged her back to their bench.

"Bye!" The pink woman waved with her free hand.

If this woman could see their vibes matching, then she was a compeer, a mage talented in finding complementary energy patterns. There was only one reason she'd be here: to work on a marriage for Edmund. His brother hadn't even mentioned it.

"Will you be pressing charges, Colonel?" Masset demanded. He lifted his handcuffs, shaking the chain near Bronte's face.

"No charges," Vincent said.

Bronte spoke at the same time.

"Colonel, I accept your offer of lunch." Her lush lips tipped into a frown. She stepped back from the handcuffs. "But I want my leaf back."

He held out the fiery leaf. "I'd give you the whole tree."

Chapter 3

Bronte stuttered to a stop outside the manor doors. Her mental alarm squealed like an out-of-tune orchestra at the sight of the empty driveway. Her violin case swayed at her sudden halt and bumped against Vincent's leg.

He stepped up beside her. "The back terrace is around to the left."

She didn't move.

"Is it too hot for you out here? We could have lunch inside, but you're going to attract the rest of the family if we use the dining room."

"Where is my car?" Her voice screeched in the quiet. Panic buzzed in her head like a bee trapped in a glass jar.

"One of the servants took it behind the house. Someone will drive it around when you're ready to leave."

"But my car keys are in my purse." Her tone shot higher and headed toward a whine. "How did he move…" She took a breath. Her shoulders drooped. Real mages didn't need keys. Or doorknobs. They didn't need to hide or to have sponsors. They didn't need to fear arrest for stealing a stupid leaf.

A soft pressure landed on her head and her hat flew off. She turned her head and glared at the thief.

"I can't see your face in this thing." He held the hat by the crown, delicately clasped in his palm. He shrugged one shoulder and tilted his head. "I can barely read your vibes." The great and powerful colonel wrinkled his brow at her, confused.

"No one can read my vibes. Let me help you out and simply tell you how I'm feeling right now." She planted her feet to face him head-on. Her violin case banged between them and came perilously close to parts he wouldn't want in contact with the hard case.

He slipped his fingers around the handle and took it from her grasp, adding it to his hand that now held her hat by its brim.

She allowed it, but only because she needed both hands for this. Finger by finger, she ticked off her thoughts, pointer finger first. "Number one, I want my car back. Number two, I want to get home before my pass expires, before I have to deal with another Chief Masset arresting me. Three, I want to get there without falling asleep behind the wheel. Four, I want people—no, I want *mages*—to stop telling me where I can and cannot go." She ticked off her last finger. "And I…" She paused. She had one more finger. She needed to use it for something. "I want my violin back. Please." She held out her hand.

He gave a firm nod. His wrinkles smoothed. "I'll take care of all that for you." He did not hand over her instrument.

She closed her eyes and let her head fall back. She took a breath for three slow counts and then lowered her chin. "No." The word was a long note filled with exasperation. "That was me telling you how I feel. I'm not asking you to fix my problems with a wave of your mage wand. You can't poof it all away like your gardener did with your leaves." She flung a hand behind her to the naked branches. They stood stark against the blue sky.

How long had she been inside? Forty-five minutes? In that short amount of time the gardener mage had erased that beautiful, bright canopy. No evidence remained of the leaves' existence anywhere. Not on the ground. Not on the branches. They'd been shaken off and obliterated. Deemed no longer worthy. Like her, they'd been banished. There were no survivors… except one. She clutched her purse against her chest.

Something hot and angry wrapped around her gut like a lasso. "You know, this season is called fall because the leaves are supposed to fall."

He squinted at her as if she'd suddenly started speaking another language. "They did fall."

"They are supposed to fall one by one. Or two by two. However they choose. Not because a mage forces them to. They're supposed to scatter down to the ground all on their own."

He studied her. "One fell right into your hand." Uncertainty drenched his tone.

"Yes, guided by mage power."

"A mage who was flirting with you. I saw it from the window."

"Mages don't flirt with me. I'm a Non." She pointed at the left side of her cardigan, bringing his attention to her N.

"Your N is a lie, though the reason you wear it is exactly the reason we control the leaves. Appearances matter. Rallis would lose respect if our enemies thought we're too weak to regulate the mages around here, much less the trees or the grass." He brushed the underneath of her chin with a finger. "Project the image you want seen. That's something you of all people should understand. You're a master at manipulating people to see what you want them to. They are completely deceived by your façade and don't look any deeper."

The brief physical touch increased the connection between his vibes and her syphon. The flow of his energy quickened.

"It's not a façade. I can't conceal my ability. People just don't notice. They assume I'm a Non."

"And you play along."

"Of course I do. I want to live. What you think I am…" She shook her head. "It's not what all those fairy tales say. I'm not the witch in Hansel and Gretel capturing lost children to feast on their energy." She pressed a hand to the bare skin beneath her throat. "I never sensed mage energy before I met you. I never have since. All those accounts in the history books of burning…syphons." There. She'd said it. The word flung from her like it had been straining at its tether, yearning for freedom. "Those poor women. They were turned over to the inquisitions by other mages."

His intent focus did nothing to stop her ramble. Instead it seemed to be the catalyst for the spill of her plea.

She continued, "Some coward of a mage was accused of witchcraft, and he pointed the finger at a syphon to save his own skin. Those historical accounts all read the same. No one else in the village or the castle knew the syphon even had a mage power. And there's a reason no one ever suspected anything! There's nothing bad about syphons." She held her hands in front of her as if pleading with him to believe her. Those words had existed inside her for years. They were finally free.

"I'm familiar with the stories." His tone reflected a scholarly expertise. "It's worse than you know. Most of the history books don't tell you that the coward who betrayed her was the only mage the syphon could sense, the only mage whose vibes sang to the syphon's soul. They handed their syphons over to a horrible death to deflect attention from themselves."

She took a step back.

"Without exception, the men who accused the syphons were very powerful mages." He stepped forward. "But their courage didn't match their power."

He bent down until his nose was mere inches from hers. "I'm not a coward." The colonel no longer sounded like a professor. "I'm not scared. Not of anyone, including you and your direct line to my vibes. You need me. Just as much as I need you. And I'll stand up to anyone who tries to sever that link."

She leaned forward an inch, refusing to give anymore ground. "Your energy might sing to my syphon, but I've survived without it just fine." She closed the gap another inch and lowered her voice to a whisper. "I don't need you. And I don't trust you."

He narrowed his eyes. "You will."

Edmund strode out the front door. "Good news, Bronte." He strode over, putting an arm around each of them as if she were family. "You don't need to rush off today. I got your pass extended." He smiled down at her. "You get to stay."

* * * *

She'd never seen a pass like this one. She'd spent years playing with musicians from all over the country, Nons with generous passes from their sponsors to come and go as needed. Never had any been required to stay in a territory that was not their home. Her parents had invented a new way to jerk her around.

Vincent read over her shoulder as she scanned the words again. "*Non-mage Bronte Casteel shall remain within Rallis Territory until noon on Sunday, September 18. At 12:01PM the aforementioned Non-mage shall cross the Ohio River into Bradford Territory under the auspices of Casteel and enter Locke Territory by 8:00PM that day.*" She supposed she should be grateful they'd allotted her a whole eight hours to drive home to Chattanooga.

Bronte tucked the pass into her purse. Deliberate and careful, she slid it next to her identification papers. A fiery tip of the leaf poked up. She wanted to yank it out and get rid of it, but then it would flutter around the yard. Completely alone. Vulnerable. Subject to the whims of mages.

She gently tucked it in and snapped her purse closed. She wasn't the only one unhappy about the pass. Vincent's dark eyebrows squeezed together. His nose flared above clenched teeth and he glared at his brother.

It's a start. Edmund mouthed the words to Vincent. She guessed he silenced the sound waves, but she'd read his lips.

"A start to what?" Bronte refused to let them exclude her.

Edmund's eyes jumped to hers. They matched Vincent's.

She glared. "It's quite rude to talk about me when I'm standing right here."

"Yes, it is rude, Edmund."

Bronte turned to face the source of the smooth voice. A tall, regal woman glided out the front door. "Maybe you'll finally take it to heart coming from this lovely soul."

"You're right, Mother." He tipped his head toward Bronte. A strand of wavy hair jumped to his forehead. It was longer than Vincent's short, military look but still this side of appropriate for a future senator. "I'm sorry, Bronte."

Bronte nodded in acknowledgement but not forgiveness. She was too powerless here to pretend everything was alright.

Vincent stepped between the two women. "Bronte, may I introduce my mother, Helen Rallis."

There wasn't much resemblance between the mother and sons, though at second glance Edmund had his mother's smile. True joy beamed from it. As his twin, Vincent ought to have inherited it too, but she'd yet to see it.

"Lady Rallis, it's an honor to meet you." Bronte nodded again.

"Oh please, do call me Helen." She walked two steps in her gleaming high heels, stooped slightly to accommodate Bronte's shorter stature, and hugged her. "May I call you Bronte?"

"Of course." How could she say no?

"Would you mind terribly if I join you for lunch?"

"Please do join us." Lady Rallis was a powerful mage, but Vincent was the dangerous one. At least to Bronte. She welcomed the buffer.

Lady Rallis took Bronte's arm. Vincent and Edmund followed behind as they made their way around to the back terrace.

"I understand you live in Chattanooga. I've never been there."

Naturally.

Chattanooga was poor and full of Nons with scarcely enough mages to oversee it. A lady of a founding family would never lower herself to venture there. But the city was the heart of the music scene for Nons. So much that even mages performed there occasionally. Other than Bronte.

"Lady Rallis—"

"Helen."

"Right. Helen. Do you have a landline I could use? Since my pass has been changed, I'm going to miss the next few performances my band has scheduled. I need to call them and let them know."

Helen's elegant brow wrinkled briefly. "Oh, how unfortunate. I hope they're understanding people."

Bronte heard the meaning behind the words. *Sorry you're not going to make it, but not sorry you're required to stay here.* Lady Rallis gave her a long look. Her classically beautiful face held the fierceness—the ruthlessness—of a queen.

Bronte held her gaze. "Understanding doesn't mean they'll forget."

Lady Rallis's small smile provided little clue to her thoughts. She silently gestured to the left, indicating they needed to pass beneath the arch of the east wing. The groomed pea-gravel path to the back of the manor matched the driveway that her old car had managed to limp down. The gardener had gone overboard on the gravel on this section of the path. Bronte sank with each step.

"Mother, you need to tell the gardener to ease up on the rocks." Edmund's wry tone made it clear he struggled too.

"One doesn't question Dell. The man knows everything."

Bronte's next footstep stayed on the surface of the path, as if the pebbles decided to stick together and support her instead of drowning her heels among them. The rush of Vincent's energy into her syphon increased.

Helen gasped. She stopped, studied Vincent and then turned to Bronte. "I can hardly believe what you do for him."

"I didn't do anything." Her hackles rose as high as the other woman's gratitude, recognizing it as a trap.

Hope softened Lady Rallis's honed look. "You're letting Vincent deflect the power of our footsteps without any repercussions for him. Vincent never wastes his mage vibes on something as trivial as walking." Her voice bordered on a whisper. "You are a true gift to all of us."

"I'm not a gift to be passed from one hand to the next."

Lady Rallis's eyes flashed. "Then be more."

"Fight back." Vincent stared down at her.

"Fight back? Now you're talking crazy. Have you forgotten your history already? I'm here for the next twenty-four hours. That's not enough time for a revolution." She glared back at the mighty colonel. She walked on, wanting only to get this lunch over with.

"As interesting as this conversation is, I'm afraid I must take my leave." Edmund interrupted. "I have work that won't wait." He patted Bronte on the shoulder as they came in sight of the terrace set with an elegant table. "I'll show you to the landline on my way."

She followed him inside, leaving Lady Rallis and Vincent behind. The coolness of the house enveloped her. They passed through a room with the chatter of a talk show on the television and into another sitting room with the landline. Edmund left her to it.

She dialed Claude's number.

Her old friend had changed over the last year. She hardly knew him anymore. And what she did know, she didn't much like. Maybe luck's grace would favor her and his answering machine would click on. Morning time came around four in the afternoon for him. Noon was the middle of his night.

He answered on the first ring. "Bronte?" The word shot through the phone. He was wide awake.

"Yes, it's me." She fired back at his abrupt greeting, but she needed to get this over with before someone walked into the room. She dispensed with the pleasantries. "I'm sorry to do this, but I'm not going to be able—"

He cut her off. "You didn't play the damn song like I told you! You needed to follow the notes exactly as I wrote them. How many times have you changed my songs? I know it was you who did it!"

Bronte wrenched the phone from her ear at his vicious yell. This conversation had been a long time coming. The middle of the Rallis house wasn't the place for it, but she was too exhausted and stressed to tiptoe around him like usual. "What has gotten in to you, Claude? I've tried to hold on to our friendship, but you've not made it easy. No one in the band wants to deal with you anymore."

"If you would just do as I tell you, then I wouldn't need to be unpleasant and rude!" Claude roared.

"I'm not even going to discuss that insane statement. I'm calling to let you know I won't be available until Monday."

"Monday?" he shrieked. "You're gonna miss two more gigs?"

"Yes." Bronte gave a curt nod even though he couldn't see it. "You have to take my place."

"I don't play in public anymore, Bronte!"

"Well, that needs to change. You need to shake off whatever made you crawl into a cave and refuse to play. If you want the group to be successful, you're going to have to deliver on this contract. I'm still not clear why you agreed to do a wedding in the first place. I'm sorry I can't be there, but it's out of my hands."

"It's because of your asshole family, isn't it? They're not letting you leave. You're their goddamn slave. Don't you see how these people treat us Normals like we're not even human? Fight back. You should be the one leading the charge against the tyranny the mages hold over the Normals."

"Quite a speech, Claude." His words were an eerie echo of Vincent's. She peeked over her shoulder. Vincent was gone, but she knew he couldn't be too far away. "But I'm not going to rehash this again."

"Blasted vibes, Bronte. They have you completely brainwashed. When you're ready to rise up and lead your people to a better life, let me know. I'll be right behind you singing your theme song. I'll compose it for you. You're practically a household name around the South. You could join up with Double-Wide."

Her whisper was fast and furious. "I will never support Double-Wide. They are terrorists who kill innocent people. Nons and mages." Time to end this. She took a deep breath. "We both know your songs haven't resonated with me in a long while. The band has been great, but it's not working for me anymore. I'm done."

"Done? As in quitting the band?"

Bronte yanked the phone away from her ear at his shout.

"No! I'm not letting you quit. I need you."

Was that a threat? For the first time since embarking on this forced journey, she was glad to be so far from home and out of Claude's reach. "It's not your choice. It's mine and I've decided. I'm going out on my own." There. She was fighting for herself—in a safe, rational manner. A thrill tickled through her. "Maybe I'll give Europe a try. The best Nons are there anyway."

She couldn't believe her own words. She'd never planned to leave, never wanted to. Now that Vincent had exposed her power, she'd be safer if she left. The world was bigger than just here. More importantly, the rest of the world was mostly *sans* mage.

"Bronnie, come on."

She hated that nickname.

Claude continued, "We're still friends. Stay with the band, and we'll play more of your stuff." His voice firmed up from a whine as he bargained. "I've got friends I can introduce you to. They already know who you are and wanna meet you. They can help you with all this stuff. They'll, you know…get you more famous, help you play where the creeps perform. You'll see. You don't want to leave. They won't like that."

"Who won't like that?" Her head was aching from this conversation.

"These people. You know, people who make things happen. You have to stay with my band."

"And if I don't stay? Then bad things are going to happen?" Her voice crept higher. She looked behind her to make sure no one was listening. "Claude, tell me that's not what you're saying." He was the only kid who'd befriended her when she'd been thrown into a strange school. He'd grown into the man who'd helped her get on stage the first time.

Now he was silent.

"I have to go now." She slowly placed the phone back in its cradle.

Claude's voice shot out of it, faint, but adamant. "Wait! Don't hang up. What time are you coming back?" He clicked into silence.

She put a hand to her mouth as if to try to contain the suspicions gnawing at her about Claude. She took two slow steps toward the doorway, her eyes on the detailed Persian rug beneath her.

She ran into a hard column of male.

Chapter 4

"What was that about?" His tone was the wrong side of polite, but her whisper hid too much of her landline conversation. Pulling sound waves toward him was not one of his strengths. He was much more adept at pushing energy away. The few key words he'd caught had his gut sending up a warning flare.

"My friend is upset. He'll have to scramble to replace me to avoid reneging on our contracts." She bit at her lip. Worry lined her forehead. It wasn't because of contracts. It was because of the guy on the other end of the connection. Claude Somebody.

If she wouldn't tell him, then he'd put one of his team's analysts on it as soon as he tucked her away, safe and comfortable. He tilted his head down to her. She stood a whole head shorter than him.

"Or bad things are going to happen? What the heck kind of friend is that?"

She narrowed her eyes. "None of your business." She sidestepped around him and headed into the next room.

Everything about her had become his business the moment she'd stepped back onto Rallis property. She was lying to herself if she thought otherwise. She sensed the tie between them as much as he did. He waved a line of energy across her shoulders, as easy as touching her with his hand. His mage energy was like another appendage, only its shape and power took whatever form he chose.

Her syphon pulled his vibes in like a warm, soft hug. She sucked in a quick breath, proof that she sensed their link. "Don't get used to it."

"Too late." He followed her into the media room where his cousin stood watching the television. He had no patience for Allison right now. He rarely did. Edmund, on the other hand, tolerated her with a fondness and sympathy that Vincent never managed.

"Oooo! Lawry!" Allison spoke to the man on the show as if he could hear her. "That was sooo good!" Her squeal never failed to grate a few layers of tissue from his eardrums. The credits rolled. She spun around. "Vinny! Did you see any of the *Dr. Lawrence Riley Show*?" Her gaze landed on Bronte, and she scanned his syphon from head to foot. Her lips puckered in a frown. "Hmm. Who do we have here?"

Bronte gave Allison a polite smile. Her Mayflower breeding was tough stuff.

"Oh." Allison's tone drooped. "A Non." At the sight of the deceptive N on Bronte's sweater, Allison dismissed her with a careless wave.

"Allison, you will give her the respect—"

"Vincent, it's alright." Bronte glanced at him, her cheeks pink. "Let's just go have lunch."

He wanted to shake his cousin along with the rest of his world. Bronte had dealt with this her entire life. She deserved better. No one would treat her like a second-class citizen in this house.

He slid his arm around Bronte's back. The heat of her skin soaked through her sweater and the sleeve of his shirt. "Bronte, may I introduce you to my cousin, Allison Rallis. Allison, this is Miss Bronte Casteel." As a mage, Allison should have been introduced first, a social slap learned at his mother's heel. His cousin's indignant gasp let him know she'd felt the cut.

"It's an honor to meet you, Miss Rallis."

His cousin gave a regal nod. "Bronte." Her eyes flashed to the N again. "What brings you here?" Her sneer lifted half her nose.

"Vincent invited me to lunch." The sarcastic tone was clear.

"Oh dear." Cynicism etched through Allison's pitying smile. "Let me explain something. Girl to girl. If you think he actually spends any time with a woman outside the bedroom, you're terribly deluded. He's not that type."

He went to step in front of Bronte, to block her from Allison's disdain, but this time, Bronte anticipated his move. She grabbed his hand, still at her waist, and squeezed hard. He held his position, but only because reinforcements had arrived. His mother's vibes fanned toward him.

"Allison, that's enough." His mother's strong voice carried through the room as she stepped in from the terrace. "Bronte is our honored guest, and she will be treated as such."

Bronte tugged him toward the terrace, a silent command to retreat.

"Aunt Helen, it's not nice to let them get ideas. Nons just don't understand." Allison caught up to Bronte. "Vincent doesn't have an emotional relationship with anyone."

Bronte tipped her pert little nose high. "That's not true. I've only been here for an hour, but even that's been long enough to see he loves his mother and brother."

Allison frowned, her mouth pinched tightly. "Just don't expect anything from him."

Bronte laughed softly. "Thank you for your concern, but I assure you I have low expectations." She stepped outside.

He needed a chance to prove his worth. She wouldn't willingly give it to him. He would have to take it anyway. It was his most urgent mission. He followed Bronte onto the terrace and left his mother to deal with Allison.

"Bronte is…different," his mother explained.

"Yes, she's a Non," Allison replied. "I see that. Don't you think we would have figured out already if Nons could help him? They can't. They didn't help Daddy, and they won't help Vinny."

He shut the door on his female family members, but it didn't stay closed. They followed right out.

"Althea!" Allison called. "Attend me on the terrace! I'm lunching out here."

Vincent clenched his jaw.

His mother gestured for everyone to be seated after Jasper brought another chair for Allison. "Did you clear your calendar, Bronte?" She beamed a smile at Bronte's curt nod. "Good. Then you're all ours."

Displeasure scribbled lightly across his syphon's face.

"I'll make it worth your while," he promised with a whisper.

He couldn't charm or flirt like Edmund. Hell, even the gardener mage had better instincts for charming her. Who knew she'd be charmed by a floating leaf? Vincent could float her every tree in the yard. Would she find that charming? Unlikely. No matter. He had something no one else could offer her, besides his own vibes. He had knowledge. He knew more about syphons than anyone. He'd use it to his benefit. To keep her, he'd use every weapon in his arsenal.

However, he worked best in private. His strategy hadn't included company. He gave his mother a narrowed glare. Apparently her faith in his ability to snag his girl equaled Edmund's. Why else would she invite herself?

Bronte met his gaze with a bemused smile as if she could guess his thoughts. She sat silently as two of his mother's maids set their lunch on the table.

The two women were recent hires. He'd read over their security profiles last month before approving them. Neither profile raised any flags. But he'd check again. With terrorists dumping bodies on their land, everyone was suspect. This included Allison's potionness, Althea. The tall, slender woman stood behind Allison, swirling two flasks of dark liquids. Her face was carefully blank, a useful expression for someone whose boss was a potion addict…or for a terrorist's agent.

Allison gave an absent wave over her shoulder without looking at the potionness. The woman moved discreetly against the wall, still swirling.

Allison clapped her hands with glee as she studied her plate. "Ooo! Non-mage food! I adore eating Nons' cuisine every now and then." She examined her food with a wrinkled nose. "But I need meat. This will not do. Take it away." As the maid complied, Allison looked at Bronte. "Vinny's a vegetarian. I'm sure you didn't know." She waved a finger back and forth over his mother's plate. "What is that anyway?"

Thank the goddess he had Bronte safely seated between him and his mother.

His mother took the question in stride. "Quinoa with roasted sweet potatoes and a touch of onion. Salad greens."

"Sweet potatoes! I adore them!" She turned her head toward the house. "Keep the sweet potatoes!" she hollered in the direction the maid had disappeared. "*The Dr. Lawrence Riley Show* was all about sweet potatoes today! Dr. Riley concocted a potion from its leaves. But you really have to know what you're doing when you use it," she cautioned. "Too much and it could kill you. Get it just right and it will open your heart and let love and peace for all burst out." Allison touched her chest and then lifted her hands as if to embrace the world.

"Sounds painful. Better avoid that one." Vincent snapped his napkin to his lap.

The maid returned with the plate, ham added.

Allison circled her finger over the orange pile on her plate. "Dr. Lawrence Riley said sweet potatoes grown by Nons are superior to those grown by mage farmers. It's something they actually do better than the rest of us! Non farmers have such dull energy they vibrate their growth less. Therefore, their sugars grow undisturbed, and they make sweeter sweet potatoes." She flashed her brown eyes to Bronte. "You like Dr.

Riley, don't you? He's all for Nons' rights and how useful you all are to mages."

Bronte smiled tightly. A drip of sweat trailed down her temple. He'd forgotten she suffered from the heat. He glanced at his mother in her suit and Allison in her black turtleneck, both as cool and comfortable as if it were a breezy, cloudy sixty-eight degrees. Allison caught sight of Bronte's bead of sweat as well. His cousin preened, pulling the neck of her shirt higher. It was a sign of power for mages to dress in opposition of the weather and regulate their body temperatures with vibes.

Bronte tipped her head to Allison. "It's good to know we Nons have our uses."

"Oh, you do! But, really, we could import all the sweet potatoes we need. I mean, how many sweet potatoes could the Republic eat? We don't need to grow them here."

Bronte sank back against her seat, resigned to let Allison win her thoughtless, intolerant games. Streaks of pale blue lined the skin beneath her eyes.

"You drove all night to get here." Vincent pushed a tendril of cool air over Bronte.

She leaned into it. "How did you know that?"

"You said your mother called you late last night ordering you here. You live in Locke Territory. You arrived here at eleven. It's the obvious conclusion."

"You must be exhausted!" His mother laid a hand on Bronte's arm. "Eat quickly and then Vincent can find you a place to rest. But do tell us about your music, will you?" She turned toward the wall where the butler waited. "Jasper, would you put Bronte's violin back inside the house? It's too hot for such an instrument."

Jasper obliged and took the damn hat as well.

Vincent directed another push of air toward Bronte's neck, where little strands of her dark, shiny hair were damp.

She met his eyes and straightened. Alarm tightened the muscles of her face as she realized the source of the breeze.

He waited for her rebuke. But it didn't come. He pushed another soft breeze at her, an example of the aid he could render her if she'd allow it.

Allison inhaled with an annoying tsk. "You're a musician, are you? That's so cute. Aunt Helen supports the musical arts. In fact, the Rallises are the benefactors of many music scholarships and two outreach programs. It's even given a few Nons the chance to watch the mage children perform. Isn't that sweet?"

Vincent gripped the table, his fingers like claws on the fine white tablecloth. “By the goddess, Allison,” he began, his tone slow and deadly.

Bronte nudged his shoe under the table. “I’m sure the musicians in the area are grateful for your support, Lady Rallis.”

“Helen.”

“Right, Helen. The Rallis Symphony is known to be the best in the nation. Obviously, you are one of the reasons behind that. I love classical music.”

“Too bad you’re not allowed to play it,” Allison quipped.

“You’re mistaken, Miss Rallis. I am allowed to play it.” Bronte’s sharp retort drew an approving smile from his mother. “You’re referring to the law prohibiting Nons from joining symphonies or having their own. Mages reserve that privilege, like so many others, for themselves.”

“Hmm, Europe has some decent symphonies.” Allison tapped a long manicured finger against her lips. “Aren’t there some Nons who left and played there? Although I doubt your training in the South was sufficient for that.”

“It was quite sufficient.” A small smile accompanied Bronte’s glare, a lady’s *screw you* expression.

Mother beamed in approval.

“Cousin, shut up,” he bit off. “Or leave. Clear?”

“What? What have I done?” Allison’s eyes were wide with confusion.

“She’s correct. I can’t think of one Southern school anywhere near as good as the music schools in the North. I was lucky. My school happened to have an exchange program set up with another school in Dublin.”

“Dublin?” Allison’s mouth made a circle of surprise. “Our Dublin here?”

“No,” Bronte gently corrected. “Ireland.” Then her eyes fired with a dangerous light. “I did play for a mage orchestra once.” She lifted her gaze to him, peeking through her dark bangs.

Vincent hummed in the back of his throat, a low vibrating growl.

“What?” Allison choked on her food.

Bronte shrugged. “It was an audition. I lied on the application and said I was a mage.”

The potionness gasped at Bronte’s confession.

“Risky.” His mother’s eyes were wide with alarm.

A dozen horrible outcomes flickered through his mind. “Do you know what happens to a Non who gets caught claiming mage status? Jail. Exile.” Worse.

Her eyes dimmed like a curtain drawn across a window. "I did get caught. But I had to know if anyone would give me a chance. I found out the answer." She shrugged again. "I survived. Now I play mostly folk music. Country and bluegrass. They're good too. Just different."

His mother put down her fork. "Tonight is the twentieth anniversary performance for Peter Leggert. He's the conductor of the Rallis Symphony. They're performing a mishmash of his favorite pieces. Since your pass has been extended, you and Vincent should both come."

Bronte laughed and shook her head.

Allison butted in. "Well, I'm not going." She picked up the tall, skinny glass at the edge of her plate and held it out to her side.

The potionness stepped forward with a sigh of relief and tipped her flasks into the glass. Two streams of dull green liquids poured out.

Bronte shrank back in her seat as if she wanted as far away from it as possible.

Allison downed it, lifting the glass and tipping her head back until her nose pointed at the ceiling of the porch. As the potion soaked through her system, she shuddered and then gave a pleased smile. "*Chrislia* is one of my favorites. It makes every bit of energy so clear."

Allison stroked the air around his mother. "Such a lovely aura, Aunt Helen."

Damn that Riley guy for hooking her on these concoctions.

"I respect Aunt Helen's love of music, but I don't share it." Allison sighed in bliss from the effects of the potion, then blinked at Bronte. Her mouth formed an exaggerated circle. "Oh, Bronte, I'm probably making you uncomfortable with my power. It slipped my mind to block my energy. Vincent forgot too, I see."

Allison leaned back toward the potionness. "That's a good one. It brings everyone's aura into such sharp resolution. We need to tell Lawry again how fantastic this is. I can see energy everywhere." She focused her eyes on Vincent with a tip of her head. "Vinny." Her voice was soft and dreamy. "Your energy. I've never seen it so relaxed. Did you finally try that potion Lawry gave you?" She squinted as if she were nearsighted and missing her glasses. "Vinny, your vibes are flowing into that Non by the megajoule!" Allison's voice reached higher as she stood up. Her chair crashed to the ground. "She's…she's stealing your power!" Allison looked down at herself, extending her arms to inspect them as well. "Is she doing it to me too?"

"Calm down, Allison," his mother began.

Allison's hands went to her hips. "Is she the reason you can sit here? You never lunch with us. For a while I thought she was just good in bed. But no. She's helping you with your power. If she can help you, then she can help my father!"

"Bronte is mine." Vincent's words trembled with power.

Allison twitched under the force.

"I beg your pardon. I do not belong to anyone." Bronte's crisp words dropped flat and powerless among them, a glaring example of her vulnerability, of her need for a protector. She would survive only if she belonged to someone.

Allison ignored her. "You are so selfish! Father has nothing. He doesn't even have me because he can't tolerate other mages' vibes! You have everything. Riches. Fame. People think you're a hero. But you stampede over anyone who dares inconvenience you. Well, I'm done with that! I'm buying her sponsorship for my father, and he won't share with you!"

Allison stomped back inside. The potionness stood against the wall, mouth gaped open. She stared at Bronte, horrified, and then took off after her mistress.

His mother gave a small sniff. "I apologize for that. Allison had a trying day. Her home is here, but her heart is with her father. He's rather… ill. Please don't let her influence your decision to come to the concert tonight. Allison's gift is almost as rare as Edmund's and even more useless. Without that potion, she can only see the auras of dark powers, not the light powers. It's a very unfulfilling ability. There are no other aurist mages registered in Rallis Territory, light or dark. No one will think twice about what you are."

Bronte's stare locked on the far edge of the table, her eyes clouded with anger for him. He did not regret his words. She belonged to him as much as he did to her.

She lifted her eyes to his mother. "Forgive me, but I don't believe you that no one will notice my power. Not if I'm out in the open. The goddess help me if anyone else learns about my power. Going to the symphony, as much as I would love to hear that music…" She paused and sighed, lost in thought for a moment. "Too risky. Besides, bringing a Non to an event like the symphony will tarnish your reputation at the least."

His mother arched a brow. The added smile softened the haughty expression. "I assure you, my reputation can withstand you."

"It doesn't need to be risky. We can slip in discreetly, hide you among us." He could give her this. He took her hand. They'd held hands thirteen years ago, too. "You'll be safe." He'd make sure of it. "And don't let Allison scare you away. You belong here."

"Why? To syphon off your excess vibes? To serve your needs? No, thank you. I already have one set of masters. I don't need another. No matter how you make me feel. I am done being under the control of a mage." She stood and pushed in her chair.

He put his napkin on the table and stood with her.

"No, dear." His mother patted Bronte's hand. "We're not—"

"Mother. I've got this."

She stood, folded her napkin, gave a nod with a closed-lip smile, and went inside.

"Bronte, I don't want to control you. I just want to be with you. You said syphons aren't like the fairy tales. You're right. I've studied them. There are cases of syphons throughout history who lived peacefully, happily with other mages. Give me a chance to prove it to you. Not all mages are like your parents."

She shook her head as if shedding his words. "This isn't history. This is my life. I'm not going to risk it. Thank you for lunch, but I am leaving now."

Every hope of making her want to stay swirled down a deep, dark drain. He'd played his only ace. If she wasn't interested in what he'd learned through hundreds of hours of research on syphons and if the connection between them couldn't lure her in, then he was out of bait.

But she wasn't leaving.

"Where do you think you're going?"

She stared back with her chin tilted up and arms crossed over her chest. "A motel. Until I'm allowed out of this territory."

He kept his voice free of mage vibes, but the intensity of his words remained the same. "You will stay here."

She jerked her hands to her hips. "My pass states I must stay within Rallis's borders. Not in this house."

He took a deep, slow breath. He had only one option against her stubborn refusal to give him a chance.

Wariness slid over her face.

It didn't stop him from crushing her illusions of getting away. "Your sponsorship is currently under Rallis authority. Therefore, your actions are subject to Rallis approval. You stay here."

Bronte swallowed hard. She took a shaky breath, blinking as if something had fallen in her eyes. "My parents would admire your methods, Vincent."

Chapter 5

Bronte stomped down the pebbled path toward the west tower of Rallis Hall, where, according to Vincent, a servant had tucked away her car. Vincent had suggested they drive to his house since it was a mile farther into the estate. A sensible plan. But she'd darn well take her own car.

He followed two steps behind her angry pace—exactly where he could stay. The heat of her fury melted every word she might have spoken to him anyway. Arguing would change nothing. She was stuck under the thumbs of twice the usual number of mages. Instead of just the Casteels, the Rallises ruled her, too.

She rounded the tower and spotted her old Volvo. It rested in the shade cast by the stone manor. A gleaming black pickup truck sat next to it. Bronte hurried to her car as if to defend it from the heavy shadows of the Rallis power. The Volvo was her only ally, her sole means of escape from too many mages all blessed with so much power a single one could crush her whole life. The strike of her heels on the stone sidewalk broadcast her anger at all of them. Only one was around to hear it.

"I'll drive." Vincent's assured tone yanked at her last thread of restraint. Apparently he wasn't listening to her shoes.

Leaping off the stone walkway to the gravel parking area, she ran. Her long strides bunched her skirt around her thighs. She made it to the car, spun around and sprawled her arms and body across the driver's door.

He was still a dozen paces behind, his pace steady and dignified compared to her frantic flight. His assured demeanor only fueled her ire.

"I. Will. Drive. My. Own. Car." She yanked the door open, jumped in the seat and slammed the door shut before he replied. With a rhythmic tapping of her fingers against the steering wheel, she fumed as he walked around to the passenger side. Temptation gnawed at her, daring her to peel out and mar the perfectly raked gravel with a pair of skid marks.

Vincent gave her a raised eyebrow, staring at her through the windshield as if he could read her mind. Her violin case hung from his right hand. Driving off before he could get to the passenger side, step in with his long legs, and sit his hard ass down wasn't an option. She might have found some silent humor about his hard ass since it reflected part of his personality in addition to his physique, but her bitterness got in her way.

Ignoring him as he slid into the car, she cranked down the window to alleviate the stifling heat. She was afraid the small, enclosed space would intensify everything she absorbed from him. But it didn't. The connection between them remained steady. Finally, one thing in her favor.

Bronte stabbed the keys in the ignition and drove out of the parking area. Gravel crunched under her tires. She turned left onto the paved private road that would take her farther into Rallis land, the opposite direction she wanted to go. She'd never been to Vincent's house, but this had to be the way. He wouldn't live near the border of the estate. No, he would live deep in the heart of the land, the better to keep out as many strangers as possible.

The better to keep her in.

Thick silence flooded the car's interior. Vincent sat perfectly still, his head cocked to one side. His vibes poured out.

She soaked them up like a sponge with an infinite capacity to absorb his energy. Too bad the rest of her was maxed out on him.

The pavement ended a half-mile from the manor house. Twin gravel paths, one for each tire, branched off to the left. With nowhere else to go, she turned. The trail meandered back and forth through the woods. Her anger lent a heavy foot to the accelerator—too heavy for the bumpy road. The car went in and out of a deep pothole. The Volvo's shocks gave a loud squeak. She didn't slow.

Vincent stayed silent, probably because he could deflect the energy of a crash should she get too reckless.

He controlled everything. Including her.

Resentment lifted its head inside her, like a seedling erupting from the ground. She'd worked hard all her life to keep that seed of bitterness unfertilized, in parched ground, so it wouldn't grow and dominate her. Vincent had stirred it up anew by stealing control over her life, even if only for the short term. She wished she could stop syphoning his power. An impossible wish. Syphons were feared partly because they could not shut down their power.

"Bronte." His tone was matter-of-fact, calm and quiet.

She took a breath. Her chest puffed and deflated. "Hmmm?" Her closed lips vibrated with the sound. If she opened her mouth, the bitterness might spill forth.

"Your car is out of tune."

Shock opened her mouth for her. She took her foot off the accelerator with a bent knee and stomped on the brake until her leg locked straight. She turned to him, her face so tense the muscles nearly twitched in protest. All the while he sat calmly in his seat, as if he'd expected the force of her stop. He probably had. It would be next to impossible to surprise a deflector mage with any kind of physical force or energy.

"That's why you've been so quiet? You've been sensing my engine?"

"I can tune it for you."

A thousand bitter words clogged her mouth. She choked on them. Finally a few spat forth. "No! You've done enough!" She wrenched open the door. Its ugly groan made it sound as if the car was on his side, moaning, *Yes! Please tune me!* She slammed it shut and stalked off.

She heard him get out, though his door neither squeaked nor moaned. The car, her only ally, had turned traitor. She marched on, as if she might walk away from everything that had happened in the past twenty-four hours.

A stream of energy brushed against her ankle like a delicate lasso. She broke its hold with a single step, only to have it happen again. "Stop that." She tossed the words over her shoulder.

"It's not me."

She spun around, ready to argue, but stopped. He was right. It wasn't coming from Vincent. Something was in the woods. Its energy sent a serene sparkle into her syphon. From her spot on the rocky road, she peered into the trees. Whatever it was, it emanated the most marvelous energy. Her anger swept away on a wave of wonder.

Vincent closed the distance between them and walked around to stand in front of her. He stroked the back of his hand against her cheek.

"Give me a chance. That's all I want." His gentle words matched his touch.

"You want more than a chance." She focused past his shoulder, peeking over his superior height. Tall trees reached scantily clad limbs into the crisp, blue sky and hid whatever shed such glorious vibes.

"I can't be sorry about this." He brushed her cheek again, his focus burning through her. Unlike her, whatever lurked in the woods didn't call to him. "Since I came into my power, I've learned to grab on to every bit of good life offers. I sensed you the moment you arrived today.

I recognized that tug on my energy as if I'd known you my whole life instead of a handful of hours thirteen years ago—your syphon reaching out and tapping my energy."

"Yes, like a pipe channeling waste into the sewer. Useful, I'll give you that."

"You mock this because you're afraid of it. But I'm not."

Easy for him to say. He wasn't the one who'd face the fire. But she didn't want to talk about this.

"What is that…power?" She pointed into the woods.

He sighed. A temporary surrender.

The little waves of energy tickled at her with delicate caresses of energy. An airy huff drifted out of her throat, almost a laugh. "It's different from you."

"It's the Rallis mark, the gyre."

"The gyre is your mark?" She knew about the special marks that claimed the land for the founding families. Each family had its own mark, but she'd never known they could be this powerful. During today's meeting, she hadn't truly understood what the senator and the Double-Wide letter referred to concerning the Rallis gyre.

"Why can I feel it?"

"Its energy's frequency is close to mine." Vincent watched her, stern and earnest. "The gyre's really intense right now. No one can go in."

"Mage vibes don't bother me, remember?" She patted his shoulder in consolation. Between his vibes and the gyre's, the energy in her syphon filled her, loosening her every constriction, as if she'd turned to marshmallow. She wanted more.

"I'm going in." She walked forward, her gaze on his for a few steps. She arched an eyebrow at him as she stepped past the first tree.

He darted after her. She ran. He caught her in two steps and hugged his thick arms around her. "It's too dangerous to go in there. It'll burn up a mage's sense in mere minutes."

She slid her arms from his grasp and pushed away his hold. She didn't fool herself. He allowed her to slip free.

"We both know I'm not the average mage. You're not stopping me. I need to go in there."

"When the energy is this high, just driving by here gives me a pounding headache."

"Then wait in the car. It's not giving me a headache. I'll be fine. And it's not like I can escape since you have the car. My papers are in there anyway." She walked off. Her heels sank slightly into the soft ground with each step.

His vibes pulled even with her before she was six paces away.

"Don't come if it's going to hurt you," she said.

He shrugged. A touch of pink brightened his cheeks. The tough colonel blushed. "I think…if I stay close to you, it might be enough to keep me from getting sick." The last words came in a rush. Such a powerful man wouldn't like to admit to such weakness. "I'm fine right now. That's never happened this close to the gyre when its energy is this high."

She gave him a small smile. "Alright, Colonel. I'll hold your hand and keep you safe." She reached for him. His hand engulfed hers, but she was the strong one here. The rush of his mage power into hers warmed her from the inside out. His energy stirred her in places that had lain dormant since that handful of hours behind a garden shed years ago.

She glanced at him from beneath her bangs. His eyes had gone dark, his blush erased. In its place was heat, desire. It wasn't longing or yearning. This was hard, demanding. The connection between them was potent and heavy and much too intense for her. She turned her back on him and took one step. Their hands stretched apart. Before she took another step, an ugly thought itched at her mind.

"Wait. The body is in the gyre. Will we see it?" Stumbling over her grandfather's body would ruin every pleasant feeling the gyre fed her.

"I don't know. If I were hiding it, I'd put it in the cave, not out in the open. Although I'm not sure even a Non could tolerate going down there." He shook free of her grip and put both hands on her shoulders. "Listen to me. If you truly can get into the gyre, you cannot tell anyone. Not until we have a solid alibi for you on the day your grandfather died and the night his body disappeared."

"I did not steal the body." Betrayal and hurt tumbled through her. "Nor did I kill him."

"I know you didn't. I believe you."

Bitterness opened the hatch for her spiel. "I didn't even know my grandfather was dead until I heard it on the radio. I haven't seen my family in thirteen years. I spoke to my mother yesterday for the first time since then. I want nothing to do with them. I certainly have no desire to touch a rotting body, much less move it." She shivered and then let her shoulders slump. The quick verbal dump had rinsed out her starch. "I'm sure I have some witnesses who will verify I was somewhere in Chattanooga working when he died."

Her rant echoed silently through the trees. The soft rasp of dead leaves dancing along the forest floor accompanied it. His lips were pulled into a thin line, his eyes gone dark with pity.

"Don't." She shook her head. "I've cut them from my life."

"But they haven't cut you from theirs."

"And I can't change that. You can't either. You said you've learned to grab onto the good in life. Well, I have too. I grab what happiness I can as I roll with their whims. I've learned to keep my head down, to move in whatever direction they push me. That's how my life works and how it will continue to work." With that, she grabbed for his hand, spun around and pulled him in her wake. She trekked through the thick buildup of dead leaves and sticks, determined to find the source of that energy. Nothing would stop her. Not high heels, not a dead body, and not Vincent.

She wobbled over a big stick buried beneath the leaves. He slowed their pace. She lost her footing again, a small hole this time, and her ankles teetered on her shoes.

"Maybe we should come back later. When you have better shoes."

"Now." She looked up at his hawkish profile.

He scanned their surroundings—right, left, and back again. The colonel was on duty.

She high-stepped through the woods to keep her heels from snagging against tree roots and fallen branches. Her cheek brushed against his shoulder as she stumbled again. It was a bumpy walk. He pulled her hand into the crook of his elbow. She leaned into his offered support.

"What exactly is the gyre?"

"It's the Rallis mark on this land, the source of our territory's energy. Each family's is different. Our mark is both above and below ground. It forms a cave that spirals down into the earth. The story goes that a Rallis created the mark on top of the land, and the goddess blessed it with her energy from within the land. My ancestors took it as a sign they'd settled in the right place."

"It must be huge to emit this much energy." She looked up at him. Despite his worry about the intensity of the power, he looked at home in these woods. She shrugged. "I don't know much of the Casteels' history, but I think the High Council moved them further west at least three times. Their marks on the land got smaller each time, as if they didn't want to spend much energy on creating one only to be forced to move again. The Casteel mark is a pool. A small, shallow one. It has a rock in the center. There's no power in it."

"No, you're wrong on that. All marks have power. You're just not tuned to the Casteel mark. And thank the goddess for that or your parents might have guessed what you are." They walked past dappled trees as he explained. "Our mark was created by an ancestor so powerful she could disperse weather systems. Or so the story goes."

"No one is that powerful." Her voice was soft.

He smiled down at her, satisfaction gleaming in his eyes.

"What?" She didn't trust that look.

"You're smiling."

She fought back the urge to reach a hand to her face to check. "This energy is hard to resist. I'm happy." That was weird. "I don't know if it's just the gyre or a combination of the gyre and you."

"I'm glad you like it. I want you happy."

Hazardous territory. She'd just handed him something to use against her.

"Back to dispersing weather systems, are you that powerful?" Not her most graceful change of subject.

He shrugged. "Never tried. But energy types tend to run in families."

Bronte gave a hard laugh. "That's probably why my parents quit having children after me. Afraid of what they would get."

He stopped in his tracks and cupped her face. Dark blue eyes stared down into her. "I'm glad they got you. And even better…I have you now. If you've never felt like anyone wanted you, let me make it clear. I do." He held her face still between his hands, leaving the rest of her wobbly. She blamed it on the shoes. Her gaze broke away from his only to land on his lips. Neither moved for a moment. Then he took her hand again and tugged her along.

She concentrated on her feet instead of the current of desire flowing between them. Her toes ached already, pushing against the tips of her pointy shoes, a definite distraction. She didn't want to admit it, but she was glad Vincent took the lead so he could scare away any snakes lurking under the crunchy brown blanket of dead leaves.

Other than the crunch of their steps, silence clouded the woods. Neither the song of birds nor the rattle of the wind dared disturb it.

As they walked, the trees grew closer and closer together until Bronte and Vincent were forced to twist back and forth among their dappled trunks. A dozen more steps through the woods and the broad trunks became all white. Tendrils of power leached from their pale surfaces as she passed them. The soft caresses passed right through her skin.

They were close.

The gyre must be on the other side of the next cluster of trees. The trees stood like sentinels, nearly shoulder to shoulder. Their trunks left only enough room for her to slip through sideways.

Vincent stopped. Her toes relaxed in her shoes with a throb of relief at the pause, but every other part of her wanted to keep going, pulled by the vibes. He turned to her, something written on his face that she'd never expected to see.

Fear.

She peered around him to find what might put such an expression on his face. Even as she looked, she knew in her soul there was nothing to fear. Ahead the energy source almost sang with the beauty of its power.

"Don't let go of me." He squeezed her hand tightly.

"No, I won't." Her voice sounded foreign in this silent place. She wouldn't leave him to suffer whatever ill effects all this energy might have on him. She squeezed back in reassurance.

He didn't move.

She took the lead and slid between a pair of pure-white trees. Her sweater snagged back and front, one side against each tree.

He exhaled sharply to make himself smaller.

She almost had to pull him through the tight space. She stopped the moment he was clear.

"What happened to the trees?" she whispered.

The remains of hundreds of white trees stood in concentric circles, each circle of tree trunks shorter than the last as they reached the inner most area. It was like a woodcutter had created a round theater out of the forest. In the very center, two taller tree trunks leaned toward each other, as if they had once touched but were cut off below their embrace. Their slanting torsos were doomed never to reach fulfillment.

"They're not really trees." He whispered, too. "Not anymore. They're rocks now. The cave spirals down beneath us. The two rocks in the center protect the entrance to the cave. The outer circle wasn't here when I was born. The mark is still growing."

No wonder the Rallis name garnered such fearful respect. Even the goddess had yet to halt the flow of her blessing upon their territory. Over two hundred years in the making and the mark still grew. An ancient potency emanated from it.

"It's beautiful." She pulled him forward, and they stepped past the first layer of former trees. They reached just above her waist. "It feels… pure." She scanned around the circle. No body in sight. She wouldn't ruin this moment by mentioning it. Instead she savored the peace of the vibes buffeting her from every side.

"It is pure. It's the energy of the goddess, after all. The family's altar is supposed to go in the middle of the mark." A bare hint of nerves hid in his tone. "This is where the thanksgiving ceremonies used to be, but the power is too intense. None of us can stand to be here for long anymore. On days like today, no one can even get in." He laced their fingers together. "Except you."

She felt a touch of pride at her own mage power. That was new. "You Rallises are too powerful for your own good." She let her free hand glide over the sides of the petrified trees as she led them toward the center over the packed dirt of the ground. The smooth ridges of the former trees vibrated with energy.

Her feet throbbed for relief, so she toed off her shoes. "Close your eyes," she ordered. She started to reach under her skirt with one hand to tug off her stockings.

"No," he replied with both eyes open. "I can't sense a thing in here. I need to see."

She huffed at his uncooperative attitude. "Don't you ever let down your guard? Of all places in the world, surely you are safe standing in a blessing."

He looked at her, steady and unmoving.

Of course the famous colonel never let down his guard. She discreetly tugged off her stockings anyway with one hand. She almost sprawled into an ungraceful heap, but she managed. Though this irresistible energy glided into her from every direction, she was still a practical girl and wouldn't risk ruining the stockings. Besides, he couldn't glimpse anything from above.

The moment her bare feet made contact with the ground, energy danced up her legs. She wanted to run and skip and jump through it, as if it were her personal playground. "I like it." Little sizzles vibrated up her legs and she lifted her head with a laugh. His face hovered higher than before. Without shoes, she'd dropped by almost three inches.

Vincent brushed his shoulder against his cheek, wiping away a line of sweat. "Are you too hot?"

She shook her head with a squint. That was the last thing on her mind.

"I can't cool us off in here. I'm afraid to use any vibes. I'm not sure how the gyre would affect me," he explained. Sunlight shimmered on the white rocks, sparkling bright rays everywhere and adding to the temperature.

"Cooling myself off with vibes is a luxury I've never had. Too hot and too cold are normal for me." Her sense of play dimmed. "Is the energy hurting you? Do you have a headache?"

He gave a short, abrupt laugh. "No headache. But if you let go of me, I think I'll explode. There's no way I could stand here without your syphon power pulling off some of the energy. And if you left me, I don't think I could make it out."

"I won't let go." She squeezed his hand. She was his only defense. "I swear by the goddess I won't let you go."

"I swear by the goddess I won't let you go either."

She wrinkled her brow. "I meant in here, Vincent. Not as a general statement concerning the rest of my life."

She ignored his lack of response and walked farther into the gyre. The rocks dropped in height as they closed in on the center. Bronte stepped on top of one and, holding his hand, she jumped from one rock to the next, using them like stepping-stones. It would make a fabulous concert arena.

Energy radiated from the stones and stretched out to her. It tickled like a thousand dandelion puffs dancing over her skin. Facing the tall, angled stones in the center, she reached out to touch one. Vibes poured over her, immersing her inside and out with magic. She tipped her head to the sky and sighed with perfect contentment, swaying on her feet as energy gently pummeled her.

She turned and faced him, leaning her back against one white trunk that acted as a roof to the entrance of the spiral beneath the ground. She couldn't keep the smile off her face. Everything else fell away—her parents, her past, her dreams, Claude. There was nothing here but pure energy. Tipsy with the power, she closed her eyes and put her one free hand over Vincent's heart. Its steady thump pulsed through her until it passed into the gyre.

Vincent sucked in a harsh breath.

She giggled. "Can you feel that?"

"Yeah." His voice was rough.

Her hand curled into his shirt. "Kiss me." She pulled him closer.

He leaned in, but stopped. She could feel him hovering just above her lips.

"Are you drunk on all this energy?"

"Who cares if I am? Maybe this is what your thanksgiving ceremonies were supposed to be like. Your altar is just waiting for this. So kiss me." She tugged again, but he didn't cooperate.

"I'd like to. But I'm not going to kiss you for the first time when you're high on energy that isn't mine."

"This isn't our first kiss."

"Thirteen years ago was a peck."

His heat waved over her.

"I dreamed…I wished you had come after me." The confession wafted from her lips. She opened her eyes to find a mar of regret across his face. His mouth pulled down like he was in pain.

She straightened and shifted them around, pressing him against the rock until it captured him and held him in place. "If you won't kiss me, then I'll kiss you. And I'll give you more than a peck this time." She slid her hand around his neck and drew him down. His breath touched her mouth. She inhaled the heat of him, surrounded by his vibes more than ever.

"Move away from him!" The cruel voice slashed through the silent air before their lips touched.

Bronte jumped, obeying the voice without conscious thought. Adrenaline snapped her out of the gyre's joyful influence.

Vincent jerked away from the rock and stepped in front of her. They fumbled at each other to keep contact with their hands. Her bare wrist ended up clasped tightly in his grip.

She moved to stand at his side. She was used to hiding, but she would never cower behind him.

Chief Masset stood at the edge of the gyre among the trees guarding the powerful place. He squinted at them, as if the gyre was a sun and radiated light too powerful for comfort. "Bronte Casteel, you are under arrest!"

"On what grounds?" Vincent's words shot around the gyre.

"There's something not right about that Non. Get away from her, Colonel."

She whispered to Vincent. "He can't get in, can he?"

"Don't know," he muttered, too soft for the chief to hear. "I wouldn't have thought he'd get this far. Get behind me."

"You have no reason to arrest her," Vincent hollered. "You are overstepping your authority, Chief Masset. And trespassing on Rallis land." Vincent stepped back, forcing Bronte to do the same. "If I say run, you go straight back to the big house," he said to her in a low voice.

"Only if you come, too. I'm not leaving you here to deal with him or these vibes. Besides, I swore not to let go."

"Don't let her pretty face influence you, Colonel. Now hand her over." The chief didn't wait. His fist closed and opened. He thrust it straight toward her. Her ears popped with his spell before it reached her.

Vincent jumped in front of her.

Without moving a hand, his mage energy expanded and shot out as if he'd wrenched open an unfathomable reservoir of power inside him. For the first time ever, she sensed the powerful energy surge of a mage's spell. She could have reached around him and let his energy pour over her hand. The more energy that flowed out of him, the bigger the reservoir grew, as if it endlessly boiled up inside him. How much could his body hold? How could he possibly control this? How did he keep it from consuming himself?

Her heart raced. Fear took her breath, but her own mage power stayed steady and true. Her syphon absorbed the excess of his energy as if she were his coolant, keeping his engine running at the highest speeds without burning out. The more energy he used, the more her syphon pulled into her.

The energy of the gyre shifted as if the mix of powers tipped its equilibrium. Her ears sizzled under the pressure. Like a chain reaction, energy gushed forth. The ground rumbled. Bronte swayed. Her syphon drank in gulps of energy—the gyre's and Vincent's—until surely it could hold no more.

Her skin tightened as if her mage power expanded within her. She fell to her knees behind Vincent. He stayed on his feet, her wrist bound in his hand. Their physical connection kept Vincent from being overwhelmed, but it didn't help her.

A loud crash like water rushing from great heights roared through the air, going on and on. Finally it faded away as if someone slowly dialed down the volume. She took a breath, easier without the rush of energy working through her. She looked around, anticipating an unrecognizable landscape after all that energy had swirled around. But from where she sat on her knees, leaning against Vincent, everything looked the same. Until she stood.

The all-white trees at the edge of the gyre—the ones so close together she'd barely squeezed through them—had lost their heads. The trees no longer stood as guards shielding the goddess's blessing. They were now a part of it. No leaves or branches littered the ground. The trees' canopies had simply disappeared. The trunks, now pale columns, gleamed like ice under the bright sunshine.

"Did you do that?" Her voice was small. Hesitation pitched the words high.

"We did that. You and I."

Bronte closed her eyes for a moment, the ramifications of that too complicated to puzzle out right now. Just a few minutes ago, all she wanted was to stand inside this magical place. Now all she wanted was out.

"Did we…kill the chief?"

Chapter 6

Vincent scanned the edge of the gyre where the chief had stood. Every nerve was alive and ready. That had been everything he'd ever been born to do. He wanted to do it again. A primal satisfaction ripped through him. He'd vanquished the mage who thought to take her from him. He'd deflected the chief's rapid-fire spell and then added his own to it.

He wanted to charge over there and make sure his foe was truly conquered. But getting Bronte away was priority one. She'd been the catalyst for the whole thing. Without her syphon power, he couldn't have cast or controlled that amount of energy. Not in here.

"Are you alright?" He kept his gaze where the chief had fallen.

"I swallowed an entire ocean of power. But I'm fine. Do you see him?" Her shaky voice clamped down on his urge to rush into another attack.

He risked a glance back to make sure she told the truth. Her hair had fallen from its tidy knot. Now it spread in shiny waves around her face and down to her arms. Her sweater hung off one side and exposed a pale shoulder.

"We should go see if he's alright," she said.

"No. We'll get you back to the big house. I'll come back."

"And how are you going to do that? You can't be here without me, remember? We have to go together."

Her fiery retort was a relief. She would be fine.

He squeezed her wrist gently and pulled her up. Her wrist was so small, he was hesitant to put too much pressure on the fine bones, but neither did he want to turn and use both hands. He didn't trust that the chief was truly down. "You can make it over there?"

"Of course I can." She sounded offended but then stumbled on the first step. "I'm fine." Her reassurance sounded like a question. She cleared her throat and stepped up beside him.

He moved to stay in front of her. “Behind me. He cast enough power to kill us both three times over.”

“Oh.” She fell silent as they got their rhythm of walking together, her close behind him with their hands clasped at his back. “Maybe it was an accident?”

The gyre’s power could have added extra energy to the chief’s spell, but that wasn’t an assumption he could afford to make. If there had been a place to tuck her away, he would have, but there was nowhere to hide here. Besides, she was right. He’d be useless without her in the gyre.

“My shoes are back there.” She tugged on his hand.

He didn’t give her any leeway. “Later.” He kept his eyes on the one lump ahead that didn’t blend with the rest of the landscape. “I see him.”

He led them to the former edge of the gyre. The chief lay flat on the ground. His eyelids twitched, the only indication he still lived. The gyre’s power was too intense for Vincent to sense anything else about the other mage, even with Bronte’s syphon.

“I don’t want to look at him. I hate mage duels.” Her voice stuttered around the words. “Mother challenged the neighbor once. She caught the woman kissing my father. The poor woman didn’t have any lips after that. They were gone. She could hardly open wide enough to scream.”

He gave her wrist a tight squeeze at her nervous ramble. He felt the shivers passing through her but there was nothing he could do to help her right now.

Masset opened his eyes. Vincent held up his hand to show Masset he was willing to finish the job if necessary.

The chief stared at him with a scowl of frustration and pain. “This Non is evil. They all are. She’s gonna kill you, Rallis. Or worse.” His voice was hoarse, but even defeated and knocked down he wasn’t giving up. “Best to hand her over.”

Bronte shifted against his back and tucked herself farther away from the man. For once she was cooperating.

“Let me take her in before she affects you any more.” Dust covered his bald head, dulling his skin to a flat gray.

Vincent kept his hand in front of him. “You don’t quit, do you? You could have killed us both in there, Masset. Or was that the plan?”

“I was aiming for the Non. You stepped in my way on purpose. The law doesn’t care about mages foolish enough to get killed defending a Non. If you’d died protecting her, no judge would do anything about it.”

“His family would do something about it,” Bronte said.

Masset ignored her. "I'm gonna get a warrant. I'm coming back for her."

Bronte peeked out.

Masset stared as if his eyes could pin her in place until he got that warrant. "This country never should have let weaklings like you in."

Bronte stepped beside him and faced the chief. "Take it up with the goddess! I was born here!"

His syphon had a spitfire button detrimental to the state of her health. "It's alright. I've got this." Someday she'd be able to stand up to fools like the chief all on her own, but it wasn't today.

"It most certainly is not alright!"

Footsteps crashed through the woods. Vincent heard them long after he should have sensed the person's vibes. He needed to get out of the gyre before someone else crept up on them, although if another enemy walked onto Rallis land, massive security overhauls would be top priority for everyone on the estate.

"Sir!" Gerald's voice came from right. The former lieutenant was Vincent's right hand man around the estate. Edmund was right beside him.

"Sir, are you alright?" The ex-soldier's eyes went wide at the destruction of the white trees.

"I'm fine. Have the sentries escort Chief Masset all the way to the property line. He went in the wrong direction as he was leaving."

"Yes, sir!" The young man saluted yet again, despite Vincent's continued orders to cease. Gerald relayed the command into the amplifier wired to his throat. The man had little mage power left. Even sending sound waves was difficult for him. "We've been combing the estate when he didn't exit through the gates." He bent down to the chief, flung the older man over his shoulder, and stomped off. Gerald's mage sense may have been permanently fried on his first mission out, but he was stronger than an ox.

Edmund surveyed the scene. His hands in his pockets, he nodded absently. "I like what you've done with the place. You two have added your own touch to the gyre. Your first undertaking as a couple. Makes a statement. Even the goddess approves. We can use this. She's definitely one of ours now."

"I am not one of yours. And Masset is coming back to arrest me! Why?" Her voice lost its strength with the question. "Does he know… what I am? How could he know?"

Edmund shook his head. "Who knows what he thinks? But Masset will never be able to arrest you." He squinted and took a step back, his hand squeezing at his forehead. "How can you stand it in there? You two are alright, aren't you? Because if you need help, please tell me you can get out on your own. I'd rather not come in."

"We're fine." Vincent was quick to reassure him. "Get out of here before you get sick."

Edmund nodded and jogged off through the trees.

He squeezed her hand, though he wanted to put his arms around her. The scared, prickly anger in her tight brow and flat lips told him such a touch was unwelcome. "Trust me on this. Masset cannot go up against my family and win."

"You want me to trust you? Then get me out of here! I should never have come in the first place." The tipsy, happy effects of the gyre's energy on her were long gone. Another charge to lay at Masset's feet.

"I should have told my mother no for once in my life. Masset is going to realize what I am!"

"He can't get you here."

"But I'm not staying here forever."

He slipped his hands toward the nape of her neck. "He's not getting you. Period. Do you think I'm going to let him—anyone—take you away?" He swallowed hard against the regret burning in his gut. She had suffered for thirteen years because he'd been too weakened to protect her. "I would have come after you. But I didn't even think you were real. When we met, I was…"

"Hurt. By a spell." She nodded. "I wondered. Afterwards."

Not quite right, but close. "You were here and gone before I could wake up enough to realize you weren't a dream. If nothing else, then trust that I'm not going to let anything happen to my only lifeline to living without pain."

Her gaze dropped to the ground.

He dared to pull her into his chest.

She went willingly.

He wrapped his arms around her small frame.

"This doesn't change anything," she muttered against his chest. "Masset is coming back for me."

He sighed. Bronte was a practical girl. She wouldn't have survived otherwise.

"And we'll stop him again."

Obtaining a warrant would keep Masset occupied. He'd never find a judge who would sign an arrest order for a Non residing within the senator's estate. But she was right. Outside the boundaries of the estate was another matter, though Edmund would be whispering in every judge's ear the moment he got back to the big house.

Because of the chief's bigotry, Vincent needed to act faster than planned. But he'd make it work. Quietly though. Bronte was sure to object to his plan. He'd spring it on her as gently as possible. Now wasn't the time.

He'd change the world for her.

* * * *

The trek back through the woods hurt. Her feet wobbled and blistered inside her grubby heels. The hike out was impossibly longer than the trip in. After the duel between Vincent and Masset, the mass of energy inside her weighed her down. How could something as ephemeral as mage vibes weigh so much? She didn't want to take another step, not in these shoes, though Vincent had retrieved them for her.

They passed a fallen tree; its long trunk lay parallel to their path. She halted. Tree after tree clogged any hint of the horizon or her car. With no end in sight, she would at least have satisfaction for her feet. Right now. Bronte plopped down on the log, jerking Vincent to a stop with their connected hands. She hadn't let go of him. She'd kept her promise.

The rough bark snagged her skirt. She shifted and a few threads popped. She toed off one shoe with an achy grimace. Vincent knelt, dropped her hand, and pulled off the left shoe.

He looked up at her, his hand firm on her ankle. She turned her head the other way. It would be so easy to fall into the rhythm that existed between them. And impossible to stay.

Out of the corner of her eye, she saw him reach up to her hair. He pulled back with a small stick in his hand and tossed it into the brush. He leaned in and scooped her off the log. It happened so quickly that her arm automatically went around his shoulders.

He held her high against his chest, their eyes inches apart. They spent a silent moment studying each other. She supposed he was giving her a chance to object. Though she had many protests bottled up inside, being denied a chance to walk all the way to her car was not one of them. She was the sensible sort.

With exhaustion as her silent excuse, she relaxed against him. His sigh of relief pressed against her body. At the same moment his mage energy released with a gentle, controlled push. The complete opposite of the way his energy worked against the chief, this was a gentle stream, not to deflect a spell but to deflect her weight. She wrapped her other arm around him, her head falling naturally into the crook of his neck. He continued through the forest, carrying her as if she was no more burden than walking out by himself.

His scent filled her. It was all Vincent, no hint of cologne, just a trace of sweat that wiped away the sophisticated veneer that had surrounded him in his family's home. The short whiskers on his jawline grabbed at a few strands of her hair from the top of her head. She let them cling, the rest of her hair already a sweaty wreck.

Vincent's steady rhythm gave her a touch of peace and allowed her to think. Her choler unwound thread by thread. She took a breath and lined up her thoughts. If she disappeared from Rallis Territory before Chief Masset could return, he couldn't follow her home to Locke Territory. There was little cooperation between founding families. No Southern Alliance family would assist the enforcer of a Central Coalition territory. For once, mage politics were on her side. She just needed to get home.

To keep her here, Vincent had crimped every pseudo-freedom she'd enjoyed for the past thirteen years. Though his vibes made her feel like she finally fit in her own skin, it wasn't worth dying over.

The edge of the woods came into view. Her car waited in the middle of the gravel road. She took another breath of him, one last inhalation of his essence.

He stopped in front of the old Volvo and reached for the handle of the passenger door. She slid out of his arms and into the heat of her car.

She grabbed his wrist as he started to back away. "You have to let me go before he comes back. You know this. Get my pass changed. Let me leave." She looked into his blue eyes as he crouched down before her. His broad shoulders took up almost the entire width of the door's opening. Even if she had his strength, she would still be afraid to take on Masset.

"Masset can't win against a Rallis. The family rules this territory."

She tilted her chin. "It seems Chief Masset and I are in the same boat. I can't win against you either."

"Bronte, you and I are on the same side. You're just too stubborn to admit it." He reached under her knees and tucked her legs into the car, shut her door and walked around to the driver's side.

"I am not being stubborn," she began as soon as he sat down behind the steering wheel. "Case in point, I am letting you drive. I just want to be free to go about my life."

"Hiding isn't much of a life."

"Neither is having your choices taken away. Vincent, you have all the power. I have none. I'm stuck following your commands."

He dared to smile. "Sweetheart, going into the gyre was not following my commands. You are freer here than you ever have been. You don't have to hide who you are. Not here. You have choices. You just have to find the courage to make them."

"I'm not that brave. Nor am I that stupid."

"You stood up to Masset in the house and in the gyre. That was brave."

"Do you think that was the first time I stood up to an enforcer? Besides, I was pretty sure you weren't going to let him arrest me over a leaf."

"Not then. Not ever. Not for any reason."

She couldn't hold his gaze. He was too intent, too powerful. Too magnetic. She looked away and smoothed her fingers over the rip in the upholstered seat. "Promise me you'll let me go tomorrow. No more pulling strings to keep me here."

"I can't keep you safe if you're not here."

"You are the biggest threat to my safety. No one knew what I was until I came here. If Senator Casteel knew why you wanted me, I'm sure he would refuse to extend my pass."

"There is no Senator Casteel."

"Thanks to the Rallises there will be soon enough," she retorted.

"Then the new Senator Casteel will be grateful for what we've done and he'll let me keep what's mine."

"Maybe I should tell him that I'm a syphon." She thrust the words like a sharp sword, but her threat held little power. She was too tired to do anything more than talk big. She glanced at the clock. 3:02. She rubbed her gritty eyes. She'd been here for a little over three hours and she was drained, a combination of driving all night and having the foundation she'd built her life on explode to bits. "That would get me out of here." And tied to a flaming stake.

"Tell them." His hard voice held a battle-ready anger she didn't share. "Tell your parents. I'll stand behind you. Beside you. In front of you. Wherever you need me."

She shook her head. A disbelieving laugh that held no humor bubbled out of her. "No. My mother would do the lynching herself. Especially if she knew I helped…" She waved her hands around, searching for a word. "Grow the gyre. That was a lot of power. A scary power. We could have hurt someone."

"Someone did get hurt. Masset." He glanced over at her. "He would have killed you, Bronte. What should we have done? Let him?"

"If anyone else had been around, they would have been crushed. What if your brother had arrived sooner?" Her voice cracked.

His hand landed on her head like a big paw. It was reassuring in a gruff, silent way. He started up the car. The keys were still in her purse. He guided the car over the gravel path. The gyre's energy faded with the distance until it was too faint for her syphon power to pull any longer. She touched the passenger window, hanging on to the sensations as long as she could.

"This part of the drive is rough. Mage power doesn't work here."

Sure enough, they hit a huge pothole and then bumped through a meadow. A one-story house sat in the middle of it. Four stone columns supported the roof's broad edge. It hung over a long porch accessible by three stone steps. The natural wood siding on the house blended with the meadow and surrounding forest. The double front doors were black with a thin strip of windows near their tops.

"No driveway?" Her voice hiccupped in the middle as they hit another bump in the field. She rolled down her window and stuck out her hand, letting the tall, thin weedy stalks that dotted the field brush against her as they drove past. They were crisp and brown with fuzzy tops that protected seeds.

His jaw hardened. "I let it grow over. Since Double-Wide's been so damn active, I'd rather no one came here anyway. Lately whenever I've been here, it's to recupe. I can't have people around for that."

"Does it work?" she asked as he turned right in front of the house and parked the car. "Does not having a driveway keep your family away?"

He shook his head with a vexed laugh and got out. Bronte stepped barefoot into the weeds and pulled her violin from the backseat. He hauled her battered duffel bag from the trunk. She'd packed it with the bare essentials, planning only for a few hours' sleep in a motel on the drive home. He waited by her side, his expression hesitant, hopeful. She couldn't imagine he looked vulnerable very often.

"I'll take the couch," he offered. "Or you could…if you wanted to… you could sleep at the big house." He fumbled over his gentlemanly offer.

The big house contained at least four Rallis mages plus their mage servants. She'd take his cabin. She climbed the steps and stopped in front of the doors. She met his eyes despite the nervous flutter in her gut. Her body was more alive, more awake than normal. She wanted to sing it back to sleep. This moment held a significance she didn't want it to have.

He set her bag on the stone porch, reached into his jeans pocket and pulled out a long key, with jagged, uneven teeth. She raised an eyebrow at it.

"There were days when using a key was much easier than using energy."

There were days…past tense…as if those days were over thanks to her.

He opened the door, picked up her bag, and waited. She set one foot over the threshold and then the other. With three paces into the cool, dark space, she found herself in the kitchen. A long table dominated the open room. Even through the dim light she could see the eight empty chairs that lined the rectangular table, as if a large pioneer family gathered around it for supper.

The room brightened as a collection of lanterns came on. They dangled from the ceiling over the table. A large fireplace and chimney took up a quarter of the wall to her right. A doorway before it led into a bedroom. There was no door to the separate room. She could see the bed pushed against the front wall with a quilt draped over it, an artistic smear of greens on a white background.

On the other side of the table, the kitchen appliances and wood counter stood. Shelves instead of cabinets lined the walls and held a minimal number of plates, bowls, and pans. The stove was chrome with rounded edges, the shape reminiscent of another era. But it was the refrigerator that grabbed her attention. She pointed a finger it, her palm facing up to convey a bit more politeness, though nothing could soften her baffled curiosity. "Your refrigerator is pink."

"Yeah." Vincent shrugged. "Edmund's idea of a joke." His voice held weary acceptance. He set her bag on the bed and then came to stand behind her. "When this house was almost complete, I got called out on a mission. I came back to find the place all done. With a pink fridge. Stuffed with food, thanks to Cook. But the color is all thanks to Edmund."

Her smile widened at the thought of Vincent returning to his brother's surprise. It was apparent even to her that Edmund strived to anchor his brother to the lighter side of life. Vincent needed that…although Bronte hardly approved of Edmund working to keep her anchored to Vincent.

She resumed her exploration of the small house. Another doorway stood down from the refrigerator, but she couldn't see where it led. Along the rest of the wall in the living area, books stood at attention on floor-to-ceiling shelves. A couch and a fat leather chair sat facing the back window.

The house was sparse. Lonely. She didn't need to ask why he'd never gotten rid of the pink refrigerator. She drifted over to the books and scanned their titles.

Mages of the New World Colonies: Power and Partnership

Mage Settlement of New England 1641 - 1775

Women's Mage Power and Life in Plymouth Colony

"Is this what you read for fun?" She reached for one, the impact of the title like a hot fist to her chest. "*Deadly Mages: Sirens, Syphons, and Necromancers*," she read aloud. Her throat clogged up like it was stuffed with cotton. The binding creaked a warning as she opened it to its middle. She stared down at a rough illustration of a beautiful woman cradling a withered man in her lap. A syphon sucking a mage dry, Bronte guessed.

He took the book from her, folded it shut, and put it back. "That one's not pleasant reading."

She turned back toward his shelves to search out other gems. One book had no title. She slipped it from its spot on the shelf. It was heavy in her hands. The leather cover was plain on the front as well.

"What's this?" She opened it and darted a glance at him, daring him to stop her.

He didn't. "My dissertation."

Surprise washed through her.

"There's a lot of downtime when you're a deflector. We have to do something while we're waiting to heal from the big blasts." Vincent shrugged. "General Wilen encourages everyone on his teams to keep their minds working. Even when they've blown their sixth senses. Long distance education is a lifeline."

She squinted at the title page, her breath caught in her throat at the next shock.

THE IMPACT OF MAGE / SYPHON PARTNERSHIPS IN PRE-REPUBLIC COLONIES

A dissertation submitted in partial fulfillment of the Requirements for the degree of Doctor of Philosophy in History

by

Vincent Bradford Rallis

Mage/syphon partnerships? She ran a hand over the words as they resounded through her. With this dissertation, he'd booted colonial syphons out of the closet. Why hadn't this made the news? She snuck a peek back at him and clasped it to her chest. She wouldn't give him a chance to take this book away from her. She made her way to the couch, took the corner nearest its companion chair, and sank deeply into the cushions. The warm light from the window glowed, perfect to read by.

"I never forgot you, even if I didn't believe the memories. I wanted you to be real. I questioned Edmund over and over about a girl with long, dark hair and red lips until he thought I was crazy. No one I talked to saw you." He stood at the bookshelf, his voice hard, a shell of anger and disappointment wrapped around it.

"I'm good at hiding."

His jaw clenched. "If I'd believed what my heart was telling me, I would have searched for you. That day is a blur. That old shed is still there. Mother wanted to tear it down, but I insisted it stay."

The horror of the end of that day had long overshadowed the beauty of the few hours of magic she'd had with him.

If the High Council hadn't insisted every founding family bring all their children to the Gathering that year, Bronte would have been left behind as usual. Instead, she'd sought out a hiding place the moment they'd arrived at the seat of Rallis power. It hadn't taken long to find one on the sprawling estate. Bushes and tall, bobbing flowers hid the small shed. She risked the bugs and sat down on the ground against the stone wall of the small building and pulled her book from her pocket.

He'd come staggering around the corner of the shed like the hounds of hell were on his heels, then skidded to a halt.

She sat motionless.

He'd leaned against the wall and closed his eyes, momentarily oblivious to her presence.

She could believe that the future colonel hadn't been himself that day.

Brushing away the memories, she stroked her fingers over the smooth page of the book. "My mother didn't think you would be here today. She said you'd moved away."

"Bronte, she lied to you. No Rallis moves from his territory. She knew I'd be here. She sent you to soften me up in hopes of getting her way." His voice was quiet to gentle the blow of the truth.

"She doesn't know what I am."

"No. But if I remember correctly, she saw that peck of a kiss. If I needed to send a messenger into enemy territory, I'd choose the one the enemy had kissed."

"Devious minds think alike?"

He narrowed his eyes. "I'll use it to my advantage. To free you."

Time for a change of subject. She wasn't going there again. She glanced down at the thick dissertation in her hands. "So now you're Dr. Colonel." She opened it and rhythmically flipped page after page of typed text.

She yawned. "I am going to read this," she stated as soon as her jaw closed.

"Go ahead."

She hadn't expected such easy acquiescence.

He sat down in the leather chair and propped his booted feet on the scarred table. From the marks on the old wooden surface, he sat there a lot. His arms and head fit into the chair that had molded to his form. He watched her.

She looked down at the book. Page sixteen. She had no idea what the first fifteen pages said. Another yawn cracked her jaw. She thumbed through it further and then stopped on a random page, her gaze caught by his text.

Katherine Carver, daughter of a Massachusetts's tavern keeper, writes in her journal of meeting John Chilton. She states that his energy "sang to her soul with a melody she could never live without should its tune halt." This sentiment is similar to other syphons' descriptions of their energy mates.

The potential of this mage-syphon match was cut short. Chilton, a powerful shielder frequently involved in skirmishes with hostile Natives, was killed by a "wild man" seven days after meeting Katherine. The syphon's sister wrote the final entry in the journal, stating Katherine starved to death three days after Chilton was killed. This is highly improbable since there were no mentions of food scarcities anywhere else in the daily diarist's accounts or in any other historical source. Even if the starvation was self-imposed, three days without food would not have killed her. The true cause of the syphon's death remains unclear."

Bronte shut the book with a bang. The cause of death was unclear? How could he not know? It was clear to her. Seven days. Seven days until she would be so addicted to Vincent she'd die without him.

Chapter 7

She turned white. The tired circles under her eyes darkened even as the rest of her paled. She blinked as if she couldn't stop flinching from what she'd read. Clutching the book to her chest, she walked around his coffee table to the back window.

"What's wrong?"

She shook her head as if she didn't understand the question. "Katherine Carver died of starvation."

It took him a moment to remember. "I chalk that up to a grieving sister's dramatic writing. Finding more information on either Chilton or Carver was impossible. I almost left them out." His research was supposed to have hooked her as much as a dry dissertation could. It certainly wasn't meant to upset her. The knowledge he'd gathered about real syphons was the only leverage he had at reasoning his way into her heart.

He scrambled to offer her a brighter side. "There are happier accounts in there. Most of the other evidence of powerful mages who mated—who paired up—with syphon mages, were much happier. They were long-lived, especially for then, and they accomplished a great deal. Things that would have been impossible for the man to do on his own."

She turned to him, leaning against the sill, her face in soft shadows with the light of the window behind her. She closed her eyes like she might fall asleep on her feet.

He closed the gap between them. "Maybe you should take a nap. You can lay your head in my lap this time."

She gave him an admonishing look, one that included a small, reluctant smile. He knew he remembered that part correctly: thirteen years ago he'd fallen asleep with his head in her lap.

That day he'd done a full-scale retreat from the Gathering in hopes of holding onto his sanity. He'd hidden behind the old kitchen garden shed. The spot radiated peace, though he hadn't noticed her presence at first.

Even then she was a balm to his soul. And it wasn't because he'd been poisoned.

"No nap." She shook her head and clutched the book tighter.

"It's either take a nap now or fall asleep during the symphony."

"I'm not going. That would be a disaster."

"We can debate that after you've slept. You'll be able to argue better then."

She pursed her lips in frustration.

What had he been thinking to turn down her kiss in the gyre? He wanted to trace her lips with his fingers, or better yet with his own mouth. He could have tasted her by now. "Come on." He reached around her shoulder, his hand firm against the nape of her neck. "The sheets are… mostly clean." He shrugged. "They haven't been on there long."

She lifted an eyebrow at him, bemusement outshining her distress for the moment. "Actually, what I'd really like is a shower."

"I happen to have one available." He took the book from her.

"I want to read that." She watched him set it on the table.

"It'll be right here." He dared to reach for her hand, so much smaller than his.

She gave him one of her slow blinks and looked up at him from beneath her lashes and dark hair.

He tugged her hand slightly, testing, pulling on her to follow.

She complied.

He tried to look at his home through her eyes. He'd never had anyone here other than Edmund, who'd stayed maybe twenty minutes at a time. This was his refuge. Bronte's presence made it even more so.

By the goddess, what he would give for it to be her refuge as well.

He picked up her bag as he led her through the bedroom to the bath. She stopped in the doorway as he set her bag on the white marble counter. He pulled out two towels from the open shelves beneath and placed them next to her bag. "Use whatever you need and take as long as you want. I'm going to check in with my team." He walked past her, taking a deep breath of her scent. He eyed the bed, just twelve feet away, and then strode out before he could get any more ideas.

With his ears and sixth sense attuned to her, he paced through the main room to his office and picked up the landline.

General Wilen answered on the first ring as if he'd been waiting for Vincent's call. Omitting a greeting, the general dove into his news. "The Casteels aren't a real cooperative bunch. They're not at all fond of their daughter. They've refused to let any of our readers in, so we've got no idea who's been in their house. I wonder what energy is floating around there. Something they don't want us to read, that's for sure. You got the daughter tucked up tight, I'm guessin'? She hanging out with your momma, or can the Non not tolerate their vibes?"

"Bronte's with me."

The general paused. "With you? You know I didn't mean for you to sit guard on her, right? If you feel like she's a flight risk, put Gerald on it. He's capable of babysitting a Non while you rest up. We need you healed as soon as possible. This whole DW thing is going blow soon. I can feel it."

Vincent felt the same way about the case. "I am healed."

"Already? How?" When Vincent didn't answer right away, the general continued, "Wait a minute. A pretty girl shows up on your doorstep and you feel all better? Huh. Must be a real special girl." The older man took a breath. "I'm…relieved. I was afraid this time you weren't…"

Vincent was surprised to hear the worry and grief that accompanied those words. "I'm fully recovered."

"Well, good." The general's tone was back to his usual clipped pace. "Check in with Sylvie tonight at the farm. Let her go over you and make sure. You can transfer the Casteel girl to our custody while you're here. Maybe her pretty looks will work on my other boys too. Besides, I want to dig into her vibes and see what she knows."

Vincent gritted his teeth hard. Possession knifed through him. Bronte's pretty looks would not be working for anyone else. He wasn't giving her up, not for his mentor and boss, not even for his men. No way was she going to the farm. The general would blast through Bronte's mind like a bomb in a haystack. He'd trust Wilen with his own life, but not with Bronte's. "She stays with me."

"Is that right?" The general strung out the words, long and slow. "She stays with you. Interesting. Let's see. Ultrapowerful mage meets powerless girl, and he feels all better. Am I getting this right? Where have I heard this story before?"

Vincent sat back in his chair to wait out the general's sarcastic spiel.

"Hmm. I believe it was you who spouted on about powerful mages and seemingly powerless girls. You know, I do listen when you boys speechify about the learning you're doing. Though I admit I'll be glad when Thorton is done with this math PhD. I'd rather not hear a whole lot more about combinatorial and linear algebraic manipulation of a matrix."

They'd all be glad when Thorton was finished.

"I got some of her history here," the general drawled. "Says she was at your family's estate once. You have anything you want to tell me about your little Bronte Casteel? Sounds like you had a little inspiration for all that research that went into your degree."

Vincent couldn't have kept it from the general for long. The man was too smart. "I met her when I was home on leave after PIT. My memories aren't real clear, to the point that I thought she wasn't real."

"Yeah, PIT's a bitch like that."

The one positive aspect about Poison Immunity Training was that you got to go on leave for a few days. The bad part was you were too sick to enjoy it. Or even remember it.

"Don't get attached, Vin. If she's involved in this DW shit, she's as good as dead," Wilen stated flatly.

"She's innocent."

"Then bring her to me and let me see for myself." The country soldier act was gone.

"Is my word not good enough?" For the first time, Vincent was prepared to use his family's rank against his mentor and boss. To protect Bronte, he'd do anything.

"I trust you, Vincent. But I don't know her." Wilen's tone lost its edge. "Let me see for myself. Bring her to the farm. Tonight."

"I can't. My mother has already claimed her company tonight. Along with the senator and the rest of the family."

"The rest of the family? Including you, eh? So you're taking a syphon masquerading as a Non to the damn symphony, I presume?" Wilen stayed on top of anything that attracted powerful mages. The theater would be packed with them tonight. "A bit unsafe. Sounds exactly like something your mother would do. I don't like it."

"You don't like it because now you can't skip out on going."

"Humph. Damn symphony."

Papers shuffled in the background.

"I'm sure your little violinist will like it though. You probably already know all this, but here's what our people have learned about Miss Bronte Casteel. She's in a band." The general's voice parsed out information, one bullet at a time. "She gives music lessons to Nons. She turned down two Chattanooga mage families who asked her to teach their children. Including the Lockes themselves. Miss Casteel hasn't left Chattanooga in thirteen years. Not since her family sent her there straight from the Gathering held at…oh look, your house." The general didn't wait for Vincent to respond. "She was teaching a class at a Nons' school when the late Senator Casteel died and was on stage in a bar the night his body disappeared. So far so good."

Vincent tensed for the coming shot.

"She has one weirdo friend." Papers shuffled again. "Claude Hines. He's quite a recluse. Angry, bitter. He books her band's gigs. Other than that, he's made no landline connections except to Bronte's house. He got beat up by a bunch of mage kids about ten months ago and hasn't left his trailer since. I hope he's showered 'cause I got Merriam on her way down there. I don't want to hear her jabber on about his stink for months."

Vincent stilled. If Wilen was sending their only veiler, then something about Claude had raised a huge alarm. With her rare talent, Merriam could sit right in front of a person and never be noticed, but she wasn't very good at anything else. It took a skilled support team to get her in place and back out.

A *thump* sounded across the line, likely the general's feet knocking on top of his desk. "How 'bout I transmit you the reports? Then you can tell me what they're missin'. Fill in those holes that must be in here 'bout the syphon that's nursed you back to health. Until I can talk to her myself."

* * * *

Vincent mulled over his plan as the landline duplicator spit out papers. He was going to make this world safe for her. Whatever it took. Having Wilen as an ally would be helpful. Nevertheless, he wouldn't put her through the general's interrogation.

The papers continued to spit out. Judging by the tall stack, the general must have put all his analysts on the two reports.

While he waited for them to finish, Vincent stood and paced to the entrance of his bedroom. There'd been no reason for a door when he'd built the place. He never anticipated anyone staying here other than him. His mother had insisted on a door to the bathroom. She'd howled at him to close off that part of his cave. Thankfully he'd agreed.

Bronte lay in his bed on top of the covers. Her arms were bared in the sleeveless silk shirt she'd worn under her sweater. A halo of dark, wet hair fanned around her and highlighted her pale skin. She was asleep but not peacefully. Her breaths were uneven and shallow, ill at ease even in her dreams, but the lions prowling around the boundaries of the estate could not get her here. Not Wilen or Masset. Not her family. Not Claude. His eyes narrowed as he came to that name on his mental list.

She stirred as if she could sense his displeasure, twisting to her side.

He shoved away from the doorframe, padded softly to the bed, and pulled the far edge of the quilt over her, cocooning her in its warmth.

She opened her eyes.

"Go back to sleep," he whispered as he stroked his fingers through her hair. The pillow beneath was wet. With a spray of energy he pushed the water out, drying both with two swipes through her hair.

She reached up, her fingers mimicking his, and brought a strand of hair to her line of sight. "My new favorite hair dryer." Her voice was groggy.

"Sleep," he ordered with a brush of his hand down her cheek. He turned and walked back to his office, though it was the last thing he wanted to do. He sent a push of energy to bolt his front door. The locks on the windows and the back door didn't move as he tried the same thing on them, already latched. It felt odd to so easily use his mage power for everyday actions.

He scanned the energy around them, his sixth sense relaxed but primed. Bronte's syphon kept him comfortable even when he was geared up. The vibes of the nearest people came from the big house, but with the gyre throwing off such intense power—even more now since the encounter with Masset—it was hard to be sure. He wouldn't let down his guard. He'd keep her safe even if she didn't want him to.

He pulled out the reports and skimmed Bronte's first. It didn't reveal much more than the general had already told him. He flipped to the one on Claude.

In the bedroom, her movement pushed at the air around her. He looked up from the report and froze. He had every sense tuned in and picked up the energy of the rustling covers before she stepped out of bed. Her mage vibes would take practice to sense. He wasn't good enough yet. Her energy signature was almost blank. Almost.

A *thump* and two clicks sounded from the main room. She appeared in front of the opening to his office with her violin and bow in one hand, the other still fingering a lock of her hair.

It spilled down her shoulders and to the middle of her upper arms, curling under softly. It framed her beauty perfectly. He'd like to see it all spread out on his pillow again.

She flicked the back door's lock, walked out and shut the door behind her.

So much for keeping her locked in.

He strode to the couch and looked out the window. She sat on the edge of the back porch. Her feet dangled over the edge. She tucked her violin under her chin and pulled the bow along the strings. Notes found their pitch and streamed out with a purity that matched her faint energy. Her melody vibrated around him and everywhere else. The universe's energy responded and vibrated in concert. Even the energy of the trees and grasses morphed to blend with her song. He closed his eyes and let the vibes she created with her song soak into him. He liked music as much as the next guy, but not classical. This, however, would turn even a rocker's head.

The landline's duplicator swished out more papers. He forced himself to shake off the bindings of her song and picked up the latest report. He needed to focus while she was busy.

The handwritten cover page read,

Meant to tell you about this. Your syphon's distracted me too.
T.W.

Shuffling to the next page, his gut tightened as he read the short report. DW had detonated another bomb, this time in Eaton Territory in a wooded area behind a mage school. It should have been empty on a Saturday afternoon. The blast occurred two and a half hours ago, a hundred yards from the school during an early festival to celebrate the autumnal equinox. The place had been packed with families. No injuries. Another bomb off target.

Vincent sat back in his desk chair and tried again to puzzle this out. The last four DW attacks had missed their mark, after a dozen being right on. Something was wrong in Double-Wide. But what? A traitor in their organization? If that were the case, it shouldn't have taken four bombs for the terrorists to notice and eliminate the problem. Vincent reread the details and studied the grainy photos.

Just then, mage vibes drifted toward him. Not Bronte. Someone was coming down his road. Three someones. His parents and brother. The cavalry had arrived, ready to plan the attack to secure his syphon's future.

He locked the reports in the top desk drawer and went to the front porch to meet them. Best to keep his mother outside. If she got in, he'd need a crowbar to remove her. Vincent leaned against the post at the top of his porch steps and stuck his hands in his pockets.

Out here, Bronte's music resonated crystal clear. Its energy waved through the air. He watched his mother absorb it the moment she stepped from the Land Rover. She took a deep breath, her eyes closing, as if she could inhale the melody.

"Good goddess. Is that her?" She paced to the edge of his house quicker than high heels ought to allow.

"You're a lucky man, brother." Edmund sauntered up the steps. "You've found a girl who's like a mythical siren for Mother. You'll never be alone again. It will always be the three of you."

His mother leaned around the corner of the house, pulled to Bronte's tune. "Is she in the back?"

Vincent nodded again.

"I'm telling Dell to cut your grass," she said. "I'm not tromping through these weeds."

"Then you can listen from here."

She gave an exasperated huff but stepped up to his front porch.

The sad beauty of Bronte's tune shifted and twisted, circling around the same melody again and again. It ventured further away each time, leaving him surprised when the melancholy string of notes returned. His bones vibrated with her sound. His heart moved in time to it. Her song captivated them all—even his father's face lightened for a moment, though he climbed the steps like every move hurt.

He'd been helping with the victims of the bombing since early this morning. His drawn face looked as if he'd spent his every vibe mending what damage he could. "All this time, the Casteels have held the answer to your sense-sickness." He looked off into the meadow and squinted against the bright light of the blue sky. "Who would have thought such an incredible gift would come from such an unlikely source?"

Vincent looked the other away. For thirteen years he hadn't believed what his heart was telling him. He should have known.

"The house of Casteel will never let her go." His mother shook her head with disgust. "If they knew she was the complement to your power, they'd probably get rid of her just to spite us."

"Bronte said something similar on the way here." If Vincent had anything to say about it, they would never see their daughter again.

His mother put her hands on his shoulders. "Vincent, she needs to be able to stand beside you. Not behind. Believe me, I know. The Hawkins name was no blessing when I first came here."

"But your scrappy, sly heritage has served you well, Mother," Edmund said.

"As it has served you, Edmund. You're fifty percent Hawkins after all, even if you grew up here," their mother said. "But back to Bronte. She cannot continue this façade of being a Non."

She moved to stand beside her husband. His parents shared a look of secrets, two experienced warriors with a long history of prevailing over powerful foes and ready for another fight. Together they were a force of nature.

"There's only one alternative." Mother's flat voice rendered her verdict.

Vincent nodded, knowing they'd drawn the same conclusion. "She has to come out of hiding."

"We'll help. You can't do it alone," his mother said.

For a moment they fell silent. Bronte's music continued to drift around to them, creating an almost physical connection between her and every living entity within hearing.

"I don't know about this. She's a bit timid, Vin." Edmund crossed his arms over his chest.

Vincent frowned. "You're wrong about that."

"Well, she uses her propriety like a shield."

"That's certainly nothing you would know about," their mother shot in.

Edmund grinned. "Bronte's lovely, and there's enough fire in her to fascinate. But it'd be easy to blow out her flame with just a breath." He rubbed a single finger over the bridge of his nose. "She not going to come out of hiding willingly."

"No." Vincent shook his head. "I'm going to have to drag her out."

"Well, make sure she still likes you afterward." His mother waved a finger in the air. "She's not one of your army mages. You can't order her around."

"Masset's already on her trail."

"Oh, yes. He's definitely working on that warrant." His mother had imported a bevy of Hawkins spies when she'd married a Rallis.

"Either Masset suspects something about her, or he's prejudiced against every Non out there now. I'm guessing the latter. He's no aurist mage." He looked at his father. "I don't know if he's the right man to be the chief of the enforcers, Dad. After that first bombing, he changed."

"Losing a son would change any father," he replied. "I'll look into it. But our mages are up in wands over the bombing. It would be almost impossible to replace the leader of the enforcers right now. He's gained a good bit of support for his strong tactics with Nons because of the Double-Wide attacks."

"Strong? He tried to kill her in the gyre." Vincent ran a hand through his hair. "We have to secure her position with us fast. And the Casteels won't simply hand her over."

"Changing history doesn't happen overnight, Vincent," Helen reprimanded. "And that's what needs to be done. The public is scared of syphons."

"The public is scared of everything these days," Vincent scoffed.

"There are some powers that should be feared," Edmund said matter-of-factly. "Though syphons obviously aren't one of them."

Vincent wasn't fooled by Edmund's casual words. His brother had a power so rare they'd had to research ancient scrolls to determine what it was. Knowing its name hadn't helped. It was still just as dangerous, just as deadly, and imperative to control. So far, Edmund excelled at concealing the depths of his power. He and Bronte had that in common. But if Edmund's control ever slipped, the devastation would be unmatched.

Vincent thumped him on the back in consolation.

Edmund shrugged him off. "Bronte's about to become the spokesperson of scary mage powers. She'll be good at it, if only because she looks like she could be knocked over with a dandelion puff."

"If that's what you think, you've been duped." Vincent would rather forget how she stood up to Masset—not once, but twice.

"The symphony's a good starting point," his mother said. "She'll like it. We'll keep her with us, insulate her from the curious. We'll arrive late, let everyone see her in the box with us, and we'll leave early."

His father took her into his arms. "Darling, that means we can't go to the dinner before or the party after."

She nodded.

"You're a sweet girl."

"I am not."

His mother had worked all year on tonight's celebration; even Vincent knew that.

"Besides, it's not a big sacrifice. Not for Vincent." She patted him on the arm.

His family rallied for a fight in his honor. They'd arrived here without waiting for him to ask for help. And his mother was giving up her big night.

"Thank you."

"Of course, darling. In the meantime, we convince the Casteels to transfer her sponsorship to us permanently. That's the first step until we can secure her legal protections as a mage."

Edmund tilted his head. "After seeing the gyre, it's obvious the land has welcomed her with open arms. She's already bonded as one of ours, though not by law. As for getting the Casteels to hand over the legal rights to her, I say we hold the medallion hostage."

Vincent straightened. "No. Double-Wide will think we're accepting their gift and giving in to them. If they share that with the public, everything this family stands for will be crushed."

Edmund shrugged. "Alright, Colonel. Whatever you say. Then we stall for now. Tell the Casteels we can retrieve the medallion in a week or so, and in the meantime we need to keep their daughter as a witness to the safety of the medallion. You know, with Bronte in your life, you could take the Senate seat. You wouldn't have to worry about the vibes of all those other senators bugging the hell out of your sense."

"No way. That's yours." As firstborn, Vincent was entitled to the position, but his overly powerful mage sense would flare beyond the tolerable at the Rushes. Vincent had never wanted the seat. He wasn't sure Edmund did either.

He focused the conversation back to tonight's plan. "We take the sentries with us to the symphony. They'll guard the door to the box and can tell everyone we're enjoying the time alone as a family and don't want to be interrupted."

His mother pressed a hand to her chest. "Why, how high-handed of us."

Edmund stepped in closer, shrinking the size of their circle. "The Eatons would back us up right now if they knew what she did for Vincent. All three of their sons struggle to control their mage sense. They hardly leave their house. The Winslowes, too. Their granddaughter just turned fifteen. They've moved her to the attic to limit her exposure to others' vibes. I suspect something similar has happened to the Nobles as well. Their daughter disappeared awhile ago."

"How do you know the Nobles' business? They're no friends of ours." Vincent frowned. What had his brother been up to?

"It's that Hawkins blood. He's a natural spy." His mother spoke absently, her thoughts somewhere else. "I'll talk to the Eatons and the Winslowes."

"I'll check in with the Bradfords," his father said. The small territory to the south of Rallis typically followed in their wake with most issues.

"That's four founding families behind us. We'd only need another three and we'd have enough of a majority in the Senate. The Lockes might be another easy one. She lives in their territory, after all." Edmund rubbed at the bridge of his nose again.

Vincent shuffled his feet at all this political maneuvering. Give him a battle, a duel, even a bomb. But the political siege rested in the hands of his family. He chafed at his inability.

"In the meantime, we'll show her off, keep mum about what she is, let everyone get used to her, and see for themselves she's nothing scary," his mother said. "We'll do the big reveal, and they can all be stunned that mages were prejudiced against this misunderstood power for so long. She'll be a hero."

"I'd settle for her being my mate." Vincent listened for a moment to the final notes of her song. It was bittersweet background music for this strategy session. "She's going to want to run."

"Well, I'm not losing her," his mother stated emphatically.

"I'm not losing her, Mother."

Edmund grinned. "Then it's a good thing I brought you that rope to tie her up after all."

"I beg your pardon." Bronte stood in the weeds at the side of the house. Her hair fluttered in the breeze.

"Hi, Bronte. We stopped by to bring Vincent some necessary supplies." Edmund grinned.

His mother swatted him on the shoulder. "Bronte! Darling! That was an absolutely lovely song. Just beautiful," she cried, bravely walking down into the weeds to join his syphon.

Bronte smiled cautiously but took a hesitant step backward as his mother rushed her. "Thank you. I haven't played that in a long time."

"Who's the composer? I don't recognize it."

"Me."

"Oh!" Mother wrapped her arms around Bronte. "Amazing! You should be on stage. Vincent, there's a garment bag and two suitcases in the car. Get them for me, would you?" She hustled Bronte toward the porch steps as Vincent obeyed her orders. "You are going to enjoy this evening. I brought you a dress and everything you could need to go with it." She turned back to him. "Oh, honey, don't drape it over your arm. It'll wrinkle. Go hang it up."

"Actually, I'm not—" Bronte began.

His mother interrupted. "We're leaving at seven o'clock. Feed her before you leave, Vincent. We'll see you in a bit." She grabbed one arm each on his father and brother. It was their turn to be hustled. "Don't come into the house. Drive your truck to the front and hop into the limo." She walked toward the Land Rover, stopping at the passenger door. "By the way, Bronte, your shirt's on inside out," she hollered, pointing delicately with her finger.

Vincent pulled Bronte back inside the safety of his house. He locked the door behind them the moment they were safely inside.

"My shirt's on inside out?" She looked down. Her mouth gaped in horror.

Vincent hadn't noticed before and still could hardly tell. But there was a fold at the bottom of the shirt that should have been on the inside.

"Oh good gracious. Your mother thinks we had sex." Bronte blinked at him, frozen with her violin snug under her arm. She was reeling in the wake his mother frequently left behind her.

Vincent crooked a smile at her with a tipped head. "My mother is a Hawkins by birth."

"Oh, no." Bronte's voice was properly alarmed. Even a Non would know of the Hawkins' reputation.

"She's smart. She's good at maneuvering people where she wants them." A useful skill for safely debuting a syphon into society.

She lifted an eyebrow. "And where exactly does she think she's maneuvering us?"

"I'm guessing her strategy is sort of like wrongly accusing someone of breaking the rules. If everyone believes you've already broken the rules, you might as well go ahead and do so. Not that having sex would be breaking the rules," he clarified.

Her eyes traced his body. He assisted with her perusal and stood motionless before her, grinning boldly when her eyes made it to his.

Bronte averted her glance in a flash, her cheeks pink. "She is devious."

Chapter 8

"This is a huge mistake." Bronte tried once more to convince him. She'd lost a dozen arguments over the last two hours. "You can't take a Non into a mage event. They're going to kick me out." She stood at the far end of the long table, keeping it between them like a wall. She needed as much distance as possible to focus on this fight. Her opponent was a major distraction. She'd never seen anyone wearing the dress uniform of the mage army. At least not in person.

The all-black suited him. The high, straight collar matched the stark, handsome lines of his face. The medals and ribbons decorating the jacket looked impressive, powerful. She had a foolish urge to run her hands over the breadth of his shoulders.

The whole house smelled like him. The scent of his shower left its aroma everywhere. She couldn't escape from the temptation short of pinching her nose shut.

He'd taken care of her this afternoon. He'd cooked for her—vegetable lasagna, guaranteed potion-free since he'd made it himself. He'd discovered how to curl her hair with his energy after she'd wished aloud for a curling iron. With everything Lady Rallis had packed in those suitcases, she couldn't believe there was no curling iron. Her hair now hung in wavy locks down her back and over her arms. The last time she'd worn her hair down in public was the day of that awful audition for the Rallis Symphony. The soft brush of it on her arms felt a bit wild, a bit out of control.

"And I can't find my Non-mage insignia. Where's my N?" The frustrated whine in her voice bounced around the room. The letter had been on her cardigan but she must have lost it in the gyre. "I could be arrested for that alone."

"They won't dare kick you out. And no one is going to arrest you," Vincent refuted. Calm and reasonable. "Not when you have an army of Rallises at your back, your front and your sides."

"No offense, but I think you're overestimating your influence."

"No offense, but I think you're out of touch with mage politics."

She pressed her fingers against her forehead. "What if someone recognizes my power? If Allison saw it at lunch, surely someone else will too." Her stomach rolled at the thought.

"Allison's power is unusual. Plus she's an addict and a damn guinea pig for that doctor. He experiments on her. She walks around drugged up most days." He stepped around the table. "You'll be safe, Bronte. I promise. I'd give my life to keep you safe."

"Please don't do that." His dissertation, still laying on the coffee table, caught her gaze. *Even if it hasn't been seven days yet*, she thought. "If someone is going to have to die for me to do this, then I'm absolutely not going."

He reached for her hand and squeezed gently. He wasn't letting her walk away from this argument. His vibes drifted inside her, an invisible caress. Her formerly dormant powers sighed in blissful contentment. She swallowed hard and ignored it. Sort of.

"We wouldn't go if I wasn't confident you'd be safe. Don't you want to hear the music? When was the last time you heard mage musicians? Other than yourself, that is."

She opened her mouth to deny that she was a mage. It was a reflex, but this time she stopped. She shifted her eyes to him. He was waiting for that denial. It was apparent in the quirk of his lips.

"A long time." She couldn't erase the longing from her voice. Mage music resonated like no other. The energy of the sound waves penetrated a body as if skin was blessed with the ability to hear. She was starved for it, yearned to hear it, to be a part of it.

He slid his hand up her arm until his palm rested on her bare elbow. He crooked a smile at her. "Let's go. Besides, you're too dolled up to stay home tonight. My mother has this whole thing planned down to the minute. We shouldn't be late." He tugged her toward the door.

She let herself be dragged, picking up her borrowed clutch from the kitchen table as she passed. Outside in the slight breeze, her wrap fluttered. It matched the silk chiffon of the dress. The black beading around the shift's neckline and down the sides was a work of art. But her favorite part was the two long ruffles attached just beneath the waist, one on each side, like low wings dancing in the air. The shift was fitted but not overly so. Despite its loveliness, she felt exposed in the sleeveless dress. On the other hand, she could cover herself from head to toe and still lack sufficient armor to face this night.

She tried to ignore the fear racing up and down her skin…tried to forget she was about to invade forbidden territory. She needed a distraction from the nerves swirling through her. She chose the first topic that came to her mind. "Why do you drive a petrol truck and not a mage engine?" She stepped up into his black truck as he held open the door.

"Mage engines give off too many vibes for me on some days. It's easier to use petrol power." He closed the door, leaving her shut in with her nerves.

It took him six seconds to walk around the truck and get in. It only took three seconds for fear to claw its way clear through her.

She thought to ask where he got the petrol, the stations being hard to find, but the sharp edge of panic severed her thin hold on the conversation.

She gripped the beaded clutch too hard. Her fingers wouldn't stay still on its threaded glass jewels as Vincent drove back to the big house. He took her left hand into his and set them on the middle console. Even within his grip, her fingers trembled.

He rubbed his thumb over the back of her hand. "Have you ever been to the Palace Theatre?"

She shook her head and listened to him describe its ornate beauty, distracting her with details she was surprised he knew. She should have tugged away, but she couldn't handle this alone. Though accepting his strength came with tight ties, for a few hours, she would take what he offered.

Just for tonight.

Accompanied by his low voice, the dark, cool night gathered around her and insulated them both from the rest of the world. The ride smoothed as they exited his meadow. Vincent leveled out the truck with his mage sense as it went over the bumps. Her syphon power absorbed the hiccups in his power each time they drifted over a pothole.

The rest of the Rallis family waited on the front steps as Vincent drew up to the house. A group of sentries lined the stairs as well, their dark gray dress blending with the night. Another man stood off to the side. He'd been at the gyre with Edmund, but Bronte couldn't remember his name. A shiny black limo sat in the driveway sandwiched between two Land Rovers. Their mage engines cast a soft glow on the ground.

Lady Rallis glided down the steps with a smile at Bronte. "Into the car, family. Quickly now. We're on a schedule. Vincent, Gerald will follow us in your truck. You'll have a quick escape home if you need to get out. Are you alright with this? Bronte's syphon can get you through, yes?"

Bronte glanced up at him. She hadn't even considered how hard this might be for him.

Lady Rallis didn't wait for an answer but continued to parse out instructions. "We are killing two birds with one spell on this expedition. While we're there, be on the lookout for a wife for Edmund. Scan the crowd." She looked at Senator Rallis. "Burr, we need someone liberal. Open-minded. One who doesn't mind a syphon in the family. Keep watch for that type of energy."

The senator gave his daughter-in-law a small bow, pressing the Rallis Medallion against his chest.

Edmund cleared his throat. "If I may, she does need to be at least a little bit pretty. More importantly, she needs to be big in the breasts and on the backside." He cupped his hands in the air, outlining his preferred shape. "I like a good, juicy squeeze in both directions."

"Edmund." Helen's voice pitched high as she admonished her younger son with a swat on his arm with her purse. "Do not be crude."

"What?" he asked innocently. "You need to know the details of my order if you're going to get it right." He rolled his eyes as his mother stepped into the car. "Which she's not," he said under his breath toward Vincent.

Edmund motioned for Bronte to get into the car. She climbed in and took a seat against the wall along the driver's side. Vincent sat next to her; Edmund sat across from them, all alone. Vincent's father and the senator sat with Helen, facing forward. Two sentries got in the front. A chorus of slamming doors echoed as the remaining sentries piled into the other vehicles.

"Maybe you should let me handle my own wife shopping, Mother."

"Absolutely not. Look at Vincent. Did you know he and Bronte met thirteen years ago? Thirteen years! Maybe I need to dig into your past and see who you've met and if anyone has any potential."

Edmund's eyes slid sideways. "Dig into my past and all you'll get is an empty hole." He smiled with tight lips and gestured to Bronte. "Let's focus on Vincent and Bronte for now. Now there's a match with the goddess's blessing."

"Wait." Bronte took a breath and set her shoulders. "I am here for the next sixteen hours. Only. That's it. There's no match here. After that, I am going to be outside the Rallis Territory border, complying with my pass. I'm not staying."

Her pronouncement rang out. Silence filled the large interior of the car. The Rallises, except Vincent, glanced around at each other. Finally Lady Rallis spoke with a placating smile. "No need to decide anything in haste, Bronte."

"It is my decision. I hope you honor it."

Lady Rallis just smiled.

Bronte sighed. Even if she had the official status of a mage, she'd still never win against this family. "All your Mayflower friends are going to think you're crazy to let your son be seen with a Non, much less the whole family."

"We've got tonight covered. We've got it all covered." Helen reached out to pat Bronte on the knee.

"You stay with me at all times." Vincent's voice filled with authority. "Please don't have to go to the bathroom."

"If anyone approaches us, we do the talking, Bronte. We know what to say," Lady Rallis chimed in. "By the end of the evening, five hundred mages will have spent two hours in the company of a syphon and have no damage to complain about. Someday we'll be riding in this car to go hear Bronte play on stage."

Five hundred mages.

Good goddess. Five hundred mages.

The car was suddenly too small for her. "I thought you were going to act like I'm a charity case. Taking the unprivileged Non to the symphony." Her head spun. Her heart beat too fast for her to sit still. She needed to be outside sprinting for the rest of her body to keep time with the vital organ.

Vincent took her hand. "No one is going to announce that you're a syphon."

Lady Rallis's smile narrowed. The expression fit with the tough, sophisticated veneer of her fitted leather jacket topping her dark dress and lipstick.

"I would hope not. I'd like to continue living!"

"You mean living the half-life you've created for yourself?" Lady Rallis criticized as if she had every right. "You know that's not good enough. Otherwise you wouldn't have auditioned for the Rallis Symphony. Yes, I asked around after our lunch." She raised her eyebrows at Bronte. "Half a life is what Vincent has too. That's not good enough for him either."

The car glided to a halt and the door opened before she was done talking. Lady Rallis tossed the last words over her shoulder as she exited the car. Her husband and the senator followed.

Cool air rushed in, bringing shivers of fear tingling through her body. "I don't think I can do this, Vincent." Fearful tears gathered behind Bronte's eyes.

Edmund scooted to the edge of his seat and winked at her as he got out, leaving her and Vincent in the car.

Bronte struggled to find enough air to make her plea. "If your truck is here, then take me home. Please, Vincent."

His face softened in sympathy. He reached out to touch her cheek, but she dashed out of the car to run to his truck.

Enough with being the good, obedient Non. She might long for mage music, but she wasn't going to die for it.

The gleaming black truck sat against the curb across the street. She jogged around the limo and fled toward it. The wide city street was filled with limos and expensive cars. Mages in formal dress lined the sidewalk. An orderly row of mage lights floating above the street held the dark of night at bay. Flashes of blue suddenly disturbed their soft, steady glow.

Everyone halted. The blue lights flickered off the windows of the neighboring buildings as a half-dozen enforcer cruisers hurtled down the crowded street. A single siren pierced the air ensuring everyone noted their approach. The pack of cruisers skidded to a halt in front of her.

She was surrounded.

Masset jumped out of the closest car.

Bronte took a step backward, and then another. Vincent's hand closed on her bare arm. His other arm wrapped around her shoulders and tucked her in beside him.

"Bronte Casteel, I have a warrant for your arrest." Masset's vicious smile gleamed in the dark night. "Approved and signed by your sponsor, Phyllis Casteel." He unfolded the paper and held it up with a shake.

A crush of Rallis sentries pressed around them.

"Hmm." Edmund appeared on her other side. "Let's see that, chief." He waited for the other man to hand it over and then scanned it. "Problem. Miss Casteel is currently sponsored by Rallis." He reached for Bronte's purse, and she let it go without a protest. He opened it and pulled out her new papers.

"Your warrant is invalid." Vincent looked at the man with hard, dead eyes.

"Consider yourself yet another victim of Lord and Lady Casteel's unethical schemes," Edmund stated. "Though a man of your caliber should see through such tactics. You must be aware of their reputation."

Masset glared at both brothers and jerked the papers from Edmund's hand. "Let me see that." He paced closer to Bronte.

She wobbled on her feet but stood her ground. Not that Vincent gave her any other option. "I've done nothing wrong, Chief Masset. I've merely followed the orders of my temporary sponsors." The words came out of her mouth with such steadiness she couldn't believe she'd spoken them.

The enforcer sneered. He shifted his gaze to her papers and flipped them front and back. "Chapman! Get over here!"

Another enforcer stepped forward. His eyes were wide with trepidation. He glanced back and forth among the sentries and the Rallises.

"Yes, sir?" He stuttered.

"Read this!" Masset shoved the papers into Chapman's hand. The pass bent with his force.

"Uh, sir, uh, I'm sure the Rallis word is truth, sir." The young man stammered around the words.

"Check!"

The younger enforcer took the papers with a shaky hand. He closed his eyes for a quick moment. "Truth, sir. No hint of any aberration, sir."

Bronte glanced back toward the theater. A crowd of mages stood along the stairs and gawked. Bronte felt like she was spotlighted on the floor of the Coliseum, fighting lions while Roman senators watched from the safety of their seats. Lord and Lady Rallis, as well as the senator, stood a few feet away. They studied the faces of every enforcer as if memorizing them. Masset's men withered under their glares.

The chief yanked the papers away from Chapman and tossed them to the ground.

"Pick. It. Up." The order came from the senator himself. His voice powered through the air.

Masset obeyed like a puppet on strings.

Bronte reached out with a shaky hand to take her pass back.

"You will pay for this," Masset whispered to her. "You Nons are all trash. This isn't over." Masset stomped back to his car, threw himself in and slammed the door. Other enforcers followed suit. The cars streamed away.

Adrenaline swirled through her, leaving nausea in its wake. She'd yet to make inside the building, and already the calm veneer she always wore to protect herself had been ripped to shreds. Masset had won in that respect. She tried to mentally gather the pieces of her composure around herself.

"Well, nothing to do but brazen it out now," Edmund said.

She was enough of a Mayflower daughter to know that.

"Too many people saw Masset's little show." Edmund's words were as sharp as she'd ever heard them. "If we left, we'd look guilty or scared. For now, smile." His voice converted back to normal. "It's a lovely night. You're a lovely lady. I hear you like this kind of music. I don't, but I'll smile anyway. Now you join in, too, for our audience."

Bronte's eyes lingered on Edmund's smile. "You are all crazy."

On the building's grand steps, their audience had shrunk by half. Only a few mages remained outside, a small enough group to perform for, she supposed. She pulled her lips up, not sure if the action resembled a smile, but she was too stiff with fear to form a real one.

"You have to do better than that. Lesson number one: always assume there are intuiters around. Always. You can't hide from them. So *be* the smile, Bronte. Feel it."

There was no smile big enough to hide her fear. So she focused on her anger, whether it was rational or not. "If I live long enough, I'm going to get you all back for this."

"That's the spirit!" Lady Rallis called out.

* * * *

The entryway of the theater opened into a gleaming lobby, empty with the exception of a few stragglers. Ahead, the static drone of a crowd radiated from three sets of open doors. Everyone else was already seated. They were almost late.

Bronte cast her gaze upward in a silent plea to the goddess for survival. Her eye caught on the domed ceiling, gilded and etched with thousands of tuning circles—enough to channel power for every mage here to pull on. This was an old building to house so many circles. They'd gone out of style since the average mage's power had escalated over the last few generations.

This place was probably torture for Vincent. He already carried too much energy of his own. He placed her hand, which was still shaky from the encounter with Masset, in the crook of his elbow and covered it with his. His energy flooded into her like he'd been drowning until he'd touched her.

All of a sudden, Helen turned back to them with a rigid smile on her face. A trickle of alarm vibrated through Bronte. Something was wrong again.

Edmund grabbed Bronte's empty hand. He held out a bouquet of red roses obviously stolen from the towering arrangement next to him.

The velvety bunch of buds bloomed into full flower before her eyes. A spell's pressure pushed at her ears.

"Bronte, you're the first pretty girl to show up on our doorstep since you last left it. But you ended up with the wrong brother. Vincent's a nice guy, but he's too serious. Come over to my arm, and I'll worship ever step you take." Edmund's voice was too loud to be talking to someone right next to him.

What in the universal blazes was he doing? He moved the flowers closer to her with an adoring smile.

Bronte lifted a hand to take the lush blossoms. It was the only possible response. Before she touched them, they exploded. A shower of petals rained down. Her syphon absorbed a gentle burst of energy. That meant Vincent was responsible for the eruption. Patches of red velvet continued to drift down slowly over the entire lobby. Vincent controlled their descent. Delighted gasps sounded from two women lingering by the theater doors. One reached out and caught a petal.

Helen looked over at the two women and waved. Her rigid smile softened. This performance was for those women, whoever they were. Maybe one of them was an intuiter as Edmund had mentioned earlier.

Vincent went chest to chest with Edmund. It was a little awkward since her hand was still on his arm.

"How about I worship your nose with my fists? Find your own girl to court. Quit trying to woo mine."

"Bronte should be able to choose whoever she wants. You're monopolizing all her time. Just because you're the one who saw her first doesn't mean you get to keep her."

"Damn straight I'm keeping her."

Bronte joined in. She'd already made it clear those were fighting words to her. She planted her feet wide between them. With a palm on each of their chests, she spoke loudly. "Boys. That's enough."

Helen nodded with rapt attention, completely captivated by the performance. Bronte was in the eye of the storm these Rallises whipped up with everything they did. "I don't belong to anyone but myself. Now behave. Both of you. Let's just go sit down." She marched off, then stopped. Going back to grab Vincent's hand, she tugged him after her.

The women gasped again. Bronte looked back just in time to watch as dozens of petals gathered back around the one single stem in Edmund's hand. He walked up to her and tucked the flawless flower behind her ear. "I'll wait as long as it takes."

"Waste of time, Edmund." Vincent strode farther into the lobby.

Bronte caught the senator's wink at her before she turned around. She followed Vincent, still connected at their hands. A dejected Edmund walked behind her.

The Rallises seemed to pull wild, crazy schemes out of the air as easily as spells. Keeping up with these people took a lot of focus. She was afraid what would happen if she let down her guard even for a moment. They'd turn her life upside down permanently.

A sharp voice rang out from the open second level. "Senator Rallis! How is your break from the Rushes?" A blond woman, her hair dancing along her cheekbones, skipped down the steps. She sparkled in her floor length gown. It was the exact color of her skin, giving the illusion she wore nothing but glitter. "Any progress on the Kadesha Bill, senator? Do you think you can persuade Winslowe and get the majority to declare the potion illegal? Any update on how many deaths there have been because of the potion?"

"No comment tonight, Chrissy." The senator's voice boomed with good nature. "The newspapers will have to wait until I'm back on the floor. Tonight I'm with my family. It's a rare occasion, and I'm going to enjoy every minute of it."

"How nice for you, senator. I'll dig deep and try to find my patience." Chrissy gave him a flirty smile and then switched targets. "Helen, darling! You missed the dinner! How could you?"

"Hello, Chrissy." Lady Rallis hooked one arm through her husband's and the other through the senator's, ready to lead the march away. "I'll explain later." She winked at the reporter as if she had a good story brewing. "I can't believe we're this late."

The lights flickered.

"Let's get to our seats, everyone. I'll call you later, Chrissy. I'm not missing a single minute of Peter's performance." Helen hustled through the lobby. Two sentries caught up and smoothly stepped in front of her. Bronte figured they had to do that a lot when it came to Lady Rallis.

Bronte followed with Edmund and Vincent. The two sentries behind them ended their parade. They hurried to a smaller hallway and through a door marked *Private.* It led to a back stairway, empty and quiet. Finally.

"You can thank me now," Edmund announced softly. "I don't think anyone suspects Bronte's terrified instead of thrilled to be here."

"Yes, good work, Edmund." There was a touch of sarcasm to Helen's voice. She shrugged, her voice turning to exasperation. "Who would have thought that Reina Parrish would be here? She never comes to these things. Intuiters hate crowds."

"Probably why she was lingering outside the auditorium," Lord Rallis stated.

"Sorry for putting you in the middle there, Bronte. You outshine that rose in your hair by a thousand lumens, but you're no good at hiding your emotions. Fear was written all over you, smile or no." Edmund patted her on the back.

"Edmund, don't think I'm blind to what else you accomplished with that little scene," Lady Rallis sounded disgusted. "You practically announced you're in love with Bronte. A soon as this gets around, no one is going to expect you to search for a bride any time soon."

"That was not my intention at all, Mother," Edmund stated innocently. "I was just trying to help. We needed a reason for Bronte to be upset. I had to do something. Keep the flower in your hair, Bronte," Edmund ordered as she reached up to remove it.

"No. Take it out," Vincent countered.

"No. Keep it in. Let that reporter get a good glimpse of it. We need her to remember it. I used big energy to get all those petals back just right. Not something one could do if a syphon was sucking you dry of vibes."

Chapter 9

Vincent lost the battle to keep her in the second row of their box. Instead, Bronte sat in the front, sandwiched between him and his grandfather. The senator had plenty of experience battling against mage spells at the Rushes, but Vincent didn't like this at all. He scanned the crowd beneath them. More than half gawked up at their box. He would have put an energy shield in front of her if it wouldn't be cause for suspicion.

He wanted to ask her if she was alright, to glance over to see for himself, but he didn't dare take his eyes or his mage sense off the crowd.

"It's going to be a long evening if you don't relax," his grandfather stated over Bronte's head.

He merely tightened his grip on Bronte's hand. A small commotion built around the aisle closest to them on the main floor. "Allison's here," he stated. He kept his gaze on the growing group.

"I thought she didn't like this kind of music." Bronte's wry tone told him she was composed enough for now. "Must be her date who likes it."

"Dr. Lawrence Riley likes anything that gets him into society." His mother's tone matched Bronte's. "He's using her as a stepping stone."

"How much higher could he hope to step than a Rallis?" Bronte asked.

"Bronte, you fit right in with us," the senator observed as he returned Riley's wave.

But the doctor didn't seem satisfied with that response. He pointed a finger straight at Bronte and then waved to her, and gave her a thumbs-up.

Vincent tensed. "Do you know him?" Energy vibrated on his fingers, ready to lob a shield in front of Bronte, but Riley turned away. His fans gathered around him.

Bronte shook her head. "Isn't he supposed to be supportive of Non-mage rights? Guess he knows a Non when he sees one."

Musicians strolled out onto the stage. The informal procession continued until the entire orchestra wandered out. The cacophony of warm-ups mushroomed into giant vibrations of sound. Vincent heard Bronte take a soft breath of anticipation. He risked a glance at her.

She looked happy for the first time since stepping into the gyre. Her lips pulled into a tight smile, as if she were fighting to contain it. From the stage, the notes solidified into one, merging into the same frequency.

As Peter Leggert took the stage, the audience came to their feet. Vincent stood with them, but only because Bronte did. She made herself a larger target than ever. She'd be safer behind him, but he kept his feet planted. Thanks to her, his mage sense flowed at full strength. Deflecting spells was easy work compared to deflecting bombs. After the early morning DW attack, his sixth sense had never been so damaged. Now he was sitting among hundreds of people with no discomfort at all.

He glared at the crowd. He'd protect this woman from anything.

Bronte looked around their seats as they sat back down. "We don't have any programs. How can you have your own box but no programs?"

The first note of the music sounded. Her head wrenched around to the stage. A tiny smile parted her red lips. She straightened as if sitting tall would help her better catch the music.

Even as the musicians performed, his family and Bronte bore the eyes of a curious audience. They were on a miniature stage in this box, and it was too dark to see their watchers. He concentrated on the space in front of their box. His speed at deflecting energy was unsurpassed. He'd have enough time to protect Bronte from a spell if he sensed it a mere inch in front of her. But he didn't relax.

Vincent spent the first three songs watching the crowd. The crowd applauded time and again. The conductor bowed each time, receiving the praise as if he'd done all the work. Seemed to him the musicians worked harder. Then the tuxedoed man walked off the stage. Two musicians moved to chairs in front of the large orchestra. The conductor walked back on. Why had he left in the first place?

More clapping. Leggert was applause-hungry.

"How much longer will this go on?" he whispered to Bronte.

She shrugged. "I don't know. I don't have a program. Just listen. Try to enjoy it."

"I am," he assured her.

She laughed.

Leggert turned to his audience. "Tonight I am blessed to bring you the music I love most. I am grateful for your support for all these wonderful years." More applause. "The next two songs are quite short, both duets. This first piece, well, there is nothing like it. As far as I know, it's never been played in public. About a year ago, we were graced with a part of the composition Manuel and Adrienne will play for you. The rest of the music was lost, much like the title states. *Lost Dreams Gathering.* I think you'll find it as heartbreaking as I do that the other movements are lost."

The violinist's first note echoed around the auditorium like a mournful ringing of bells at the ashes ceremony. For the first time, Vincent was as swept up in the music as the rest of mages here. The energy pouring from song was like nothing that had been played tonight. Less than a handful of notes into the music, he recognized it.

This was the song Bronte played this afternoon.

He leaned forward to see her face. Her chest rose in shallow, fast breaths. It hurt to see the sad, longing on her face.

"Oh my heavens. Bronte, this is your song!" His mother hissed from behind them. She was as stunned as Bronte. "Where's a program?"

She found one and thrust it in front of Vincent. It read *Lost Dreams Gathering, B. Castle.*

The song wrapped through the very fiber of the building until it cradled the audience. From the corner of his eye, he saw his mother wipe a tear from her cheek. The cello sang in, creating a deeper, mournful tone. The song was richer for it, but Vincent preferred the way it sounded on his back porch.

The notes reached high, pleading for something he wouldn't have understood without meeting the composer herself. The ending of the song balanced between highs and lows, giving the impression there was hope if not happiness. The last note hung in the air. The audience sat stunned. Mage music was full of brilliance, but this outshone everything else played tonight. The mass of mages stood, nearly perfectly coordinated as a group, and erupted into a shattering mass of clapping.

Bronte turned to him, her face pale. "I want to leave. Now."

"How did he get that piece of music?" His mother stuck her head face between theirs.

Vincent thought Bronte was going to ignore her. The audience's noise blocked her soft voice. He struggled to pull her sound to him

"I left it behind. It was an accident. That day I auditioned." Bitterness streaked through her words. "Can we leave? Please, Vincent."

She stood. Her gown caught on his knee and showed him a glimpse of her slender leg. As he followed her out, he noticed his mother nodding at someone as she applauded with the rest of the appreciative audience. He followed her eyes to the conductor's surprised gaze on their box.

* * * *

Her own song deadened her nerves to everything. It wasn't the mages who had scared her off. No. Her own creation was the catalyst to her flight. The irony of it struck her. A bitter breath escaped from her lungs, the doppelgänger of a laugh. A layer of ice had solidified over her heart with the final note of her song, a cold anger that seethed and pushed her feet down the quiet hall.

A sentry spoke behind her, keeping pace with Vincent. "They're splitting up. Jackson, move inside the box. The senator is still there. Colonel, I thought the plan was to stay together. Is there anything I should know?"

"We're leaving," Vincent replied. "Escort us to my truck. I'll take it from there."

"Yes, sir."

"Bronte, wait." Vincent's sharp order was loud enough to carry into the other boxes they passed. She marched on.

It was the cello. She knew what the violin sounded like, had played it a thousand times herself, better than they'd heard tonight. But since no mage would ever consider playing with a Non, she'd never found anyone equal to her skill to play the cello part.

Vincent's hand cupped her elbow. "Remember how we talked about sticking together?"

"You're right on my heels. That's close enough," she snapped softly as she met his intense blue eyes, his eyebrows pulled in a fierce scowl. His expression was enough to scare away any enemies. It didn't intimidate her, though.

"Let's aim for closer. The conductor knew you'd written that song. He looked at you."

"I seriously doubt he remembers my face." Her heels stabbed at the thick, red carpet.

"Your music must have made quite an impression on him. It certainly impressed the audience. Way better than all that old stuff." His legs easily kept up with her shorter ones as they flew down the stairs.

"Vincent, they took my song." Her voice was too loud, too high, but she couldn't find enough control over it, even though another woman lingered down the hall. "I have a lot of songs, but I love that one." She stabbed at her chest with her finger. "I wasn't allowed to make it sound like that. Even though I can!" She ground to a halt in front of the ladies' room. Her shawl fluttered around her. "I forgot my purse!"

"Mother will get it."

"It has my papers in it."

"It will be fine."

She heaved a sigh. "I need a minute. Just give me one minute."

Yanking her arm away, she pushed the door of the ladies' room open and strode in. She locked herself in the first stall. She closed her eyes and tried to catch her breath, her sanity, her focus.

The ladies' room door opened.

"Bronte." His voice was calm. "Remember that plan we talked about? It hasn't changed. You stay with me." Vincent's shoes poked beneath the stall's door.

"You cannot be in here."

"I second that!" A woman's disapproval chimed from another stall. A lock clicked followed by the sound of high-heeled footsteps. "Outrageous. Simply outrageous."

Oh good goddess. He needed a rescue. She twisted the stall's knob. The door swung in, but a buxom, older woman brushing cheeks with Vincent blocked her way.

"Outrageous. But it's wonderful to see you out, darling Vincent. Tom said he thought you'd be down for weeks after that explosion."

The lady turned her gaze on Bronte. Her wide, brown eyes were too shrewd for her jolly expression. She looked Bronte up and down. "She must be something," the woman drawled. "Lucinda Wilen." She introduced herself, though she offered neither a hand nor a cheek, just a bosom bustling in front of her like a barge moving down a river. "I'm General Wilen's wife."

Bronte took a step back into the stall. "Bronte Casteel."

"Well, my goodness. Look at the expression on her face, Vin. Perfectly smooth. Not a ruffled feather on this little bird. You'd think she has hostile encounters in ladies' rooms on a daily basis. It's bred in, you know. That perfect composure only happens if you have fifty generations' experience of hiding you're a witch. My family never had it and never will. Lordy, we survived the inquisitions by an ancestor or two each time."

She poked a finger in Vincent's uniform-clad chest, revealing the fading tuning circles tattooed on her fingers. "I'll tell you one thing we didn't do, colonel, and that was invade the other gender's private bathrooms. Now. You. Out."

"Right. Sorry," Vincent clipped, reaching a hand for Bronte. "Please, Bronte."

"For pity's sake, boy. She'll be out in minute. Let the girl pee already. Goodbye." Lucinda waved with a flap of her fingers.

"I need a minute." Bronte's voice sounded small compared to Lucinda's.

"I'll be right outside with the sentry." Vincent conceded, sticking a thumb in the sentry's direction, his voice a warning. His footsteps sounded like he was trying to pound his shoes into the floor. The door sighed open and then softly knocked shut against its frame.

"I'll tell you one thing." Lucinda stared her down. "You don't feel like much. Kind of weak and flat. There's no fizz to you. Wouldn't think you'd be strong enough for Vincent. In fact, I'd think you were almost dead if I couldn't see it for myself." Lucinda shook her handbag at Bronte like a finger. "No wonder you've fooled everyone into thinking you're a Non."

Bronte shut the door in her face. The slam resounded through the bathroom. Bronte wanted to stomp her feet and insist that she had fizz.

"You've certainly got my Vin tied up in knots, Bronte Casteel." Lucinda's voice faded slightly, as if she'd moved away from the stall. "Who would have thought? He's a tough one. They're all tough though. Powerful. And lonely. Every single one of them. 'Bout breaks my general's heart. They've no idea he's such a softie."

The sound of a short zipper wrenched through the air accompanied by the soft clatter of Lucinda's purse. "My Tom loves those boys like they're his own sons. Never had any kids of our own. Wouldn't know what to do with a baby if it came with instructions as fat as *Mercurio's Potion Treatise*."

Bronte peered through the crack in the stall and watched as Lucinda touched up her face. *Hurry up and leave*, she thought.

"My general's damn good at dealing with powerful mages. 'Specially the weird ones. Those who have a duty to step up and protect our country. Mmm hmm. Big on that. He's protective of his boys. He wants to make sure no one's gonna break their hearts, lie to them, abandon them, betray them, use them." She itemized the misdeeds like a bulleted list. "He's gonna see to it those things don't happen. He's gonna find out what the truth is."

Lucinda spun around and leaned against the counter, her arms folded under that chest. She squinted at the stall door.

Bronte quickly jerked her head from the crack and spoke, trying to cover up her spying. "It's nice to have someone look out for you. Although I'm sure Vincent can handle himself."

"Probably. How 'bout you? Are you too weak to take care of yourself?"

Bronte wasn't sure if Lucinda was threatening or challenging her. Did Vincent know his boss was suspicious of her? "I've taken care of myself for a long time."

"Really." Lucinda's sarcastic surprise echoed through the bathroom. "I don't know if you're very good at it, Bronte. Doesn't look like you've gotten too far in life. If you ever had any potential, it's already faded away, honey. You've never grabbed the bull by the balls, and you never will. You'd rather run away from it."

Bronte gasped. "I'm here, aren't I? That's not running away."

"Oh pish posh. You're here because Lady Rallis made you. Now, you coming out of that stall, darlin'? Or are you just being polite and not peeing when I'm talking?"

Since the woman couldn't see through doors, Bronte indulged herself. She stuck out her tongue and gave a mean scrunch of her nose at her.

In the mirror, Lucinda lifted an eyebrow.

Damn these mages.

Bronte schooled her face and exited the stall. "I needed a moment to find some peace, that's all." Stepping toward the mirror next to Lucinda was like a gazelle approaching a water hole when a lion was partaking.

"Not much of that in here for you. I sent your peace out to the hall. If that's what you're looking for, go get him."

"I will. It was nice meeting you," Bronte said as she sidestepped to the door.

"Ha. Look at those Mayflower manners. Fizz-less. I'll tell the truth even if you won't. It was very interesting meeting you, Bronte Casteel. We'll meet again soon, I'm sure."

Chapter 10

Grab the bull by the balls. Fizzless? Pish posh.

Bronte shoved the ladies' room door open. It banged against the wall.

Vincent stood a foot away. His dark eyes pinned her before she even opened the door all the way.

A muttering wave came toward them. Louder and louder. Intermission.

The first of the concertgoers appeared around the corner, followed by an aristocratic deluge. Vincent's expression hardened, his jaw tight, determination etched deep in his face.

She took his hand. She wouldn't let him face the mob of vibes alone.

Bronte wanted to face them down simply to prove the rude woman wrong. But she was out of her element among these mages. All she could do was syphon Vincent's vibes. She could not conquer this crowd. It was too mighty of a bull for her.

They swam against the current of mages, mostly women, streaming toward the restroom. Though the sentry followed behind them, without the protection of Vincent's family, Bronte was a minnow among very big, toothy fish that liked to play with their food.

Vincent's scowl cleared a small path. Mages stepped aside to avoid not only the power he naturally deflected back at them but also the broad shoulders. *Bull* was an apt description.

"Rallis!"

She heard the man's voice sounding from behind them. Vincent dipped his head an inch and kept going.

She looked back to see a bald man in a uniform quite similar to Vincent's. This had to be Lucinda's other half. Formidable. That was the word to describe Vincent's boss. She met his eyes over the crowd and dared to hold his stare for a second. There. He could report back to his wife that she was not fizzless.

A tune drifted to her ears over the noise of the crowd. She looked away from the general. She recognized the melody. Someone hummed one of Claude's songs. It was from his current batch of completely horrid compositions. His songs rarely made it out of the South. Who would know it here?

The tune floated above the din of the crowd. The screechy melody hovered, as distinct as oil floating on the surface of a puddle, unable to mix with the depths of the pool. It should have irritated every ear after the beautiful music this crowd had soaked in.

She glanced around to see who it was, but found no suspects. The bald man was the only other person who even seemed to notice it. He, too, was looking around the crowd, except his eyes kept traveling back to her. The scowl on his shiny face was a clear indicator that he, like his wife, disapproved of her.

She turned back to focus on maneuvering through the crowd, and the loud volume of the newly freed audience soon smothered the awful song.

They zigzagged through the glittering throng, but not fast enough for her taste. She would have run if he had let her lead. She was surrounded by the enemy left and right. Faces became a blurry blend of toothy smiles and penetrating gazes that threatened to undo her. Inquisitive stares lodged in her skin. She squeezed Vincent's hand until her nails dug into him. Her heart fluttered with fear, but she kept her head high and her face masked in serenity. There was nothing to do but ride this out. Calm confidence her only weapon.

Bronte ran into Vincent's back at his abrupt stop. Lady Rallis cut them off twenty feet shy of the door. His mother gave her a smile. Bronte assumed it was supposed to reassure, but it fell quite short of its mark. She recognized the man standing next to Lady Rallis with a zing of shock.

"Bronte," Lady Rallis began as she slipped Bronte's forgotten clutch back into her hands, "I'd like to introduce you, or rather reintroduce you, to Peter Leggert. He abandoned his post to meet you again! And Peter, this is my son, Vincent," she added offhandedly. "But you really don't care about him compared to Bronte."

"Helen!" The reporter's sharp tone was unmistakable as she slithered into the conversation. "There's not a mage soul in the world that wouldn't vibrate at the chance to meet a Rallis son."

"Oh, Chrissy," Lady Rallis waved the woman's comment away with an eyeroll the reporter couldn't see. "This lovely treasure, who my son is lucky enough to have gracing his arm tonight…it's B. Castle." Helen whispered the last with glee, as if it was an exciting secret spilling out into the world. "She composed that last song. That amazing song."

"It's a great honor to meet you again." Peter Leggert's deep voice boomed through the lobby. "I've never stopped regretting that I didn't have the courage to hire you on the spot. I kept your song. Obviously. You are such a talented musician and composer. I've followed your career occasionally through the years. I'm glad you were able to find…a measure of success."

The evaluation sounded uncomfortably like Lucinda's. She'd worked hard to achieve her position among the Chattanooga musicians. But he was right. What she'd accomplished as a Non was nothing compared to a mage's potential.

"I wish I'd known you were going to be here. You could have joined us on stage and played the song yourself."

Her most fervent wish. She sucked in a hard breath. To stand so close to it—the stage, the audience, the musicians. Her song. Still, that dream was beyond her grasp. Close but not close enough.

And it never would be. She could never stand before an audience of mages and risk them finding out her secret.

Oh goddess, it was salt in a wound.

Peter smiled wistfully. "Maybe you could have played the rest of it, the part you kept with you. I'd love to hear it sometime."

"It was quite beautiful." Chrissy butted her face in between Leggert's and Helen's. She held a small notebook and a pen. "Can I get a quote from you, Miss Castle? Your thoughts on tonight's performance?"

"Later, Chrissy." Helen squeezed the woman from the conversation. The reporter took the hint, but she lingered close by.

Peter smiled sadly. "I must get backstage now. I made my musicians nervous when I ran offstage after you. They likely thought I was abandoning them. I'm glad you're back." The conductor turned away.

"We're leaving." Vincent's words were harsh and stern. Not even his mother dared to counter the commanding voice of the colonel. He narrowed his eyes on the door, a target blocked by dozens of mages conversing, socializing, probably ready for a lynching at a moment's notice.

"Colonel, if it's alright, I'll take point this time," the sentry said.

Vincent nodded, said goodnight to his mother, and charged after the sentry. Bronte followed in his wake, one hand in his; the other grasped the beaded bag. A squealing lady cut off their access to the door. She threw herself in front of them like she was a matador's red cape to a charging bull.

"How's the date, you two?" she bubbled vivaciously. It was the pink lady who'd waited for a meeting with the senator this morning. Was it only this morning? The woman still wore pink, brighter and bushier than before.

"Sir?" the sentry asked.

Vincent brushed his concern away.

Pinkie had lost her handler—Frederick, if Bronte remembered correctly—in the mass of mages. Bronte spotted him fighting through people to get to her. Lady Rallis was on her way as well, throwing "excuse me"s back and forth. Her sentry hurried to catch up and looked ready to toss her over his shoulder.

"Lady Rallis," the pink lady called out as Helen came into hearing range, "there's no wife here for Edmund. I know where I need to look. Frederick won't let me tell you right now where that is, but I know what I'm doing." Pinkie turned back to Bronte. "Now what kind of mage are you?" Even Nons knew it was rude to ask such a question. "I can't see a lick of your energy, but there's something…an absolutely perfect connection between you two. Perfect like a fairy tale!" Her high, nasally voice squawked with animation.

"Betty!" her handler yelled above the crowd. Betty ignored him. She curled a strand of hair around her finger absently.

"Whatever you are, we need more of you. Many mages these days can hardly tolerate others. It's a growing epidemic. A pandemic even. Let me tell you, when mages are too powerful to tolerate other mages' power, it's an economic hardship for us matchmakers. Now, they're nothing like him." Betty shook a finger at Vincent. "He's a bit extreme. But my goodness, so are you!" She giggled.

Frederick made it to the compeer's side. Finally.

"Oh, Freddy!" She sobered a touch at the man's scowl. "Frederick," she corrected. "Look who it is! These two are leaving early. Wonder why!" She gave a wink. And then another. "Enjoy!"

Vincent nodded at the sentry. The man took his cue, pushed past Betty, and opened the door for them. The cold air wrapped around Bronte's legs as she walked out. She looked back as the door glided shut behind them and drowned away the deep murmur of the crowd. From inside, Betty waved to her, unaware that Chrissy stalked closer. Frederick saw the reporter coming and pulled his pink puffball away. Bronte lost them in the crowd.

The only life outside was the chauffeurs who kept warm in their cars. Gerald, Vincent's man, did the same in his truck. He made a U-turn in the middle of the street and pulled up right in front. Vincent helped Bronte in, the leather warm from the heated seat. Gerald exited the driver's seat and, along with the sentry, headed over to the Rallis limo with a nod to Vincent.

The cityscape faded as her stoic colonel drove them back. The land morphed into pitch-black countryside. Slowly, the safe solitude of the truck lent her a touch of calm. Fear unwound its tight grip. She leaned her head against the soft leather of the seat.

The image of the violinist and cellist onstage burned in her mind. The musicians had played her song beautifully. Melodic perfection. Sitting in the Rallises' box, she'd recognized the song immediately. If Lady Rallis hadn't been surprised as well, Bronte would have thought the woman planned this.

She thought back to the scene of her audition in front of Peter Leggert, a hard memory to relive. He had liked her, had listened intently. Her playing distracted him from her lack of personal mage vibes. He'd been ready to hire her. But she'd dropped her purse and her Non papers had fallen out.

The whole idea of auditioning had been foolish. If he'd hired her, she could never have hidden her power, or lack of it. She'd been doomed from the start. This Non-mage disguise…it had been itching for a long while, she realized. Somewhere inside her, she'd chafed to strip it off. Daring to audition had been a symptom of her malaise.

She turned her head toward Vincent as she leaned against the seat. "Peter Leggert put my song in the program because it's one of his favorites." She gave a soft laugh. "Can you believe that? When I look at it like that, it's hard to stay angry. Tonight was worth the risk." Her words waved through the comforting quiet that existed between them.

It had been worth facing down Masset and the encounter with Lucinda in the bathroom. Bronte had grabbed hold of that bull, regardless of what the other woman thought. "To hear my song like that…" She would have done almost anything.

Vincent studied her before looking back at the road. "It was the most beautiful song of the night. But he should have asked for your permission. He knew where you lived if he was tracking your career. And you should have been on that stage playing it."

"But, Vincent, that's never going to happen. This is as good as it gets for me. This is me grabbing the good."

He lifted his eyebrow, questioning her reasoning, but he stayed silent, letting her work through this on her own, as if she would draw the correct conclusion if she'd think hard enough.

He pulled through the gates of the estate. Her syphon absorbed the hitch in his energy as he pushed at them. The stars in the sky twinkled as if they, too, sensed him. The darkness hid all but a few details on his face—the glint in his eye, his stern, proud nose and the sharp cut of his jaw. The lights on the dash were too dim to see much more. Even in the dark, he exuded intensity, power.

She was already accustomed to it.

A dangerous thing.

It was almost time for her to leave.

She turned toward the window and craned her neck to view the stars until the trees surrounded them. They passed the woods that held the gyre. Memories of their almost-kiss bubbled inside her.

The last twenty-four hours had been a crazy, scary adventure. She'd accomplished her task for her mother, heard the mage music she'd longed for her entire life, and encountered the perfection of Vincent's vibes again.

The truck's clock read 9:49. A little over fourteen hours before she had to cross the Rallis Territory boundary. This would be her only night with him, the man whose power sang to her syphon. She would never have this again. This night, with its music, and with Vincent, needed to last her a lifetime.

She smiled as Vincent drove through his meadow.

* * * *

Bronte led the way into his house, slowly feeling her way in the dark, though she'd already memorized the simple layout. The lanterns above the table brightened to a soft glow as Vincent stepped in behind her.

"Thank you. For tonight." The words floated up through her, heartfelt and sincere. "I never would have had to courage to do that without you, much less had the opportunity to go. I am grateful I got to hear my song."

He took her hand and raised it to his lips. "It's only the start."

"No, Vincent. It's the end. Almost."

"We'll get your pass extended again. Edmund is working on it. Your parents can't say no." He placed her palm against his cheek. The short roughness of his whiskers rubbed against her hand.

"You're wrong. My parents can always say no. When it comes to me, they always do. But let's not talk about them."

"So long as you know this isn't the end." He bent down to her, nose to nose.

"I'm leaving tomorrow."

"No." He was emphatic.

She was too. "We have a deal. Now be quiet. Because this isn't going to be a soft peck. This one counts." She was grabbing the bull by the… horns. She had fizz and it coursed through her in magical places. Standing on her tiptoes, she clasped his face and pulled him in to meet her. Every tense knot in her body let go. She pressed her lips softly against him, waiting for him to respond. Bronte made a soft hum in the back of her throat, surprised she'd managed to catch him off guard. The warrior had yet to react to her assault.

Slowly, his arm crept around her waist as if he were unsure she would stay. In the next second, he closed off any option of her leaving and pulled her into him. His body was hard beneath his uniform. He opened his mouth and took over the kiss, tasting her, teasing her, letting her do the same to him.

A new tension glided through her, as demanding as her former fear. Her body tightened in places that hadn't responded in a long time. Heat moved along her skin and she dropped her shawl to the floor. She stepped her feet between his, bringing her hips into him. The new contact made her want to crawl up his body.

He surrounded her, his scent, his vibes, his strength. She reveled in it, drew it in to her as if it alone could sustain her. Tilting her head, she cooperated with delight as his lips moved from her mouth, to her cheek, to that spot under her ear.

She wanted to run her hands over his skin, but that handsome uniform stood in the way. Her hands felt along the front, searching for a seam, but it was smooth, no line of separation for the jacket to come apart. He helped her.

A stream of energy flowed from his finger, unlatching the fibers that had woven together to hold the jacket shut. She couldn't have taken it off him herself.

Her syphon power pushed into overdrive and boiled over with Vincent's energy. It was hard to breathe around it. But more than air, she wanted him. The jacket slid from his arms to the floor. Now only his white t-shirt blocked her touch. She reached for its hem, but he stopped her.

"Let me take care of you." He stepped behind her, a move too fast for her lust-drenched senses to track. Her arms were left empty of his warm strength. That was not what she wanted, even if he was back there to pull down her zipper.

"But I want to touch you." Her voice was breathy with want.

"Plenty of time for that," he whispered as his lips found the spot under her other ear. She let the back of her head rest against his chest. The zipper hissed in the air. The dress fell to her arms. One wiggle and it dropped to the floor.

Her bra and panties matched the dress. Creamy, lacy bits. She'd never stood in front of a man in undergarments that his mother picked out. At least Lady Rallis had good taste. She lifted her hands high and reached back to touch his broad shoulders. He cupped her breasts through the bra. She arched into his touch.

"You think this is goodbye." His wary whisper traveled down her neck with the brush of his lips, his hands skimming down the soft skin of her belly. "It's not." He stood tall and controlled behind her, while she might have melted at his feet.

She hadn't anticipated this cautiousness. She turned to face him. The tips of her nipples brushed against the shirt he refused to relinquish. As the teasing touch rippled through her, he steadied her, his hands around her arms.

A hard line creased his brow, revealed in the dim light of the lanterns. "Trust me, Bronte."

"I do." It was the rest of the world she couldn't trust.

He leaned his forehead against hers and shook his head, as if he knew her thoughts and denied the truth of them. But she would not let the rest of the world silence this sensuous tune building between them. She rose to tiptoes, meeting him as best her height allowed and brushed her lips against his, enticing him further into her song, into her hold as if she were a siren mage. She closed her eyes. Her lashes drifted over his cheek…a signal of some sort to him, perhaps, since he tightened his hold around her. Melting the colonel into a pool of lust was a challenging task, but the rewards beckoned.

She let her tongue skim across his lips, giving him a taste of her own teasing touch. He must have liked it. The kiss turned so powerful she might never escape. Did she really want to?

He lifted her, holding her close for a moment, only to pull his heat away as he laid her on the bed, the cool blankets a sharp contrast to her hot skin.

He braced one knee on the soft surface next to her hip and slid her bra straps down her shoulders to reveal tight nipples that craved his attention.

She curved up to him with impatience, but he was not to be hurried. She went breathless under his gaze, anticipating his touch. "Vincent…" The single word held her complaint.

"I want to look."

A soft laugh escaped in a huff. "It's too dark to see." But she realized the truth even as she spoke.

"Not for me. You've never been with a mage, have you? I'm your first." He bent his head and brushed his lips against the top of her breast. "And your last. You are all mine." He closed his mouth over her nipple.

A broken hum vibrated from her lips.

She was his.

But this is all they would have.

She thrust the thought away as his tongue played over her hard tip again and again until it was so sensitive she was ready to beg for something more. He drew her into his mouth. The sound of her cry snapped through the air. He moved to her other side and repeated the process, taking his sweet time yet again.

She tingled beneath his touch, needing more everywhere.

"I can taste your power." His words vibrated through her nipple sending delicate heat dancing down her skin to her center.

"Not possible," she denied with a shiver.

He drew back and moved onto the bed, his knees between her thighs. He hovered over her, balanced on his hands and knees, touching her exactly nowhere.

"Quite possible. And true." He hovered over her. "You are beautiful. I never thought I'd have a chance at anything like this." He bent down and kissed the fullest part of one breast, and then the other. "You are a gift."

With her bra pulled down to expose her nipples and lacy stockings framing the tops of her legs, she must look like a nymph. She certainly felt like one. And she liked it. She slipped her fingers beneath the hem of his shirt.

He shuddered at the contact and reached for her hands, preventing her exploration. Instead, he laced his fingers through hers, connecting them. He leaned forward and kissed her stomach, so sensitive she jerked in response. He worked his way down, softly. Light brushes of his lips fired every nerve he touched and left them awake and yearning for more. He laved care to her hips, one side and then the other. He drifted down to her inner thighs, skipping past her most needy parts.

"Colonel, you're a tease. I never suspected." It bordered on a complaint.

"I believe in doing a thorough job." His lips trailed over her skin with his words. "I carry out every mission with total attention to detail. It takes time to do things right."

"Surely some missions require speed." She shook her head back and forth on the pillow as he pressed a kiss on top of her mound…inches shy of where she wanted him, and blocked from her skin by her panties.

"This isn't one of them." But finally, he pulled off her panties.

She sighed with a touch of desperate gratitude and lifted her hips to assist.

He dipped back down to kiss the sharp edges of her hip bones, now exposed without the stretch of lace.

She arched up again, wanting to move him, to make him touch where she burned the most.

He dodged her, fanning his hands along the tops of her thighs, creeping in toward her feminine core. "This is meant to be savored." He ran one finger right down her center, pressing over that most sensitive of places and entered her, once, twice.

Every nerve point inside her fired. She dug her heels into the bed.

He passed his tongue over her clitoris, once and then again in rhythm with his finger.

She shattered wide open.

His vibes poured into her in places she hadn't known existed. A cry echoed. She reached for him as sensations drowned her. She grasped blindly but failed to connect from her lack of focus on anything but the waves of pleasure swelling through her. He found her though, grabbed her empty hand, and grounded her as the spasms of heat and energy rocketed through her.

He caressed his way back up her stomach, bestowing gentle kisses on each nipple and then reached her lips, caressing them with his.

She panted beneath his attention and, after a long moment, looked up at him with a slow blink. She smiled. "Well, colonel, I'd say that was a successful mission." She'd never heard her voice sound so sultry. He was powerful enough to turn her into a siren mage, after all. She poked a finger into his chest. "Now. You take off that shirt. It's my turn."

* * * *

Vincent obeyed. Anything to please her, to keep her right where she was meant to be. In his bed.

His shirt shot to the floor like a bullet. He froze, surprised. His power had crept beyond the boundaries of his control while he'd devoured the taste of her, and he hadn't even realized it.

She giggled.

His cheeks burned. Hell, he couldn't remember the last time he'd lost control. And it had never happened in bed.

"I felt your power," She touched herself low on her belly. "Right here. Do that again. This time with your pants."

"Bronte." A growl. "You're playing with vibes so hot they're gonna burn us both." His gaze caught on her perfect breasts, framed by her pulled-down bra. He reached beneath her and flicked the clasp. He cupped her softness with both hands and passed his thumbs over the tight pink nipples as the bra whipped to the floor with his power.

She arched into his touch, her head pressing against his pillow. "Not my bra. I said your pants." The airy words weren't much of a command, especially considering the smile that graced her lips. Her body was replete with a pleasure he would build for her again.

She skidded her fingers along his shoulders and chest. Her touch left a blaze in its wake as she made her way to his waist. But like his coat, she wouldn't be able to remove his pants, not with the mage fastenings.

Despite the years he'd worked to earn this uniform, he suddenly resented it. If she wore clothes he didn't have the power to remove, he'd be really pissed off.

He swung his feet to the floor and complied with her order before she realized the situation. He didn't want anything to make her feel inadequate. Because she wasn't. She was the most miraculous being who'd ever graced this land, and he would prove it to everyone. Including her.

Her gaze followed him as he surpassed her command, taking his underwear and socks with the pants. His hard erection bounded free. He sucked in a breath and gritted his teeth as she reached for him, closing around him.

She closed around him, running her touch along the length of him.

He squeezed her wrist and pulled her hand away. A pretty pout took form on her lips.

"Next time, beauty. I want this to last." He leaned his hands on either side of her head and bent to kiss the pout away.

She anchored him by his shoulders to hold him in place and opened her mouth beneath his, humming beneath his kiss. It rocked him clear to the tip of his cock.

She lifted her legs and caught him by his hips, locking her ankles behind his back. The mischievous minx smiled.

He braced himself. He hadn't deterred her a bit.

She reached between their bodies and stroked his cock in her hand. "Let me, please." Her husky whisper blew along his neck, her soft hand making him harder than ever. Pressure built and demanded an answer.

He closed his eyes.

"Take off my stockings."

He felt his way around along the lacy tops with shaky hands and traced a path around her thighs. "I like them."

She moaned. "But I want to feel your skin on mine."

Leverage. Somewhere in that statement was leverage. Eyes still closed, he fought for the power to think up a bargain. He was too close to the edge. "If you want me to move, you havc to let go."

"Oh." Disappointment clouded her voice, but her legs fell from his back, and with one last stroke, she released his cock.

He opened his eyes to see her very core spread beneath him. He held on to control by the last thread of a frayed rope. He rolled one stocking down and then the other, letting his power toss them to the floor.

She gasped.

With his lips over her clit, he licked and teased until she was as high on that wave of need as he. High on pleasure, desire…love.

"Oh please, Vincent, come inside me. Let me feel all of you." She pulled at his shoulders, trying to make him comply. "Now." A breathy, begging word.

"Impatient, are you?" But so was he. His energy broke the remainder of the dams he always kept tight around his sixth sense. It overflowed and crashed onto her, into her. His vibes worshipped at her banks like waves lapping at the land, offering its very self to the shore. Never had anyone accepted him like this. Never had it occurred to him that it was even possible.

He swept his lips over her taut belly, working back up.

She arched under his caresses, tilting her chin and exposing the graceful curve of her neck. She draped over his bed like a goddess to be adored and treasured. "Please hurry."

"Such manners," he gasped. The head of his cock had already found her. "But happy to help." He entered her slowly. She stretched around him, her walls quivering as he slipped inside. Liquid heat surrounded him.

"Oh, thank you." Her eyes fluttered shut.

It had been so long…so long since he could tolerate being this close to a woman. And it had never been like this. He moved inside her, deep and tight. Bronte's legs came around his waist and urged him faster. He thrust with more force, careful to not hurt her, but she wasn't having it. And he couldn't hold on.

He reached between her legs to caress her clit. He was taking her with him. He jetted into her. His mage energy flowed. His essence poured straight into the heart of her syphon power. She spasmed around him, on and on, until his body and his power were drenched in this ultimate pleasure.

He was slow to recover. Panting for air, he went down on one elbow. He wrapped one arm around her, twisted around and lowered himself to the bed. He pulled her with him until she lay draped over his chest.

Bronte hadn't caught her breath either. Mission accomplished.

She traced the line of his jaw.

He reached up, brought her hand to his lips and then tucked it against his chest. Tossing the quilt over them, he held her tight, catching his syphon close enough to pull her into his dreams before a deep sleep closed in on him.

Chapter 11

Bronte opened her eyes to darkness. Her restful sleep faded in an instant. Vincent lay next to her, flat on his back, motionless except for the rise and fall of his chest. He slept like he did everything else, intense and focused. Even in his dreams he had straight, smooth posture. His leg pressed against hers. She didn't mind.

But it was time to go.

Instinct told her to say a silent goodbye or risk a pointless argument. The time allotted to her faded away, almost gone. There was nothing Vincent could do about it. Her parents held her strings.

A bittersweet ache built in her heart, a storm cloud of tears and loss ready to rage. She shoved it aside. It would have to wait. It could have its reign when she was far away, when she could afford to remember what had been.

She sat up and crawled over him one limb at a time and stepped to the cold floor. She gazed down at him, waited, but he didn't wake up. Vincent was sound asleep. It seemed out of character for him to be so blind to his surroundings. The aftereffects of the sex, she thought. She almost smiled.

She padded to the bathroom and groped around in the dark for her bag she'd left on the floor. She pulled out the jeans she'd saved for the ride home. Though she patted around the sparse contents of the cheap duffel, nothing felt like a shirt. Tiptoeing back to the bedroom, she spotted a lump of shadows on the floor. Clothes of some kind. She felt around. Her hand met her bra, stringy and wiry, and the thin cloth of Vincent's t-shirt. Their pale colors almost glowed in the dark. She slipped them on.

She picked up the heels she'd worn to the symphony. They were the only shoes within view. Had they been a gift from Lady Rallis, or were they a loan? She hoped for the former, since they were all she could find. She grabbed the beaded clutch.

At this rate, Lady Rallis could have her arrested for theft if she was so inclined. The Rallises would have to catch her first. Bronte was confident that even their all-powerful reach wasn't enough to infiltrate Locke's boundaries. Assuming she could get there.

She picked up her violin and stepped into the quiet night. The chatty crickets stood as her only witnesses. They hushed as one unit when she stepped off the porch, as if they were in silent awe that she dared to flee from the intimidating Colonel Rallis.

Her breath rasped loudly through the quiet night as she moved toward the car and stepped into the spotlight of the almost full moon. She tiptoed. Her sore feet went quickly numb, her shoes still in her hand. Their *clip-clip* would be too loud for a sneaky escape. She opened the driver's door. For once it didn't squeak. Maybe her car wasn't the traitor she thought.

She placed her violin on the passenger seat and glanced one last time at the house. No Vincent on the porch. But his vibes flowed into her syphon almost as easily as if she lay next to him.

She sucked in a hard, scratchy breath. She refused to miss him already. Squeezing her eyes shut against the sensation, she started the car. The engine turned over, smoother than before. He'd done something to it. When had he managed that?

The car bumped through the meadow in the dark. She didn't dare turn on the headlights. Vincent's vibes stretched, thinned, but stayed with her. The gyre's influence picked up as she drove toward it. Its energy syphoned into her. Gravel cracked and crunched beneath the slow turn of her tires until she came to the paved road that led to the big house. The gyre's power faded, but Vincent's energy still whispered within her. How long would it last?

The little clock on the dash was dark. Bronte pushed the button for its minuscule light to shine. 3:02 AM. No one else should be about.

She drove down the smooth road, passing the big house on her right and steering around the front of it to the straight lane leading to the gates. Along the driveway, the dual border of naked trees loomed blacker than the night sky. Their branches stretched over the path like a tent of bony fingers. She passed under them. Vincent's energy dwindled to a wisp. She stilled, trying to sense him a little longer. But it was useless. Her syphon's reach had a limit. And she'd just passed it.

Her hands shook on the steering wheel—grief, instant loneliness… heartbreak. It was withdrawal of the heart, not from addiction. But that didn't stop the hurt. She tried to box it back in and focus on the dark drive.

The gatehouse was straight ahead. Its two halves straddled the driveway with ample space for cars to pass beneath it. Her gut knotted at the lights shining from the right side of the small building. Someone was awake. Worse, the gates were closed.

A lump of dread settled in her stomach. By the stars, she'd forgotten about that. How would she get the gates open? Brute force? Prayer? She had to figure out something. Instinct told her if she didn't get out now, she never would.

She slowed, hoping a slower, quieter engine might go unnoticed by the gatehouse's occupants…hoping the gates would open automatically as she approached. She guided the car under the gatehouse at a crawl.

A door opened. The light from inside silhouetted a female form.

The shadowy person hailed her.

"Bronte?" Allison's loud holler carried through the car's windows. Heck, the woman's shout probably carried to the big house.

Bronte stopped the car as the other woman bent over to peer in the passenger window. "What are you doing? Are you leaving?" Allison asked.

A man came up behind Allison. The light inside the gatehouse kept his face in darkness, but Bronte could guess who it was.

She stepped out of the car and stood in the doorway. It was easier than cranking down the passenger window. Her bare feet made contact with the driveway. They couldn't get any colder.

"I was just looking for a little bit of space to clear my head." That was a lie. She'd remembered too late that she shouldn't lie to a mage. She'd spent too much of her life lying. It was a habit.

Allison didn't seem to notice. She nodded. "I get that. This clan can be rather 'do this, don't do that, shame on you.' I escape from here on a regular basis. I'll open the gates for you. I'll be here for another hour if you want back in. After that, you're on your own." Allison turned her head toward the gates, and they silently opened in.

Lonely freedom yawned on the other side. She turned to Allison, but a shout from outside the gates grabbed her attention.

"Freeze!" A clatter of footsteps from the road drummed toward her and onto the driveway.

Bronte obeyed, as did Allison. Her date did not. His shadow disappeared.

Mage lights blinked into existence, blinding her with their brightness. A small army of enforcers stood in front of her. Guns and blasters targeted her.

Bronte's mind splintered, too stunned to catch a single thought of the jumble spinning through it.

"Step away from the car! Hands up!" The mage lights glittered against their metal vests formed of connected tuning circles. They were ready to channel as much energy as possible to handle her. Bronte had seen the vests in newspaper photos, worn by enforcers when capturing deadly mage criminals.

"Great," Allison muttered. "Now I'll really be in trouble."

Bronte moved away from the car as ordered. The strength in her legs disappeared and left her with enough energy for only a few steps. She locked her knees to keep from falling.

"Turn around." The man's voice was softer this time but no less deadly. Disdain dripped from each word. "Arms on the car."

She knew what was coming. Cold handcuffs girdled her wrists one by one, the kind of restraints used for mages. The hard metal squeezed tightly and bruised her thin wrists. The cuff's sharp square angles prevented a mage from channeling extra energy into his sixth sense. They would have no effect on her. Not that they'd believe her if she told them.

"Why are you doing this?" Adrenaline coursed through her and awakened every sense to the max. It was all too intense for her mind to process.

"Shut up." The man shook her hard and then yanked her from the car. His rough gloves scratched her bare arms, exposed by her short sleeves. Vincent's short sleeves. The enforcer marched her down the driveway. His hard shoes kicked against the back of her bare feet. Rocks cut at her soles as he shoved her toward the road. The mage lights floated with them.

She walked out through the Rallis gates. This wasn't freedom.

"Thank you, officers," a man called from the down the road.

The guns and blasters came out anew, pointed into the darkness.

The unknown man, shrouded from her view by the night, seemed to ignore them. "General Wilen is grateful for your assistance. I'll be sure to give him all the details about how helpful you were. We'll take her from here."

Her captor whispered a string of foul words. "ID," he demanded.

"Of course." Two men came into range of the mage lights—one dark-haired and bearded, the other clean-shaven and blond. Their black army uniforms were instantly recognizable, though this wasn't the formal one Vincent had worn tonight. No, these uniforms sported an array of pockets and sheaths loaded with a dozen weapons.

The bearded soldier lifted a card from around his neck and threw it to the ground in front of the officer. "Miss Casteel." He beckoned her with a quick bend of two fingers. "If you would?"

She grasped at the possibilities their politeness might hold. "Could I contact Vincent—"

He cut her off. "Colonel Rallis? The man you were leaving in the middle of the night? You looked like you were done with him."

The sarcastic words loosened a flood of pain through her heart.

He shrugged. "You can call him later. Maybe. General Wilen has a few questions for you."

The enforcers abandoned their quarry without another word. Wilen was too great a power to battle against. Defeated, they stomped to their cars. The mage engines powered up, a low hum in the otherwise silent night. They disappeared into the darkness as the gates to the Rallis estate closed, quietly shutting her out of their protective embrace.

Alone. Defenseless.

The blond soldier strode forward.

She dropped her gaze. Goddess, she couldn't even look him in the eye. "Could I…" Her voice failed. She tried again. "Could I get my papers?" The words stuttered, caught on her tongue. They might have been a whisper. She could barely hear them over the utter loneliness ringing in her ears.

He took her arm. "This is a terrible idea, Dane. She doesn't even have shoes on." His reluctance didn't stop him from escorting her to their vehicle. "Vincent is going to blast our asses to specks when he hears about this."

"Please. I'm a Non. I need my papers. They're in my car."

"Naw." The bearded man shook his head but not at her. "They'll be bigger than specks when he hears we kept her from being arrested by Masset's men. Probably more like chunks."

"I don't know about that. Guess it all depends on what Wilen plans to do with her."

Bronte swayed. Her legs fell out from under her, but her new captor pushed her into the car without missing a beat and shut the door.

She leaned forward to take the pressure off her bound hands. Her chest rose and fell, but there was no air inside this vehicle. Only fear.

The blond got in on the other side, sitting in the back with her. Two others took their places in the front.

She kept the Rallis gates in sight for as long as she could as the vehicle sped her away.

* * * *

Moonlight, not headlights, lit the road. Another benefit of a being a mage—they could use their sixth sense to see in the dark as easily as their eyes saw light. For Bronte, the darkness added another layer to this nightmare. They were on the road that followed the Olentangy River. The twists and curves of the vehicle crushed her back against her hands.

"Why the hell haven't you shut her down already?" The words burst from driver as if he could no longer hold them in.

Bronte jerked at the sudden shattering of the silence.

"Why should we? She's not doing anything." The calm statement of the warrior next to her was a sharp contrast to the driver.

"She's a syphon. Don't you know what they do? We ought to pull over and drown her in the Olentangy."

The bearded man turned around to face his colleague. "Why do we always get stuck with him?"

Bronte could feel the blond man staring at her like he was looking through a microscope. "Her energy is like the space between stars in the sky."

"Oh blasted hells, Gregor. Don't start with the poetry crap."

She turned away from the uncomfortable inspection and looked out the window. The darkness passed them by. She had no clue where they were taking her. They weren't heading into the city. She was sure of that. Empty fields, shorn of various crops, quilted the land.

She was lost.

Whoever and whatever she had been before, Bronte knew with a certainty there would be no going back. Why hadn't she fled the country instead of obeying her mother's orders? Her family was completely capable of negotiating with the Rallises without her. They'd taken the easiest way out by sending her. Her anger built, melting away the blanket of fear that wrapped around her mind. She sat up straighter, taking the pressure off her wrists.

She caught the wide-eye gleam of the driver in the rearview mirror. He yanked the car into a turn. The unexpected move slammed her into the door. Her head banged painfully against the metal seat belt hanging from the wall of the car.

"Damn it, McIssac!" Dane shouted. "If you can't drive, stop the fucking car and get out."

"It's a straight shot from here. Surely the corporal can handle that." Sarcasm from Gregor to her right. "As soon as he's done, he can take his pig-ass back to his own base." Another minute and they came up beside an old white farmhouse. McIssac stopped the car and made to get out.

"No, thanks, McIssac," Gregor said. "We'll take her from here. You stay there."

McIssac froze halfway out of the car, an unnatural position. The soldier beside her had iced him there. Fear bubbled at the amount of mage power and control that man must have. Ice someone too much and his heart would stop. She shivered.

Bronte's door opened. Her handler pulled her out. They walked around to the back of the house. Dozens of buildings sprawled among the fields, dark blotches against the night. A helicopter sat off to the left in an empty field, its rotor circling slowly, each blade visible. Two men walked away from it as if they'd just landed.

Despite the quaint house, this was no farm.

The blond mage guided her inside and then straight down a set of stairs that lined the interior wall of the house. The musty smell of a basement filled each breath. She felt her way into the pitch-black one foot at a time. For all she knew, there was a pit ahead of her ready to swallow her up for good.

The soldier stayed with her and plunked her down into a metal chair. The gap between the back of the chair and the seat gave her space for her cuffed hands. Bronte gave a small sigh of relief. No pit.

"You can't see, can you?" he called.

She shook her head. "No." The word was hardly more than a puff of air.

His shoes whispered against the steps. He was leaving. He didn't care that she couldn't see. She bit back a cry and converted it to a whimper instead.

Non-mages were at a complete disadvantage in the dark compared to their so-called betters. No Non trusted the dark.

A quiet thought flickered in her mind. She wasn't a Non. But it made no difference here. Her mage power was useless.

Bronte nearly wept when the light over the stairs flicked on. Metal clacked to the floor as her cuffs released without a physical touch. She slumped, let her shoulders droop forward and dragged her numb arms forward until they hung free of the chair. Feeling returned slowly and brought painful pins and needles. She wrapped the cold appendages around her body.

Despite the light, there was nothing to see, no other furniture, just plain, gray walls. She rocked back and forth, trying to comfort herself in the stark surroundings. Her chair wobbled against the uneven concrete floor.

She should do something, she thought. Fight for freedom. But she was too afraid to move. They weren't going to let her simply walk out. A sob burst from her throat. Or maybe it was a laugh. She wasn't sure. She waited, as if another sound might take the initiative and pop out as well. But no. She was empty. As empty as this room.

Her mind crept back to Vincent, like scared prey sneaking to safety. Was he still asleep? Maybe the absence of his energy was why the gauge of her soul was on E. Maybe it had nothing to do with being captured.

Syphons were always captured. And killed.

Footsteps drummed down the stairs. A pair of legs appeared. She turned her head away before she could see his face. What did it matter?

Somewhere inside her she'd always known this was bound to happen—that she would be revealed as a syphon and punished accordingly. Maybe that was why she'd never found the courage to leave the Republic. Since she couldn't escape fate, she'd stayed and waited for it.

The man walked over to her, dragging a metal chair behind him. He put it directly in front of her, but remained standing. She glanced up at him. It was the bald man from the symphony.

"Sorry to keep you waiting, Miss Casteel." He smiled at her. "Do you know who I am?"

Bronte dropped her eyes and stared straight ahead. "General Wilen, I presume." Her dry, scratchy voice fell flat, barely reaching past her ears.

He sat down. Their eyes met. A scuffle of shoes came from deep in the gloom to her left. Another person hid in the shadows. Either he'd been down here all along or the darkness concealed another entrance.

"I understand you like music, Bronte," the general said.

She nodded.

He didn't say anything else. She shifted her gaze back and forth from his eyes to the floor. He stared. She squirmed.

Finally, she blurted it out. "I'm a syphon."

His expression stayed frozen, unmoved by her confession. His dark stare stabbed at her mind.

She hated his eyes.

"Your friend, Claude, likes music, too." He crossed his legs. "You know what else Claude likes? Newspaper clippings." He smiled. "You don't get any newspapers though. You're not known to read them. We asked your friends. They seemed to find that as odd as we do. Everyone likes newspapers…gossip, scandal, comics." He paused.

Bronte had nothing to add to the silence. She'd long since stopped caring about the doings of mages, avoiding even the written accounts of their lives.

Finally, he began again. "Claude has scrapbooks full of clipped articles. We found them when we searched his trailer. Someone mails the articles to him. He saves the envelopes and glues them into the scrapbook too. According to Claude's mailman, he never mails anything back. Each newspaper clipping focuses on a particular event or location, for instance a mage school or hospital, a shopping center. Within one week of the articles appearing in the newspaper, the location was bombed by Double-Wide." The general paused. "You startin' to see the problem here?" He raised his eyebrows high. They looked like they might climb onto his bald scalp.

If Claude had newspaper articles about places that were bombed, there might be a problem. She just wasn't sure exactly what it was.

He didn't wait for her answer. "Also. Claude has a lot of maps. You know anything about those?" At the shake of her head, he continued, "Well that's a darn shame. Because you're pretty much the only person we know who Claude talks to. You show up there every now and then, right?"

"Yes." Her hoarse voice barely carried the word. She cleared her throat. "I go there to pick up copies of his music. Sheet music. His compositions."

"Right, right. That's what we heard too. You go into his bedroom?"

"No! Never." She shook her head. "Claude and I are…friends…though I wouldn't call him that anymore."

"The maps are marked up with the longitude and latitude of specific places in the Republic. Is Claude some kind of explorer or cartographer? That a hobby of his?"

Her stomach dropped with every bit of information the general revealed. "Not that I know of. He doesn't leave his house anymore."

"Yeah. That beating he took must have done him some mental damage."

Bronte scrunched her brow. "Beating?"

The general feigned surprise.

She didn't need to be a mage to recognize the expression was a lie.

"You don't know about this? He got beat up outside Tremont Tavern by a couple of mages. You really don't read the papers, huh? And he didn't tell you?" The general kept going as she shook her head. "Probably too embarrassed to admit to his best girl that he got beat up. As far as we can tell, that's when he started hunkering down in the craphole trailer he lives in. November 11 of last year. Sound about right?"

Bronte could hardly think straight, but the timing was possible.

"The only thing that goes out of his house is the sheet music he gives to you. You play it. And then you know what happens?" His voice got softer and softer.

Bronte shook her head, swallowing hard.

"Things go boom," he whispered.

Chapter 12

"The Double-Wide terrorists set off a bomb every two days after you play one of Claude's new songs."

Bronte's heart stuttered and stopped, cycling through the pattern again as the general's words rebounded through her head.

He continued, "We have the music. Confiscated it from Claude's house along with the scrapbooks and the maps. One of the code guys played the songs on the piano. Sounded pretty weird to me. But what do I know about music? The code guys are the smarties, not me."

She didn't believe that for a minute.

"According to the smart guys, it's a pretty simple code once you know what to look for. A specific note corresponds to a specific number. Play the notes in order and you can decipher the coordinates of the location for the bomb. Best we can figure it, you stand on stage and play the music, and, if our Double-Wide agent can recognize notes by hearing them, he knows where to set off the bomb. Now, I can't recognize one note from the next. But I'm told there are people who can do this." He stilled. "Can you?"

She nodded, her neck muscles almost too tight to move.

"The notes of the chorus represent the longitude and latitude of the bomb sites. It's possible the verses hold the code to the staging areas for the explosives. We're still working on that part. You know anything about this?"

Bronte shook her head vigorously, feeling sick to her stomach.

"Four bombs. Four. In the last eight weeks. Not gone as planned. The code guys say the music we got from Claude's house contains the coordinates for logical targets for Double-Wide's bombs. A school, a hospital, a playground and a market. But none of them were bombed. The explosives were planted off target. One by less than a mile. One by over fifty miles. What I want to know is this: what happened to make the bombs go off in the wrong places? And who comes to listen to you play when Claude gives you new music?"

Bronte's lips felt numb. Her head spun and somewhere down the line, sooner rather than later, she was going to be sick. "I changed…" She had to clear her throat. "I changed the music. Claude's stuff wasn't good anymore. I told him multiple times that I didn't like what he was writing. I got tired of putting up with it. I changed the notes. On stage. Only a little. It didn't take much. I improvised during the performance. The rest of the band followed along. We're pretty good at that."

"Uh-huh. Do you remember what you played?"

She cleared her throat again. It kept getting clogged. "Yes. I always remember what I play." She squeezed her eyes shut, dizziness spinning the room.

"Well, that's great. We'll get you a viola, and you can play it for us."

"Violin."

"What about your fans? You got any groupies that show up on regular basis? Somebody who knows all this music stuff. Enough to hear the notes and know what they are."

"No. Maybe. I don't know." She shook her head. She could picture the bar in mind, looking out from the stage, the lights not quite dim, but dark enough to hide the dirt embedded everywhere. "We have a good number of fans. We're rather well known for a band of Nons. But there are three men. Boys, really. Younger than I am, I think. They certainly act like it." She could see their faces in her mind. They usually sat against the wall. "They always made me uncomfortable. They…leered. At me. The band started calling them Broupies…for 'Bronte's groupies.'"

She took a breath and looked off to the left into the nothingness. "They were overly touchy. I started to avoid them as best I could, getting offstage as quickly as possible, or taking the last seat at a table of regulars. Friendly ones. I don't know for sure that they all know about music. But one of them asked me about my violin once. He claimed he had a Stradivarius."

The general's eyebrow twitched. It was against the law for a Non to own such a cultural emblem.

As she tattled, she violated an unspoken Non code of ethics, betraying her people. But they weren't really her people. She had no people. No other syphons existed, to her knowledge. She had to save herself. "He said it played like nothing else he'd ever touched. He invited me over to try it." She shivered from the ugly memory. "I declined."

She shrugged as best she could with her arms still aching slightly. "After that I made sure to stay close to one of the band members whenever those guys were around. But none of that means they'd be involved in... Double-Wide."

The general sat back in his chair and crossed his arms over his chest. His expression was flat, as if no plea for mercy would ever penetrate him. "He's breaking the law already if what he told you was true. We'll find out. We always get the truth."

A woman spoke from the gloom. "Well, Tom, darlin', you got the truth this time. She's honest." Lucinda. Bronte recognized the voice from the bathroom conversation. The woman stepped forward until she stood next to her husband.

"Hi there, Bronte." Her smile wasn't friendly.

"Mrs. Wilen." Bronte nodded.

"Oh now, call me Lucinda. After our girl talk in the loo, let's not go back to being all uppity." Lucinda waved her hand in the air and mage lights coalesced in the air along with a burning pressure in Bronte's ears. The lights didn't extinguish the gloom of the basement.

"Did you grab that bull?"

Bronte narrowed her eyes at the woman and then stood, as if rising to her feet from the chair where she'd been dumped exemplified her fizz. She dusted off her jeans and smoothed the wrinkles from Vincent's undershirt.

"Oh ho! You did grab that bull. It's written all over you. But you foolish girl! You didn't hang on! Otherwise you wouldn't be here. Now come on. No more running away." Lucinda slapped her on the back. "You get out there and try again. Make me proud."

Footsteps clattered down the stairs, fast and familiar with the terrain. Shoes, then legs came into view. It was the blond. "Vincent's on his way. He's mad." His voice lilted up on the last words.

"Well," Lucinda began with a huff, "Vincent was a wuss. He let down his guard. Take note of this, Gregor. See what happens when you don't take care of your things? Someone takes them from you. Law of the universe."

Gregor ran a hand through his short, spiky hair. He was tall and broad enough for the uniform, but his face didn't match. It was too boyish. Too cute. "Speaking of laws of the universe as pertains to mystical energy... General, sir, you might be interested to know no one has been tempted to fight in the last forty-five minutes. That's a record. We're a cohesive, content team at the moment. Not counting McIssac. The syphon is working enough energy off us that we're kind of...relaxed."

She was? Bronte was completely blind to it.

"Maybe, Miss Lucinda, ma'am…maybe…you could tell Vincent she's just going to stay here? Since, you know, she left him and all. He might take it better coming from a, uh…lady. What do you say?"

"I say no." Bronte planted her feet and straightened her shoulders. "I decline your offer. Thank you for *asking.*"

Lucinda shrugged with a lift of her hand at Bronte, acknowledging her answer.

Just then, waves of energy spiraled into her. Another clatter of feet pounded down the stairs. A grunt, and a hard thud followed. Gregor's feet dangled from the floor as Vincent pressed him into the wall.

His vibes had forecasted his arrival.

"Sorry, colonel." The blond's words were a barely audible gasp. "We saved her. Enforcers. Came in the gate."

"You took her." Vincent shook him. "And brought her to the basement." His thick growl vibrated with such anger that Bronte could hardly understand him.

"My bad." The blond's words were as strangled as his throat.

Lucinda leaned down to her ear. "Bull. Balls. It's the only way to handle these men. It's good advice that no Mayflower momma is ever gonna give you."

Gregor's face turned red, then purple. His eyeballs bulged, though perhaps they were just watering. It was hard to tell in the dim light.

"Vincent, stop, please." Bronte shuffled closer, coming within arms' reach.

He looked at her, eyes wild with rage. He dropped the man to the floor.

"Thank you."

The blond gasped for breath as Vincent stepped past him. He wrapped one hand tightly around her waist, the other around the back of her neck. His hands burned against her cold skin, which had soaked in the damp chill of this awful room. His mouth came down on hers, hard and demanding. She forgot to be embarrassed. His energy swirled into her syphon like a storm's wrath. In his kiss, she tasted his desperation, his hurt.

This kiss wasn't about lust.

He broke away, but didn't let her go. His eyes no longer held a hint of blue. "We are going to talk."

Bronte nodded. Fear loosened its grip. She hadn't realized it held her so tightly until his presence unwound it. He'd rescued her.

The ache in her heart contracted. Guilt, remorse. She'd hurt him. He didn't—couldn't—let many people get close to him. He'd let her into his life, and she had walked out—for good reasons. But he would not see it that way.

"Where are your shoes?" The demand in his voice was coated with a helpless fury.

She looked down at her feet, silent. Her missing shoes belonged in another lifetime. She didn't want to explain here.

"Well," Lucinda sang. "I am going to make breakfast." She strode to the stairs, put her hands on her hips and looked down at Vincent's victim. "You wanna come help me, Gregor? Or are you gonna sit on the floor and pout all day?"

Gregor looked up at her with bleary eyes.

She shook her head with a disappointed frown and marched upstairs.

Vincent turned his glare on General Wilen.

"I had to find out," the general protested calmly, though a hint of regret tinged his voice.

"You should have called me the moment you were planning to take her!" Rage punched through his words.

"Don't take it personally. I woulda done it to anyone to stop this damn group of terrorists. Besides, I left you a message. You didn't check 'em, did you?" The general shook his head. "You're new to figuring out how to handle love and the job. But be quick, boy. We don't have time for mistakes."

"You called last night while we were at the symphony. About the codes in the songs. You did not call to tell me you took her! At the very least, as her temporary sponsor, the family should have been notified." Vincent prowled toward the man. "She did not deserve this."

The general held out a hand. "Alright. I'll call the next time."

"There won't be a next time." Vincent's roar hurt her ears.

The general shrugged.

He wasn't guaranteeing anything, Bronte thought.

Wilen shifted his gaze to her. "Remember that tune somebody was throwing above the noise of the symphony's crowd?"

Bronte blinked at the general's abrupt switch of topic.

The general continued. "That song was bomb number three that went wrong. The code boys played those songs over and over. Someone was humming that song in the lobby during intermission." He turned to Vincent. "I think someone is coming after her, Vin. Maybe they're mad she switched the songs up? Seems a likely scenario." He nodded to himself. "If I wasted all those pounds of explosives, I'd be mad too. 'Course, it wouldn't have taken me four bombs to understand I had a problem with my system. That's one thing we have going for us. They're not as smart as we are."

The general paced the scuffed floor. "It ain't Claude who was humming that song. I know that. Because he's on his way to my basement. I'm hoping our hummer is also our newspaper clipper. That would solve two problems in one. It'd be convenient."

"What about one of the musicians?" Vincent asked. "Is one of them sympathetic to the plight of the Nons? Or the conductor? He said he'd been following her career. Maybe he's been in her audience."

"I would have seen him. I think." Bronte tried to remember the faces in the crowd, but everything was a blur in her mind; she was too drained to think.

"Disguised maybe." Gregor groaned as he sat up.

Vincent studied him and then shifted to her, worry etched in the grim line of his mouth. He cupped her cheeks in his hands. "You have to stop running away, Bronte. You need to stay where it's safe. And I can't keep you safe if you leave the gates." He dropped his forehead to the top of her hair for a moment before he looked her in the eyes. "For your own good, consider yourself housebound."

"Good idea," the general said. "Nobody gets in. Nobody gets out. Nice and safe in your little cabin."

Disbelief barreled through her so hard it ought to have punched through Vincent as well. "If you think you're going to spell me into your house, think again! I will not tolerate having my freedom taken away. Besides that, all spells make me feel awful. I can't even stand to be around them."

"That's not true. My spells don't affect you like that."

"Vincent!"

He couldn't hold her glare; neither did he recant. She sighed, searching for some sort of mental equilibrium. This teeter-totter of emotions, from terror to guilt to anger, was nauseating.

"I need out of this basement," she whispered. She stepped over Gregor on the floor and climbed to the top of the stairs to a bright, sunny kitchen she'd not noticed on her way down.

The bearded man leaned against the counter. He had two black eyes and a tissue stuffed up one nostril. He glanced up at her from the newspaper spread between his hands. "You all talked out already? The general usually goes for hours."

She stopped in the middle of the floor, her eyes widening at the headline of his paper. *Syphons: Dangerous Powers or Two-Bit Mages?*

"Mage reporters are an imaginative bunch," he said. His gaze fell back to the paper.

Another newspaper covered the kitchen table. She walked over and scanned the headline. *Syphon Pregnant with Rallis Heir,* followed by its subtitle, *Council Calls Dibs on Syphon Baby.*

"Oh, goddess." Her heart pounded too hard to breathe around. "How did this happen? Where did they get this information?" Questions pirouetted in her head too quickly to grab them all. The world spun. Bronte slowly lost view of it.

A chair met the back of her legs and her chest touched her knees as Vincent pushed her down. "Breathe." The hand against her neck burned hot against her clammy skin.

"I'm okay." She pushed against his hand as she spoke through numb lips. Thick strands of hair fell around her face, blocking the light. She wiggled, but it was a minute before he let her sit up.

He brushed the hair from her eyes.

A glass of orange juice appeared before her, along with Lucinda's command. "Drink."

"Her name's not given," the bearded man said as he closed the paper. "Someone kept that to themselves, at least. It's just B. Castle. Is that your stage name or something?"

Bronte stared at a corner of the kitchen, seeing nothing. "I compose my songs under that name, but no one ever saw them. Except for one song."

He folded up the paper and rapped it against his leg. "There's a photo of the two of you in here. It won't be long before someone connects a syphon named B. Castle with Non-Mage Bronte Casteel."

"And somebody thinks you and Vincent have done the dirty," Lucinda observed as she cracked an abnormally large amount of eggs into a bowl.

That woman thrived on embarrassing and tormenting her. Bronte closed her eyes and gritted her teeth. She hated Lucinda at that moment. Purposefully turning her back on the other woman, she moved her gaze to Vincent. "Your mother?" she asked.

"She'd never leak anything to the press."

Bronte swallowed hard. Did the culprit even matter? The heart of the matter focused on one thing: her escape. "Can you get me out of here, Vincent?" She leaned her elbow on the table, twisting her shoulders to face him.

He nodded. "I have to meet with the general one last time and then we'll go home."

“No.” She interrupted him. “That’s not what I meant.” This wasn’t the time or place for this conversation, but she couldn’t bring herself to stop. “Get me out of the Republic.” She stared at him, her chest rising and falling too quickly. “I can’t stay here. It’s not safe. If I leave now, I can salvage this. Switch names. Make it so no one can connect me to B. Castle. If anyone discovers who I am, no one will hire me in Europe either.” There weren’t a lot of mages outside the Republic. They were considered spooky, dangerous people. “Help me get out before it’s too late. Please, Vincent.” She bit her lip. Worry, pain and fright all flooded into her until she thought she might burst.

He took her face in his hands, the blue of his eyes still dark with fury. She could see his answer in them before he spoke it.

“No.”

She closed her eyes. A tear dripped down her cheek and twined through his fingers.

He brushed her cheek dry. “We will figure this out.”

“There’s nothing to figure out! If I stay, I face the penalty for being a syphon. If I go, I live.”

How had she come to this?

She should have fought harder against the Rallises. Against Vincent. They’d twisted the rules on her, but she should have thought of something… thrown a tantrum maybe. They wouldn’t have taken her to the symphony if she’d been kicking and screaming. She should have defied the Casteels as well and refused to deliver their message. Her mother’s call had been her cue to move out of the Republic. She’d missed it, blind as her life’s conductor lifted his baton to direct her. And she should have refused to play Claude’s wacky songs from the start. Another cue missed. She could point to a half-dozen of them when she could have prevented all this from happening. She’d done nothing, clinging to the charade she’d invented as if it were armor. It laid it tatters around her now.

“It’s going to be alright,” Vincent said. His placating tone flamed her anguish.

“It is not! ‘Alright’ is the life I had before. *This* is awful.” Though a dark cloud of regret enveloped her, she caught the hurt that blinked across his face.

Lucinda shook her head and frowned, disappointed.

Bronte ignored her.

“We need to prove syphons aren’t dangerous.” Vincent was calm, logical. “We’ve already started.”

"We?" She was shouting. She never shouted. "We? You and your family, the great and powerful Rallises have orchestrated all of this." She shook her hands in the air as if she trembled before them. "I've had no say in any of it! And I am done with that! I will come up with my own plan to get out of this mess!" She put her hands on her hips and exhaled, reaching for mental control, a lid to contain this tirade of emotions she'd never allowed freedom.

She would not continue to bow to the whims of these powerful mages. If Vincent wouldn't help her get out, then it was up to her. She had to find a way to fix this, to grab the bull and ride instead of letting it kick her around.

She'd come up with a plan. She'd fight back, take control.

Somehow.

* * * *

Vincent focused on his energy spilling into Bronte's syphon. It was a convenient way to keep watch on her proximity. The connection between them flowed steady and strong. Though he couldn't see her, he knew she sat in his truck—unhappy, scared, frustrated.

If he wanted to be honest about it, she was pissed off.

So was he.

He'd refused to let anyone take her back to Rallis Hall. She'd have to wait. He didn't trust anyone with her right now. Hell, he couldn't even trust her.

At his order, Gregor was on guard duty. The man was a powerful mage. He had the heart of a poet, but his soul was pure warrior. After their confrontation in the basement, the man would keep her safe. He was too afraid to fail.

Vincent gritted his teeth as he replayed the man's words about keeping Bronte here so the farm could use her syphon.

Keeping her.

Fuck that.

She belonged to him. No one else. If that was too possessive for his little syphon's taste, then she didn't need to know about it. But he'd damn well make sure everyone else knew.

He rubbed his hand over his face and tuned back in as the general droned on. His boss recapped what they knew about DW to his warriors, most of them deflectors, like Vincent, but of varying degrees of power. He eyed them from his spot against the wall. They'd all gathered in the front parlor of the old farmhouse, sprawled out on chairs and couches, resting up while they could. Energy wafted around the room, one deflector after the other bouncing it away, but there wasn't as much as usual. Bronte's effect.

Wilen's speech continued. Not a single man here needed the recap, but they were all accustomed to the general's chatter. The man would wind down soon. Surely. If not, Vincent would walk out. He had a good excuse. Who knew what Bronte would try next if he wasn't timely enough?

She'd scared him.

He'd dropped his guard. Vincent couldn't remember the last time he'd slept so deeply he couldn't hear his front door open. How had he not sense her syphon powers disappearing into the horizon? His heart had stopped when he'd woken to find her gone.

He'd known instantly that she was far, far away. No hint of their connection had been left to his sixth sense. He'd had no idea how long she'd been gone. All he knew was that he'd slept for hours. Of course, now he knew her fear outweighed her trust in him. After all, it wasn't the sex that had scared her away. She'd wanted him as much as he'd desired her.

Though what did he know?

Obviously he couldn't trust his gut to predict her reactions. He'd thought she was as connected to him as he was to her. Maybe she never would be. His vibes flowed into her; her syphon power gave him peace. But she did not share anything of herself. It was the nature of her power.

Even now, she grounded him with her presence, her stubborn heart. She refused to let him do the same for her. Refused to accept his influence, which could clear a safe path to her dreams.

She wouldn't get a chance to run again. The moment they got home, Vincent would bar Allison from the gatehouse. If his cousin wouldn't abide by their security plan, then she'd have to stay away from the exits to the property. Or she could move out.

Allison had told the gate guards they could have the night off. She'd wanted a little private time with the doctor. She hadn't even watched the whole scene play out as Bronte was taken, telling the entire family, whom he'd gathered in the senator's office, that the enforcers had arrested her. Vincent had brought the wrath of the Rallises on Masset's force before Gregor had managed to make the correct connection on the landline to the big house.

The general's silent pause grabbed his attention. The dozen men in the room shifted in their seats, recognizing their boss was finally ready to deliver the pertinent information.

"Now, about last night's incident," the general said. "Peter Leggert's car was bombed at oh-one hundred. He's the conductor of the symphony, for those of you not up on your cultural arts. DW has claimed responsibility via their usual MO of letters to major newspapers. A couple interesting details from the explosive guys: the size of the bomb was smaller than normal. Also, it wasn't plastic explosives. It was a potion."

The implications raced through Vincent's head.

It was what they'd long suspected.

There was a mage in Double-Wide.

Vincent could see the pieces of this case start to come together. They'd been stumped trying to determine how a bunch of Nons could travel to different targets occupied by mages, get in without anyone noticing and set the bombs. No Non-mage had that kind of freedom of movement.

"We're hoping a little time in the basement with Claude Hines will help shed some light on the identity of our traitor. I'll keep you posted. Dismissed."

Vincent pivoted and headed toward the kitchen, flipping through the memory of whom he'd seen at the symphony last night.

"Rallis!" Wilen hailed him. "You're recovered?"

"Yes, sir."

"Then you're back on duty at fifteen hundred." Wilen spun back toward the front room. He shouted orders for updates from the analysts working in the dining room.

Vincent kept strict control over his face and hid the dread those words brought. He needed time to secure Bronte's future. But his duties here had always been priority. He exited the house and marched briskly to the truck, reviewing what to delegate to others when he had to leave her.

Gregor sat on top of the hood. He gave Vincent a wary nod as he slid off. "She hasn't moved. Quiet out here."

Vincent nodded back. "Be at Rallis Hall at eleven hundred. Bring Dane with you." One problem solved—they'd guard Bronte in his absence. Those two owed him.

"Yes, sir."

Unlocking the door with a whiz of vibes, he climbed behind the steering wheel. She huddled in the passenger seat, her arms over her chest. He pushed enough energy around her to warm her and reached behind his seat to the blanket he always kept there. Half afraid she would reject his offering, he gently draped it over her. He let go of his breath as she gathered it around herself and shifted to her hip toward him, like she was settling in for a nap, but too much tension lingered around her for that.

He pointed the truck home, his gaze on her more than the road. He knew the route and could sense the energy of the road and the utter lack of life around at the early hour. He could afford to stare.

His beautiful girl was completely bedraggled. His t-shirt hung crookedly around her shoulders, too big for her small frame. Beneath the blanket, her bare feet stuck out, a mix of purple and white. The white worried him. He should have made her wait in the house, but she'd insisted on the truck. He sent a spiral of energy at them and held it there. She grimaced. He knew the pain of rewarming frozen digits. She bore it without complaint. His girl was tough. It took longer than he expected for her toes to turn pink.

"Why?" The word burst of out him. "Why did you leave?" He had to know, unable to wait any longer. Maybe the conversation would go better after they had a little distance from it, or when Bronte was more rested, but he didn't have the patience for it.

She sighed with a quick glance up at him, but she wouldn't hold his gaze. "There is no future for us, Vincent."

His chest clenched at her hard stab to his heart. He had to take a breath, two breaths, before he could get control of his tongue. "Without you, my future is more of my very recent past." He reached out a hand. He could almost see his vibes flowing into her. "I want this. I want what you and I are together."

She didn't say anything, just looked at him from under her tired brow.

"You want me, too. I know you do. You may think leaving me is a step toward your future, but it's not. You're running away from it. Blasted hells, Bronte, of all the syphons I've studied, you're the only one who's run away from her match. Not once, but twice. And if I gave you the opportunity, you'd do it again."

"Are you implying there's something wrong with me?"

He'd offended her. Good. He was offended too.

"Well, go find yourself a new syphon then," she said.

He ignored her outburst. "You left without saying goodbye! Snuck off like we're some quick fuck!"

"You never would have let me go!"

"Damn straight! And you wouldn't have been kidnapped by the enforcers or by my boss." He stared at her, let her see the fear in his eyes. He watched her recognize it and grow wary. And then fear lit her eyes as well.

"Vincent, I am leaving. Don't let me break your heart."

She already had.

Chapter 13

Bronte's cheeks burned for the remaining of the drive back. Anger, hurt and guilt all vied for space inside her. She turned her eyes to the window. The sky brightened, a stark contrast to her dark mood. Orange and pink glowed over the flat horizon of the shorn fields. A new day.

The day she was supposed to leave.

A sliver of dawn's light lit the woods. The road narrowed, leaving barely enough room for two vehicles to squeeze past...and only if they had skilled drivers behind their wheels. Mage drivers. Driving was something mages did quite well for all their highbrow aversion to creating machines themselves. Even creating mage engines was considering dirty work, left to dark mages.

They pulled into the gates, Vincent opening them with his vibes as they neared. Her syphon power absorbed the hitch in his energy. She wondered if she'd ever get used to it, ever stop noticing it.

"I want to drive my car back." It sat beneath the archway of the gatehouse.

"I'll have someone take care of it for you."

"Vincent, stop the car." Her order was clear and firm. With a heavy exhale, she turned to him.

He yielded.

She pulled the door handle. It was locked. "Vincent." A one-word warning.

"Bronte," he countered, "you scared the vibes right of me when I realized you weren't here this morning. So please. For me. Let's go back together."

She flipped the lock up. She swore she saw his soul hanging in his eyes. She stayed tough.

He sighed.

She won.

"Go to the big house," he ordered. "Park in the front. Go straight to the senator's office. Everyone is waiting for us. I'll follow you."

"Why?"

"Meeting about the newspapers. Do not stop. Do we agree on this?"

She nodded, weary of everything. "Straight to the senator's office. I'll see you in a minute." Bronte tiptoed to her car. Her feet were in desperate need of a hot bath. At least they weren't frozen, thanks to Vincent, but the aftereffects of the cold lingered in them. They were stiff and tired.

The car keys hung in the ignition, her purse on the seat. Vincent waited as she backed away from the gatehouse and did a six-point turn that he probably could have done in two. She drove between the stark trees now visible in the early morning light. The far reach of their branches hung over her like the long arm of the Rallises' power. She lifted her chin, determined. She would stand among this family as an equal. Or she'd leave.

The stone house rose in front of her. A grand, black car sat in the curve of the driveway. Apparently more people than the Rallises were attending this meeting. She slowed.

Vincent honked loud and long behind her as he sped his truck around her Volvo, forcing her to brake. He cut her off, screeching to a halt in front of her and blocking her from going farther. Her heart pounding, she put it in *Park*.

She jumped out of her car. "What was that? I told you I'd come straight here."

He stepped right up to her, swung her around to his left, slammed her car door shut and hustled her up the steps.

"What are you doing, Vincent?"

"Just please get into the house." He moved to swoop her up, but she sidestepped away.

"My shoes are still in the—" She looked back and saw for herself.

Her mother waited at the bottom of the steps. Her father stepped out of the dark chauffeured sedan. She hadn't seen them in thirteen years.

A hard knot rose in Bronte's throat. Hate. She swallowed it back down. It would only end up hurting her. She knew this from experience. Though she was tired, and it had been a terrible morning, she wouldn't turn it into an excuse to wallow in lazy emotions that would smother her soul.

Ten stairs separated them.

Her mother looked the same—trim figure, smooth face, and sleek, dark hair. Her pale gray suit fit appropriately for a Mayflower matriarch. Pearls adorned her ears, visible with her hair pulled back into a bun. By comparison, her father's hair was pure gray. The wrinkles around his eyes were deep enough that his eyelids drooped slightly. Time had not been as friendly to him.

Phyllis Casteel looked her daughter up and down. Bronte knew what she saw—a disheveled mess wearing a man's undershirt. Her bare feet were the icing on a cake turned upside down.

She didn't care.

Vincent leaned down to her ear. "Don't stop for anything. Remember? I thought we agreed to the plan."

"We did," she whispered back, not taking her eyes from the pair in front of her. "But this is such a remarkable sight I had to change the plan."

"A remarkable sight, indeed," Phyllis sniffed. Her mother's hearing outshone that of any mage Bronte had ever met. "You look quite the worse for the wear compared to the last time I saw you."

Bronte put a hand on Vincent's arm, a silent message to keep quiet.

He growled in resignation.

She tilted her head at them. "It's a surprise to see you after all this time, Mother."

"Don't call me that."

The past leaped through thirteen years and landed on Bronte in one fell swoop. But she wasn't sixteen anymore. She looked up at Vincent. She'd stared at him then, too…behind that garden shed…as her mother yanked her away. Phyllis had screeched a bushel of insults on her for daring to tryst with a noble son. Bronte remembered her own confusion. She'd thought the boy she'd held hands with, the boy she'd kissed and cradled in her lap as he slept…she'd thought he was an overworked, disrespected servant. Not a firstborn son.

How could she ever make that mistake?

Regardless, her mother couldn't yank her away this time.

Phyllis climbed the steps. Her husband followed. "You still haven't learned to keep your head down, have you? Too late now. But don't worry. You won't have long for regrets." Her smug smile glowed in the early morning light.

"Dear." Her father rubbed his hand against Phyllis's back. "Now is not the time."

"Of course. It will wait until after this pointless sponsorship hearing." Phyllis gave an evil, satisfied smile. "But we all know what we're really here for."

"This isn't a judge's chamber, Mother."

Phyllis laughed sharply. "I see the Rallises have kept you properly ignorant. Well, good for them. It's highly inappropriate to keep one such as you in the family's circle." She gestured gracefully to Rallis Hall. "The Rallises have kindly offered to host the hearing in their home." She sidled closer to Bronte until they could have reached out and touched. With a sneer at her daughter, she spoke. "Husband, your ancestors must have greatly displeased the goddess somewhere down the family tree to have produced such defected daughters." She lifted her hand.

Bronte froze, every muscle flexed hard, a worthless shield against the coming spell.

Vincent's energy spiked with a rush into her syphon.

Her mother jumped back.

"Ahh!" Phyllis looked down at her hand as if she expected to see damage. From the energy pouring into her, Bronte expected to see smoke rising from scorched skin, but her mother was unmarred.

"You dare to spell me?" Anger morphed her mother's face into a dark cloud of hate, but Vincent's fury outmatched hers by a dozen of the bombs he deflected.

"Watch where you step, lady." His soft tone was the minor chord before the booming crescendo unleashed its destruction. "Those who encroach upon a Rallis do not live to do so again."

Though Bronte could never be the target of his energy, chills ran along the back of her neck from the prickle of his menacing warning.

Her mother was wise enough to retreat. Phyllis clutched at her injured hand and swallowed down her retaliation, cowed in the face of a superior mage. It was a temporary defeat. Her mother never gave up. Behind her mother, the future senator of Casteel scrambled down three stairs before he seemed to reign in his fear of the famous colonel.

Vincent wrapped his arm low on Bronte's back and guided them up the steps, steering her in front of him. His power hovered at the forefront, ready, yet contained.

The door opened. Jasper stood on the other side. "Miss Casteel." A genuine smile lit his face. "We are so relieved the colonel found you. Welcome back." He bowed slightly.

"Thank you, Jasper." She sounded like she'd claimed the role of lady.

Jasper looked down the steps, curling his lip at her mother.

It was good to have allies.

Safe inside the walls of Rallis, she contemplated her mother's words as they walked through the grand foyer of Rallis Hall. "It's not going to be a sponsorship hearing."

"No."

"She wants me dead."

"Never going to happen." He reached for her hand as they sauntered along. "Your mother is no one. Not compared to Wilen. Not even Masset. And you've survived both." He lifted a sardonic eyebrow. "So what's your plan for this?"

Bronte took a breath. "Well, I don't have a plan, to be honest. Do you?"

He smiled, the first smile she'd seen on his face since…since she lay in his bed, a few short hours ago. Hours that had tumbled her life to pieces.

He chuckled. It had a wicked edge. "I have an army at my disposal."

She gasped. Her bare feet squeaked against the shiny floor as she came to a complete stop. She put her hands on his chest to hold him back. "You would go to war over this? Vincent, no. You can't do that." She could envision the blood of the bounder mages, the borders guards loyal to one family, spilling into the land as her parents refused to surrender. The bounders were simple farmers nowadays. The last territory dispute had been over a hundred years ago. They no longer even trained for battle. They didn't deserve an army descending on them. Even if her parents did.

"I'd like to."

"But you'll use a different tactic instead?

He sighed as if she were taking away his favorite toy. "For now. I'd request a hearing with a wise judge instead. You know, if I were coming up with a plan." He placed his hands over hers where they rested against his chest.

"A judge who would rule in favor of a syphon?"

Vincent nodded. "A judge who would rule in favor of what is best for her people and their society."

Bronte slowed her pace as the office doors opened, stunned at Vincent's words. A syphon's power benefiting society—she'd never thought of it like that.

Chapter 14

Bronte entered the senator's office. This time she walked into a circle of allies instead of feared enemies. They knew all her secrets. She had nothing to hide. A sense of hope—for a different, brighter future—floated around her like a wispy cloud. But it was too ethereal to grasp.

She took her seat in front of the senator's imposing desk, terribly underdressed for a meeting with the Republic's most powerful family. She straightened her oversize t-shirt and tucked her bare feet under her chair. The grateful smiles on Helen's and Edmund's faces at her return, and their lack of admonition, set her at ease.

As before, the senator sat behind his desk, Edmund to his left. Lord Rallis, Vincent and Edmund's father, was next in the circle. Beside him, Helen's proper posture hid her ruthless streak. Allison sat slightly behind them, as if she knew she wasn't part of the family's inner circle. Vincent took his seat next to Bronte, his chair touching hers.

"My parents are here." She made the announcement to the entire room.

"We know, dear." The lift to the senator's brow softened his stern expression.

"Yes, sir, but my mother has superior hearing. It won't matter where she is in the house, she'll be able to hear what you say."

The senator flung his hand with a quick snap of his wrist. Pressure squeezed at Bronte's eardrums.

"Sound spell. Standard procedure for all official matters of family and state."

Her ears strained to pop. She resisted the temptation to pinch her nose shut and blow to try to relieve the sensation.

"We weren't expecting them until this afternoon." Helen pinched her lips into a frown. "They spelled a message through the gates requesting to search through the gyre for the medallion on their own. I could hear it from my study even though Jasper refused to let it past the front door. We refused, of course."

"I don't think I'd have let them in if I were you." No sense of guilt trickled through her at denouncement of her parents.

"Keep your enemies close, Bronte. Better they're here than consorting with the mages of Rallis Territory and contaminating our people." Helen's explanation was a reminder of the difference between Bronte's life and the political elite's sophistication. To live on her own terms among such savvy would require a cunning mind. She had to adapt.

Vincent's anger pulled her attention, bubbling against her, as if the longer he'd sat in silence, the hotter the emotion boiled. Though it wasn't directed toward her, his agitated energy pressed against her. She put a hand on his arm.

"Allison," he said. Here was the source of his anger. "From here on, you are barred from the gatehouse. You are not permitted to open the gates to anyone who wants in or out, other than yourself."

The younger woman squeezed her face to hold back the tears that surely flooded behind her closed eyes.

Helen twisted around to her niece. "We have no idea what Masset would have done to Bronte," she scolded. "Nothing pleasant, that's for sure."

"Allison was trying to help me." Bronte could not let the girl be scolded over something that wasn't her fault. "She thought I was coming back."

Vincent whipped his head toward her, their faces inches apart. "Allison knew better, and now, so do you." He sliced her open, hurt pouring like blood.

She staunched it quickly, packing the cut with her own anger. "I am not a prisoner here, Vincent. Remember?"

"You *were* a prisoner! Wilen's. You almost ended up as Masset's prisoner." He rubbed a hand over his face. "Bronte, I thought Masset had you. You would have been an outlet for his hatred toward Nons. And what if he'd managed to find out what you are? Who knows what he would have done to you then? You walked right into his hands.

"As things stand now, you cannot leave here. Not with the truth about your power floating around. Please tell me you see the wisdom in that. You can blame me if you want. Or you can blame Claude for getting you mixed up with Double-Wide. Or blame your parents for making you deliver their message. It doesn't matter. The only place you are safe right now is within the gates of this estate, and they will remain closed to anyone without prior permission to cross them."

Her eyes were so dry they hurt. She wrenched them away from Vincent and stared out the towering window with a stubborn anger.

"I've never been so scared in my life." His rough words scraped against her with their anguish. "I wish you wanted to stay."

"It's not that I don't want to stay. It's that I don't want to *have* to stay." Bronte shook her head mindlessly. He would never let her go free.

She could never trust a mage.

Her breath stuck so tightly in her throat she almost choked on the thought. She closed her eyes as the impact of her own prejudice hit her, absorbing it like a blow. Her shoulders collapsed.

Her long-held beliefs against all mages had kept her safe for years. She'd seen, though, that not all mages were like her parents. She wanted to trust Vincent, but she was so afraid. She used that fear as an excuse to run from her dreams.

The anger drained out of her.

"You won't have to stay on the estate forever." He caressed her cheek with the back of his hand. "I will make this Republic safe for you one territory at a time if I have to."

"I'm doing the planning, remember?"

He looked at her with his brow lowered. "You're so stubborn."

"You're so bossy."

Someone nodded. Bronte glanced over to see Lord Rallis's head bobbing up and down. Helen's too. Actually everyone was nodding.

"You'll stay?"

"For now. But you have to stop orchestrating my life." She looked at Lady Rallis. "And not just Vincent. You all have to stop. I decide what I will and will not do. Deal?"

Vincent gave a curt nod. "Deal."

No one else responded, though she gave them plenty of silence to speak.

She narrowed her eyes at Vincent. "Will you respect my wishes and let me leave when it's safe?"

He narrowed his eyes right back. "For now."

She wasn't fooled. "But I can't leave now."

"I know. We can renegotiate later."

She gave an exasperated sigh. Gaining ground with the Rallises was like one step forward only to be gently, but firmly, pushed off the trail. No matter. She'd walk a different trail. They could follow her. As if to give credence to her determination to direct her own life, she moved away from Vincent, stepping out of the circle of Rallises. She walked behind the senator's desk to stand by the huge windows. The senator patted her on the arm as she passed by.

She hardly recognized the person she'd become—someone who could walk around Senator Rallis's office as freely as she would her own house, who was important enough to be the subject of a meeting held by the country's most powerful family. She leaned against the window to face them.

Vincent rested back in his chair, his fingers a pyramid of thoughtfulness as he studied her for a long moment. Finally, with a quick glance at his parents, he spoke. "Let's talk about the newspaper leak."

A bit of tension left Bronte as he switched the subject, or maybe it was the warmth of the sunshine beaming through the windows. It heated her shoulders and relaxed her muscles.

"Chrissy got Bronte's nom de plume from me." Helen confessed immediately. The words spilled from her as if they'd been waiting on her tongue for their opportunity to be divulged. "I didn't talk to her again last night."

"Someone did." The senator's voiced boomed against his sound spell. "Bring in the compeer," he ordered.

Edmund strode away. The doors opened before him. The sound spell remained in place as he walked out. Bronte had hoped for a respite. She tugged on her left ear.

"Do you need a break?"

Bronte cast her gaze at Vincent to find herself the subject of his intense, eagle-eyed look. She shook her head, uncomfortable to have everyone knowing the spell bothered her. "It's only been a few minutes. I can handle it."

"For Bronte's sake, be efficient, family." Helen gave the order.

Edmund led the compeer and her handler in. The door closed behind them.

Betty, the compeer, had lost her puff. Her bright pink suit matched sad splotches on her face. Her handler stood as if his joints had frozen. A slight breeze might shatter him to pieces.

Betty sniffled. "I'm so sorry." Her voice shook with tears. "That lady reporter cornered me in the bathroom. I really had to go." She crossed her legs and squeezed them together, as a demonstration of her past urgency. Despite the seriousness of the topic, Bronte bit her lip to stifle her smile.

"Freddy couldn't come in with me, of course." She jerked her thumb over her shoulder at the man behind her. His throat bobbed with a hard swallow.

"Of course." Edmund's sarcasm threw the woman even further from her composure.

"Oh, I think he could have," Vincent added with a dry tone.

The handler dropped his jaw at the improper suggestion.

Bronte didn't blame the man. She walked back to her seat, bringing Vincent within kicking distance.

Betty scrunched up her red face. "Well, no, he couldn't because he's—"

"Betty." Her handler's whispered rebuke cut off her ramble. Silence fell.

"Continue," the senator boomed.

Betty jumped. She looked at Bronte beseechingly. "I didn't tell her your name. I didn't tell her anything. She kept asking question after question." She wrung her hands like a wet sponge, despair dripping with each twist. "Every time she asked the right question, she somehow knew the answer. I think she must have read it in my face. I'm no good at hiding things." She sniffed again, and her face crumpled with it. "It's why Freddy doesn't let me go anywhere without him."

"She asked you if Bronte was a syphon?" Vincent questioned.

Betty nodded. "She listed a whole bunch of other mage types first. She asked if she was a siren, a static. I think she listed nymph and oracle. There might have been a few more. I kept saying no, no, no. I didn't say yes when she asked if she was a siphon, but I realized that's what your match must be. I didn't say anything, though." She waved her hand in the air. "Oh, it doesn't matter." Betty began to sob. "It's all my fault. And your energies are perfect together. I've never seen two mages match like you do." She lifted a hand toward Bronte. "And now you're going to be executed."

Bronte gave Vincent a pointed look. Betty's attitude reflected the mindset of every mage out there. There was no eraser big enough to rewrite the opinions of an entire nation of mages. Vincent could work on it until Bronte was wizened and gray, and still the world would not accept her.

He scowled at the compeer.

Bronte poked her dirty, cold toes against his shin—a warning not to lash the poor woman. She was reining in that bull. A current of warmth circled around her feet. Energy spilled into her syphon.

Vincent's expression turned pensive. "Betty, do you think Bronte deserves to die?"

His bloodline peeked out with the question. Founding families played the politician's game like no others, manipulating their opponents' thoughts and words like pawns on a chessboard. Poor Betty was far outmatched in this room.

"Well, no." Words shot out between sobs. "No one listens to me though."

"Chrissy Harney, the reporter, listened to you," Vincent countered. "She heard everything you said and then some. You have a powerful voice."

Betty straightened with a sniff. "Well, yes. I am powerful. But she used my words against me." She slumped. "Or more like my not-words."

"That would be your silence," Edmund offered helpfully.

"Right. My silence. And, usually, I don't have much of that. And I never will again. It's dangerous." The room filled with her sobs. "Oh, Lady Rallis, I'll waive your fee for your other son's match. The one you originally contracted me for. I've narrowed down the spot where she is. It's quite close, quite promising too."

"It's alright, Betty," Edmund said. "You don't need to find me a match. I'm in love with Bronte, too. And don't go being silent about that. I could never take a wife now. However, I am looking for simple, short-term consolation for my broken heart. Just a night's worth of solace. You can blab about that with your words and your not-words."

"Oh, for the love of the light, Edmund!" Lady Rallis dropped her head into her hand.

"Alright." Betty nodded at Edmund, and then her face fell. "Oh. I'm fired."

"Yes. You're fired," Lady Rallis snapped. "Now tell us what you said to Chrissy Harney about a baby."

"Baby? You're going to have a baby?" Betty's eyes widened in horror. "Oh no."

"You didn't tell Chrissy Harney that my son and Miss Casteel are going to have a baby?" Lady Rallis asked.

Betty shook her head a hundred eighty degrees.

"Did she ask you about a baby? Perhaps you were silent about it?"

More shaking. If Helen kept up the questions, the compeer's head would spin in complete circles, Bronte thought. She almost laughed out loud. Goddess, she was tired.

"Truth," the senator stated.

Someone else had leaked the false story.

Lord Rallis stood and approached the pair. "Betty Howland and Frederick Daniels, you are hereby released from your contract with the Rallis family. You are sworn to never mention any work you have done for us, nor anything you have learned about the Rallis family, or about the person who currently calls herself Bronte Casteel or B. Castle to anyone, at anytime or in any form."

The pressure of Lord Rallis's heavy spell crushed her ears. She clenched her hands to them, a useless protection from the force. The powerless could never block mage energy, but it didn't stop her from pushing her index fingers into her ear canal as if she could prevent the thin membranes from exploding. She heard herself make a noise as the spell finally fell onto its targets. She relaxed a little at a time and slowly brought her hands away.

The doors opened. Betty and Frederick walked out of the room.

Vincent draped his arm around her. "Alright?"

She nodded.

"Does it bother you when Vincent casts energy?" Helen studied her, concern etched in the grim line of her mouth.

"No." This time Bronte didn't resist pinching her nose shut and blowing to pop her ears, though it didn't work. "When other mages cast, it's like my syphon is trying to absorb the power, but it doesn't fit…like it's too big. Vincent is the exception."

"Okay, family," Helen began. "Two spells at once are too many for Bronte. Let's remember that."

"From now on, I cast the sound spells when Bronte's around." Vincent sat up in his chair, arms draped over its sides, a king's declaration.

"You're no good at it." Edmund shot out as he strode back.

"I'll practice, which I can afford to do with Bronte around."

"So who the hell is the baby leak?" Edmund demanded as he walked back to lean against the desk. "Is it right? Are you pregnant?" He pinned Bronte with a beam of his eyes.

"I've only been here for one night!"

"It only takes once."

She shook her head more vigorously than the compeer. The blushing flames on her cheeks burned. "No. No." She gave a sideways glance at Vincent, hoping for backup, but the speculation in his eyes made it all worse. She hadn't used any birth control last night, nor had she sensed a spell that would indicate Vincent used energy for it. She probably should have thought that through before she'd seduced him. She drummed her fingers against her chin and desperately filed through her mind for knowledge on how to change the subject.

Allison saved her. "It's my fault." Everyone spun to the other woman at her confession. "It was an accident. I didn't set out to do it." Allison gestured toward Bronte with her hand. "I asked Lawry if he thought she'd have a syphon baby. He's a doctor. I thought he might know. You were only a few feet away from me, Aunt Helen. It was right before we sat back down after intermission. That reporter was still hanging around. I think she heard me. I never mentioned anything about the Council taking it, though." Allison sounded as if that ought to make everyone less angry with her. "I said that if she had a syphon baby, we could give it to Daddy. Then he could be here too. He could come to family meetings with the rest of us."

Bronte's own shock was mirrored in every Rallis face. To use a baby for its mage power was a brutal fate. She bit her lip. Though her horror outweighed it, a touch of sympathy whispered through her. Allison's impossible yearning to belong to someone was a familiar feeling.

"Allison, what the hell is wrong with you?" Edmund did not share her sympathy. "You want to steal the future Rallis heir from its parents and give it away? You sound like the High Council justifying taking babies for their powers."

"I know. It's terrible. I know. I can't even believe I thought it, much less said it. It's just…this potion I was trying had all my thoughts bubbling up in my head. I was thinking things no one ever should. I was so relieved when it wore off. I had to tell Lawry it was no good."

"You need to tell *Lawry* that you're done taking his damn potions." Lord Rallis stood to face Allison.

The woman melted under her uncle's gaze.

"My brother has not been an ideal father," Lord Rallis continued. "We are all aware of that. Your home is here. You are part of this family. But the potions stop. Get off them. Now. We'll help, but you're done."

She gave a watery nod. "I think," she began, stopped, and tried again. "I think Lawry might have talked to the reporter on his own. I saw them talking together when I went over to the bar." She wiped away a tear. "But I only heard them talking about a death warrant."

* * * *

Vincent drove them back to his house, quiet in his thoughts.

Bronte interrupted them. "What's a death warrant?" A shiver passed through her at the ugly phrase.

Vincent looked at her with a raised eyebrow. "It authorizes an enforcer to execute a mage for extreme misuse of energy that has resulted in another mage's death or death of their mage sense." He recitation sounded as if he'd memorized it. "If someone claims grounds for a death warrant, they have to prove it at a hearing. It's impossible to fake. No one could prove such a charge against you, that's for sure. I've studied syphons for years, and I have the degree to prove it. I know their power doesn't harm."

"Are death warrants common knowledge among mages?" She slumped in her seat at his nod. "My parents will probably give it a try someday."

"They'll lose." He pulled into the meadow and followed the smashed twin trails now lining his front yard. They hadn't been there when she'd first arrived.

"Is there anything else I don't know about?" It had been one surprise after another around here. She could do without more for the next three to five years.

He parked the truck and rubbed his face, looking almost as tired as she felt. "I know you want to devise your own plans, but there's no avoiding the fact that you must be declared a mage. Soon."

She shook her head. He caught her, cupping his hands around her face.

"Hiding can't be part of your plan anymore. Not after the newspapers. There's no other option. It will be alright. You have the protection of the most powerful family in the Republic." He took a breath.

She recognized its type. "But…" She braced for his bad news with a grip around his wrists.

"Once you're declared a mage, the Casteels can claim you as one of theirs—a Casteel mage belongs in Casteel Territory. They would have legal right to do whatever they wanted with you."

"That's bad." Her shaky words puffed through the air. She searched for a silver lining. "But they'd need a death warrant to kill me?"

"Not exactly."

Silver tarnished to black. Maybe staying under the wide, strong wing of the Rallises was for the best. Maybe she didn't need freedom. The moment she thought it, her soul wilted. No, freedom was a necessity.

"Founding families are the exception to the law. They can deal with their own mages however they like. But they won't get away trying to claim you. If they refuse to relinquish their claim, we'll hold their medallion ransom until they agree."

"I thought you didn't want to do that. It's against your principles."

He stroked a finger down her cheek. "You're worth violating my principles." He got out of the truck and walked around to her side.

She sat motionless, cowed by this new set of hurdles to leap.

He opened her door. "Besides, it might not even be necessary."

"Yeah, a judge could sign a death warrant." Her knees fell out from under her as she got out of the car.

He caught her and held her against his body. "Not going to happen."

"Anything else I should know about?"

"The body." Vincent listed the next issue as if it was a minor problem. "The gyre has yet to flux down to lower energy levels. There's an envoy from the High Council here who needs in there. Senate murders are Council business…if this is a murder. She's demanding your help to retrieve the body. Apparently Masset told stories that somehow got to the Council's ears." He put his arm around her and escorted her up his porch steps.

"How can I help?"

"You syphon some of the gyre's power. That's why I could get in. I think it's why Masset could get so close. The envoy wants you to escort her in. My mother says the woman is pushy. But you are not to help her until you've been declared a mage. A Rallis mage. The Council is not getting near you without that."

She slumped against the wooden walls of his house.

"You don't have to be involved in any of it. My parents, Edmund, the senator…they can handle it all."

"No. I will be involved." Adamant, she straightened from the wall. "I suppose if the envoy needs a syphon's help, that can't be a bad thing." She pulled her eyebrows down. She had no desire to go find the body, but Casteel needed its medallion back. "Anything else?"

He zapped the lock. They walked in and she threw herself into the first chair at the large kitchen table and cradled her head in her arms. He stood beside her and ran his fingers through her hair. "I don't think there is anything else. Claude is being transported to the basement, but that doesn't involve you."

She lifted her head. "I want to talk to him."

"Out of the ques—"

She crossed her arms over her chest.

"We'll discuss it after he arrives."

She could save her arguments for then. She nodded to herself, an absent gesture that half put her to sleep. "I could deal with all of this."

He crooked his eyebrow at her.

"Except that I'm just so tired." She hated the whine in her voice. "But I don't think I could sleep."

"I can get you to sleep. Go get on the bed." He held out his hand for hers.

She looked up at him from under her bangs. "Is this a ploy? I'm tired enough to fall for it, but I have really bad dungeon feet."

"Go take a shower. Don't get dressed afterwards."

"I'm getting dressed, Vincent." Into what, though? Her bag was in her car parked at the big house.

"Waste of time. Shower fast. Come to me naked. Get in bed."

He commanded her like she was one of his men. She quirked a brow but obeyed, pivoting on her heel toward the bath. She went as fast as she could, lathering bubbles to rinse off the grime. Too bad death warrants and rumors in the tabloids couldn't wash down the drain with it.

When she came out, Vincent sat on the bed, elbows on knees. He'd pulled all the blinds closed, but a line of soft morning light streamed in through the edges. He was still dressed in his black army gear, including boots. Bronte tugged her towel tighter.

"You look all business." She leaned against the door, not venturing any further.

He shook his head. "No, this is all pleasure." The words were low and rough. He patted the mattress next to him. "Come sit." She pushed away from the door and padded silently to the bed.

"What are you going to do? I'm a little nervous." She sat next to him. His greater weight pulled the mattress down. Her hip tilted into his. She gave him a quick glance with her admission, then dropped her gaze to the floor. Their feet were side by side. Her toes looked very squishable next to his big boots.

"No reason to be nervous." He took the thick mass of her wet hair into his hands, threading his fingers through it. Her syphon power gobbled up his energy as he used his mage sense to remove the water. "I know exactly how our energy works together."

"How could you know in such a short time?" She silently calculated the amount of time they'd been together, but it reminded her of the doomed syphon in his dissertation. She quit adding. She didn't want to think about that right now.

"Instinct. I can't resist your warmth. I'm solid ice, cold and sharp. You melt all my rough spots with your pull, your strength. I feel like you have a place inside you that's only for me."

She leaned in, buried her face in his neck. His honesty tugged at her heart, almost too intense to face.

"You are the most important thing in my life. I will defend this from anyone, from anything." He pulled away, cupping her cheeks and looking her in the eyes. "I want to be your safe place. Like you are for me. I want to be worthy of you."

She sucked in a breath. He was worthy. That had never been in question. She opened her mouth to tell him, but yawned instead. She covered it with her hand and a blushing apology.

He smiled. "I might fall asleep too." He bent over and untied his boots, lining them up under his bed. "Although not as deeply as I did the last time."

She didn't miss the warning. "Yeah." She looked away. "You were pretty tired."

"That won't happen again. Take off the towel."

The sun went behind the clouds. The light in the room dimmed, but the intimacy blossomed. He reached to the side to open the bed's covers. He held them, waiting.

Bronte searched deep into herself for a last bit of boldness. She stood. The towel fell to the floor with a muffled *thump*. From his seat on the bed, he was eye level with her nipples. They hardened with his glance.

He closed his eyes. "Get in." He stood so she could crawl to the far side. "Lay on your stomach or your side. Face the wall."

"Why?"

"Because if I keeping looking at your breasts, this is never going to work." He tucked the blankets around her.

"Have you done this before?"

He gave a low laugh. "No, Bronte. I have not done this before." The bed moved as he got in next to her. His weight held down the covers as he stayed on top of them. She was trapped between the wall and him. "Relax."

She tried, letting her body sink into his.

He helped, wrapping an arm around her and securing her against him. "I'm going to fill you up with slow vibes." His voice was as sleepy as the energy her syphon power was soaking up.

She had no control over it, never had, never would. Vincent could control her power better than she could. She focused on the sensation. The whole universe seemed to decelerate with her. Though the energy drifted slowly, she was full with it. Her eyes closed, but only for a moment as a thought came to her. "Don't do this to me without my permission."

"Never. Now be quiet. I have to concentrate."

"How are you doing this?" Her mind evened out, her muscles relaxing.

"I'm forcing my energy to lose its focus. It's kind of like when your eyes lose focus. Hard to do on command. And hard to hold it there."

"So why did I have to be naked?"

"That was just a bonus for me."

She laughed as her eyes closed.

* * * *

Her breath evened. Joule by joule he let his energy spring back to its normal state, careful not to pull her from sleep. Her syphon power continued to draw his vibes without a hint of disturbance. He relaxed, tipping his head down, burying his nose in her hair. She'd used his shampoo again. He took a perverse pleasure in his scent mixing with hers.

He hadn't told her everything. He hadn't told her he needed to return to work, though he'd be by her side for the hearing at noon. He hadn't wanted to admit to her that his leave was up. He wasn't sure when he'd be back. But he'd come home to her.

He loved the sound of that. Closing his eyes, he sent up a silent prayer of thanks.

Gregor and Dane would be here soon. He hadn't told her that either. She wouldn't like it. But there was nothing she could say or do to change his mind.

He took another breath of her scent. Leaving her with two guards was not enough. He wanted some kind of claim on her…a promise that he'd be back for her, something to hold her to him.

Primitive of him. She did that to him.

A way existed, an old way—an energy weave. No one did it nowadays. The tradition of the weave had fallen off with the colonization of this new land. It was a mark of two mages' power. They merged their energies together in one small place on their skin. Since Bronte had no power to offer him, there would be no blending of their energies. It would be his energy alone, a vibrating tattoo of his vibes.

There were mages who still respected the tradition. Maybe it would make some people think twice before they touched her. Maybe it would keep her a bit safer.

He squeezed his eyes shut. He had yet to recover from her latest escape. His gut still clamored for revenge, still hadn't forgiven anyone for their part in it—not Wilen, not Allison, not Gregor or Dane, though the two would excel at their task of guarding her all the more for it.

While he was gone, they'd ensure no one took her from him. And he'd ensure she carried his energy.

He tucked in closer to her, his nose buried in her hair along the nape of her neck. With his hand on her arm, he closed his eyes and focused his power to the tips of his fingers. With a deep breath, he pulled her scent into him. The delicate hairs on her nape stirred as he exhaled and let his power flow over her in a small circle. He felt it unite—end melding with beginning, sustained energy vibrating in an endless loop. He lifted his fingertips from her arm, careful to keep his vibes even so he didn't disturb her sleep.

He loved her. She held his heart. Now she held his power, both within her syphon and on the outside. A coil of tension unwound inside him.

He lifted his head to look at her arm, squinting closer. Her skin was blank, unblemished. A pressure in his chest squeezed as if his heart had taken a punch. His weave had not worked.

Chapter 15

She woke up alone. In that moment she understood how he'd felt when she'd snuck away—lost, lonely, afraid. He'd held her for a while as she'd dreamed, anchoring her with his presence. Without him, she slipped her moorings of hope and possibility. She needed them back. What left her so melancholy?

She rolled to the bed's edge and peered at the floor. His boots were gone, but her syphon hummed with his power. He was still here, but his energy weighed heavy and sorrowful. That was the source of her sadness.

Just then he appeared in the bedroom doorway. His grim expression matched his black uniform. He'd added a variety of black straps and holsters along his chest, his left arm, and around one thigh. They all held weapons. She recognized some of them—guns, at least one knife, an energy blaster. He painted a ferocious image standing in the doorway like that.

"You're leaving? What happened?" The words were scratchy with sleep.

"I was trying to be quiet so you would rest." Even now his voice stayed soft. He stared, blue eyes studying her, but she couldn't quite see beneath that expression.

She swung her legs to the floor, sheet clutched to her chest. "What's going on?"

"I have to go to work. Earlier than I thought. There's been another attack."

Those words brought down the curtain she'd refused to look behind. This was his life.

"Was anyone hurt?"

"Yes."

"Badly?"

He nodded. She couldn't bring herself to ask if anyone was dead. Had her music played a role in this? A wave of guilt washed over her…because worry for the victims wasn't her first concern.

Her first thought had been that he was leaving her. Her second thought: she really would have to stand on her own. Despite all her insistence that she make her own decisions, the small patch of ground she stood on no longer seemed solid. The life she'd built was gone. No matter what happened to her now, she would never go back to Chattanooga. The roads before her were so steep it was easier to avert her eyes.

In her mind, she'd always thought of him as being here—an unrealistic image. He battled bad guys who had bombs. These bad guys had killed over three hundred people and injured many more.

"Now the world's best deflector mage flies off to the rescue. Not an easy job to do."

He tilted his head. "Easier with you." He looked away. "This is the second time those bastards have targeted Rallis territory." His nose flared as he spoke, and a cord of muscle clenched in his jawline. The tight control on his anger was evident. She wondered to whom he'd told his problems and concerns before she showed up. Who listened to him talk about his day?

She pulled the sheet free of the bedding and wrapped it around herself as she stood. The room was too cool for a mere sheet. She missed his warmth. "I thought you worked before and during the attacks. What do you have to do after them? If they've already gone off, what power is there to deflect?"

"Considering this is the third bomb in thirty-six hours, almost everyone is being called up. If we get a lead on their next target, we can move faster."

The rhythmic drum of a helicopter sounded in the air. She'd only heard them a few times in her life.

"I don't know when I'll be back. I can't be at the hearing. And I might not be here when you go into the gyre with the Council's envoy." He leaned his hands high against the top of the doorframe. "I'm sorry."

"I'll be alright." If he could go fight a bunch of bad guys, she could fight her parents.

One half of his mouth pulled up. He gave a soft, fast laugh but it was coated in sadness. He walked over to her. Two steps and his boots nearly touched her toes. His fingertips rested on her arms. "I know. You're very brave. Sometimes too brave. There's nothing you have to do at the hearing. You just have to be present. Edmund and Mother have it all handled. They'll do all the talking. I would have been there for support. But the gyre…"

"I'll be alright," she repeated. "I've already been in once with no problems." She thought about Masset. "Or almost no problems."

He closed his eyes and groaned. He was remembering Masset, too.

She traced a line down his chest in between straps and weapons. The helicopter sounded like it was landing on the roof. "Is that your ride?" She looked up at him through her bangs.

"Yes." He slid his hands to her cheeks and bent his head to brush his lips against hers. Tingles tightened over her skin and over her heart. She leaned forward into his warmth, into the press of his mouth…almost closing the gap between them but not quite. Those weapons were intimidating. With her sheet secured, she draped her hands over his shoulders. He was strong and hard beneath her hands.

This wasn't a kiss to tumble them into bed. No, this was a kiss to say goodbye.

He pulled back and his fingers slid down to her shoulders, then squeezed gently. "Gregor and Dane are outside the house. They will stay with you until I get back." The helicopter's rhythm and sound changed, as if the drummer had switched drums.

"Gregor and Dane?" Her words were too loud for the house, even considering the coming helicopter.

"Dane's the guy with the beard, two black eyes and broken nose. Gregor was the one you stepped over at the bottom of the basement stairs."

"I know that! And no. No, no, no."

"Gregor likes you. Dane doesn't like anyone, so don't take it personally."

"I'm not fond of either one of them. And I hope they do take it personally!"

His shoulders went up and down with a sigh. He rested his head on hers. "I'm not leaving you here alone. They'll do their job."

"Because you'll strangle them if they don't! That's not a very good reason to do a job." She stepped away.

"It's the best reason." His eyes hardened. "Someone in Double-Wide has targeted you, Bronte. They know who you are. More importantly, they know where you are. They knew you were with us at the symphony. They got onto the estate once, and I have no idea how they did it. I don't know how they got through the security spells, or how they got back out without setting off any alarms. They're blowing up buildings and people in the heart of Rallis Territory." He closed the gap she'd created. "Gregor and Dane stay."

She folded her arms over her chest and brushed up against a hard black cylinder in a sheath strapped to his chest. She shivered and stepped back. That one housed a potion, though she had no idea what kind of weapon it was.

"You don't have to talk to them," he said. "They'll spend most of the time outside the house unless it's an emergency."

"I don't like this."

"I know." His jaw twitched as he closed his eyes for a moment. "If you really don't want them, I'll reassign two sentries from the big house. Would you rather have that?"

She'd rather have none, but he wouldn't settle for that. He was trying to compromise. It was a start. "If General Wilen has called up everyone, how can those two be here?"

"The security of the estate has already been compromised. We could have Double-Wide agents here and not even know it." He picked up a black bag and stepped into the kitchen area. He must have taken her question as a capitulation. "The landline number to the big house is on my desk. I guarantee my mother is waiting for your call."

She followed him to the door. He leaned down and kissed the top of her nose. As he opened the door, bright sunshine and crisp fall air rushed in. The rumbling thump of the helicopter sitting in his meadow pounded through the floor and into her body. The pilot turned his head her way, sunglasses encasing his eyes. Bronte jumped behind the door, but stuck her head around.

"When will you be back?" she hollered. This house would be lonely without him.

"Could be tonight, could be…another night. I'll be back as soon as I can." He walked backward across the porch, keeping her in view.

This was so fast, so abrupt. She peeked out after him and locked eyes with Gregor, who leaned against the outside wall. She stepped back in the house and slammed the door. And then opened it right back up. "Be careful!" she yelled louder than she could ever remember yelling. The noise of the rotor was stiff competition.

Vincent turned in the middle of the meadow and waved. She closed the door, muffling the pounding *thump*, and watched from the window.

Goddess, but he was handsome. And overbearing. And controlling. And now he was gone. She was standing on her own. This was what she'd wanted, wasn't it?

The helicopter lifted off the ground. At the edge of the meadow, trees shuddered from the violent wind. Bronte followed the huge black bug with her gaze, murmuring prayers of protection for him. It shrank to a speck in the sky as it flew away and then disappeared.

She padded over to the bed, sat on the edge and pulled her knees up to her chest. The sudden quiet of the house seemed to wait for her as if it were a cognizant presence. It held its breath to see if she'd accept what she'd been offered. A home, a heart. As if to dwell here without him was to accept this as her place too. She scanned his sparse bedroom. Its openness declared there was plenty of room for her.

Regardless, dwelling in a sheet was not an option. She padded to his dresser where he'd neatly piled her clothes. She pulled out her skirt and inspected the snags and splotches of forest dirt. It was no longer up to snuff after its adventures in the gyre, but she had to wear something. She picked up her silk camisole and flapped it through the air in a fruitless attempt to wave out the wrinkles.

The knock at the door didn't stop her inspection or affect the pace of her movements. She would ignore Gregor and Dane.

But she couldn't ignore the rap on the bedroom window accompanied by Lady Rallis's hollered hello. Bronte scrambled into the bathroom to throw on the skirt and another t-shirt as quickly as she could.

Not fast enough. Lady Rallis zapped the front door's lock and opened it.

"Hello, Bronte! Are you alright?" Helen called in. "I want you to know…Vincent may be gone, but you're still in good hands. I don't want you worrying. You have enough to handle already."

Bronte stepped out of the bedroom to find Vincent's mother standing in front of the couch. "Lady Rallis, yes. I'm fine. Thank you for asking."

"I'm glad to hear that, Lady Casteel." Sarcasm peaked from behind Helen's Mayflower manners.

Bronte huffed with dropped jaw. "Helen."

Helen tipped her head, acknowledging the correction. "That's better. Though you do have a right to the title, you know." Helen walked over, her high heels silent. The pressure of the sound-muffling spell pushed at Bronte's ears. Casting such energy was second nature to the aristocratic mage. Clacking across the floor was plebeian—yet another example of how Bronte would never blend in. She was going to stand out if she lived among mages.

Assuming she lived.

Helen tsked with a worried frown. "I can't believe Tom Wilen dared to touch you! I hope Vincent straightened him out." She didn't wait for an answer, lifting a big shopping bag. "I brought you something to wear."

"It's very thoughtful of you to keep me in clothes. I'll pay you back." Bronte headed to the bathroom with the large bag.

"You certainly will not."

Bronte ignored her. She donned gray tights, a long-sleeved crimson dress that skimmed her curves and a pair of black boots. They were tall, fuzzy on the inside with a flat heel and good tread. They would more than suffice for a quick escape should any be necessary. Her feet would stay warm in these. She brushed her hair with her fingers, pulled it into a twist, and secured it with pins from her bag.

She walked out of the bedroom, if not a new woman, then a more respectable one.

Helen looked her up and down, gave her a nod of approval and hustled her toward the door.

"Wait." Bronte dragged her feet. "I thought the hearing was at noon."

"We started early. I want that woman and the Casteels—except for you, of course—out of my house. Sooner. Not later."

Bronte had no idea to which woman Helen referred, but she wasn't going to stir the pot by asking. She had another pot to stir. "You started? Without me?"

"Not to worry. It's all going perfectly."

Gregor took the lead as they walked off the porch. "Miss Casteel, Lady Rallis," he nodded. He was dressed similar to Vincent, all black and covered in weapons. The bearded man, Dane took up the rear. Bronte didn't like having him behind her.

"It would be my pleasure to drive you back to Rallis Hall," Gregor continued.

Helen gave a small nod to the man. She expected nothing less.

Dane opened the door for her and she slid into the backseat on the passenger side.

Bronte climbed into the other side. Gregor closed her door with a wink and got behind the wheel.

Helen steadied herself against the door as they bounced away. "I'm giving you a driveway as a wedding present."

Pushy woman.

"There's no wedding on the calendar. And if you marred Vincent's meadow with a strip of pavement, I think you'd find yourself on the wrong side of the gate he's sure to install."

Helen nodded. "Perhaps you should give him a driveway."

"No."

Dane turned to Bronte with a speculative look. There might have been a touch of respect in them.

As the house came into sight, Helen sat up straighter. "When we get into the hearing, let Edmund and I do the talking. We know what to say."

"That sounds very familiar," Bronte replied. "The last time you said that, I ended up being exposed as a syphon in the newspaper. Thank you, but I'll do my own talking."

As Gregor pulled into the back lot, Helen looked up toward the low ceiling of the vehicle like she was searching for patience. "Vincent warned me you would say something like that." She spread her hands wide. "Bronte, I know what I'm doing here. I know the people who are waiting for us. And I know the law. You don't. Darling girl, I don't think you know how bad it is in Casteel Territory, how far that family has fallen, how desperate they've become." Helen patted her knee. "When your mother kicked you out, she did you a favor. I think she's lost her mind. A lot of mages in Casteel's territory seem to have done so in the last decade. But…" Helen's word was long and conciliatory. "If this is what you want, I will stand behind you. And when you get in trouble, I will be there to fix it." Helen gave her another pat, got out of the car, and walked into the back wing of the house.

Bronte didn't move for a moment, though Dane stood next to her open door. Gregor stayed in the car with her. The cool fall air reached into the vehicle, waiting for her to step out into it, to accompany her to the house where everything would change for her.

"Are you getting out?" Dane's voice was carefully neutral. Vincent would have been tugging her out.

"Will he be alright…out there?"

"The colonel's the best at what he does, ma'am."

That wasn't an answer to her question, but Dane didn't offer anything more.

"We don't have to do this. We can go back to Vincent's if you want." Gregor met her eyes in the rearview mirror.

"No, we can't. Who knows what the Rallises will do if I'm not there to stop them?" Finally she slid from the car, nerves keeping pace with her, and strode toward the towering house. Its stark gray lines reached high, broken up by regular intervals of windows and the double wooden doors. Gregor reached for the knob to open one. She stepped into the biggest kitchen she'd ever seen. Large appliances gleamed silver throughout the work area. Pale yellow walls softened their imposing presence. There were two of everything—sinks, coffeepots, ovens—one of which had something savory baking inside it. Its scent drifted through the air.

Helen waited for her by a swinging door. She smiled and led the way through a butler's pantry lined floor to ceiling with cabinets. Dane blocked Bronte's view as he stepped in front of her. Gregor followed behind. They paraded into a huge dining room with a table so shiny Bronte wished for a pair of white gloves to avoid smudging anything. The table could seat twelve, with a great deal of space around it to expand. It was unusually wide. Bronte could have lain across its width, stretched her hands over her head, and still not spanned it. It would be inconvenient for passing the salt, but quite comfortable when it was her parents who were on the opposite side of it.

The two sat side by side. Deep frowns marred both their faces. Her brother sat next to them. She guessed it wasn't hard to tell they were brother and sister, though he was fifteen years her senior. They had the same dark hair and pale skin, but Todd's face was etched with an unhealthy gray, as if he'd spent years steeped in anger. He studied her with a glare that hid neither his curiosity nor his hatred.

She could face down prejudice and snobbery. Outright hatred was much harder. But she wasn't running anymore. She tipped her chin up at the threat in his eyes.

Helen walked along the table and gestured Bronte into the chair at Edmund's left. He was one seat shy of the head of the table. Helen sat on Bronte's other side. Dane and Gregor stood at either corner of Bronte's chair. She was surrounded, a reassuring fact as her family muttered angry secrets among themselves, pausing for the occasional glower at her.

Bronte didn't know the remaining four people at the table. A pale blond woman sat at the head of the table next to Edmund. The other three were at the far end, tucked together and intent on their own conversation.

Edmund smoothed his tie and jacket as he leaned into Bronte. "You haven't missed much. Just long-winded introductory statements, at least on your parents' part. My introduction was succinct and compelling." He squinted at her as his gaze caught on her hair. "What's in your hair?" He fingered through the hair at the nape of her neck.

"Edmund," Bronte whispered as she pulled away, "One doesn't tease at a hearing." She cupped her hand over her mouth so her family wouldn't hear, though her parents and brother had started their own whispering session. Bronte was sure she was the topic of their conversation.

"No, I'm serious," he whispered back. He put his hand on top of Bronte's head and wrenched her toward him. She was surprised her bodyguards didn't stop him.

Creepy shivers started down her back as she realized he wasn't joking. "Is it a bug?"

He fingered through her hair. The loose knot she'd fixed began to droop.

She scrambled to repair it.

"A bug?" he sounded incredulous. He pulled away from her to see her face instead of her scalp. His mouth gaped. "Very funny. It's a wea…" His whisper stopped abruptly.

She wrinkled her eyebrows and shook her head slightly. "A wea?" She touched the back of her head tentatively but didn't feel anything crawling around. She caught the eye of the pale blond woman. The firm line of her mouth and drawn brow didn't encourage Bronte to ask for her opinion.

Edmund was slow to speak. "It is…" His voice was a bare murmur. "A wee little bug?" He stared at her, his eyes making a close study of her face as if she were a book with very fine print. He shook his head. "I can't believe my brother let you out of the house without telling you there's a… bug in your hair. My brother is way dumber than I am."

"He left before I got…" Dressed. Too much sharing.

"Remember this, Bronte. Years down the road, when you realize you chose the wrong brother, remember I warned you Vincent isn't very smart."

Helen poked her nose in. "Edmund, do not insult your brother. Vincent is a very smart man, Bronte."

Phyllis's ears perked up despite their quiet tones.

Bronte studied him. "Was there really a bug?" She couldn't believe she was asking this at her own hearing. Edmund gave a shaky laugh and patted her on the shoulder.

Helen stretched her neck to see Bronte's hair. "You have a bug in your hair?"

"I've got it, Mother. No need to get excited." Edmund's voice turned vehement. "In fact, let me check again." He yanked his fingers through her hair. Her knot disintegrated. Pins tumbled to the seat of her chair and down to the floor as her hair fell to her shoulders.

"Edmund!" Helen admonished. "Manners. Please."

Bronte frantically fingered her long tresses to arrange some semblance of an ordered coiffure. She was adding this to the list of the crazy things the Rallises had done to her. She touched the back of her hair, one last check for that bug. There was no creeping little body, though one section felt different—thicker maybe, as if something coated it. But her fingers slipped right through, unable to grasp anything. A thorough shampooing was in order.

The pale blond stared through the whole episode. Was she the judge? She looked about the same age as Bronte—young for a mage judge. Bronte smiled at her, but the woman's expression didn't change, frowning as hard as her mother. Her nose was quite proper, small and pointed, and her lips were true red. She wore a high-collared black jacket similar to Vincent's dress uniform, minus the medals. Black wasn't her color, though she'd be quite lovely if even a hint of happiness glimmered within her.

Helen whispered in Bronte's ear. "That's the High Council's envoy. She's here to retrieve your grandfather's body. She insisted on attending this hearing. At the other end of the table are Judge Eaton, her reader mage, and the recorder mage."

Two cracks banged through the air. Bronte flinched, her ears popping at the judge's spell to bring the room to attention. "Now that the subject in question is present, we shall bring this hearing to its conclusion."

Every gaze in the room shot to the judge. She was dressed in a white turtleneck, and her short, red hair was spiked at the ends. The effect was an angelic devil.

Phyllis screeched, her face red enough to burst. "Conclusion? I'm not anywhere near finished."

The judge lifted an eyebrow.

Phyllis huffed and looked away, outranked by the other woman.

The judge continued, "In light of the evidence presented, Bronte Casteel is hereby declared a mage according to the laws of the Republic."

Declared a mage. Just like that?

The verdict rang out. The walls of the room vibrated with the force of its energy. Bronte gripped the arms of her chair as the spell passed through her. The pain in her eardrums seared as the pressure built and then eased. Her vision narrowed to the table before her. The wood gleamed like ice. She would not let her head collapse against it—no matter how heavy it got or how fast the room spun around her. She could only imagine the smudge of forehead grease that would be left on its shine. She gripped the chair tighter.

"To the next order of business, I have here before me a transfer request from Rallis to Casteel regarding syphon mage Bronte Casteel. It is unusual for a transfer to be presented before a judge on its first request, but given the circumstances, I will allow it. How say you, Casteel?"

"Denied!" Phyllis spate the word through bared teeth.

Edmund cleared his throat. "Judge Eaton, if I may?" The judge nodded and Edmund took the floor. "Rallis has a final offer for Casteel." He turned to Phyllis, "Lady Casteel, your medallion currently resides—"

The Council's envoy interrupted. "Look at your daughter, Lady Casteel." The steely blonde's cold voice could have frozen the air. "Poised, calm. Good breeding, despite her power. But you kicked her out. So she's likely seething under it all. Ready to take you out in a flash of mage vibes if you don't grant this wish to be transferred to Rallis Territory." Her voice was full of threats—heavy and scary. But there was no point to it. The envoy was misinformed. Bronte had no weapons against her mother.

"She doesn't have mage vibes!" Phyllis screeched. Leave it to her mother to straighten everyone out, Bronte thought.

The icy blonde laughed. "Oh, right. I'm getting confused. Who knows what I'll say if I keep going?" She leaned forward in her seat. Her dark blue eyes pinned Phyllis with a malicious stare. "I'm sure your daughter will continue to live quietly as always…if you make the right choice and transfer her to Rallis."

The judge chimed in, "The court recognizes the wisdom of the High Council envoy's advice to Casteel to transfer the mage to Rallis."

The envoy nodded once in acknowledgement and then turned back to Phyllis. "If you do not sign her over, who knows what your daughter will do?" She smiled coldly. "She knows so much about your household. I wouldn't trust her to keep her mouth shut about family secrets and the like."

Bronte knew only one family secret—that the Casteel daughter was a syphon. That wasn't such a secret anymore. Her brother looked as confused as she felt.

Phyllis snorted. "Fine. They can have her. She can die by their hand instead of mine."

"Mage transferred by law," the judge immediately declared. The same power washed through the room. A thousand pounds of pressure pushed against her ears.

"It is left to Rallis to bind her to the land," the judge said.

She'd forgotten about that part. Since Nons were not invited to binding ceremonies, she had never witnessed one. She rubbed her temples, dreading another dose of spells. How else would a mage be bound to the land? Glancing across the table, she caught her mother's gaze. Phyllis's small, evil smile sent a shiver through her. Her mother stood. "Judge Eaton."

Bronte knew what was coming. Of course she knew.

"I call for the death of the syphon mage for causing irrevocable harm to another mage."

"Your evidence, Lady Casteel?" The judge's put-upon sigh sounded as if she'd expected this too.

"I place before you records of energy readings of my son, the Casteel heir, taken when he was fifteen years old." Scrolls floated down to the judge, one of her mother's talents. Phyllis waited for them to reach the judge and carefully lowered them to the shiny table. "As you can see, his levels spiked quickly and then leveled off, sadly short of his potential. Bronte was born the moment they leveled off. She sucked the energy right out of him and permanently restricted the growth of his mage power. Her syphon destroyed his potential." Her eyes narrowed on Bronte as she sneered. She sat down slowly, her glare staying in place.

The reader to the left of the judge picked up the scroll and examined it. She nodded. "The energy readings are Truth."

Judge Eaton nodded back and then stared at Phyllis. "And where are the records of Bronte's energy readings when she was born?"

Phyllis scoffed and gestured with her hands. "No one has records of infants. Everyone knows babies have no discernible energy until three days after birth. Even at that time, nothing showed up on her recordings other than the background energy of the land."

"Exactly." The judge's voice was as sharp as her hairdo's spikes.

"No one knows how syphon mages function," Phyllis spat. "They could be different from the rest of us. She was syphoning power from the day she was born. I know it!"

"You have no proof that a brand-new infant caused your son's power to level off before he was strong enough to suit you. As you said, babies have no power when they are born. Therefore, the death warrant is denied." The words cracked through the air. Though they seared like hot, slender knives slipping into her eardrums, they had saved her life. That was… easy. Too easy. She glanced behind her. Gregor and Dane were focused and alert.

"Judge Eaton, this girl has warped your mind! Her presence affects everyone. I told you we should finish this before she arrived! Can you not feel it? We should all be scared, frightened, to know a syphon is in our midst. And yet you sit here calmly, as if she is not consuming your power by the megajoule."

The judge's gaze hardened. "Fear of the unknown, legends, myths… none of those things has a place in the law or at a death warrant hearing.

This is not a witch hunt, Lady Casteel. That would go against the sacred, founding laws of the Republic."

"I'll tell you what goes against the laws: a judge who won't enforce them!"

"There is no antisyphon law on the scrolls." The High Council's envoy spoke. Her cold voice sent a shiver down Bronte's back.

"What? Of course there is!" Phyllis steamed, though instead of growing red with anger, her faced paled and tightened.

"The High Council has erased them. Look at your Scrolls of Law when you return home. There are no longer any laws prohibiting any type of mage power." The judge nodded. "It is our own fear that holds us back. That has no place in the law." She flashed a glance toward the recorder mage. "Strike this next part from the record."

The recorder mage bobbed her head in consent.

The judge turned a withering glare on Phyllis. "Lady Casteel, you are as sour as the energy radiating through your territory. You have embarrassed both your children at this farce of a hearing. Go home. Address the problems that dwell in your land if it's not too late. If everyone in Casteel is as affected as you are, I don't think there is much hope. The least you can do is cease to contaminate the rest of us with your ill-will."

Phyllis stepped back, her chair falling. "If you will not listen to me, then I invoke the Right of Creator." She pointed a finger at Bronte.

Bronte had no idea what that meant. Nothing good, though. Helen and the judge gasped. Edmund's mouth dropped, his usual witty comeback absent. Dane and Gregor each stepped forward and put a hand on her shoulders. Bad signs all around. Phyllis had taken them by surprise. Only the High Council's envoy remained unaffected.

"Lady Casteel." The judge's voice was hard. "That law is intended for long-term spells. Dangerous spells. It is not intended for children."

Phyllis's eyes glowed like flames. "There is no description in the law limiting it to spells or potions." Phyllis lifted a scroll, already twisted to the correct part. "Whoever brings into existence a creation formed of universal energy shall be responsible for it throughout its lifespan and has the right to destroy it even if it is no longer resides in their possession."

"Again, Lady Casteel, it is intended for deadly spells and aggressive potions." Judge Eaton leaned on the table. Her fingers pressed against it. She wasn't afraid of leaving fingerprints. "If the creator no longer wishes to allow such negative energy to hurt or kill, then they are allowed to destroy it. It's a salvage-your-karma kind of law. Not a kill-your-baby law."

"You did not create her alone." The white blonde spoke. "It took two universal energies to make Bronte."

"My cocreator agrees with me." Phyllis looked down at her husband. "Don't you?"

The future Senator Casteel twitched. It might have been a nod. It might have been a spasm.

The Council's envoy glared at both elder Casteels. "Do you want the mages of Casteel Territory to know you willfully killed your daughter? Such an action is unlikely to soothe your people. The High Council has reports of riots, of bounder mages leaving their posts and general mayhem in your cities. They are planning to place an envoy in your territory to evaluate the state of your rule."

Phyllis gasped. "That's unheard of! And unlawful. The High Council has no authority to do that."

"The High Council does whatever is necessary for the good of the Republic."

"I'm hardly going to take the word of their insignificant little flunky."

"You don't have to, Lady Casteel. The Lady Glender will tell you herself." The mere name radiated authority and power. "Her summons will arrive soon."

"So be it." Phyllis dismissed the Council envoy. "To the topic at hand, I hereby invoke the Right of Creator." Ritual words. They vibrated with power. "Bronte's presence in our family has been a burden since the moment her complete lack of mage power was revealed. To discover that she's a syphon, that such a creature would be born to a family like ours, ought to strike fear into each of you. Mayflower families have no place for such an abomination. We have done a disservice to our great country by letting her live. In the name of our great ancestors who survived the Inquisition, I erase our world of you." A buzz vibrated through the room.

Bronte clapped her hands over her ears at the pressure.

Phyllis lifted her hand, pointer finger extended. Bronte's chair was yanked back—either Gregor or Dane, she couldn't see. Hard hands grabbed her. The Council envoy shot up. Bronte was tossed from her chair to the ground. A heavy body pushed her into the rough carpet. Chaos sounded above her. One loud scream, a high grunt. A splinter of wood cracked like a gun. She burrowed against the floor as if she could dig through it.

"Stay down, Bronte," Gregor commanded.

As if she wanted to stand.

"Get that woman out of here!" Edmund's shout reigned over the room. The noise faded until the loudest sound was Bronte's heartbeat.

"Clear." Dane threw his voice to them with a spell. Gregor rolled away and stood.

Bronte watched from the floor as he scanned the room and then offered her a hand up. She accepted with a shaky reach.

The judge and her two people huddled against the far wall. Helen's hand hovered in front of her chest, as if she was ready to throw mage energy. Edmund mirrored her. His gaze followed Lord Casteel, who carried Phyllis's limp body out of the room. A chair lay crumpled against the floor on the other side of the room.

Most frightening was the Council's envoy. She lay in the middle of the table, her back to Bronte. Her silvery hair splayed across the dark wood.

With a soft *click*, the door closed, shutting out the Casteels and leaving the room frozen in shock.

"What happened?" Bronte finally asked. No one answered. Shock drifted through the air like autumn leaves, settling among the witnesses and sealing them in silence.

Bronte brushed past Edmund and shuffled around the table. "Is she alive?"

He found his voice. "No one could have survived that spell."

The envoy's blue eyes stared at nothing. A drip of blood from her nose blemished the pale perfection of her skin. Bronte reached out, slipping her fingers under the woman's collar to feel for a pulse. A tornado of power zapped into her. Her ears popping with the explosion, she jerked back. Her fingers stung, so charged they might shoot lightning. The envoy sat up. The collective gasp was a chorus of shock.

"Are you alright?" Bronte's hesitant words dripped

"Yes," the envoy hissed. "You took the edge off."

* * * *

Creamy walls enclosed Helen's private sitting room, a stark contrast to the dark formality of the dining room. The envoy lay on the couch where Edmund had deposited her. She didn't move. She didn't talk. Her face was a perfect blank. Bronte wasn't sure if she was in terrible pain or just the silent type.

After a few minutes, Bronte broke the silence. "Edmund is summoning a healer. He told me what happened. You took the spell meant for me. Thank you."

The woman said nothing.

"What is your name? I feel like I should know the name of the person who saved my life."

"Selene. Glender." She added the last name as if it were a separate entity. Her voice was as sharp as ever. She didn't sound as if she had just blocked a death spell.

Bronte smoothed her skirt, unsure how to proceed. "Is there someone you want me to contact for you? Friends or family?"

Selene huffed a laugh and tented her hand over her eyes. Her fingers were long and thin. Good musician's hands. "No friends. And family? The High Council disapproves of things like that."

"Oh."

The blood still dripped from Selene's nose. Bronte handed her a tissue from a basket on the side table.

"Not many people want to be friends…or family…with a necromancer, a bone witch, a corpse whore, whatever you want to call it. The High Council's official term is 'forensic mage,' but no one's fooled." Bitterness leached from her lips.

Selene's loneliness reminded her of Vincent, except there was no resentment in him.

"I understand having a mage power people are afraid of." Mage power. Those words felt strange on her tongue. "There are some people who'd like to kill me for it."

"Obviously." Her voice was void of sympathy.

Considering Selene's disinterest in the social niceties, Bronte let her own curiosity have its reign. She leaned forward against her legs, bringing her closer to the necromancer. "You weren't…dead before I took the edge off, were you?"

"That's a stupid question. Of course I wasn't dead."

"Oh. Well, how did I take the edge off?"

"I was clogged up with our mother's killing spell."

Our mother? Bronte barely caught the rest of the woman's words.

"It's hard to use a death spell on a mage who resonates with death's energy." Selene shrugged. "You're her syphon daughter. I'm her necromancer daughter. It only makes sense that all of our powers vibrate. Though you certainly didn't take much of the power off. If you're a typical example of a syphon, they're not very powerful."

"You're my sister?" Bronte sat stunned. The insult in the envoy's words only half registered.

"Don't tell. The Rallises might not want you if they know you're related to a bone witch." Selene laughed with bitter glee. "Yes, you're the favored Casteel daughter. You got to stick around for sixteen years. She threw me out three days after I was born, when my necromancer power surfaced. The Council took me in. So don't worry about me. I'm fine."

To throw out a baby—how could they? Bronte's estimation of her parents dropped to the darkest pits of the universe.

Selene stood and walked to the door. "Be at the gyre's edge at seven thirty." Her voice was as icy as ever.

Chapter 16

Bronte chose a rock the height of a chair, three rows away from the center of the gyre. The sun streamed through the branches of the white guardian trees as it headed back to the horizon. She'd endured Helen's company at the big house for as long as she could. The news that she had a sister burned her tongue. She'd kept quiet, though Selene was wrong about the Rallises. They'd still want Bronte regardless of her necromancer sister.

She had a sister. Bronte sat on her white rock, the words reverberating through her mind. She was due some peace to think it all through, and no one could get to her in the gyre. The only other person in here was dead.

Dane and Gregor lingered on opposite edges of the gyre, frowning and frustrated that they couldn't get to her. She ignored them and opened her violin case with a flick of the clasps. The case's velvet lining was worn and dotted with bald patches. She pulled out her instrument and bow.

She was a mage. It was officially on the Republic's record books. And she was going to play like one.

She tuned the four strings until they vibrated with perfect harmony. It was the antidote to the tension coiled inside her. She caught her first deep breath in hours. The rocks of the gyre absorbed her notes and sang back to her. Constant and steady. The only constant in her universe at the moment. She had no idea what was next in her life other than pulling the bow across the strings and letting the song building inside her have a life.

The notes danced out of her one at a time. The gyre's power magnified and stretched the music until it seemed as if her creation would go on to infinity. The first stars in the sky were reaching for it when she heard her name. She lifted her bow from the strings and noticed night's darkness for the first time. The dropping temperatures penetrated her skin.

Her time to herself was at an end. Selene stood among the trees enclosing the gyre. After playing for so long, it took Bronte a moment to bring her into focus. The shadows complicated the task. She studied her sister and waited for some sense of connection to form. It didn't.

Selene disappeared back into the trees. The gyre's vibes were probably too uncomfortable standing that close.

Bronte packed away her violin and stowed the case against a rock. She started toward the tree line, weaving in and out among the petrified tree trunks in an uneven maze to the gyre's edge. The tight trees standing sentinel let her pass through. A mass of mages gathered on the other side.

The Rallises were all present—except Vincent—as well as the judge and her court. Bronte wasn't sure why they needed to be here, but she wasn't going to ask. With a twist of bitterness, she noted her parents' presence. Phyllis sat in a chair that someone had dragged through the forest for her. She certainly hadn't performed the task for herself. She either still suffered from the effects of Selene's defense or had fooled them into believing it. A Casteel sentry, his uniform silvery-gray with a yellow sash, loomed behind Phyllis. Bronte remembered dozens of them guarding the Casteel house. He watched her, his focus visible in the moonlight.

"You're late." Selene's flat tone didn't carry far in the damp night air, but Bronte heard her clearly enough. The necromancer had changed out of her black suit and into brown canvas pants dotted with pockets and tucked into short boots. Her fleece jacket buttoned on the diagonal and had two more pockets. A black stocking cap hid her hair and accentuated her pale face. Bronte would have asked her how she was feeling, but she didn't think the frigid woman would welcome the inquiry.

Selene looked Bronte up and down, disapproving of her attire with a silent sneer. Bronte still wore her dress and boots. They weren't warm enough, but she wasn't going to complain in front of Selene.

Helen came to her rescue. She carried a coat and held it open. It was long, lined, and warm. Bronte slipped it on, colder than she'd realized.

"Thank you." She noted the gleam in Helen's eye. Not maternal pride exactly. More like a queen sending her army into battle and anticipating victory. She supposed a Rallis always expected to win, though what prize was there here?

Bronte searched for pockets to warm her fingers, but her hands slipped right down the front of the coat. No pockets. She used her sleeves as an impromptu muff.

"That was a beautiful song, darling. Sad though." Helen's breath puffed a cloud of condensation with each word. "Button up that jacket."

"It sounded like a funeral song. Appropriate for the occasion." Selene stared straight ahead, her gaze pointed beyond the white trees shining in the dark.

"That was not my intention at all." Bronte bristled to think someone would connect her new song to her grandfather—a man she'd hardly known and who had never done anything to help her. But considering Selene had saved her life and been injured in the process, Bronte decided not to take offense.

"His ashes would tremble to know that you dare hold yourself in such high regard." Phyllis's injuries had not damaged her nastiness. "Why would you possibly think you would have the honor of gracing him with music?"

Bronte was grateful Vincent wasn't here to witness this. She ignored her mother and focused on Selene. "Are you ready?"

Helen took up the battle for her. "Contrary to your point, Lady Casteel, you are the one who will miss the honor of hearing such music. You are blind to the gifts bestowed on your family, and you are no longer entitled to them. You'd be wise to curb your tongue since Bronte is helping to retrieve your medallion. She could just as easily hand it over to Edmund or me, or hold it for Vincent. Or she could put it around her neck and take the seat herself."

"Impossible!" Phyllis made to stand, but Bronte's father stopped her with a hand on her shoulder. His consoling pat had Bronte wanting to roll her eyes. Her father seemed meek compared to Phyllis, but Bronte didn't trust it.

"Let me be clear," Helen continued. "We tolerate your presence on our land only so you can remove the body corrupting the Rallis mark. The High Council asked us to permit your attendance. Know that the next time I see you, I will wipe your vibes clean of this Earth." The promise rang with power, multiplied by gyre's influence.

Apparently, Vincent got his warrior powers from his mother. Bronte wished she had some for herself.

"Let's begin before this night passes into dawn." Selene took charge.

Three men stepped out of the shadows, armed and fierce, with heavy glares for Selene. She ignored them.

"Miss Casteel, how long can you channel the power of the gyre?"

"I don't know, Miss Glender." The chances for a sisterly relationship appeared slim. "I've yet to discover a limit on how long I can be in here."

"If you lose control of the power when we're in there, it would be detrimental to my well-being."

"I don't anticipate it being a problem. If that changes, I'll let you know." Bronte's retort bounced off Selene's snooty demeanor.

"Yes, do so. As soon as possible." Selene turned to her men. "Stay prepared and keep your wires on." Selene tapped her ear. "I expect you to be standing ready when I exit the gyre. If you are not, the Council will be notified."

They stood with their arms crossed. Their sneers made it clear they would run right over Selene or leave her behind if they were allowed. They held no respect, much less affection, for the necromancer.

She turned to Bronte. "Instruct me on how you will make the gyre's power level appropriate for me. You were in it a moment ago, but the energy was still too much to cross."

Bronte took a breath. "When I did this before, I held Vincent's hand. And somehow it worked." All she received for her explanation was a glare. She tried again. "I think I channel enough power in my immediate vicinity to keep it away from anyone who's touching me." It sounded possible.

Selene extended her hand, a regal gesture. Bronte chafed but she took it and stepped backward toward the gyre. Selene didn't move. Their arms stretched between them. Bronte waited. Her sister slowly lifted a foot and placed it over what must have felt like a barrier to the gyre, a test for safety. Bronte took another step in.

Selene nodded, satisfied. "Let's go." Another step and the two walked through the circles of moonlit stones. Their joined hands formed a bridge between them as they went around the rocks.

Bronte bit back her questions until they were far enough in that no one would hear. "How did the High Council end up raising you?"

"How did you become so callous you could ignore the state of the Casteel people?"

Bitterness flung so hard and fast Bronte wanted to duck. "I didn't ignore them. I was kicked out. I survived on my own."

"Bullshit. You were plopped down in a private school."

"Look, I know nothing about the Casteels' problems. Even if I did, I couldn't have changed anything. I lived as a Non. I kept my head down to save my life. I stayed away from anything to do with mages in case one of them recognized what I am."

Selene huffed. "And now that you're through hiding, are you going to work for the good of the Casteel mages and Nons? Or are you too scared? The Casteel Territory's power is out of control. Their mages suffer." Her sour laugh echoed around the gyre. "Goddess, it all makes perfect sense now. The Casteels' salvation was handed to them in the form of a syphon who could regulate the land's power. And she ran away from home."

"Kicked out, envoy. And everything was fine when I left." Bronte looked away with a heart turned heavy and hard. Their dark walk was a perfect setting to share secrets and confidences. No one could get to them. It would have been just the place for two little girls with dozens of giddy secrets to tell each other. Selene's presence was a mirror of what might have been.

"Of course it was all fine. You were doing your job. You syphoned away the excess vibes. Then you abandoned your post, and it all went to hell for the people who live in Casteel's territory."

"If that's what happened, I didn't know. I couldn't sense it at all. The only vibes I can sense are Vincent's and this gyre. Leaving Casteel was no more my fault than it was yours. Why don't you go take up the cause of the Casteel people and better their land?"

They made it to the center where the tall, leaning stones formed the partial covering into the cave. This was as far as she'd ever been. Selene planted her feet. "I'm indentured to the High Council for one more month."

"Indentured? I thought only Non-mages could be indentured."

She shook her head like Bronte was an imbecile. "After that, I will have paid them in full for raising me. My service to them started when I was fifteen. It ends at the close of my thirtieth year."

What kind of childhood had the Council had offered Selene? It went a long way to explaining her personality.

"What will you do when you're done?" She couldn't help asking, though it was none of her business.

"What are you going to do now, syphon?" Selene countered. "Anything worthwhile?"

"What do you think I should do? Go back to Casteel Territory? Would that please you?"

Selene's pale skin glowed under the light of the waxing moon. "If you're looking to please people, you're bound to fail." Her tone turned absent. She looked away as if she couldn't hold Bronte's gaze. "The Council has two necromancer apprentices other than myself. They are two and four years old. They also have a siren, a dispirit, an oracle and three statics. But they are all of age, serving out their apprenticeships. Those two necromancers are practically babies. They have no true home within the Council. No mother. They will never find acceptance when they're freed. They have no hope for happiness. No one likes the dark side, after all. No one."

Selene's flowery mouth squeezed tight. The night's shadows washed over her and seemed to coax the darkness of her death power to bleed through her skin with a frightening glow. Bronte erased the thoughts as quickly as they came. She was falling prey to the prejudices that ran through mage society. She'd thought herself above that. "So what are you going to do? Take the kids?"

"Take them where?" Selene sounded as if she'd thought on the subject for quite a while and had yet to think of a suitable solution.

Bronte lifted her face to the moon, no longer full, but its white and gray glowed in the sky. "You could move back to Casteel and live with Mom and Dad. You seem to intimidate them. I'm sure you could use that to your advantage. Blackmail them. Tell them you'll expose them as coldhearted, horrible parents if they don't hide the kids." Bronte paused, her words snagging at threads in her memory. Was that what Selene had been trying to do at the hearing? Had she been saying that she would expose their parents' secret necromancer daughter if they didn't sign Bronte over to Casteel?

Selene raised an eyebrow. "A bit weak, sister."

Bronte shrugged. "I thought it was just a myth that the High Council took children."

Selene gave a self-deprecating laugh. "Of course they take children! Any child that will do them good. Any they want! And the good Mayflower families conveniently look away and let the Council have their head in most anything so long as it doesn't bother them.

"And you are the worst offender of all, did you know that? Poor, helpless little syphon. Doesn't even rank on anyone's scale of power until the badass colonel rubs up against you, or you step your delicate little toe into his gyre. Beautiful, independent Bronte Casteel thrown to the winds by her family, just keeps her head down, doesn't look around to see how anyone else might live who's right there in the winds with her."

"Selene, your bitterness is getting old. I'm sorry I didn't rescue you. But I didn't know you existed. Get over it." Bronte glared at her until Selene finally looked away.

A far away holler reached her ears and faded quickly, as if the sound was too exhausted to linger after traveling through the thick magic of the gyre. It was Gregor, she thought. "Everything alright, Bronte?"

Bronte waved her hand. "Oh yes," she said too softly for him to hear. "We're just fine, fast friends out here." She turned to Selene. "Let's finish this and get out of here."

* * * *

"It's going to be dark down there. Do you have your flashlight?"

Selene squinted at her. "Mages don't need flashlights."

"This mage does."

Selene circled her finger in the air. Instantly the entire gyre glowed with the power of a white sun. Bronte's ears burst with the pressure as a scorching pain burned her eyes. Reflexes forced them closed, but even the speed of a blink was too slow to protect her vision. The light seared through her eyelids. She buried her face in the crook of her elbow as the pained protests of those who stood watching them drifted over. Selene's hand jerked away from Bronte's for the briefest moment. The light flared uncontrollably, penetrating the minuscule cracks in Bronte's makeshift barriers.

"Hellhounds!" The swear sounded as if it were yanked out of the woman and stuffed back down at the same time. Selene groped at Bronte's arm until she found her hand again. The light extinguished. "Damn it to the stars but that hurt. I can't see a shitty sacred thing."

It was no comfort to hear that Selene couldn't see either.

"Maybe a flashlight would be safer than mage light." Her words were muffled beneath her arm. "I think the gyre makes it harder to control your sixth sense."

"I do not have a blessed flashlight! How about we use yours?" Selene's sarcastic lash was woven with embarrassment over her lack of control.

Bronte stayed silent.

"What?" Selene continued, "Don't you have one handy in your pocket?"

"You're the one with all the pockets!"

Bronte moved her arm from her eyes but kept them closed. The inside of her eyelids flamed red. She slowly lifted them, but the view didn't change. The world was on fire. "It wouldn't do me any good at the moment anyway."

"Your vision will come back." Selene's voice was clipped. "Nothing's dead on your eyes. I can tell from here. You smell nothing like rot, not even the smallest nerve."

"How reassuring. Thank you." Even as she spoke, her peripheral vision slowly returned. The red bleeding across her line of sight collapsed in and left the edges of her vision clear. "How about you? Are you rotting anywhere?"

"No more than usual. I can't believe I did that in front of everyone. The Council guards aren't going to forget it." Selene's head drooped. "I suck at mage light. It's at the opposite end of the spectrum from death energy."

"Don't feel bad. Vincent was hesitant to even try his mage power in here."

Selene's head shot up. "Why the hell didn't you tell me that before we came in here?"

"Because I didn't think of it before!" She waited for the insults, but they didn't come. "We still need a light. Should we go ask if anyone brought one?" Besides, it was a good excuse to put off the inevitable dead body search.

"No!" Selene's protest shot through the air. "We are not going back there without accomplishing our mission. We return only when we have something to show for all this." Selene had a dot of a light going before she finished. Bronte's ears whispered a protest at the spell, but the pressure was manageable.

The light hovered above Selene's fingers like a baby bird undergoing a growth spurt so rapid its feathers burst from its body. Sparks drifted down to the ground and disappeared into the dirt. When the light spell steadied, it was no bigger than the tip of Selene's pert little nose. The utter blackness of the cave would devour that meager beam. They'd probably trip over the body.

"Let's go." Selene's words sounded defensive, as if she'd heard Bronte's thoughts. The necromancer led the way, their arms stretching between them before Bronte moved her feet. The light went first. It moved between the two tall rocks in the middle of the gyre and then down into the opening in the ground. It lit the cave walls with a golden glow. Selene descended like she stepped down a spiral staircase, most of her body still above the ground as she turned once, and then Bronte was pulled down with her onto the descending ramp.

Instantly the power of the gyre changed. Its energy deepened as if somewhere down here the heart of the goddess beat. Life pulsed from it. She was in the presence of the sacred. She opened her mouth to tell Selene.

"It's not far. I can smell it." Selene's glee sizzled through the cave.

Bronte closed her mouth with a snap. Selene was unlikely to appreciate sacredness at the moment. Instead, her sister murmured about the decay rates of mage bodies, a forensic mage on the case.

"Do you track down bodies in caves often?"

"Not in caves, no."

Bronte decided she didn't want to know where Selene worked. The woman probably traveled all over since it was unlikely that bodies showed up in the Council House frequently. Or maybe they did. Considering they took babies, Bronte was quite uninformed about how they worked.

They walked down the twirling cave in single file, the passage so tight in places Bronte's shoulders brushed both sides of the cave at the same time. They descended farther. The circumference of the tight circles loosened wider and wider. The energy spiraled up to meet her. She could have closed her eyes to luxuriate in the feeling.

Except she risked tripping over a dead body.

Reaching out a hand, she let her fingers run along the wall as they walked by. It was grooved with a thousand tiny channels as if water had rushed by them in individual currents the width of a thread. But it wasn't water that had marked them. It was the goddess's energy.

"I wonder who brought him down here," Bronte whispered.

"You could have done it."

"I didn't!" Surely she wasn't about to come under suspicion for this. General Wilen would have questioned her about it.

"You're right. You're too wimpy. It would have taken someone brave. Bold. Willing to take on a fight for the good of others. Someone courageous enough to take the Casteels' power and hand it to their enemies in hopes that this family could help."

Bronte stumbled to a halt. "Really? Is that how you describe Double-Wide? Bold and brave?"

Selene halted and spun around. "What?"

"Double-Wide. They took the body."

"No, they…" Selene shook her head with a squint of her brow. She closed her eyes and slumped against the wall of the cave. "Blasted hells." She dropped her head with the whispered curse. "I suppose it doesn't matter anymore."

"What doesn't matter?"

Selene opened her eyes. "Nothing that concerns you." A sneer accompanied the snide comment.

"You know, I'm tired of your attitude." She took the lead and yanked Selene down the gyre, circling through the cave with a fury.

Selene halted after a half-dozen turns. "We're close. Let me take the lead. I want to see the body before you trip over it." She slid past her and led them for a single loop down the cave before she stopped. She cocked her head, focused on something in front of her. The body.

Bronte froze, keeping her eyes on Selene's shoulders, but avoiding visual contact with the body didn't work. Her sister crouched down and pulled Bronte with her, giving her a glimpse of dark shoes and suit pants at the other end. Selene leaned over his head, blocking her view.

"He's amazingly well-preserved. The embalmer did a superb job." Selene held out her free hand over the body and let it hover over his torso.

"Great," Bronte squeaked, staring firmly at the wall.

"Oh, don't act like a Non. It's part of life, and it's going to happen to you too. I swear by the universe, I don't understand how Nons can live so detached from death. It's time to face the life cycle, sweetheart. Move your hand to the back of my neck. I need both hands free to find out if he died of natural causes. Not that I'm sorry he's dead. I would have killed him myself if I'd had the chance."

"That sounds like a confession to keep between sisters. If I told people that, you'd probably become a suspect, especially considering you're his discarded granddaughter."

"Does that put you under suspicion too?"

"I think I was for awhile."

"There are a lot of people who wanted him dead. He ruled a territory filled with his enemies, Nons and mages alike. Now, do you think touching me on the neck will work? Or is touching a bone witch there too much for you?"

Bronte sighed long and slow. Keeping her right hand clasped in Selene's, she took her left hand and placed it on the back of her sister's bare neck. Then she let go of her sister's hand. "Does the attitude come with the gift?"

"Does cowardliness come with yours?" Selene's hands hovered above the body and froze, her head bent slightly.

"I'm so glad we've had some time to get to know each other better."

"Poison." Selene spat the word.

Bronte nodded. It was a good way to describe their time together.

"Ingested at the mouth."

A good murder weapon, too.

"There are still traces of it despite the powerful cleanse. Did it absorb in the mouth, or in the gut? I can't be certain. Most likely in the gut." Selene conversed with herself. She leaned farther over the body, forcing Bronte to do the same to keep touching her neck. Selene leaned over the senator's head until she was close enough to kiss his lips. If only Selene's hair had been out of its hat, Bronte wouldn't have witnessed it.

"Tell me you're not going to kiss him. Please tell me that." Bronte put a knee on the ground to keep her balance.

Selene looked over at her. Her face glowed eerily with the mage light floating above the body. She smiled and pulled the senator's mouth open with a finger on his chin.

"Oh goddess."

Selene turned back to the body. Her mouth hovered over his. Bronte felt the breath pull into her sister. The pressure in her ears tripled and then eased as Selene moved from the senator's face. His cheeks looked pink… surely because of the light.

"This is a new one." She sounded troubled. "No potion I know feels like this. And I know all the potions." She sat back on one heel. "I can get him out." Her tone was confident, but there was something dark in it. Something that made Bronte not want to inquire how exactly she could do this. "But the medallion has to come off before I can do that."

"Then you have a problem."

"You take it off." Selene said "you" as if Bronte were a nameless subject in the presence of a royal personage. "Come on. This is your chance. Stick it to our family. They threw you out like a sick, disfigured pup born to a pedigreed dog."

"A colorful description, but I decline your kind offer."

"Come on, Bronte. This is your chance. It has to come off. The only other choice is to bring our father down here and have him do it. That makes two of us you'll have to guide. And even if you can do that, you don't want him down here, do you? He'd muck up the energy of this place you love."

"You do it." Bronte had no desire to touch that medallion.

"Death magic may affect the medallion," Selene admitted. "I don't know for sure. But there's a good possibility. Once death magic has touched something, it never un-touches. If the medallion soaks up what I'm about to give the senator, it will never work again. The people in Casteel Territory will truly lose what binds them to the land. The latest riots and fights will be nothing compared to what will happen if the medallion loses its control over the territory." Selene raised her eyebrows in a what-do-you-think-of-that expression. "Since you're a Casteel, it should come off for you."

"I don't know how to take it off." She looked down at her grandfather. Selene had closed his mouth and now his lips were overly smashed together. He looked as if he disapproved of all this. His closed eyes were tipped with stubby eyelashes. His crop of white hair stuck up everywhere. A definite case of bed head. Or rather dead head. Bronte was certain Selene would not be amused.

The medallion drooped to the left side of his chest, a golden gleam in Selene's light. Plain in design, the pendant was a golden, hollow circle, about four inches in diameter. The chain was made of thin, circular loops, each about an inch long. Such a simple item to cause so much trouble, to symbolize a claim on one of the Republic's territories, and to hold so much powerful energy.

"Oh, fine," Bronte muttered.

"Great." Selene sounded like Bronte had just agreed to go out for a night on the town. "I'm going to need both hands to shift him in order for you to reach the clasp. You'll need both hands too." Selene still sounded way too enthusiastic. "Push your sleeve way up and we'll put our bare arms together. That way you can still touch me. Goddess help us if I lose contact with you. I'll lift his head. You reach under and unclasp it."

Bronte did as ordered, maneuvering the right sleeves of her coat and dress high enough to bare her arms, an awkward process without being able to take her hand from Selene's neck. Maintaining the connection was vital for their safety. Her sleeves squeezed so tightly above her elbow the nerves tingled down her arm.

Selene scrunched up the sleeves of her left side. Bronte placed her bared right forearm next to Selene's left, and then removed her hand from her neck. Without another word, Selene lifted the senator's head off the ground and exposed the chain of the medallion. Bronte slid her bare arm under Selene's, their skin rubbing together. She reached for the chain with both hands. The medallion came apart at her slight pull and fell free of its former owner.

"Now put it on and tuck it under your shirt. Keep the thing protected from what I'm about to do."

"Very funny. I am not putting this around my neck. If it fastened around me, I'd be stuck as the Casteel senator and zapped to death by a spell the first time I had to step onto the Rushes. Unless you plan to throw yourself in front of me every time. Which means you'd have to hang around me constantly. Sound like fun? If I had a pocket, I'd put it there, but I don't."

"Pockets won't work. To keep it safe, it has to be next to your skin. How about you stuff it under your sleeve?" Selene's voice sounded long-suffering. "Then you can hand it over to your sponsors like the good little Non you used to be. Rallis is the only family strong enough to take over another territory. Just be sure to keep it next to your skin. If the safest place for me is next to your skin, then the same goes for that old artifact."

"Fine. I'll stick it up my sleeve." They carefully switched their contact point so Selene held Bronte's neck. Bronte held the medallion against her right arm and wiggled her sleeve over it, going slowly since it was a tight fit. She tucked the chain inside the tight fabric as well.

She shivered as the medallion's power moved across her skin. Energy never did that to her, not Vincent's, not even the gyre's. Their powers went inside to her syphon. They didn't crawl over her skin. She tried to ignore it.

"Satisfied?" Bronte asked.

Selene rolled her eyes and muttered something about a wimp. "Let's get him out of here. We're going to move down to his feet."

"But he takes up the entire space. There's no way past him." Bronte's protest went unheard as Selene took her hand and then stepped down the length of the body. The toes of Selene's shoes slipped under him as she shuffled down the wall. It was either that or step on him. Bronte shoved her boot under Grandpa's shoulder. The boot's fine suede grabbed at his suit. His arm flopped and landed against her shin. A moan gurgled from her throat. She kicked his arm away. It landed with a flop against his chest.

As soon as they passed him, she stepped behind Selene, giving her room to do whatever she had planned. At least, that was her excuse.

"I'm dousing the light for a minute. I need to concentrate on one energy at a time." Selene's glow dimmed until it disappeared. A black ocean surrounded them, so viscous it held Bronte immobile. It didn't matter how widely she opened her eyes. Darkness consumed her world. She reached for the wall, needing the reassurance it still stood beside her in the utter black.

A series of shuffles sounded in front of her. Her ears squeezed from the pressure. Finally the light's glow returned, increasing the pressure in her ears, but she'd take it. Anything to wash away the darkness.

Before her stood the late Senator Casteel, eyes closed, mouth closed, belly protruding a breath away from Selene, and his head inches from the ceiling.

A note of fear sang out of Bronte. She tried to clip it short, but it stopped only because she ran out of air.

"Hellhounds, it's so weird down here." Selene sounded amazed.

"Yeah," Bronte agreed shakily.

"It's so easy it's almost hard. I barely need to pull any vibes at all." Selene gave a little move of her head, not quite a nod, more of a brief thrusting of her chin. Senator Casteel's body stepped backward along the spiral.

"Um, do you think you could make him turn around?" Bronte was careful to keep her volume low, her tone calm, her panic buried.

Selene gave a weary sigh.

He spun around.

It was a slow procession. Weren't they a freaky parade? A dead man controlled by a necromancer who held hands with a syphon. Her parents would vibe out of their senses.

As she stepped up the incline, a sense of relief poured through her. It was almost over. She relaxed as much as possible with ears ready to burst, all while following a walking corpse. Energy from the gyre flowed through her faster as if calming had decreased its friction. The senator's feet lost their rhythm for a moment, and he walked into the cave wall.

"Syphon, what the hell?" Selene stopped to recover control of the body. "Control it."

"My apologies, necromancer. I don't have much experience at this."

The air cooled as they approached the cave's opening. Wind swirled past her as they stepped into the night air. The senator's hair moved with the breeze. Selene's mage light glowed as they walked through the stones of the gyre. It danced above them like a little white moon. She was probably showing off to prove to the Council guards she had enough control for this.

Selene's light impressed a moth at least. It fluttered around before they were ten feet out of the cave.

The crowd ahead grew noisy at their approach. Bronte recognized her mother's squeal above the rest. The waiting mages stepped to the edge, standing among the white trees guarding the gyre, too close for comfort, but none moved away. Even Phyllis was out of her chair.

"Sergeant Tyler, throw the body bag to my feet!" Selene's holler cut through the air as they reached the edge.

"He's alive!" Phyllis shrieked. Selene disagreed and tried to explain it, but Phyllis had a long habit of not listening to anyone, no matter the message. Bronte remembered that well.

"Can he speak?"

"Only what I tell him to say. And since I don't know precisely what killed him, I can't make him say it, if that's where you're going with this.

I'm taking him back to my lab. You'll get the body back when I've taken energy samples."

"Where's the medallion? Where is it?"

Selene ignored their mother as the sergeant tossed the body bag on her right foot. She bent down to open it.

Bronte, feeling like a coroner's assistant, helped. Together they were two-handed. Even this close to the edge of the gyre, the power would be too intense for Selene without Bronte's touch.

Selene unzipped the flat, crisp material, and dropped to her knees as she stretched down the length of the long bag. Then she stood, brushed off her pants with one hand and nodded at the senator's back.

He lay down on the bag like a trained dog.

Bronte helped enclose him within the plastic, a task requiring multiple hands since some of the bag was stuck under the body. His weight was almost too much for them. She huffed in disgust every time she had to touch him. Finally Bronte zipped up the bottom half and Selene finished the top part.

An absurd sense of satisfaction drifted through her at a job well done.

"Where is the medallion, you lousy girl?" Phyllis hissed. Bronte looked over to respond but found that Phyllis was looking at Selene. To speak to the Council's envoy so disrespectfully was risky, even for her mother.

"Bronte, grab the other corner here." Selene ignored Phyllis and picked up one corner of the foot of the bag. "We're going to drag it over to the trees. The guards can pull it the rest of the way out."

Bronte did as instructed. The two struggled to haul the 200-pound body a mere five feet. The Council guards pushed Phyllis aside, disregarding her protests. They reached in and yanked the bag out. The broadest of the guards slung the body bag over his shoulder.

Bronte swallowed hard and looked away, trying hard to forget about the contents of the plastic.

The trio of men departed and headed toward the road. They ignored the gardener mage, who stood behind a tree, peeking his head around in a halfhearted attempt at hiding.

Tonight's performance had attracted quite a crowd.

Phyllis hobbled after the Council's men. "Stop! I need the medallion!"

Her husband added his own demands with the righteous anger of the privileged.

Selene's soft voice cut through it all. "Bronte has it."

Chapter 17

Her sister threw her to the wolves with the simple words. Bronte swayed against the force of every gaze shifting to her. They stared from between the tight trees like an army ready to storm her defenses. She held her ground. Phyllis prowled forward to the edge of the gyre. Her injuries forgotten, she radiated an energetic violence. The woman had more reason than ever to invoke the Right of Creator.

"Spells can come in," Bronte whispered the warning to Selene as softly as she could, not wanting to give her mother any ideas. Vincent wasn't here to shield her this time. Gregor and Dane were ready to pounce, but they couldn't get in.

Gregor waved for her to come out of the gyre.

Bronte took two steps to scramble to their side, but Selene yanked so hard on her arm her shoulder joint popped a warning. Worse, her fingers ached with a sharp pain from Selene's squeeze.

"Don't you dare hurt my fingers or I'll…suck all your power out," Bronte hissed.

"Pfft." Selene rolled her eyes at Bronte's words, though her gaze was directed at their mother. Selene wore a tiny, vicious smile. Her sister had a lot of little teeth.

Phyllis tossed her head back and laughed. "Isn't this sweet? Two monstrosities united at last. You won't win."

Bronte shook her head. No, she wouldn't win against her mother. She didn't even want to play her games. Phyllis was too powerful. Bronte opened her mouth to surrender, but Selene squeezed tighter. Crushed fingers would not glide over violin strings.

She glanced at Dane and Gregor. Dane thrust two fingers in the air and pointed them toward his own eyes and then at Selene, as if he wanted Bronte to poke Selene's eyes out. He nodded encouragingly…and then rolled his eyes as she just stood there. He changed tactics and wove through the trees toward Phyllis.

"Actually," Selene began with a voice loud enough to carry through the woods, "I think we might win."

Time to put an end to this pointless scene.

"The medallion is safe in my sleeve." She looked at Selene. They were the same height. "I don't want it. I'm stepping out of the gyre now. You can either come with me or not." She wanted this medallion gone. It was the catalyst for the entire mess stewing around her. If it hadn't gone missing, she'd still be in Chattanooga playing music…and helping Double-Wide kill people, she thought sourly. And never experiencing the pleasure of her syphon pulling at Vincent's energy, a little voice in her head added.

"Go ahead. Give it to them." Selene led the way out through the trees and then looked back at Bronte with a daring spark in her eyes. That proud little smile still graced her lips.

Dane and Gregor gathered around her the moment she stepped out of the gyre. Selene kept pulling her, holding tightly to Bronte's hand so that slipping free would take an aggressive effort. She stopped in a clearing large enough that all the mages could gather around. Evidently her sister wanted the audience to have a clear view.

Selene held her mage light between them.

Bronte ignored the pressure in her ears as she gathered her sleeves up her arm.

"Don't any of you touch it," warned Phyllis. "That medallion belongs to no one but my husband." She crunched through the underbrush toward them but halted when Gregor stepped forward. Phyllis bristled in silence.

The medallion, tucked high up the dress sleeve, was being stubborn about coming out. Bronte caught a link of the chain and, working it back and forth, slid it free of the soft dress. It slid down her exposed right arm and got stuck at the top of her hand.

She wiggled her arm to set it free, a loose shake that reverberated through her body until the tremble took on a life of its own.

Get off, get off, get off. The words chanted through her head. An order, a plea, a prayer. She clenched her jaw to stop her chattering teeth.

The golden hollow circle, the symbol that represented the Casteel claim as a founding family, clung to her arm. The chain had threaded through the open design of the medallion, ensnared it, and then wrapped around her. The medallion had clasped itself to her.

Its golden circle lay flat on the top of her wrist. She tried to slide it off. It didn't budge. She squeezed her fingers together, making them as small as possible and tried again, but no luck. The slippery, nervous sweat coating her skin made no difference.

Her horror at the metal clinging to her stole her breath. "I didn't even put it on." Her airy words floated away into nothing. "I just…I just stuffed it up my sleeve."

"Mages, we have a new Senator Casteel." Selene's smile encompassed her entire face.

Bronte jerked her head up to stare at her sister. She'd been wrong. Happiness did not add even a hint of loveliness to the necromancer's face.

"Phyllis, I'd watch what I threw out as trash from now on. Hard to know what's going to come in *handy* in the future." Selene grabbed Bronte's wrist and shook her hand like a rag in the air.

"Are you crazy?" Bronte cried.

"Yes, that was a terrible joke," Edmund cut in with a dry, bored tone.

Bronte's face squeezed almost involuntarily, but she bit back the sob just in time. "Did you know this would happen?"

A sound spelled popped into place around them. Her ears clogged with the pressure as Selene began to whisper. "You are the only hope the Casteel mages have. I can't risk being senator, although I would be a better one than you." Selene must have felt Bronte tense. "Oh come on, don't be offended, you big baby. I've lived my entire life with the ultimate politicians. I've learned a thing or two. But my power would kill the medallion. This has gone even better than we'd planned. Now, dear sister, live up to expectations." Selene pulled back her energy cast.

Bronte's ears readjusted. She wanted to shove her sister away, to rail at her for this betrayal, but she refused to break down in front of her mother. She'd just become her mother's number one enemy. Before this, she'd been an embarrassment who'd ruin her heir's power. Now she'd stolen Phyllis's husband's inheritance and their claim to political power.

Phyllis sped toward her in the dark forest and grabbed the medallion. Bronte's wrist was wrenched apart. Her skin peeled into layers as her mother pulled. "Stop it, Mother!" Streaks of energy jolted into her arm.

"Never call me that!" Phyllis heaved with anger.

The Casteel sentry hurried forward, but Dane beat him. He shoved Phyllis to the ground, pulling Bronte behind him. The woman landed flat on her back.

Helen stepped forward, battle-ready. "You may not consider her your daughter, but I consider her mine. No daughter of mine is to be treated like that. Your presence is no longer welcome on Rallis land."

"Our sincerest apologies, Lady Rallis." Bronte's father spoke, conciliatory and placating.

Helen lifted a brow and looked down her nose at him. Quite a trick, since Lord Casteel was five inches taller.

He stepped over his wife's prone figure. "If you would give me a few moments to get the medallion off, I'm sure the chain will release at my touch." He turned toward Bronte, but kept talking to Helen, as if Bronte was of no consequence. "You have no idea the strain my wife has been under because of this…" Though he gestured at Bronte, he broke off, political smarts serving him in that at least.

"Take it. I don't want it." Bronte thrust her wrist out to her father. It brushed against both Gregor and Danc, who stood in front of her. That slight touch shot streaks of pain into her. Her mother had done some damage.

Selene crossed her arms over her chest and looked away.

Lord Casteel bent over, pulling a mage light close to her wrist, and examined it until her arm wanted to shake from holding it out.

"Just pull," Bronte ordered. "It will come apart somehow. That's what I did, anyway."

"Pull where?" The frustration in her father's words grated against her exhausted nerves.

"Anywhere!"

He grasped the chain with both hands and yanked. Her stomach rolled over and over at the sensation. Her nausea tripled as a force vibrated over the medallion. Her ears strained to pop as he used a spell to get it apart. She closed her eyes and breathed through the pain. He jerked again using physical force and physical magic—a duo that did nothing.

"Stop." A shove against his hands accompanied her demand. She couldn't take it anymore. Her two guards stepped in front of her.

Phyllis bellowed in rage, but Lord Casteel obeyed. He collided with his wife as he backed away and bent to whisper in her ear. His voice carried in bits and pieces. "Let her… Rushes… spells…when she's dead…"

Perfectly staged, Bronte thought, her suspicions about who was the real force in the family growing. Or perhaps they were equally dangerous.

Selene smiled triumphantly and walked off into the woods with a breezy wave to Bronte.

The Rallis gardener stepped out from among the trees and fell into step with her.

Bronte's breath echoed in her ears. The medallion around her wrist might as well be a rock tied to her ankle, and Selene had shoved her into deep waters. Bronte could do without that kind of sisterly love. A syphon mage as a senator would be nothing more than fodder on the floor of the Rushes. Her parents knew it too. Phyllis's laugh reverberated through the woods as she and her husband left the scene.

Bronte placed her right hand over her chest and covered the medallion with her left, hugging herself. She could almost imagine Vincent's arms around her. He'd tell her they'd get through this together, or if he was in colonel-mode, that he'd take care of this for her. Lies, both. No one could conjure a remedy for this. But right now, hearing his reassurances would have been a mental life preserver against the wave of fear threatening to crash over her. As it was, she'd have to find her own way to ride out her fear. She pivoted and walked back to into the gyre.

"Where are you going?" Dane called.

"Violin."

The energy of the gyre was a faint comfort. Her tired feet dragged over its bare ground. She picked up the cool handle of the black case. None of her tension eased, but simply holding the instrument was like being in the presence of an old friend. She'd take whatever consolation she could find.

The long walk out of the gyre and through the woods stole the little stamina she had left, but she refused to let anyone else carry the instrument. The Rallises led the way as if they knew she wanted to be left alone. Dane and Gregor were silent as they surrounded her on either side. Somewhere above them an owl called out. Far away, another hooted back.

Finally they broke out of the woods. Two cars waited on the gravel road.

A man called from behind the group. "Senator Casteel!"

Bronte spun around. Gregor stepped in front of her. Both of her guards pulled weapons from hiding spots she'd not noticed before. She tried to peek around, but Gregor shuffled back and forth with her and prevented her from seeing the speaker.

"Another step and I'll shoot," Dane warned.

"I mean no harm to the senator. My name is William Ansel. I am the head Casteel sentry. As she is now the senator of the territory, it is my job to guard her, the medallion and the land. It is a duty I take very seriously."

"Guarding her is a duty I take seriously as well." Dane's voice growled. "And I guarantee you are not getting any closer to her, no matter who you are." A crunch of leaves sounded. A bright red light flashed through the darkness. A groan and a *thump* followed. "I'm a man of my word, Ansel."

"You shot him?" Bronte's voice pitched high with shock. She leaned around Gregor only to have him block her.

"The Rallis sentries are on their way," Dane continued. "They're gonna escort you to the gate, close it behind you, and stick a nice spell on it. You should go find a healer. You can take this up with the colonel when he gets back. Until then, his lady is under my watch."

"Senator Casteel." The word was forced through gritted teeth. "Please listen. Your people need you."

The headlights of three vehicles sped their way—the Rallis sentries racing toward them.

"Later, Ansel," Gregor crooned. He shoved Bronte into the first vehicle after Helen and practically sat on top of her as he got in.

"You shot him?" she rasped at Dane.

"Bronte, senator," Gregor corrected himself, "that man lives with your parents. He hid in the woods to get to you. Until we know differently, we assume he's on their side. Besides, he'll be fine. Dane shot him in the leg, not the heart."

She let go of a shaky breath and closed her eyes, resisting the urge to ask if Vincent was back. If he were, he'd be here. She bit her lip to stop its tremble. The driver turned the car around and started toward the big house.

"Wait." Her voice broke, and she had to clear her throat before she could go on. "I…want to go back to Vincent's. Would you turn back around and drop me off first?"

The driver looked at Helen in the rearview mirror. She shook her head discreetly and turned to Bronte. "Darling, it's empty out there. Come back to the big house and let us take care of you. Just for tonight." She kept talking over Bronte's protest. "If you stay at Vincent's, Gregor and Dane are going to have to stay out on the porch all night or sleep in that little cottage with you. And there's no door on the bedroom."

"Lady Rallis, neither Dane nor I would ever…"

Helen held up a hand. "I know. But it will be more comfortable for everyone if Bronte stays in a house with multiple bedrooms and full of sentries. Vincent would agree, I'm sure."

The Rallis matriarch got her way. Within minutes Bronte found herself ushered into a bedroom upstairs in the big house. As Helen bustled around the grand room and its connected bath, Bronte mulled over ways to get the damn medallion off. As if there were a real solution.

Allison stuck her head in. A nervous energy radiated around her. "Did you find the body? Do the Casteels have their medallion?"

The water came on in the bathroom, and Helen briskly stepped out.

"Shower's ready. Bathrobe is on the back of the door." Helen steered Bronte into the bathroom. "I'll bring up a tray of food. You need to eat something. You barely ate a thing for lunch, and you missed dinner entirely." She shut Bronte into the steaming room.

"Well?" Allison asked.

"Bronte has the medallion," Helen said. Her voice carried through the door.

"Oh! It's as good as ours then." Allison's giddy enthusiasm was audible behind the closed door.

"I know," Helen's eager tone faded away.

* * * *

She had to get rid of this thing before it killed her. She pulled her right hand from under the bed's soft blankets and lifted it in the air. Dawn light shimmering through the cracks in the damask curtains glinted against the golden links. The weight of the medallion and its chain was strangely light, though its hard bulk was an alien presence on her wrist.

She'd wallowed in despair for most of the night. Her pillow was still damp with tears. Alas, her emotional frenzy had not repelled the medallion. Like a noose around her future, this chain strangled all her options and all her dreams. A senator could not make a living as a violinist, nor could a senator move out of the Republic. A senator stayed with her land.

As Vincent would stay with his, she thought. Her syphon power wasn't so tuned to his energy that she'd become dependent on him. Not yet. Though he was gone, a faint thread of his energy hovered around her. It made sense that it would linger within his own home. Living in Casteel, she'd be empty without him. A fresh round of sobs threatened to bubble up. She bit them back. She faced bigger problems than a lonely heart.

A senator could not be defenseless against spells.

The Casteel medallion had to go.

It was time to get physical with this thing. She stared up at the molded ceiling and plotted possible solutions. If she coated her hand in butter, maybe it would slip off. Or if she numbed her hand in an ice bath and then wrapped hot towels around the golden chain, she could shrink her hand but expand the metal. If neither of those plans succeeded, she could cut the chain. Perhaps the gardener had a pair of metal cutters.

Short of that, she could cut off her hand. A sob jerked out of her so hard it hurt. She put her hand over her eyes, and the medallion clunked against her nose. An ache spread across her face, a painful prompt to action.

She tossed off the heavy covers and slid down from the tall bed. Helen had left her a silk robe draped across an upholstered chair. Bronte tied herself securely inside it and headed down the hall and the long stairs to the kitchen.

Dane strolled beside her. "Breakfast time, senator?"

"Yes." It was easier than explaining.

He stepped into the cavernous room first, powered the lights, and inspected the area. "I can't cook," Dane stated. "Gregor can."

"I wasn't asking you to." Bronte's calm voice belied her tumultuous night. "You don't have to stay in here."

Dane narrowed his eyes. "Really."

"I'm not going anywhere. I'm in my robe."

He tipped his head. "You stay in the kitchen, and I'll wait in the hall."

She gave him a quick nod in agreement. The moment he was gone, she searched out a stick of butter from the broad depths of the gleaming refrigerator. Standing over the sink, she rubbed the yellow, fatty substance over her hand. The medallion and every link on its chain got a hefty coating as well. Maybe getting dressed first would have been wise. The robe's wide sleeve fell around her lubricated wrist and stuck among the butter. She sniffed, residual tears leftover from the night. She should have blown her nose first, too.

With half of the stick gone, she placed the butter on the counter and analyzed every possible position of her hand to determine the smallest circumference. She pushed, pulled, and tugged so hard the skin on either side of her hands gleamed white around the golden chain. Already sore from her mother's treatment, her hand and fingers swelled red and then blue. She forced herself to breathe through the pain and didn't stop tugging until black spots began to grow before her eyes.

By the time she gave up, purple bruises encircled her wrist and hand. The flutter of the kitchen door coincided with her sorrowful sigh. She looked over her shoulder to see Allison, bleary-eyed and a bit green.

"Good morning, Senator Casteel." She peered over Bronte's shoulder. "Wow. You want some toast to go with that butter?"

The door whooshed again. "I'll take care of that toast for you, senator." A soft lilting voice came from the doorway. "Straight up, no potions." The speaker was a tall, broad woman with gray hair, an apron and a generous smile. "And for you, Miss Rallis, some tea?"

Allison nodded and sat down at a bar stool while the cook busied around the kitchen.

Bronte watched, uncomfortable with having someone make her toast, but she could imagine the cook's reaction if a senator offered to cook for herself.

In no time the cook placed it before her on a porcelain plate marked with the Rallis crest. With no appetite, Bronte pretended to nibble at the toast with a freshly clean left hand. The right one was too sore to move.

Allison stared at her. "Your new car is supposed to be delivered at three-quarters morning."

"New car?" Bronte didn't bother trying to calculate mage time. It had been a relief to hear everyone using standard time around here until now.

"Guess Aunt Helen thought a senator to ought drive something other than an old clunker. The new car will match the new clothes she ordered for you. I'm probably ruining the surprise, huh?" Allison took a sip of tea. "But you don't look like you need anymore surprises. She also ordered a whole bunch of notebooks and scrolls with music staffs in them instead of regular lines. What do you call those?" She didn't wait for an answer. "She wasn't sure if you preferred notebooks or scrolls, so she bought both.

"She's suiting up for a new senator to take residence here. She's ordered the maids to clear out a room to use as your office, since Vincent's house isn't big enough." Another sip of tea. "I think she's kind of lost it really. I mean, everyone knows a senator lives in his own territory unless he is at the Rushes." The brunette looked at her hard. "If you don't like the clothes, give them to me. I made sure I liked them before she placed the order. So don't return them to the designer."

Bronte shook her head, searching through her shock for her voice. "I don't want or need a new car."

"Too bad. The old one is already gone as of a quarter of dawn. I heard the guy drive away. I can't sleep at all, coming off these potions." She sighed roughly. "Oh dark vibes, if I could have just one potion, I'd feel so much better. I even know the one I'd choose. A little *calminia*. I could sleep." Allison sounded wistful. She sniffled. "I miss Lawry. Even if he messed up. I mess up too, you know? All the time. It's not fair that I can't see him anymore just because he talked to a reporter. It's what he does! He talks to people. On television even. And he creates potions."

Bronte interrupted her. "Where did they take my car?" This family was driving her nuts. They got rid of her car without asking?

"Junkyard probably. By the stars, Bronte, nobody would want that thing. If the metallist is smart at all, he'll put your car at the top of his to-be-crushed list."

Tears burned Bronte's nose and then spilled into her eyes and down her cheeks. Her car had been a loyal ally. She blinked another tear free as the beginnings of a plan formed in her head, but it did not include rescuing her Volvo.

"Oh, Bronte, don't cry. The new car is much better. Sleek, shiny white. They took off the standard spell to keep it clean. Aunt Helen wasn't sure if you'd be comfortable in a car with a spell. But they can always put it back on. It has a petrol engine instead of a mage engine. Except for that, it's a real beaut."

"My old car was a real beaut too!"

"Right." Allison leaned back at Bronte's vehemence. "Sure, senator."

"Where is the junkyard?" With its metallist, she added silently.

"Somewhere in the Drainpipe. But no one goes to that neighborhood. Who would? It's mostly dark mages there, and nobody likes the dark. I can't believe you had to work with a necromancer yesterday." Allison shivered and then waved a hand in the air. "The metallist is somewhere on the other side of the Scioto. Dell might know. The gardener. He knows everything."

Bronte hustled back upstairs, picking up Gregor along the way, thankful he'd taken over from Dane. He stayed outside her designated bedroom as she tossed on the dress and boots she'd worn the night before, not bothering to look around for any new clothes, though she suspected her fairy clothes-mother had poofed in.

She dashed out of the room and back down the stairs without a word to Gregor.

"Big plans, senator?" Gregor asked as he slid in front of her.

"Yes." She paused at the bottom of the staircase. "Which way is the front door?"

"You leaving?" Surprise and caution pulled his voice higher.

Bronte chose to go straight ahead. It dead-ended into a hallway with three doors. Backtracking, she tried the left and strode past a portrait of a Rallis ancestor in a military uniform so decorated he must have been commander of the entire army.

"Because we should go over the ground rules if you're starting to feel adventurous." Gregor marched along beside her with as determined a pace as hers. "Number one, you're not leaving. Number two, don't go within sight of the gates. Number three, don't go anywhere on the estate without either Dane or I."

Success this time. The gleam of the foyer appeared ahead. She rushed down the hallway to the open space. Gregor sprinted around her.

"Number four, Dane or I go in front of you. All this would be much simpler at the colonel's house."

"Then you should have voiced your opinion last night." She stepped close to his heels all the way out the front door and down the broad stone stairs. As she circled the entire house, her brisk stride kept her warm in the cool fall air, despite her lack of coat. She walked around twice before she found her target.

"Dell." She moved one step in front of Gregor.

The gardener looked up from stacking branches into a vertical bundle. The sticks all stood on their ends. He smiled, and with a wink of his eye, the sticks fanned into the air to create an arch. It was quite a trick, though it hurt her ears. She wondered if he pulled extra energy through the tuning spirals tattooed on his temples for such a fancy maneuver.

Dell stepped beneath his arch and bowed low. "Senator Casteel." The dark-haired man was much taller and well-muscled than she remembered. He straightened from his bow as if he were standing at attention.

She turned to Gregor, who eyed the gardener as if he were a danger.

Dell eyed him back.

"Gregor, would you mind standing over there?" She pointed at the corner of the house in front of her. "Conforming with rule number three, you will be in front of me."

Gregor squinted at Dell for a long moment. He complied with her wishes, but he walked backward to the corner. Dell never broke eye contact until Gregor stopped moving. Even then, the gardener shifted so that his back was not to her guard.

"I hear you know everything," Bronte stated softly.

He lifted his eyebrow, a look of cautious amusement falling over him. "To which 'everything' do you refer?"

"The everything that includes where the junkyard is." At his look of confusion, she continued, "My car was taken there by mistake. I would like it back."

"I can make sure it is returned to you, senator." He made the offer with a half-bow.

"No, thank you. I would like to search it out myself." She realized she had no paper or pen. "I'll be right back. Will you be here? I forgot something to write it down with."

Dell lifted a hand toward a pocket.

"Hey!" Gregor shouted.

Bronte jumped, startled at his furious voice.

"No hands, gardener."

"Of course." Dell held both hands up as if he were harmless. "Just getting a piece of paper and pencil out of my pocket, if that meets with your approval." He reached in slowly and calmly, as if he dealt with guards on a regular basis. He turned to Bronte. "I knew I would need these today. I just didn't know why." A simple map took shape on the paper as he narrated. "This road goes all the way into the city and eventually runs parallel to the Scioto River. Three left turns and you're there. It's on Whittier. Do you want me to call them so they save your car and don't crush it?"

Bronte looked away. "Sure. Thank you." That was a logical action if she were really going to save her car. "Would that be the metallist that you would call?"

He nodded. "He does the crushing."

"That would be wonderful." She smiled. "By the way, thank you for the leaf." She took one step toward Gregor and stopped. "Do you happen to know my sis…Selene Glender?"

Dell paused. "I spoke to Miss Glender last night as she was leaving. She is a solemn lady." He drew himself up straight again, shoulders back. Power radiated from his frame. "Senator, if there is anything else I can do for you, anything, you need only call out to me. I will hear you."

"Thank you." She smiled and tucked the paper in the tiny pocket on the outside of her boot. She'd had no idea what one would put in a boot pocket, never having seen one until this pair, but now she knew—covert directions to secret places where one would undertake daring action to solve deadly problems. "Actually, there is one thing." She lowered her voice as much as possible but still have him hear. "Do you have a vehicle on the estate?"

He gave her a sideways glance. "Of course, senator."

"Would you pick me up at the road in front of the gyre at five minutes to three-quarters morning?" She said the words slowly as she calculated in her head. "That would be nine fifty-five standard Non time?"

"Ten twenty-five." The corrected time rolled off his tongue easily. "And yes, I can pick you up and take you…"

"To the front of the big house."

He opened his mouth as if surprised. "Is this a dangerous idea, senator?"

"Are you a dangerous driver?"

He shook his head.

"Then, no. Lady Rallis has ordered a new car for me. I want to see it the moment it arrives."

He crooked an eyebrow.

"Um, that is, so I can make sure I still want my old car instead." She donned her most convincing smile and prayed he couldn't sense her lie.

"I'll have you there by the time the gates open."

* * * *

Her plan hinged on a half-dozen factors. Almost all of them were beyond her control. If this idea failed as badly as the butter, then she'd figure out something else. For now, Bronte focused on her current strategy. She wandered the stones of the gyre as if it were a labyrinth, and she was deep within a meditation, though a trickle of nervous sweat ran down her back. This was the only place where she had a chance of shaking off her guards.

Dane and Gregor stood guard at opposite points around the circular space. Gregor rubbed his forehead, pain written in his expression. She felt a little guilty about that.

Standing at the edge, the men followed her with their gazes, but there were two places where she was hidden from both. She'd make her exit at the blind spot closest to the road and run to meet Dell.

She peeked down at the hourglass she'd stolen from the kitchen's smallest stove. It measured one hour. She'd started the countdown at nine twenty. The last few grains slipped through. Though it wasn't as accurate as a watch, it was the best she had. She had five minutes to run through the forest to the road where Dell would be waiting. Hustling to the spot where neither man could see her, she broke into a sprint and fled straight to the road as fast as she could. Her legs burned, but she pushed on as if powerful senators were flinging life-threatening spells at her back. Dashing around a huge tree, she leaped over a fallen branch just in time to keep from tripping over it. Her breath was so loud in her ears she could not hear Dane and Gregor behind her, but if they weren't in pursuit already, they would be soon.

The woods went on and on, longer than ever before. Every tree looked the same. How did people ever find their way around in the woods? The best she could do was run in the straightest line possible. She thought she heard a shout behind her. She ran faster. Her legs were on the verge of tripping over themselves. Finally, the break in the trees glimmered just ahead. She shot through it.

Dell waited on a vehicle with four wheels and a bench seat.

"Hi," she huffed and ran around to the other side.

He sped off the moment she sat down. "I'm going to get fired for this, you know."

"Oh, no!" she panted. Worry tightened her face. Everything else was already tight from muscle strain and stress. "I'm so sorry," she gasped. "I don't want that. I shouldn't have involved you in this."

"It's alright. I'm not needed here anymore," Dell shouted over the sound of the wind blowing past them. "But I'll see this through." He looked at her as he floored the pedal. "Your people need you, senator. We'll get you out. I can drive you right up to the gates. You can slip out when your new car arrives. William Ansel, the Casteel sentry, is on the other side of the gate. He's a friend. You can trust him."

"What? Who are you?" Had she just climbed into a vehicle with an enemy? Vincent's warning about Double-Wide being on the estate whispered through her mind. She glanced down at the ground. It whipped by in a blur, too quickly to jump out, not that she had any idea how to go about such a stunt.

"I'm just the gardener." He looked at her, briefly taking his eyes from the bumpy road. The set of his grim lips was somber and determined.

"Take me to the front. Not the gates." She used her closest imitation of a senator's commanding voice.

It must have worked. He responded with a, "Yes, ma'am." They took the circle around the front of the house with such speed she had to hang on to the seat or risk being thrown off. She stopped him. "Here. This is good." She could just make out the tall, black gates far down the drive. They glided open, and a sleek, white car turned in with an older sedan right behind. The two cars passed under the stately gatehouse.

She looked at the gardener. "Thank you. You should go now. Maybe they didn't see you." Though truth was, she didn't care much about the security of his employment. A friend of the Casteels was no friend of the Rallises. But whoever he was, she needed him gone to carry out the rest of her plan without interference. As he obeyed, she dashed behind the first tree lining the driveway to hide from whichever Rallis servant would greet the delivery service. A horrible thought occurred to her that they would deliver the car to the back of the house.

But luck was with her. The two cars pulled up to the circle in front of the big house and stopped. Bronte snuck out of the trees and climbed into the back seat of the older car, the one that would take the other driver back.

The driver wrenched around. His eyes widened at the sight of her crouched in his backseat.

"Hello." She waved to him. The medallion twinkled on her right arm. "I'm Senator Casteel." She sunk down below the car's windows.

"Uh, uh, Sss…senator." Beads of sweat popped up around the bald spot on the front of his head. He bowed—a seated, twisted version.

"Thank you so much for delivering the new car." Bronte tried to sound pleasant and calm instead of breathless with stress. She pushed her wind blown hair into order as she spoke. "What's your name?"

"Frank Ritzman, Lady."

"Mr. Ritzman, you are to be commended for your promptness. Excellent service. Since you and the other driver are leaving, would you mind taking me with you and dropping me off around the Scioto River? I have a map." She twisted around to get the slip of paper out of her boot's pocket.

"Uh, of course, Lady. Senator." His eyes hadn't yet shrunk to normal size. Bronte watched as Jasper came down the steps and took the keys from the driver of her new car. The gray-haired deliveryman nodded to the butler, walked toward Mr. Ritzman's car and climbed into the passenger seat in front of her. He, too, acquired wide eyes at the sight of her crouched down in the backseat.

"Uh," the driver began, "we're going to take *Senator Casteel* to the Scioto River somewhere."

"Yes, that's right." Bronte kept her voice calm and poised despite her awkward crouch below the windows. "I'll give you the specifics as soon as we get on the other side of the gates. Quickly now. Let's keep up your record of promptness." Bronte peeked out the back windshield as they pulled down the drive. Dell stood with his hands cupped around his mouth, his stare intent on the gate. He wasn't yelling. No, he was too still to be forcing much air through his vocal cords. He was throwing his voice to someone. She could guess his target—the Casteel sentry on the other side of the gates.

Just then Dane and Gregor sprinted around the house and jumped over a row of hedges in their way. Dell's hands dropped immediately as they came over the hedge. He spun around to face them. Guilt heated through her. Vincent would be furious. But what choice was there? No one here would help her get rid of this thing.

The driver turned out of the driveway. The tall, black gates closed behind. She sat up and took a breath. Her hands were shaking, but she was free. She needed her luck to continue so this medallion would let her free as well.

In lieu of polite conversation, Bronte sent up a steady stream of prayers as the car passed through the countryside. A mix of small farms and woods dotted the land until they entered the city. Block after block of shops and offices lined the streets, city mages at work. The atmosphere deteriorated with a surprising abruptness as they crossed a bridge. The river ran beside them and then disappeared into a thick forest too dense for human eyes to penetrate.

Bronte sat up straighter even as she shivered. "Turn here." They were close.

"This is the Drainpipe. We can't take a lady here." The gray-haired deliveryman whispered the words to the driver with an alarmed glance at Bronte. She caught sight of the driver's wide eyes in the rearview mirror. He hissed something back to the other man, too soft for her to hear.

Mr. Ritzman decelerated as they approached an old dingy shop on the right. Beyond, stacks of crumpled metal were compacted into rows and rows of towering walls, a looming labyrinth she never wanted to roam.

The driver cleared his throat. "Uh, Lady Senator, ma'am. Are you sure this where you want to go?"

"Yes, Mr. Ritzman. I am." She needed to project confidence. It was up to her to get the medallion off.

"No offense, senator, but it looks a little rough. See those mages there? I think they're about to fight." He pointed toward the building. In front of it, a group of men crept closer together, aggression written in every stance.

They drove by.

"I do believe you are correct, Mr. Ritzman. But this is the place. I need the metallist's office. Or shop. Or whatever it's called."

Mr. Ritzman looked around. "That must be it—that shack—back where those men are." His words fell slowly.

"Then back we go." She studied the building behind them. The second half of this plan looked a bit more dangerous than the first. Vincent would throw a fit.

The driver stuck out his chin with a harsh swallow. "Yes, ma'am." He spun the car around in the middle of the road. The vehicle behind them screeched to a halt. The driver stared at her through the window. The gray of his uniform was visible through the glass. She hadn't factored the Casteel sentry in her plan.

"You can drop me off in front. Quickly. I'll hop out and you can be on your way. Thank you, gentlemen. I do appreciate it. Casteel is in your debt." The car slid into the parking lot. Mr. Ritzman pulled the car so close to the metallist's office he only left her a few feet to open the car door. She climbed out among broken bits of concrete sidewalk and slipped inside the dingy building.

The interior was a smaller scale of the junkyard outside. Metal hunks of various sizes sat on shelves and tables and spilled onto the floor. Larger slabs of metal engines and tools swayed in the air, hanging from chains and hooks screwed into the ceiling, like a butcher shop with metal carcasses instead of meaty ones. Oil scented the air, heavy and sticky against her nose.

A crash echoed from deep within the building. The noise morphed into a groan, as if the metallist altered the very essence of the metal he was working. The spell crept toward her. Her ears ached. She fingered the medallion as the sound filled the building without end, wringing out the suffering of the material. She wanted to plea for it to stop, but there was no one to ask. She put her hands over her ears. Goose bumps rose along her skin.

She should leave. This was a mistake. The thought pounded in her head so hard she nodded with it. But her life depended on this. The medallion had to come off.

She took a breath and bravely stepped along the single path that trailed through the crowded room and led into the next. She needed to talk to the metallist before the Casteel sentry walked in, although for all she knew, maybe he didn't find her a suitable senator. Maybe he wanted her to remove the medallion.

The miserable sound stopped before her slow pace brought her halfway along the path. In the doorway to the next room, a man wobbled out, big and lopsided. By the light of the dirty windows, she could see he had one blue eye and one made of solid, shiny metal. She bit back her gasp. If his metal eye allowed him to see, it violated the Law of Natural Physique. Even Nons knew it was forbidden to use mage power to augment or replace body parts. His teeth were capped and shined just as bright as his eye, but each tooth was too small, as if they'd been shrunk before being coated with silver. His nose was bumpy with scar tissue.

She took a step back and ran into a sharp, heavy metal slab on the floor. He looked her up and down, taking in her dress and her form beneath. She shivered.

"Good day to you, sir." Her voice wavered. She took a breath to flatten it out. "I am in need of some metal work. I have a bracelet wrapped around my wrist. It's spelled shut. I was wondering if you could remove it?"

"Show me," he snarled with a sharp lift of his chin. His long, greasy hair flopped against his cheek. "Some man bind you as his whore?"

It wasn't a man, she thought as she held out her wrist. The medallion gleamed against her skin as if it preened before all these hunks of drab, old metal, used and discarded.

"Casteel's power." The hiss fell from his mouth even as his blue eye shined with lust. "What are you doing in Rallis territory?" He spoke to the medallion as if it would talk back.

Bronte held fast to her serene mask but ignored his question. "Can you get it off?"

"I'm willing to try." His teeth flashed in a vicious smile.

"There is a gentleman following me. I'd rather he didn't get in here." She cleared her throat. Fear clogged it. She couldn't believe she was about to say this next part. "Could you spell the doors shut? And the windows?" She wouldn't be able to get out unless he withdrew the energy of the spells.

He studied her with his mismatched eyes for a moment and then hobbled past her to the door. Instead of locking it, he opened it. An argument filtered in. "The boys are keeping him busy. Don't know what they're waiting for. Usually they're punching into 'em by now. They must have had a long night." He turned back to her. "What's he want?"

It took her a moment to understand his grumble.

"I don't know. I think he might be dangerous." She'd tell him whatever was necessary to keep the sentry out.

"I'll spell the door shut. The rest of the place is already sealed. It'll be just you and me in here. And the medallion." His gaze stuck to her, as oily as the scent that pervaded this hut. She felt the spell pop into place, but it was nothing like the force of Senator Rallis's powerful sound spell.

He yanked her wrist up. "Let me see it." His fingernails, tipped with metal points, poked at the chain. One sharp nail slipped off and pierced her skin between the chain's links.

She tried to pull her arm out of his hold, but he only tightened his grasp. "You're hurting me."

He smiled, those little teeth gleaming, as if he savored her pain. He yanked on the chain, taking away the slack. Dots of blood squeezed to the surface from the punctures in her skin.

She leaned away from him. “Let go.” Her sharp order worked too well, and she stumbled against an old engine lying on the floor behind her as he suddenly obeyed. Anger mixed with fear. Her heart pounded. “Can you get it off or not?”

He tapped a long, sharp fingernail against his metal eye as if he were thinking. “Gonna hurt you. And your people. But I’ve heard they’re used to the hurt. Heard there isn’t much good going on in Casteel. Ain’t this proof of that! Guess you aren’t up to the challenge of being the leader of a bunch of no-gooders like the people in Casteel.” His voice was gravelly. “It’ll be like cuttin’ out your own vibes.

“I can’t feel it.” She didn’t know why she bothered to lie to him. He didn’t mind her pain. He raised every internal alarm inside her mind, but for the first time since she’d discovered the medallion around her wrist, she had real hope of getting it off. She faced him with a determination to survive.

He must have read it in her face. “You think you’re tough enough to make it through the hurt? These type of things merge with ya. Medallions are the most powerful of all. It’s why they don’t fall off after death. Someone else who can merge with it has to touch it. I can’t share its power, that’s for damn sure. But I’ll harness it into something.” The glee on his face contrasted sharply with the rest of him.

“You may not keep it, sir. I am leaving with it. I just don’t want it attached to me.” The medallion may have chosen poorly, but she wouldn’t let him confiscate it.

“Then no deal. I ain’t doing this for free, lady. It’s a risky business. No one’s ever removed a medallion from a living mage. By now the things have soaked up so much energy they could almost be alive. Removing it might kill you. Then I’d have the enforcers, the Council, and the Senate down on me. You want it off, I’m keeping it.”

She could not walk out of here without trying. “If you can get it off me, you can have the link of the chain you break.”

It was the only bargaining chip she had.

“Alright. A link. Let’s give it a try.” His chin jutted forward, his mouth full of dull mirrors flashing. “Come on through. My tools are in the back.” He spun around.

She followed slowly, fighting her instinctive desire to flee. This had to be done, she told herself. Senators were powerful. She was not.

She walked under an arched doorway, four feet thick and made of stone, to find herself in a chamber that belonged in a castle’s dungeon, not in a crumbling building in a junkyard. The room contained a huge wooden block, big enough to function as a table, and a collection of sharp metal tools that hung from hooks in the wall. Thick chains swayed above high above the table. Their ghostly creaks whispered through the air. The floor felt like dirt beneath her boots, though it was too dark to see it. There were no windows. The three mage lights hovering beside the walls did little to cut through the darkness.

"I can't see very well in here." Bronte began. "Don't you need brighter light to see what you're doing? I don't want you to accidentally break my hand instead of the chain."

Break? More like chop it off.

"You don't need to see," he grumbled. He tapped his metal eye. "I can see everything I need to."

Despite the openness in the room, the walls threatened to collapse on her. Her feet would barely move her any farther. She came to a stop in the middle of the room. Yes, this would hurt, she told herself. But she'd live. Otherwise, she'd be alone among dangerous strangers—the Casteel mages in her family's territory and the powerful senators at the Rushes. And Vincent wouldn't be there.

"Put yer hand here." The weathered man placed his hand near the end of the solid wooden block. A hundred gouges ran its length as if other medallions had been here before her. He picked up an ax and closed his real eye as he rubbed the tool in circles along a smooth rectangular stone. The whispering of the metal and stone sounded like undecipherable secrets swishing through the air. Bronte could not find any reassurance in the rhythmic hiss.

Every muscle tensed; her body rebelled against her. She had to clear her throat to get any words out. "Is it as simple as brute force?"

His blue eye opened, glared. "Nothing simple about a Mayflower Medallion. Probably a link isn't payment enough if they come after me. But I like shiny, pretty things." He smiled. There was nothing pretty about that shine. "Like to take their power until they fade to dull. And there's nothing more powerful than that." He flicked a finger at her wrist. "Now are we doing this or not? Put your hand here," he growled, the finger tapping at the table.

His words prompted her terrified mind. This had to work.

She took six steps to his table and placed her hand on it. It was cold, unnaturally so, as if all the warmth had been drained from it.

His metal fingernails slid under the little slack in the chain wrapped around her wrist. "Not much room here. Easier to hack off your hand and slide it off that way if it'd come. But it probably wouldn't. It'd just tighten up so it won't fall off."

It was good to know in advance that the hacking-off-her-hand plan wouldn't work, she thought. She leaned against the table. A wave of dizzying fear pulled her in all directions.

"Don't move."

Bronte shook her head and panted, eyes wide and brow tensed. She couldn't close her eyes, but if she watched, she would move—a simple survival instinct. She tried to take a slow breath. *Don't move, don't move, don't move*, she chanted silently. He raised the ax. She stifled a scream. It stuck in her throat as if she'd shoved a rag down it.

The medallion's guillotine came down with a whistle, slicing through air molecules as it reached the chain. The force slammed against it and vibrated into her arm, up and down the length of her torso. Every cell of her body trembled. She tried to get away from the razor-sharp energy but it reverberated inside her. The pain echoed again and again.

No escape.

A scream rattled her eardrums. A black wave collapsed over her. She drowned in merciful darkness.

Chapter 18

Vincent punched a blast of energy at the gates and forced them open. He sped through with just enough space to clear them. They rebounded behind his vehicle and boomed shut, their locks slamming into place. Gregor's frantic confession replayed in his mind as he flew down the driveway. Vincent stayed focused on his objective: find her. But beneath that thin layer of concentration, a storm of fear brewed. It grew stronger with each minute.

She'd slipped away. Again. Only this time she had a damn medallion wrapped around her. His Bronte was the senator of Casteel. Pain stabbed at his chest as he contemplated the ramifications of that. He gritted his teeth and huffed it away.

First step: find her.

Gregor was combing the city roads for her and her only possible accomplices, the two deliverymen. All three had vanished. Finding the new Senator Casteel was national priority since according to the High Council's envoy, a mysterious potion had killed the last one and the murderers still were on the loose. Vincent had pulled two trackers from the bombsite to hunt her. He would have done it even without her upgraded status.

He slammed the brakes as he took the circle in front of the house. The tires squealed against the smooth pavement of the driveway. He jumped out and sprinted up the steps. Jasper met him halfway.

"They're in the kitchen, sir. The lieutenant said something about the readily available knives there."

Vincent tromped past him, hoping Dane had skewered the damn gardener with them. The front doors slammed open against the interior walls of the big house. His energy was out of control. Bronte would be horrified.

"Has he talked?" His boots pounded through the corridor and announced his arrival. Let them hear him. Let them sense the vibes of his fury.

"No, sir."

The clusters of servants grew thicker as he approached the kitchen. Behind him Jasper reprimanded them with a harsh, nervous whisper to get back to work.

Vincent shoved open the kitchen door, ready to crack open the mage who'd infiltrated his family's home. He surveyed the ridiculous scene before him.

The cook and her staff hovered by piles of chopped vegetables that dotted the counters. Dane leaned uselessly against the bar sharpening a knife. In the sitting area by the windows, Dell slumped on the couch with a bloody nose and a bruised cheek. His feet were propped up on the coffee table, while Mother sat holding his hand.

"You have to tell us where she is. She's out there all alone," she crooned.

Vincent marched up to Dane. "What the hell is going on?" His voice was a deadly murmur.

Dane held out a hand toward his mother and shook his head with a helpless drop of his jaw.

Vincent turned to the two on the couch. "This is not a counseling session, Mother."

She flinched back at his roar, a hint of fear in her expression.

"Clear the room." He tossed the last words over his shoulder and the cook and her people scurried out. "What the fuck, Dane? Why do you not have answers for me?" The lieutenant was a hell of a warrior and a decent energy reader—a good combination in a bodyguard, able to defend and accurately anticipate a possible attack. His skill at getting people to talk was almost unsurpassed. Only the general topped him.

"She wouldn't let me," Dane explained.

Vincent spun to his mother.

She stood, hands up as if she would plead for mercy for the traitor who had thrown the woman he loved to the other side of the gates. "Vincent, Dell says she's alright. He's an oracle. He would know."

"The gardener is an oracle." He gave the man a dead look. "That's not in your employment file."

Dell didn't move, as if he knew to stay frozen. "I know Senator Casteel is alive. I've seen a vision of a young woman with the Casteel Medallion at the Rushes."

"A young woman. Not Bronte?"

"It has to be her, who else would it be?" Dell sat up as if he'd realized an answer to his own question.

"Where is she?" Vincent roared, flinging vibes against the man so hard he flattened to the couch, his lungs unable to pull a breath. The pots and pans hanging from the ceiling rattled. His mother scrambled behind him.

"She's safe. Protected. Ansel is with her." The words were raspy against Vincent's pressure. Dell's dusty brown boots slipped against the floor as he battled to get away.

He'd been gone for one night, and his syphon's life had turned upside down again. Blasted hells, what was she going through now? "Who the hell is Ansel?" Vincent approached the couch with a steady stomp.

"Casteel sentry," Dane snapped, stepping up beside him. "He was here last night. He wanted to talk to her after she was crowned senator, but we kicked him outside the gates. I shot him in the leg." He nodded toward Dell. "You might want to let him get a breath."

He took Dane's advice and pulled his energy back from the man's throat, leaning down to wrap a hand around it instead. He yanked the gardener off the couch, keeping Dell's arms down with an easy push of vibes. "Where did Ansel take her?"

"She left on her own. He'll take her home. Where she belongs."

"She belongs with me!" Vincent dug his fingertips into the man's throat. He'd already known she'd left on her own, but hearing the words was like a claw swiping through his gut.

"She belongs in Casteel," Dell gasped. He fought against the energy restraining his hands, but Vincent held him easily. "She's safe. Ansel wouldn't let anything happen to her."

"I've already heard that. She's slippery. Does he know that? She got away from me once. She just got away my two best men. And I doubt Ansel is that good, considering his late senator was murdered on his watch!"

"Ansel was the best sentry I ever worked with!" Dell panted, anger pushing at his words. "He protected the territory's mages better than the senator. Ansel was the one trying to make their lives better in Casteel's territory."

"So you were a Casteel sentry, too, huh? Becoming a gardener is a long way for a sentry to fall, oracle. How exactly did that happen?"

Dell grabbed at Vincent's hand, straining to pull it from his throat. "About seven years ago," he gasped. "A bunch of the sentries left and scattered around the Republic, hoping to find a mage from a founding family willing to temporarily take over Casteel until a suitable blood relation could be found." Dell wheezed for air. "We needed a steward that would hand it back if there was ever a proper heir."

Vincent eyed Dane. His lieutenant nodded. Dell was telling the truth.

Vincent scoffed. "That's ridiculous. No founding family mage would deign to be a steward. He would keep the land for himself." Mages gobbled up unattended territory. A heritage of hiding from witch hunts had left them needy for as much safe land as they could claim, and once they had it, they never abandoned it.

Vincent let go of the man's throat, but kept his arms pinned down with vibes. Dell gingerly tilted his head left and right. "You're right. A man wouldn't leave the territory once he claimed it. We were looking for a woman. Females of founding families are raised knowing they'll leave their territory. We thought a woman would be more inclined to move to Casteel, claim the seat and then relinquish it." He tried to clear his throat. "We've searched for years. None of us had found any candidates to be a steward. So when the senator died, we took the best choice we had. If the medallion were to fall off for a Rallis, then at least we'd have an ethical senator, even if it meant losing our founders and becoming a Rallis Territory. The whole country knows Rallis looks out for their people. And you have the army behind you."

"The Casteel sentries stole the body?"

Dell nodded. "Ansel stole it. He left the note behind. The note was tricky, trying to explain our gift to the Rallises without the Casteels realizing what we'd intended."

"Uh-uh. Something's off about the note. It's not the full truth." Dane crossed his hands over his chest as he leaned in with crooked head, examining Dell as if answers were written on his face.

"Did one of the Casteel sentries kill him?" Vincent kept up the questioning while Dane penetrated the man's mind for answers.

"No," Dell protested vehemently, shaking his head. "We all took our vow seriously. We protected Casteel. There isn't a single sentry who would ever harm the Casteel senator."

"You didn't protect your senator. You abandoned him by leaving your post."

"For the good of the people and the land," Dell retorted. "We did not kill him. Until last night, we thought he'd died of a heart attack.

"You put the body in the gyre." The breach in security that Vincent had puzzled over had occurred seven years ago when Dell had been hired as the gardener. He just hadn't done anything to act on his deception until recently.

"Must have hurt going in there," Vincent said.

"Like a thousand knives."

"And Bronte?" No way had she been part of this scheme. If they'd planned for her to take the medallion, they could have arranged for her to remove it from the body while it was still in Casteel Territory.

"We thought she was a Non. We never knew she had a power. And we never expected her mother to send her to get the body back. A lucky break for us. We thought Lady Casteel would call the enforcers when they found out the body was gone, or call in the army, or even come here herself. Any way around it, the note would have gotten to the Rallises because it stated the body was here. You all are smart enough to recognize you were the intended recipients of the letter. But the goddess was smiling on us. She had a plan all along. She's given us a Casteel heiress. We just didn't know it. Now we don't need the Rallises or any other founding family. We have a good-hearted senator, and we're taking her home."

The man had guts to throw such a threat in his face, especially when all Vincent had to do was push. Dell would go through the window. It would be simple to ensure a sliver of glass sliced into his heart. "Let me tell you what you've done, gardener," he growled. "You've shackled a defenseless woman into being your senator. Bronte cannot protect herself against any kind of energy. She'll step onto the Rushes and crumble with the first spell that hits her. You've taken her life and have traded it for the good of a rotting people."

"Bronte doesn't want to be the senator." Allison stood behind him. "She was trying to get the medallion off this morning with a bunch of butter."

"She doesn't have a choice." Dell's voice was softer as he looked at Allison. "Just as we don't get to choose our family or our mage power, we don't get to choose our destiny. We just have to hold on until we find some good."

"Butter," Vincent spat. "Bronte has a habit of going to extremes to get herself out of situations that have been forced on her."

"You just met her, Rallis. You hardly know her."

"I've known her all my life." It felt like it, he'd dreamed about her for so long. Their connection was automatic. "If she couldn't slide it off her, she'd probably try to cut it off."

Dell shook his head as he fell against the couch, his face going pale. Vincent pulled his mage sense away from the man. He didn't need it anymore.

"Oh, no. She asked about a metallist this morning. At breakfast..." Allison's voice trailed off. "Surely she knows that wouldn't...I'm sorry." She talked through tears. "I've messed up again. I told her there was one. That Dell would know."

He spun to Casteel's agent. "Did you tell her how to get there?"

"She went to get her car back," Dell protested, his voice going weak. He pressed a hand to his chest. "I'm telling you the truth. You can back off with the torturing vibes, colonel." He took a raspy breath.

Vincent tilted his head. "I'm not touching you." He jerked his chin at Dane. "Tell Gregor to get to the junkyard. Smythe and Hobson, too."

Dell struggled for breath. "Look, no one can cut off a medallion, not even the most talented metal worker. No one would ever try that. It's impossible. And stupid. The backlash over the land and the mages tied to it would be incredible. Everyone knows that." He gasped between words.

"Bronte doesn't know. She might have spent sixteen years at Casteel's seat, but no one bothered to teach her about being a mage. She tried to get it off with butter!" Vincent spun toward the kitchen door. "Mother, banish the gardener from the land with the strongest spell you can." He'd let the Rallis sentries deal with the spy. "Dane, you're with me."

Dell coughed, clutched at his heart, and fell to the ground. Vincent paused at the door. "What the hell is wrong with you?"

"You're right," Dell panted. He crawled to his knees. "If that's not you, must be her. She's cutting it."

If it was strangling Dell, a Casteel mage, from miles away, what was it doing to Bronte? Vincent ran out the door, desperate to get to her. Goddess, let him make it in time.

* * * *

The smell washed into her nose with a shallow breath, thick and greasy, the scent of nightmares. A desperate need to flee seethed through her, but the heavy pressure of this place smothered her.

I want to go home. The thought danced through her like a song.

She could see the place in her mind, the soft light of lanterns hanging above a long table, a cozy bed topped with a quilt. The mental picture was a stark contrast to the darkness that surrounded her now. Escaping from this black was impossible.

A low, male voice responded, as if she'd spoken out loud. "Let's just give you a minute before we go anywhere, senator." She could barely hear the man's words over the sizzle crackling in her eardrums. She didn't recognize the voice, but his words held clues.

She was still a senator.

"It didn't work." Her voice broke with the whispered words. She didn't need to see the medallion to know it still clung to her. The uneven ridges of the chain pressed into her skin under the weight of her arm. Her right side burned, from the tips of her fingers all the way to her shoulder and the side of her face, as if a bolt of lightning had struck her. The rest of her just ached.

"It didn't work, no." The blunt words penetrated the static in her ears.

She opened her eyes. The Casteel sentry hovered over her, an angry set to his jaw. Bronte couldn't remember his name.

"Don't try to get up. I have some business to finish." He limped away.

Even her eyes ached. She closed them for a minute. A hard, low *thump* vibrated through the floor and into her body. She craned her head back to see. The dim mage lights illuminated little except for a single glow on the eye of the metallist. He lay on the floor ten feet away. The silhouette of a knife protruded from his chest.

A blade of panic sliced into her own chest. A whimper shook from her throat. She scooted away. Her body scraped along the rough, dirty floor. Her arm dragged uselessly in her wake. She got to her knees. The walls of the room undulated. She leaned hard against her left hand to keep from collapsing. The burn radiating from her right wrist spread upward and reached out to envelop the rest of her body's nerves. Bronte couldn't catch her breath between the sight of the dead man, her pain, and the dizziness that almost erased her vision.

"You killed him."

The sentry walked toward her. She shuffled back.

"Yes." He stopped moving, his hands out to his sides. "But I would never hurt you. You don't need to be afraid of me."

A hysterical laugh escaped from her mouth. "You killed him." She'd already said that. "This is my fault." Hot tears cooled against her cheeks.

"He knew the consequences. Everyone knows the consequences for messing with a medallion." His eyes locked on her, piercing her face with pinpoint accuracy.

She sat up straight on her knees. "I didn't know."

"You do now." A simple statement of fact. "Let's go home."

That was exactly where she wanted to be, but she didn't want to go anywhere with him. "Where is home?"

"The Casteel seat."

"No." Her whispered denial was accompanied by another voice. She twisted her neck to see Gregor in the thick arched doorway. He didn't look at her. He glared at the sentry.

"Ansel." Gregor nodded. "Did you break the break the spell on the door, or was that someone else?"

"Me." The sentry followed Gregor's cold eyes to the dead metallist. "That was me, too."

"You gonna take your knife back?" Gregor's everyday tone rattled Bronte's gut.

Ansel gave a quick jerk of his head. "It's a message."

"Effective." Gregor gave a curt nod. "Shame to lose a good knife though. Could just carve your name in his face. Then you could have your knife back."

"He's dead. We need to call the enforcers." Bronte struggled to work her hoarse voice.

Gregor stepped in front of her. His tall body blocked the view of the dead man. She looked up at him. His blond hair stuck out at odd angles, his pale eyebrows pulled down in concern.

"The enforcers won't do anything." Ansel explained it as if it were common sense. "Taking a medallion off a living bearer is an automatic death sentence. That law has been decreed since the medallions were created at the landing. The medallion chooses. I protect." He hit his chest with a hard *thump*. His words shrunk to the bare minimum as if his calling consumed his power of proper speech.

"That was no reason to kill him," she cried. Had there ever been more useless, powerless words in the history of language?

Gregor crouched down beside her. "Bronte, no sentry can allow a threat like this to go unanswered. They can't afford to be seen as weak." His soft voice did not console her. "The Casteel sentries must be especially vigilant. They just lost your grandfather to a murderer who's still out there."

Bronte shook her head at him. "You're on his side? I should have known. You people all stick together." She glanced back and forth between them. The brutality of this land of mages hit her anew. She'd been sheltered from much of this. Her banishment was a blessing in that regard. Nons were much more civilized. They had to be. They were held to a higher standard. If they failed to maintain that standard, they were stripped of their sponsorship.

Bronte forced one foot under her and then the next. She accidentally flashed Gregor a glimpse under her dress, but she didn't care. She was getting out of here. Gregor wrapped his hands around her arms and helped her. She cried out from the pressure on her right arm. It was alive with a ceaseless burn. He instantly stepped back.

"Take me to Vincent's," she whispered.

"He's on his way. He called out to tell me where you were. I was closer so I got here first."

"Bet he's really mad at me."

Gregor's frown deepened and Bronte's shoulders drooped. She needed just one thing to go right. She took a step, and then another, teetering out of the room, cradling her right arm. She felt as lopsided as the metallist's eyes had looked. Gregor's hands rested on her shoulders and kept her straight as she wobbled down the path outlined by metal pieces and chunks.

The Casteel sentry pushed in front and shoved open the door. Already crooked on its hinges, it crashed to the ground. Outside, the sun beamed bright and yellow, but its powerful rays couldn't permeate the shadows housed inside this shack. Ansel stepped out, surveyed the scene, and then moved aside, standing at attention as she passed.

The sun greeted her with a spray of heat, but it did nothing to warm her. Still holding her arm, she walked toward the vehicle that had to belong to Gregor. It was similar to the one he'd tossed her into when he'd arrested her. Today it was a means of escape instead of capture.

A black truck skidded into the dirt lot. Vincent. Relief unwound a coil of tension inside her. She stumbled as it loosened. He jumped out into the dusty cloud his tires had stirred. He paced to her, wide steps that closed the gap with such efficiency she didn't bother to meet him halfway.

Her lower lip trembled. She bit it. It didn't stop. A flood of tears that had built beneath the surface gushed forth. With no choice but to give them free rein, she buried herself into his chest.

He wrapped his strong arms around her, warmth finally pressing against the chill she'd yet to shake.

She leaned into him, unable to hold on to him as she cradled her injured arm.

She'd caused a man's death. She'd been ousted as a feared syphon. She held a title that required a quick draw on mage spells, but her holster was perpetually empty of weapons. For all that, one thought swirled above the rest.

"What if it doesn't get better?" Her words were muffled against his chest. "My arm. I can't hold a bow."

"Oh, love, we'll find the best healer in the land if we have to, but it will get better." His voice rumbled against the top of her head. She felt his kiss against her hair. "Let's go home."

* * * *

"She needs to go to Casteel Territory." Ansel argued with Vincent, but Bronte knew the man had already lost. She sat in the backseat of Gregor's tall vehicle. Angry voices filtered through the closed door. Bronte studied the sentry, finally able to see him in the light. It was hard to judge his age, since his hair was a premature gray. He was tall and lean and didn't look like he smiled much. Was everyone unhappy in Casteel?

"She's coming home with me, sentry." Standing with his arms crossed over his broad chest, Vincent didn't put much force into his argument. He, too, knew he'd won.

Gregor stood next to him; Dane leaned against the front of the vehicle. On the other side of Vincent's truck two army mages stood in front of another Land Rover.

Ansel narrowed his eyes. "Then I want inside your gates. She's my senator. I have the right to guard her." His hands hung slightly away from his hips, ready to move. But he was outnumbered.

"No." Vincent opened the back passenger door of Gregor's vehicle and stepped in with one leg. "Dane, drive my truck home, and when you get there, tell the senator that Rallis Territory needs a new metallist. Then find out where the hell the gang is that's supposed to guard this place." He closed them inside the backseat and gently pulled her into the crook of his arm. She soaked up his heat as Gregor slid into the driver's seat and pulled away from the awful place.

Vincent's energy merged into her with a shudder of sharp vibrations. It burned like a harsh swipe over raw skin. Was her syphon damaged, too, from trying to get rid of the medallion? His energy twisted into her, crooking back and forth as if the edges of her syphon were jagged and torn. She forced herself to relax into his vibes, to open up to them, but everything intensified as she did, including the pain in her arm. As if he could sense her struggle, he stroked her cheek. He whisked away the strands of hair clinging to her neck and face. She closed her eyes. Despite the hurt and worry that gnawed through her, warmth flooded her insides. The throbbing in her arm slowed. Her eyes were too weighted to open. He was doing it again…escorting her into sleep with his vibes. She intended to protest, but the next thing she knew, Vincent was pulling her out of the car and carrying her up his steps.

"Thought I told you not to do that without my permission." Her mumble was groggy with sleep and pain. He didn't say anything, just glanced down at her. His eyes were tense and alert, matching the pinch around his mouth. He was keeping a tight rein on his anger and fear. He stepped through the doorway of his house and turned toward his bedroom.

"No, not the bed," she protested instantly. "I'm too…" She searched for the right word. "I'm too contaminated from that place. The couch, please."

He obeyed. She closed her eyes as he set her down on the large brown couch, unable to look at the expression she'd brought to his face.

The door opened behind them. Gregor or Dane, she supposed. Vincent stepped away as a woman in a long plain dress came around the side of the couch.

Bronte sat up at the unexpected sight, but didn't get far. Her shoulder screeched its disapproval. She sank back under the examining eye of the Rallis family's healer. Who else could the woman be? Bronte imagined the summons the healer must have received. She must have dropped everything to get here so quickly.

She tilted her head at Bronte. "Much sadness in you, senator." The healer's soft voice matched her appearance—round cheeks, long gray hair, and deep laugh lines.

Bronte met her compassionate eyes. Unless the healer could get the medallion off, no cure existed for this sadness.

"Will my arm heal?" She stayed focused on the only problem that might have a solution.

The woman kneeled before her, placing her hands an inch in the air above Bronte's wrist, and closed her eyes. They stayed like that for so long, Bronte closed her eyes too. Her arm burned and ached without end. Nausea rolled in her belly along with it. Vincent had done her a favor by helping her sleep through the drive.

The healer suddenly dropped her hands. With a shake of her head, she gave a sigh. "That jolt of energy would have killed anyone else." A hint of outrage colored her voice, at odds with her gentle demeanor. "I would guess your unique power is the sole reason you are alive. You are lucky to be a syphon."

Bronte raised an eyebrow. Surely this was the first time anyone had ever said that phrase.

The healer mimicked Bronte's expression. "If you weren't a syphon, then I'd say your arm would not heal. In fact, you would not have survived. There would have been no place for all that power to go. As it is, I sense some damage, but not enough to impede normal activities given time to heal. All this energy that surrounds you now, the medallion's and your mate's," she added slyly, "it all needs a chance to settle down inside you. I'd tell you to take the medallion off for a while and let your body and your power re-equilibrate, but since you can't, stay away from any sizable energy sources for a few weeks. Your sixth sense has been fried, as they say. There's nothing I can do. Only time can heal this. Especially since the medallion is on the injured arm." The woman stood. "You'll want to keep it supported in a sling. I'll leave you something for the pain."

"I don't take potions. They don't work on me. At least not how they're intended to work."

"I know, senator. Colonel Rallis was quite adamant about that when he summoned me. I am adding Non-mage medicine to my bag from now on. In case you need me again. Or I happen to find another syphon patient." The healer smiled gently.

Bronte opened her mouth to say both conditions were unlikely to happen, but Vincent was already escorting the woman out. After a curt thanks and a click of the door, he returned and sat down on the coffee table next to her. "You should stay out of the gyre until you heal."

She gave him a sad smile, her heart aching as badly as her arm. Falling for this bossy, handsome warrior had never been in her plans. "Vincent, I won't be here. I have to go to Casteel."

He leaned toward her, hands on knees. His expression looked hollow, his eyes bleak, as if she'd syphoned everything out of him, not just his excess vibes.

"No. Before any decisions, first you heal." He shook his head, angry bewilderment. "Bronte, what were you thinking?" His harsh voice had a quiet edge. "You walked in there asking him to kill you. There is no other way for a medallion to come off. Do you understand that?"

Her own anger lifted its head in answer. "I cannot be stuck with this!" The feeling in the pit of her stomach was awful. She'd messed up, but she refused to back down. She shook her left hand at the medallion. "I had to try something! I need it off. I'll die on the floor of the Rushes." The words flew from her mouth, propelled by guilt over her sneaky escape and a near-suffocating sense of failure. She had not fixed her problems. She'd made everything worse.

"What you tried almost got you killed!" The fury in his voice was tempered by the fear shining in his eyes. "You don't know what you're up against with that medallion." His hand stroked down her cheek and his voice softened. "You have to know the rules to survive here. This isn't

Chattanooga. Let me show you how it works before you go waltzing off by yourself. I know you think I'm controlling you. I swear I'm trying to get better at that. But you have to talk to me. And if I'm not around and you don't want to talk to Edmund, or my parents, or the senator, then you'll just have to wait. Between Double-Wide looking for you, the prejudice against syphons that we haven't had a chance to address, and the fact that you're a senator…you have too many enemies. I can't protect you if you're running away all the damn time. And you don't know enough to protect yourself."

"Fine then." Tears streaked down her face. Her guilt scraped at her again, leaving a prickly, defensive anger in its wake. "I know this: if I have to be the Casteel Senator and go to their territory, then you're not coming with me! Are you?" She pushed the words out of her throat, clogged by tears. "I may not know much, but I know that. You won't leave here."

The shuttered look in his eyes was answer enough. She didn't want to hear him say she was right, so she switched subjects. Now was as good a time as any to tell him. "I think there's a chance that Double-Wide didn't hide the body in the gyre. So your estate might be safer than you thought."

Vincent sat back, studying her. He wasn't reacting with the surprise she'd thought he would. "Yes, I know. Quit changing the subject. We're not done talking about this. I will find a solution, Bronte."

Her shoulders slumped. "There is no solution." She had to leave—exactly what she'd been fighting for since the moment she arrived on this estate. But now she'd give anything to stay.

* * * *

"She's right." His brother walked in the front door, a cool breeze accompanied him.

"Not now, Edmund." He should have locked the door, Vincent thought. He needed Bronte to himself for a while, long enough to recover from the fear, time to reassure himself that she was safe, and to figure out how to keep her that way.

"This isn't going away, Vin. There is no way to get the damn thing off. You're stuck being senator," he said to Bronte as he walked over to them.

Vincent glared. "Do you think I'm going to let her walk out and move to Casteel?"

"Yes, I do. What alternative do you have?" Edmund pushed his hair off his forehead. "Casteel's mages are going to demand she go there. They'll come get her themselves if they have to."

"No one gets through those gates." Vincent stood with such force that the low table rocked backward. His bound dissertation fell to the floor. "I'll merge the territories before I let someone take her."

Edmund flung his hands in the air. "Rallis territory does not border Casteel! You cannot merge something that doesn't touch."

"Then we'll take over Warren Territory. It's just a slip of land. All that family does is blow in the breeze anyway."

"Love has driven you out of your mind, Vincent." Edmund shook his head, stripped off his jacket, and threw it to the other side of the couch. He loosened his tie with a yank. "You're proposing war against two territories so you can be with her?"

"It's only attacking one. We already have Casteel. Warren is weak. We could walk all the way to their mark without encountering resistance."

"Vincent." Bronte's tired voice reached out to him. Her sad smile hurt his heart. "You're being ridiculous. You're not going to declare war for me." The sun shone on her hair. Dark gold glistened.

He studied her face, lovely even through her pain, as she reclined against the cushions. He sat back down on the old table, resting his hand on her legs. "Then I'll go live in Casteel."

She stilled, a faint glimmer of hope kindled in her face, but it was gone in a blink. "No. You won't."

"What the hell, Vin!" Edmund shouted. "No man leaves his land. We've earned this heritage from the blood of our ancestors."

"Spare me the lesson."

"Apparently you need to hear it! Wilen is retiring as soon as DW is stopped. You're next in line. After two generations, Rallis is going to be back in control of the army that occupies our land. You cannot turn your back on that."

Bronte's shaky breath sounded through the room, reaching into his heart. She leaned over the edge of the couch and laid her head in his lap. "Visit me," she ordered softly. He could hear the tears in her throat.

She was giving up.

His sweet little syphon had been pushed around by powers greater than herself all her life. And now she'd been shoved to the top where she had no way of defending herself.

He stroked her hair. A little touch of his energy tangled inside it. He stilled, recognizing it immediately. He fingered through her hair until he found it. His energy weave glimmered at him, camouflaged in her hair's natural shine. How had that happened? He closed his eyes, remembering.

His nose had been in her hair as he'd breathed in her scent. He smiled, unabashed. Something had gone right. Finally.

Edmund threw his voice to Vincent's ear. "Yeah, what the hell were you thinking, brother? She doesn't even know it's there."

Vincent shrugged, the smile still on his face.

"Don't you think you should have asked first?" Edmund's thrown voice was a whisper. "I had a hell of a time hiding it from Mom. She would have expected grandchildren or something. Promptly delivered in nine months. Not anymore though."

Vincent stroked his fingers through her hair again. It wasn't where he'd intended the weave to go, but he gladly accepted it. "I'll think of something, Bronte. I will never give up." He felt a tear soak through his pants to his skin.

"Fine," Edmund agreed softly. "But while you plot world domination, let's talk about how Bronte is going to get Casteel back up on its feet. Because it does fall to her in the meantime."

"How do I do that?" Her soft voice wrenched at his heart.

"First off, don't ever try to cut the medallion off again, Bronte. Hellhounds, we'd thought we'd lost you. Mother is in tears. She thinks she came on too strong. Plus she was the one who hired Dell." Edmund came around the couch and sat down on the leather chair. "You cannot—I'd like to stress the 'not' part—tell anyone what you did. William Ansel knows. Dane and Gregor know. As does Dell. The rest of our family knows." He gave a weary sigh. "If anyone asks, the only reason you went there was to get your old car back. The metallist attacked you and tried to get the medallion off you. He's dead. He cannot say otherwise."

Bronte sat up and started to object, but Edmund spoke over her. "Bronte, if anyone finds out, they're going to draw the obvious conclusion that you don't want to be the Casteel senator." He held his hands wide, exasperated. "And from here on out, that's the deepest, darkest secret you've ever kept. And we all know you've kept a doozy. The territory of Casteel cannot afford to have a senator who wants to cut her ties to them so much she'd risk death. Clear?"

Vincent had to bite his tongue. He wanted to focus on how to get her out of this, not teach her how to rule. He watched his little syphon nod. Though he was still furious with her for taking such a foolish risk, his heart ached for what she faced, what they faced.

"They aren't going to want a syphon for a senator." Bronte shook her head, her frown so deep it pulled at her eyes.

Edmund scooted to the edge of the chair, shifting closer to where Bronte sat on the couch. "They don't have to like you. A senator takes care of the land and the people. You're a vast improvement on what they used to have."

"Selene, uh, the Council's envoy, blames me for the state of the energy in Casteel. She thinks my syphon ability helped them control it. When I left, things went sour."

Vincent shook his head. "You're powerful but not that powerful. One mage wouldn't have that big of an impact."

Bronte looked down at his lap, opening and closing her mouth as if she fought against saying something. Vincent waited as she circled a finger around the wet tear spot on the knee of his uniform. "About Selene," she began, "I think she might have been involved in putting the body in the gyre."

He waited for the rest of her story, but nothing came. He gave her a prompt. "It wasn't DW. But why do you think the High Council's envoy is involved?"

"I was going to tell you about this, I just haven't had the chance. I found out yesterday. Selene is my sister."

Vincent straightened in surprise.

"Our mother gave her away when hints of her necromancer powers showed up." Bronte tilted her head, her hair falling across her cheek. "When we were in the gyre, Selene said it was a brave and bold action to move the body there, to hand over Casteel's power to the Rallises. She feels sorry for the Casteel people even though she wasn't raised there. A lot more than I do. She said I was too wimpy to help them." Her mouth tugged back down into a frown.

He took a breath. Bronte's explanation brought clarity to Ansel's plot to overthrow Casteel's rulers. He'd bet Bronte was correct—Selene was involved, though it didn't matter now. The damage couldn't be fixed. Bronte wore the medallion, but Selene's words to Bronte had been needlessly hurtful. He shifted to sit next to her on the couch and carefully wrapped her into his arms. "You are brave and courageous, Bronte." He stroked one finger down her sad face. "Too much so. You should just stay home, meaning here, and behave."

She snorted and looked at him sideways. A tiny spark came back into her eyes that he was grateful to see.

"Your sister…" The words held a note of disbelief. "Wasn't the one who moved the body to the gyre. Dell did. He's a Casteel mage."

"That makes sense. He helped me get out of here. I probably should have mentioned that earlier. How did you find out?"

"He told us." Vincent didn't want to tell her the next part, but she needed to know. "He collapsed in the kitchen when the metallist tried to cut into the medallion." He took a breath. "If the metallist had succeeded, the mage energy in Casteel Territory would have gone out of control."

"Ooh." The sound pushed out of her like someone was squeezing her insides. "Do you think the entire Casteel land felt it?"

He put his arms around her, pushing her head back onto his chest. "Yes."

"Oh goddess. I'm sorry." The words came out as sobs. "I didn't know."

"You do now. I don't think my heart can take much more of your escape artist tricks. Next time, tell me your plan before you execute it." He stroked her hair while tears of regret spilled from her eyes. Visions of kidnapping the Casteel Senator and taking her to the other side of the border to live in mage-free Canada flitted through his head. Having a plan B seemed wise.

Edmund stood and walked over to the window that looked over the back of Vincent's meadow. He rubbed his finger over the bridge of his nose. Vincent recognized his plotting pose from a hundred childhood schemes. "Remember the story. It's not your fault. All that pain Casteel Territory experienced was the metallist's doing. Plus, the healer said only a syphon could have survived the attack. We'll use that too."

Vincent gritted his teeth. "How did you know that?"

Edmund shrugged. "I ordered her to tell me everything that occurred between her and the senator of Casteel. The healer is a mage of Rallis Territory. She knows her duty."

"Bronte is not the enemy. You may not use her as a pawn in your games."

"Come on, Vincent. They're your games too. Your woman needs to learn how to play. You're right, though. She's not the enemy. She's our newest ally. Becoming senator is exactly what you need, Bronte. You can only make things better for the Casteel mages. I think the public-relations issues surrounding your mage power just got a whole lot easier."

"But what about the Rushes? I can't defend myself against the spells that fly around there on a regular basis."

Anger bubbled over in Vincent. "If anyone dares to touch you, they will have the wrath of Rallis to deal with. I have the army at my back. You may be the Casteel senator. For now. But you are mine. No one wants the warrior mages on their land."

Edmund nodded in agreement. “It’s a decent threat. It’s what allies are for.”

“Everyone is going to think I’m being controlled by the Rallises.”

“What does that matter, if it keeps you alive?” Vincent turned his attention to the door as a knock sounded. How the hell had he not noticed that another mage’s vibes were so close?

Edmund turned, guilt highlighting his face. “I’ve got this.” He strode to the door and pulled it open. William Ansel strode in like this was his house. Vincent hadn’t sensed him at all. Hell, he was off his game.

Bronte stiffened at the sentry’s arrival.

“Rallis will not control the Casteel senator, lady.” Ansel stood at attention in front of Bronte.

“This isn’t about control, Ansel. This is about keeping Bronte safe.” Vincent glared at Edmund. His brother had let the man inside the estate and then left him on the porch. The man had been listening at the door.

“The first hurdle is the Gathering anyway,” Edmund interjected. “It’s in two days. The Senate won’t meet again before it.”

“No, the first hurdle is her security,” Vincent objected. “Bronte doesn’t know you, Ansel.” The other man started to protest, but Vincent cut him off. “If she doesn’t trust you, she’s not going to take your advice on staying safe. You need to assign someone to her that she can trust.”

Ansel narrowed his eyes. “Who do you suggest?” The sentry’s gray hair and uniform matched his steely expression.

“Gregor and Dane?” Vincent suggested with a look at Bronte.

“No. They’re loyal to you.” Ansel replied.

“Gregor.” Bronte’s gentle voice was a counterpoint to the angry men. She leaned back against the couch and closed her eyes, her mouth tight with pain. With the single word, she’d stepped into the game whether she knew it or not. The sentry wouldn’t refute an instruction from his senator.

Vincent nodded and looked at the sentry. “You need to kick out her parents and brother.”

“That is up to the senator, Colonel.” Ansel eyed him. “But, as it happens, I agree. They should meet with an accident.”

“No more killing,” Bronte ordered.

“Use whatever force it takes to keep her safe,” he directed Ansel.

“You can trust that I will do my job, but I will do as I see fit.”

“She may be your senator, but she is mine first.” His voice snapped at the sentry.

“Not anymore, colonel.”

“Vincent, there is one more thing I need to do before I leave.”

He looked over at her in time to see her brush a tear away with her left hand.

"I want to see him."

He'd hoped she'd forgotten. "Nothing good will come of this, Bronte."

"I'm running out of time. I want to see Claude."

Chapter 19

She exited the long, black car and studied the two uniformed soldiers guarding the side door of the farmhouse. It had taken multiple long arguments with Vincent and over twenty-four hours to plan for a senator's visit to the general's dungeon, but she was here. She suspected the long planning time was Vincent's doing, allowing her a day of healing before facing down Claude.

The guards' salute to Vincent was swift as he escorted her to the house. Their black coats puffed around their bodies, though there was nothing soft about them. Bronte knew they were padded with weapons because Vincent's coat matched. The three soldiers were a trio of blank faces.

"Sir, the suspect's in the chair. He's ready for you, Senator Casteel," the guard closest to her stated with a sharp voice.

"And the general?" Vincent questioned.

"General Wilen's baking muffins, sir."

Vincent nodded as if he'd expected this. He looked at her, eyes veiled with caution, his face tense. She wanted to reach out and touch his cheek.

"You don't have to do this. It's not too late to change your mind. Gregor will take you back home."

"I want to talk to him." She felt small surrounded by all these soldiers despite the high heels on her pumps. It was the men's width, more than their height. She smoothed the N on the outside of her long, creamy, wool coat. The symbol already felt foreign, but it was part of her disguise. Claude might open up more if he thought he still knew her.

Vincent jerked his head toward the door. Gregor and Ansel filed past and stepped inside. Their complete lack of noise was like watching a movie with the sound off. Bronte was well versed on the plan. Vincent, her sentries, and the reader mages would sneak down first, muffling their noise with their mage power. They'd hide in the basement's plentiful shadows. Bronte would walk down by herself, leaving Claude to assume they were alone.

Vincent caressed her cheek with a gloved hand and walked inside. The connection she felt with him lingered despite the growing distance, but it had nothing to do with his energy or her syphon. It was her heart, desperate to cling to him while it could.

The guard nodded for her to go in. The others were already safely concealed in shadows. Her shoes tapped against the wooden stairs and announced her presence. She paused at the bottom, searching. Vincent had merged with the darkness, deepened with a mage's power, but his energy reached for her always.

Claude sat in her old chair, exactly as she had, facing away from the stairs. From the light of the stairwell, she could see his restrained arms and shackled ankles. His smell drifted over, sweat and fear. She waited for the pang of sadness at his suffering, but nothing came. She was numb. It was uncomfortable, this lack of sympathy. But Claude had killed and tricked her into playing a role in those deaths. If she'd only questioned him more, dug around to discover why playing his terrible songs note for note was so important…but she couldn't go back and fix it. She could only move forward.

A spotlight flicked on above Claude. "Ahh! Give me some warning, assholes!" His shaggy, brown hair smashed flat against his head. He wore his usual jeans and grubby t-shirt. No shoes. Was there a policy against shoes for the basement's prisoners? Her feet chilled at the memory of her own barefoot experience.

She strode to her designated spot four feet in front of him. He noticed her finally. His mouth fell open and then closed with a sharp frown that dimpled his fat cheeks. He sneered. "Bronte. Now this is a surprise. Guess you figured it out. Didn't think you were smart enough." Sarcasm bled through his voice. "So you were the one who told. A traitor to your own kind." Spit flew through the pool of light.

"I didn't figure it out." She felt no shame in admitting it. "The people here did, although I suppose they looked at you because they were digging through my life." She studied him, detached. How had she missed the anger and resentment inside him?

"Why would they ever investigate you? Pretty, insecure, little Bronte. Never colors outside the lines, never breaks the rules, a proper, powerless Non. All respectable in your white suit. Untouchable."

She shrugged away his disdain. "They suspected I was involved in my grandfather's death."

"You?" His laughter cackled harshly in the darkness. "Fucking vibes, that's rich. He wasn't even supposed to die."

Her heart jumped at the information.

Vincent's words tickled at her ear. "Get him to talk to you. Ask him what he means." Her syphon drank down his power.

"Damn it!" Claude screamed. "They're driving me nuts. The creeps are everywhere around here. How can you stand there so calm? All these damn mages and their creepy energy."

Bronte shrugged. "I suppose I'm used to it." Her mind raced behind her calm words. "What do you mean he wasn't supposed to die? What was supposed to happen to him?" Bronte wanted to cringe. Interrogation was not her strength. Specific questions to ask would be helpful. Too bad she couldn't throw her voice and tell Vincent.

"His heart." Claude rolled his eyes, his words loud and exaggerated. "His cold-ass heart was supposed to open up and pour out love for us Nons. He would have helped solve all our problems. He might've liked you, Bronnie, once his heart was opened with that potion. He might have invited you back home."

"A potion? You were working with a mage?"

He laughed again, short and sharp. "You'd never guess who. Those vibrating freaks will never guess either. He's one of their own, after all." Despite his bindings, he shrugged. "You'll know soon enough anyway. When the fucking powermongers let him in, he's going to make everything all better for the Nons."

"Why would he do that? If he's a mage, why does he care about the Nons?"

He closed his eyes and breathed in as if there were a sweet smell. Maybe the scent of the general's post-torture muffins had drifted down to him. "I've always loved your voice. Did you know that? It's what I liked best about you. It wasn't your playing, or that pure white face that makes me want to rub some mud on it. It was your voice." He opened his eyes. "Maybe they'll put you in jail with me since you helped me do all this. Then I can hear you forever. Talk, talk, talk. Even if you have betrayed your own kind. You could have been the queen of us, you know." He gave a laugh. "Our own Mayflower Non. These fucking mages are on their way down. Down to the pits of hell!" Fire and brimstone burst through his voice.

She stepped back. The fast move jostled her arm painfully. She tried not to wince as she tucked her arm against her chest with her left hand. It had been hanging unsupported for too long. The burning pain was making her sick, but she refused to wear a sling in front of him.

Claude kept on with his rant. "The mages are losing it. Too much power eating at their minds. Their strength has become their weakness." He leaned forward as much as his arms would let him. She tried not to scramble back into the shadows. Even now they held secrets she couldn't see. "Now is the time for Nons to step up and demand a fair take."

Wanting to get this over with, she tried again. "So who's going to keep working toward your cause now that you're locked up?"

He glared at her. "Never fear, Bronnie." His words fell slow and angry. "The work will go on. And if the damn mages know what's good for them, they'll go along with it. There's a whole bunch of senators who are going to be mighty sorry if they don't. All of them, actually." A laugh vibrated from his throat.

She looked into the darkness from where Vincent's vibes flowed. She wished her eyes could penetrate the shadows. "With all those deaths, I'm sure the senators already regret what's happened." She certainly did.

"Not like they're gonna! It's about to get up close and personal," he whispered dramatically. "But don't tell. I don't want to ruin the surprise." He leered at her with a grin stretched across his face.

"I wouldn't think there's much you can do from in here, Claude." A nervous shiver ran down her back.

"God, you are so stupid sometimes, Bronte. There are other people I have working for me. They're competent enough to do the job on their own. You'll have to wait and see. Don't worry about me though. As soon as my man gets the power, I'll get a pardon. We've had this part planned for a while now. Thanks in part to you," he taunted. "Double-Wide is grateful for your loyal service. We enjoyed using you, though I didn't use you as much as I wanted. I've always liked that ass of yours, rocking back and forth on the stage." He sighed and shook his head. "We were going to have to switch communication methods soon anyway. You weren't doing a very good job."

Anger pushed away any remaining numbness or fear. "I wasn't doing a very good job helping you blow up people?" The wall she'd erected between his ugly emotions and her own feelings cracked with the question. She had to know. "How many people did I help you kill?" The question bubbled over. It had been brewing since the moment she'd understood the role she'd played. She hadn't found the courage to ask until now.

"Bronte!" Vincent's tone bit at the air while William Ansel rang out with his own warning at the same time.

"Miss Casteel, it's time to go." The two came out of the shadows.

Claude flipped his stringy hair back and gave a low, hard laugh. She felt more tortured than when she'd sat in that chair. Spinning on her heels, she walked away, conquering the steps at a fierce pace, leaving her former friend behind.

She took the first landing with a quick twist and sidestepped around the guard at the top of the steps. The air in the kitchen smelled sweet—the general's muffins. The scent and the bright color of the room felt wrong, too close to the hell below for this much happiness.

"Hello, senator. You didn't talk long. Not much to say to your old friend?" General Wilen stood beside the oven removing muffins from tins one by one, his black uniform and bald head pristine and perfect under the lights. "We needed a name, Bronte. Muffin?" the general offered with one raised eyebrow. "They're hot."

"She got us the name and more, general," Vincent said behind her. "If he's taking out senators, then the Gathering has to be the next target. General, you're going to need to get the High Council on the landline. We've got less than twenty hours before the senators arrive there." Vincent walked up to her, kissed her on the forehead. "Good job, love."

The general pulled apart a muffin. Steam billowed out as he faced Vincent. "We're invading the High Council? I've been wantin' to do that my whole career. That's just the way I'd like to go out." He smiled into his muffin.

Chapter 20

Bronte withstood the stares of over three hundred mages as she lingered at the edge of the High Council's mark. She stood alone. The rest gathered at the fringes of the cavernous room, avoiding the mark as best they could. Avoiding her? Perhaps. She let them look their fill, safe for now under the Order of Truce that bound all who entered the High Council House. Safe due to the feared might of Rallis that promised deadly retribution should the new senator of Casteel come to harm.

Tonight's Gathering had pulled every founding family to the mark that bound the Republic together. She was the sole representative of Casteel. Unburdened by her isolation, she studied the High Council's huge sanctuary. Above her, a domed glass ceiling let starlight twinkle through. The enormous dome was supported by white marble columns that stood close to the walls of the round room. In the center was the mark, a series of thirteen connected spiral labyrinths set flush in the stone floor.

Its long-dead creators had extracted a deep cross section of rock, laid it on its side, and forced the layers to spin into the complicated maze that spanned most of the floor. It must have taken enormous power. But unlike the Rallis gyre, which was alive with the goddess's blessing, no sense of sacredness dwelled here. It was consumed with itself, with ambition and authority.

The uneasy crowd, segregated by family, was solemn and quiet despite their ballroom attire. Dozens of warrior mages stood guard outside the massive room, ready for the attack that the majority of those present were unaware of. The High Council had forbidden Vincent and General Wilen from sharing the threat they faced, even though the extended families of all senators were present, from the youngest to the oldest. No, it was not the expected DW attack that inspired their fear. Nor was it being in the presence of a syphon. It was the threat of the mark's power that had them shivering in their finest garb.

Vincent leaned against a column near the rest of his family. He gazed at her as if she were on the other side of an impenetrable divide. The sadness in his eyes matched her heavy heart. She gingerly held out her right hand to him. It wobbled in the air, and the medallion clattered around her wrist. Her courageous warrior mage walked forward, daring to venture closer to the powerful mark.

He bowed to kiss her hand and then tucked it back across her stomach. He wrapped his arm under it like a living sling. With his other arm encircling her back, he pulled her into a sideways embrace. She savored the moment with him, even it if it was under the eyes of the most powerful mages in the world. After a lifetime of avoiding mages, her lack of worry was a new experience.

She leaned against him, his uniform scratchy along her bare shoulder and upper back. The elegant navy dress, courtesy of Helen, displayed her every curve. It had a sleeve for her left arm, but the right arm was bare. It showcased the medallion—the wretched thing. But she wouldn't let her resentment of it pollute this time with Vincent. She closed her eyes and focused on his energy. He'd been distracted since they'd left the basement, security uppermost in his thoughts. Though she'd spent last night in his bed, she'd been alone. He'd worked, finalizing defensive measures for this event, and coordinating a quiet search for their main suspect.

"Is there a solution to the maze?"

Vincent chuckled. "No. The thirteen families are symbolized in the mark. No one gets in. No one gets out. The labyrinth is too powerful to walk anyway."

A small whisper of voices slowly built. Vincent's laugh had caused a stir. The crowd relaxed a bit as they took their cue from the colonel.

His lips brushed against her skin. "Can you feel the mark's power?" he whispered.

She ought to be able to, considering the intensity of the last Gathering here had killed three senators and two Council members. That had been a quarter of a century ago. The mark's power had grown since then.

"Barely. It's nothing like what I pick up from you or the gyre. A soft hum, nothing more."

"It senses you. I can feel it brushing against my vibes as you syphon it away. Some of its energy anyway. Enough for everyone to stand inside this room."

"Is it too much for you?" she asked. "The energy? The mages?"

"No. I can handle anything with you. I was seven years old when the Gathering was last held here. Mother nearly passed out. Grandfather couldn't be moved for three days afterwards, so we couldn't go home. But right now, I'm fine. As is everyone else."

Bronte glanced around at the mages lingering along walls. "I feel like I was born blind. All this energy that I don't know exists until someone tells me it's there."

"It's the goddess's way of making sure you can't take advantage of the rest of us." Behind them, an old woman's crackly, loud voice rang through the sanctuary. The crowd hushed.

The crone walked up next to her. "It allows the rest of us to take advantage of you though." Long gray hair hung in thick waves to her knees. Her face was finely wrinkled all over. Bronte was the exact height to look the woman in the eye. Except the woman's eyes were stitched shut.

The remaining seven councilors, clad in white ceremonial robes, stood behind her. The blind woman reached out and plucked at the medallion wrapped around Bronte's wrist. "An improvement for Casteel. If you weren't a senator, I'd keep you for the Council." She shifted to Vincent, patting his cheek.

He let go of Bronte's right arm slowly enough that she could take over supporting it, and he bowed to the woman.

"Lady Glender." He greeted her with a cold, formal tone.

"Such a handsome man, you are." Lady Glender stepped up to the edge of the mark and took Bronte's bare elbow. The move ousted Vincent from Bronte's side. "She's mine now, colonel."

Bronte met Vincent's eyes over the old woman's head. She couldn't find a smile for him. He seemed to share the same problem. She could almost hear the damn clock carelessly ticking away, a countdown to the dissolution of the bond that existed between them. They didn't have a future. Vincent could never be bound to Casteel Territory. He was a Rallis clear through to his soul. She was the Casteel senator. They only had now. She smiled after all, bittersweet and small, but there. He narrowed his eyes. He hadn't given up. Yet. Her heart cracked a little more at the hopelessness of it all. He turned away.

The other councilors floated around the room and took their positions along the huge labyrinth. The remaining twelve senators left their families at the walls of the sanctuary and filled the spaces between the councilors. Vincent's grandfather stood on the other side of Lady Glender. The only other woman senator stood four mages away. Bronte was the youngest by at least twenty years.

Behind them, the founding families moved forward as other spectators crowded in along the walls of the room. The High Council's entrance was the lower guests' cue to cross the threshold of the sanctuary. Selene stood among them, her white sheath, the color of the Council, blended with the rest of her coloring, elegant and frosty.

"The Gathering is the time that each family renews our commitment to hold a free land for all mages." Lady Glender's voice permeated the vast space. "We devote our lives, our blood and our energy to the goddess's gift of this Republic. Let the heirs come into the labyrinth to represent the people of the land, and we will seal the circle."

"No," a young mother protested, clutching an infant to her chest, her eyes wild with fright. Other parents joined in. "I won't do it. The last time—"

"This time is different, Annabelle," Lady Glender snapped. "This time the power is muted thanks to our newest senator. Your babe will be fine. You, of course, will go in with her. Choose your marks, children." One by one the heirs walked into the labyrinth. Some were young, others adults. All were tense as if they expected to be thrown out by the force of the power. Everyone knew their history.

Edmund walked in for Rallis, winking at Bronte as he passed by. Apparently he wasn't tense.

"Now there's a big boy," Lady Glender chuckled.

The heirs stayed in the spirals closest to their senators. The circle in front of Bronte was empty.

"Casteel needs an heir." The High Councilor's tone slashed through the air, her sightless face stared at Bronte. "Call my daughter to you."

"She's not your daughter," Bronte retorted. She held no fondness for Selene, but the High Council had left her sister devoid of warmth and love, her heart welded shut without a touch of lightness. It was a dismal way to raise a child.

Lady Glender cackled. "The brave senator defends her people already," she announced to all. "Now call your sister." She threw the last words to Bronte's ear.

Bronte looked through the crowd until her eyes found Selene. Her sister was oblivious to the situation, focused on a tall, dusky man whispering in her ear. Selene shoved him away, her face narrowed in a scowl.

The man stumbled back with a grin.

"Sister, come stand as my heir." Bronte revealed their relationship with the single, bitter word. The crowd's murmur rose as Selene strode out of the audience, rewrapping herself in her usual cold grace. She passed between Bronte and Lady Glender. Bronte had yet to forgive her.

"See, I told you she likes you," the old woman said to Selene.

The moment Selene stepped into the spiral in front of Bronte, something snapped. The mages jerked like it had touched them. Complete silence fell.

The councilors and senators held out their hands, palms up, elbows only slightly bent, but the circle was too large for anyone to touch. Bronte looked around her. She could not reach out her right arm for long. It was too sore.

"Just stand there, Senator Casteel." The high, sweet voice came from the councilor to her left. "You can't throw out any power anyway. We'll close the energy's circle into you." The young woman, draped in a councilor's robes, was no more than twenty. Her golden hair fell around her shoulders in fat ringlets. Lush red lips turned into a snooty smile.

The air grew heavy. A slow current moved through it and blew Bronte's dress against her legs. The force batted her back and forth from the inside out. Selene stared with wide eyes. Her chest moved in shallow, quick breaths. She was scared. Bronte had no words of reassurance to offer.

A whispered hush pressed down from the top of the room, so heavy it held everyone under its weight, as if the goddess's unseen hand came down and closed around them. Bronte felt pulled into the circle, as if she might fall into the power of the mark and into Selene, into something beyond, a vastness she didn't recognize—the goddess gathering her people anew into this land, a place of safety and freedom. She closed her eyes.

She wasn't sure how long it lasted—hours, days, mere seconds. No formal closure ended the silent ceremony. The pressure simply eased. The energy level dropped to normal, dragging her strength with it. She could have lain down and slept, but everyone else seemed energized. A glad cheer swept through the room. Parents gathered their children, heirs fled the labyrinth's spirals and they all swarmed past Bronte to the exit. She wavered in the wind of their departure.

Vincent appeared at her side, his stern brow wrinkled. He wrapped an arm around her and pulled her from the room. No lingering allowed. "That was exactly what the healer said you didn't need."

"I'm fine."

They stepped into the gleam of the sanctuary's large outer chamber where the Republic's finest mages gathered, outshining the gleaming floor and polished walls of the grand room. Vincent guided them to a stop between two of the numerous elaborate staircases that rose with a graceful twist to the balcony. He raised a brow as she leaned against him. "You are not fine."

"Tired, that's all."

"We need to get you out of here then." He motioned to Gregor, who waited against the wall along with Ansel.

"That's not allowed, remember?" She wouldn't be the one to break the rules, nor would she get Vincent in trouble for helping her do so. Attendance at the Gathering was mandatory.

"Bronte, there isn't even a place to sit down."

"I noticed." Mages took *show no weakness* to extremes. "All the more reason to stay. The first syphon mage to come out to the public cannot sneak away because she's tired. Besides, you're here…even if you're not standing next to me." Her voice faltered, but she refused to cry. "I'm not giving up my last minutes with you because I need a nap."

He pressed his mouth to her ear. "Then leave because this is the scene of DW's grand finale, Bronte. Please. I can get you out."

"No. You can't." Lady Glender's mouth joined Vincent's at her ear.

Bronte jumped back.

Vincent thinned his lips into a hard line, a barrier for angry words.

Bronte reached for his hand as Lady Glender gave them a sly smile.

"I'll stay with Gregor. Would that suit you?" She watched Vincent scan the balcony with a trained eye. The high space was dotted with prominent mages who hadn't been invited into the sanctuary.

"No. It doesn't suit." He scowled and at the same time nodded a greeting to two guards stationed at the foot of the nearest staircase. They eyed the crowd, extravigilant.

"If that scowl is for me, then look at me when you do it. You're confusing your own men." She reached up on her toes to kiss his cheek. "Go. I'll be safe enough. After all, Lady Glender is here." She spared the councilor a sideways glance. "I'm sure she wouldn't insist on everyone staying if it was unsafe. She has the best interests of all the mages at heart."

The old woman nodded and walked away as silently as she'd arrived.

Vincent brushed Bronte's cheek with the back of his hand and then nodded to Ansel and Gregor. "Take care of her." *Or else* hung silently in the air. She followed Vincent with her gaze until he walked out the far end of the room and disappeared down the corridor. Somewhere in the building, his team had a temporary headquarters.

Loneliness swamped her. The joy of the celebrating crowd didn't touch her. She glanced around and locked eyes with Selene, who graced the balcony directly in front of her. Her sister jerked her head, wanting Bronte to come up. Bronte merely raised an eyebrow and discreetly shook her head no. She had nothing to say to her heir at the moment.

Selene rolled her eyes. "Please." The word popped in her ear.

Bronte sighed and made her way to the staircase nearest her sister. The crowd gave her a wide berth, but curiosity dwelled in their stares instead of hostility. Gregor and Ansel mounted the stairs with her. She was panting by the time she reached the top. Next year she would insist on a chair for the post-party. She stopped at the top to catch her breath. Her two guards turned away to face the crowd.

Selene closed the distance between them. Bronte's ears popped as her sister conjured a thick soundproof spell, cutting them off from everyone else. She shivered as the pressure pushed against her. The crowd's noise disappeared.

Selene glared. "You can't cut the medallion off. That was stupid." At least no one else could hear her sister's insults, Bronte thought, not even her sentries standing six feet away. The crowd below gazed up, intent on their silent sister show. This balcony was a stage.

"I'm too tired for a lecture, Selene. If that's only reason you summoned me here, I'm leaving." Bronte took two steps away, but Selene's hand on her left arm stopped her just short of the edge of the spell and the first stair down.

"It's not." Her eyes softened. "I want you to know…I believe in you. The mages of Casteel need someone compassionate, someone to focus on their needs instead of squeezing every joule of power from them for the sole benefit of their founding family. You can lead them."

She studied her sister. They were strangers. Selene had no idea what kind of leader Bronte would be. Bronte couldn't help but question the motivation behind Selene's words. Was this another ploy by a mage to use her in their political games? She shrugged her sister's touch away. "Thank you for the encouragement. I'll certainly do my best." Something stabbed Bronte hard in her ribs. "Ouch." She put her hand on her side only to encounter something cold and hard that had no visible form. She tried to brush it away.

"Uh-uh," a man said next to her, but there was no one there other than Selene. The man continued, "That's a gun, Bronte. I wouldn't just push it away. Might go off."

"Selene." Bronte's voice wavered with alarm.

"I heard," Selene stated calmly, not sounding the least bit intimidated. "We have an unexpected guest. A veiler."

"Pop the spell," Bronte ordered. Help stood on the other side of the sound spell.

"No, no. I wouldn't do that." The man dug the gun's barrel deep into her side. "The bullet would be in your gut and I'd be free of this room before she could pull her heavy spell off the two of you. This is one thick spell. Thank you for closing me in it with you." His sarcastic glee turned Bronte's stomach.

"Dr. Riley, I presume." Selene was calm and cool, as if she dealt with this everyday. The High Council must have told her about the main suspect.

"You already know? How disappointing. But no matter." His cultured, smooth voice was perfect for a television host.

Bronte strained to make eye contact with Gregor or William, but their backs were turned. Her efforts earned her another poke in her side.

"Behave, Bronnie. Isn't that what Claude calls you? Eyes on the envoy." A low laugh accompanied the words.

Selene nodded. "I've caught a few of your shows. Very interesting. Especially the potions. I'm especially intrigued by the sweet-potato potion. I've never encountered anything like it. Would you tell me about it?"

"Ah, yes. Sweet potatoes are only a small part of the potion, actually. I'd never give away my secrets. That particular spell is designed to open the heart of a mage to spill with love for all."

"It sounds like my parents could use that." Selene's laugh tinkled out.

Bronte wanted to berate her to quit playing games.

Selene continued, "I was speaking with Colonel Rallis recently. He suggested that perhaps you didn't mean to give the late Senator Walter Casteel such a large dose. Granted, the late senator's heart needed quite a large crack to let any love for Non-mages in."

"Love for Nons." Another laugh, bolder and louder. "The colonel is not quite as smart as he thinks he is. That's obvious, though, isn't it? I mean, here I am. And where is he? You only have half the story," Riley continued. "Double-Wide…it was just my cover. This isn't about the Nons and all their whining for equal rights. This is about me. You see,

I needed an ally in the Senate. The potion was supposed to open that pretentious bastard's heart to me, the national expert on Nons. Then, after a few more DW bombs strategically placed in Casteel Territory and a few hundred mages dead, the freaked-out senator would turn to me, his new friend, and beg for my help. I'd locate the nasty Nons in DW faster than the army ever could, and I would be the hero. I'd probably be appointed to the High Council."

Bronte interrupted. "But the Nons in Double-Wide would tell everyone who you are."

"Oh please. You're as stupid as the colonel. No one knows my identity, other than Claude. It would only take a single dose of the right potion to shut him up permanently. Senator Casteel's death was due to a slight miscalculation on my part. But no matter. I have another plan. One more bomb will do the trick. After tonight there will be very few powerful mages left. The founding families, so conveniently gathered, are about to be wiped out. The most elite squad in the army is going to be decimated as well. It will be my duty to step up and lead the Republic out of the grip of those repulsive Nons."

"Fascinating." Selene nodded as if this were an everyday conversation. "But I'm curious. Why bomb the symphony conductor's car with an exploding potion?"

A *tsk* came from his invisible presence. "Ah, that. The blame for that was supposed to go to Bronnie. Make them think she was leading my silly terrorist group. She has quite a legitimate grudge against magekind, after all."

"A desperate choice and a miscalculation, doctor. Syphons can't tolerate spells or potions."

"Thank you for sharing that with me, Envoy Glender. I do enjoy expanding my horizons with new, accurate information."

The gun stuck Bronte in the ribs, hard enough to bruise. "I want to thank you, Bronnie, for your service to DW. You could have done better, but it wasn't too bad. Now it's time for my grand finale. Bombs away," he whispered.

Bronte felt his presence disappear. Selene's spell popped.

A shock wave ripped through the world.

Chapter 21

All was calm and quiet on the streets surrounding the High Council's home. Vincent surveyed the northeast lawn from the roof of the sprawling building. Bronte was three stories below and two wings over in the sanctuary's antechamber. The distance wasn't enough to cut off his connection to her syphon; no distance could sever her hold on his heart.

"Balcony north door. Spell fouled!" The shout vibrated over Vincent's mage wire.

Adrenaline flashed through him. He bolted down the metal stairs that connected the roof to the attic. Fear and determination battled through him. His world honed to getting to her.

"The door's open, but all's clear." The blunt voice of the team leader inside the antechamber crackled through his wire. "No one's near."

Doors didn't open on their own. He should have realized Riley was more than a potioner mage. "He's a veiler. He was already inside," Vincent shot back. "Team Two, north corridor." If Riley was powerful enough, he could have been waiting in there undetected for over twenty-four hours. "Deflects ready." He threw the orders into his mage wire and sprinted down the corridor to the outer chamber. The explosion ignited the moment he entered the antechamber.

The shock wave vibrated, a mirage of energy. Instinct took over. Vincent slammed his power against the explosive wave. The air rumbled, a thundercloud of terror. Screams tore through the air. He blocked it all out. His heart pounded a vicious pace as his mage power held back the pressure, forcing it down. His vibes flowed against it without end, an infinitely strong muscle.

One by one, his team of deflectors failed as the power overwhelmed them. The bomb's energy pushed too hard and fast against them. And then it was just him. Time slowed, seconds stretched to minutes. He could almost see his vibes working against the energy of the bomb. Riley had buried it under the floor in the center of the room.

Vincent thrust his hands in front of him as if their physical strength would add to his sense's force. He shoved more vibes than he'd thought possible toward the explosive. Like a sudden flick of a switch, the power of the bomb shifted. Its energy collapsed with a roar.

The implosion shook the building one last time. Vincent stumbled. Blinked. His breath echoed in his ears. He should never have been able to do that. No one was that powerful. He could see the stunned mages huddling around the room and heard his men reassuring the crowd.

He'd just deflected a bomb big enough to take out a dozen city blocks.

His men's voices drifted into his foggy mind. Their chatter focused on hunting down the culprit. The crowd was silent, too shocked to move. Despite years of training, he felt the same.

His head rocked with power, too heavy for his neck. He caught the looks of amazement from his team, unable to believe he'd deflected the overwhelming energy.

"How'd you do that, colonel?" The warrior's voice sounded far away.

A trickle of horror touched his mind. He knew how he'd managed it. Bronte. He'd just shoved the residual effects of all that power through Bronte's syphon.

His horror built to a flood.

Vincent scanned the crowd, circling around, desperate to see her. A high sob filtered down to him, carrying easily over the quiet room. He raised his eyes to the steps. Gasps of horror echoed around him.

Bronte and the envoy necromancer were on the north balcony. His syphon was so close to the edge of the staircase that her dark, shiny hair tumbled over the first step. Her face was turned toward him, her eyes closed, her body lifeless.

Selene kneeled next to her, lifting Bronte's hand to her chest.

"Bronte!" Her voice was a desperate snap. "Open your eyes!"

Wide-eyed mages parted before him as he sprinted up the stairs. Goddess, he'd done this to her. His heart clogged his throat so tightly he couldn't get a breath. He slid an arm under her shoulders. Her head fell back against him. Pulling her close, he stroked his fingers through her long, shimmery hair. His weave, buried in the strands, still swirled with his power. He leaned down until his forehead touched her, breathing her in.

"Bronte, don't leave me. No more running away. Remember?" His voice was a bare whisper. He wouldn't have cared if the whole world heard his plea, but he couldn't catch his breath. His sweet little syphon had taken everything he'd forced on her. She'd saved every person in this room.

Metal clattered to the floor. Selene's cries ricocheted around the silent room.

Bronte's energy reached out to him for the first time, brushing against him, impossible for her to do in life. The soft touch of her soul wrapped around his heart, but he pulled away. He reacted before he could think it through and deflected that energy right back into her. She jerked in his arms.

"Breathe for her," Selene ordered.

Gently, he laid Bronte flat against the hard, cold floor. Her lungs moved under his force, once, twice. The horror at seeing her chest expanding from his air was mixed with a desperate hope she would do it on her own, as if he were showing her she could do it. She took over on the fourth one.

He waited for her to open her eyes. It took as long as that bomb had taken to deflect. Forever. The midnight blue of her eyes was the most beautiful thing he would ever see.

* * * *

"What happened?"

Crouched over her, he barely managed to catch her airy whisper.

His relief faded and guilt flooded in. This was his fault. "I'm sorry, Bronte. I poured so much energy into you that I…" His voice disappeared. "I killed you."

"Obviously not," she whispered. He thought if she had the energy she would have rolled her eyes. She lifted her head as if she wanted to sit up.

"No. Please don't move."

Her brow wrinkled.

"I need a chance to recover, even if you don't." He slid his arm under her shoulders, lifting her against him. Her right arm dragged to the ground. She grimaced as she tried to move it. He helped her support it against her stomach.

Bronte gasped. "The medallion. It's gone."

A tear dripped down the necromancer's cheek. "I didn't want it. I'd rather have you alive than have this." She held up her arm where the medallion had attached.

Bronte looked up at her sister. "I guess you get both. Death magic doesn't hurt the thing after all."

Selene swallowed. "I didn't know for sure. It…affects other magic things. Really, Bronte. I didn't know."

"You'll be a much better Senator Casteel than me."

Bronte let her head drop against his shoulder. She looked up at him with those lovely eyes. "Take me home. Please. Your home."

That worked for him.

Gregor crouched beside him before he could move, whispering in his ear. "Got him leaving out the front doors. Cuffed and ready for transport to the farm."

Vincent gave a curt nod. "Tell Team Two to wrap up. Pull everyone else out." He carefully lifted Bronte into his arms.

She wrapped her left arm around his neck. There was a cheer as he carried her down the stairs.

Selene followed them.

Lady Glender waited at the bottom of the stairs and greeted Selene with a short nod. "Senator Selene Glender."

"It's Senator Selene Casteel, actually," Selene corrected as she came to the last step.

"Taking the name of the parents who abandoned you?" Lady Glender gasped as if she were offended.

"No, I'm taking the name of my people."

Lady Glender nodded. "I'm sad to see you go. You've been a valuable envoy." She looked with blind eyes at Bronte, a greedy smile on her face. "But we'll take good care of your syphon sister in your place."

"The hell you will." Vincent's shout echoed through the damaged room.

Lady Glender ignored him. She smiled at Bronte. "You'll stay with us, my dear. And it's thanks to your colonel's weave that you can. It's such an old-fashioned tradition, but beneficial for a syphon. You will always have a source of his power. Being addicted to his energy won't be an issue."

"A weave?" Bronte's bewildered eyes shifted from the old hag to him.

"You can't have her."

"I can. I will."

"What's a weave?"

He looked down at Bronte and opened his mouth, but nothing came out. He halted around an explanation.

A knowing look came into her eyes. "What did you do?"

He would have preferred a more private moment. "I wove my energy into you. A weave marks a mage as…claimed. Usually two mages combine their energy, weave it together and leave a mark on each other. But you…"

"I can't."

"So it's just mine."

"It's in my hair, isn't it?" She muttered something else. It sounded like something about a *wee little bug*.

"You didn't tell her?" Lady Glender asked. "Very unorthodox of you. Deceitful. You would make a good Council member, colonel. Instead, Bronte will serve the Council. She will syphon away the heavy power weighing us down, burdening our senses." She gave that fucked-up smile to his syphon. "It's what you were born to do."

The mages below protested, their voices a mass of sound. Above the roar, his mother shouted the loudest.

"No." He would battle to the death if he had to. "You will not do that to her."

Rumors of mages who disappeared behind these walls were prolific, but never proven.

"What are you going to do, colonel? I can defeat all your weapons." The old hag took a step forward. "You can't defend her with a spell at the moment. She's so sense-sick already, yet she can't stop syphoning your vibes. If you cast now, it will just make her worse."

Bronte gasped. "I'm weakening you?"

"No. Never. We're a team. Partners. You make me stronger."

She pushed at his chest.

He gently slipped his arm away and made sure her legs were strong enough to hold her.

She turned in his arms, resting her cheek against his chest and giving Lady Glender her back.

"You can't stop me from taking her." Lady Glender's voice boomed through the room. "I am High Council. Our actions serve the best interests of all mages—the greater good, not the individual. The syphon has done that herself tonight. It certainly wasn't good for her to absorb all that power, saving every person here. With your help, of course. From this moment on, she will serve all magekind by assisting the Council."

"Gregor." Bronte whispered just loud enough to be heard above the crowd. "Give me your knife."

Vincent didn't dare take his eyes off Lady Glender, but from the way Bronte stirred in his arms, Gregor complied.

She turned to face the High Councilor.

"Lady Glender." Bronte's soft voice summoned silence through the room, an impressive feat considering the volume level. She waited until she had the attention of every mage in the room. "I decline your offer to stay in the High Council. I will not hide here. Or anywhere else."

Lady Glender's voice resonated. "You think these mages will tolerate your presence?" She gestured to the crowd below. "That you'll be allowed to live freely and without threat of harm? That is not what usually happens to syphons, you know."

Bronte took a step forward. The knife glistened in the folds of her skirt. Lady Glender lifted a brow and pursed her lips. She knew the knife was there. The council guards didn't. Yet. But the old crone could summon them with a thought.

Vincent caught Gregor's eye. His lieutenant was primed to cast, ready to defend Bronte from their own rulers.

"My power does not harm. As you said, tonight was a demonstration of that." Bronte swayed.

Vincent tightened his grip around her.

The old woman leaned in to Bronte, her whisper audible through the whole room despite its soft tone. "And if I demand you stay? What then?"

Bronte looked the woman straight in the face, as defiant as he'd ever seen her. She smiled, rebellious and cold. He could see a resemblance to her sister in the expression.

Silence reigned as the two faced off. The crowd stirred as the tension pulled tightly through the grand room.

"Fine then!" Lady Glender capitulated.

What was her game?

"Keep your freedom. Take your chances!" The high councilor spun to the crowd, without eyes but not without sight. "Next year's Gathering will be here even if the power in the mark grows tenfold." She raised her hands in the air. "And it will be here the year after that! And so on until I decree otherwise." Her voice rebounded through the room like a mini-bomb. She pointed a crooked finger at the mages. "Keep that in mind."

She turned toward him. With a chuckle, she tossed off the mantle of her power like an old, tattered rag. Suddenly she looked like nothing more than a mischievous old woman. She reached up and patted his cheek. "How's that?"

He nodded, his mind scrambling. "That's…good."

The old woman was tricky, and after everything that had happened, he didn't have the focus to keep up with her.

"Then thank me."

"Thank you."

"You're welcome. But you owe me." The quiet words vibrated with power.

Vincent nodded. Bronte was worth it. He swooped his syphon off her unstable feet, clutched her close to his heart and left the crazy woman behind.

* * * *

Vincent pulled up to his house as the sun rose over the trees. Bronte had insisted on going home immediately. With his help, she'd slept most of the trip. She leaned against the seat, too deeply under to know they'd arrived.

Her dark hair spilled over her shoulder. Her pale skin gleamed against it. The handle of Gregor's sheathed knife stuck out from the top of her dress. His lieutenant had handed her the sheath before they'd left. Bizarre. The man adored his knives.

Vincent had tried to take it from her as she'd slept, but she'd stopped him every time. He frowned at the other man's gift lying against her breasts. Had he ever given her anything? He would remedy that first thing, shower her with gifts until she forgot about Gregor's knife.

He slipped silently from his truck and carried her into the house. Her hair spread across the pillows as he laid her on the bed. He reached for the knife one more time.

Her left hand slapped on top of it. She opened her eyes. This time, they stayed opened.

"Why do you have Gregor's knife?" He couldn't stop from asking any longer.

"He said I could keep it. You're right. He does like me."

A wave of jealousy rose inside him.

She gave him a tired smiled. "The knife was part of my plan. I did have a plan, you know."

"Half-conscious, you came up with a plan?" He undid the fastening on his jacket as quickly as he could. He wanted nothing more than to lie down next to her.

She nodded sleepily. "It was a bit risky. You'll probably say I should have consulted with you before I implemented it."

"Whatever it was, I'm glad you didn't do it. We need to do something about this bad habit of yours. You tend to think up the most dangerous plans possible." He lay down and pulled her in close, moving an extra pillow to support her arm.

Goddess, he was so lucky.

"What was this plan?" Better to know so he could close off whatever avenue she was pondering.

"I was going to cut off my hair. Get rid of your weave."

His heart stuttered at the words. "You wouldn't have had any of my energy on you if your syphon power truly needs mine. If you really are addicted to my energy, you wouldn't have survived for long."

She narrowed her eyes. "Did you know about that addiction thing?"

"No." He narrowed his eyes right back. "But the high councilor obviously knows. Someone needs to infiltrate the High Council and expose their secrets."

"Uh-huh. So long as that person is a Rallis and only tells you all."

"Of course."

She rolled her eyes. "Anyway, you're right. If I'd cut it off, I probably wouldn't have survived. I was betting they'd rather have me alive and with you than have a dying syphon on their hands. If the only known syphon in existence died under their watch, it wouldn't be very good for the Council."

"Risky, Bronte. But brave. And smart." He closed his eyes in relief that she hadn't needed to go to such extremes. That knife wasn't getting anywhere near his weave.

"Sometimes you have to take a chance." Her soft voice warmed him. "Fight back. Defend yourself and the ones you love."

"That's my job."

"Well, I guess I've learned something from you, because tomorrow I'm going to call Peter Leggert and see if he'll let me audition for the symphony."

Vincent wrinkled his brow. "Maybe you should give yourself a few weeks to rest first. Let the arm heal. But I'm sure he'll let you audition. Hell, you won't even have to audition."

"Vincent." Her voice morphed into a sharp warning. "You are not to interfere. Neither is your mother."

He wasn't intimidated. She couldn't even move off the bed.

"Are we clear?"

"Love, I just want to help. You're beyond good enough to play with those fools."

"Fine, then. Help me. And next time, I'll go with you and help you deflect the bad guy's bombs." A determined light glimmered from her eyes like stars in the nighttime sky.

He sighed and leaned his forehead against hers. "Never." Behind the whispered word lay a determination that matched hers.

"Hmm." She teased him with her smile. "Are we at a stand still already then?"

"As long as you're standing next to me, I don't care where we are."

"Then do we have a deal? No interference?"

He kissed her nose. "Deal."

"For now?" she asked, still testing.

"For always."

Meet the Author

Anise Rae has long been frustrated by the fact that superpowers are nearly impossible to come by for a mere human. To compensate, she dreams up alternative realities where people just like her (and you) have magic, worlds populated with heroines who dare to stand up to society's expectations and be true to themselves and heroes with plenty of savvy to fall in love with such brave women.

Despite her lack of supernatural magic, Anise has come to realize that the true magic within us is our own unique creativity–a gift we must nuture as frequently as possible. It's why her house is littered with crayons, craft kits, legos, yarn, and paper and pens. Or it could be because she hates to clean. Though she lives in the suburbs of Atlanta, her favorite place to vacation is in smack in the middle of the real Rallis Territory, where cornfields wave in the summer sun like an ocean of green speckled with golden tassels. You might want to come see for yourself.

Acknowledgements

This book has been my baby for a long time, but as the saying goes, it took a village to raise it to adulthood. It never would have made it relying on me alone. In fact, I'm quite sure Vincent and Bronte wouldn't want to show their faces to the world without our army of molders and shapers.

First, hugs and kisses to the people who read the first drafts and didn't laugh: Cheryl and Christine, who were with me with I took my first firm steps on the writer's path; Katie, who read multiple drafts and probably needs a new red pen since she likely ran out of ink correcting my mistakes; and Larissa Reinhart, my fabulous critique partner and author of the Cherry Tucker Mysteries.

Next, many thanks to all the people who listened to me blather on about my stories and the ups and downs of writing, and kept on encouraging me, though they had to be sick of hearing me talk about it: my kids, (rest assured, I never mentioned anything about the good parts of the story), Julie, Dad, (once again, I left out the good parts. And, Dad, please tell me you'll skip those parts), Sandy, the Clandestine Book Club, Jill, Renee, Mac, Cecilia Dominic, Terri L. Austin, and LynDee Walker.

Also, big thanks to Lyrical Press and Piper for the opportunity to release this story into the world.

Last but foremost, bushels of gratitude to my mom, who has always been behind me every step I've taken, who taught me to read when I was three, and provided a home filled with books, including some of my grandmother's old romance novels. It was a fateful day when I discovered those in the cabinet. When my father caught me, he said to my mother, "Should she be reading those books?" My mother responded, "Probably not." Then she walked away. And I kept reading.

And to you, dear reader, thank you for taking a chance on a new author. I hope you enjoy Vincent and Bronte's story. Edmund's turn is next.

57136297R00154

Made in the USA
Lexington, KY
07 November 2016